Jane Austin

# Mrs. Beauchamp Brown

Jane Austin

**Mrs. Beauchamp Brown**

ISBN/EAN: 9783337241407

Printed in Europe, USA, Canada, Australia, Japan

Cover: Foto ©Raphael Reischuk / pixelio.de

More available books at **www.hansebooks.com**

*NO NAME SERIES.*

"Is the Gentleman Anonymous? Is he a great Unknown?"
DANIEL DERONDA.

———◆———

# MRS. BEAUCHAMP BROWN.

"Though the mills of God grind slowly,
Yet they grind exceeding small;
Though with patience He stands waiting,
With exactness grinds He all."

BOSTON:
ROBERTS BROTHERS.
1880.

I DO not believe, dear little sister, that any other public will ever care for this story as much as you do. I am quite sure that none other could have cheered and encouraged me while writing it as you have done; and I most devoutly hope that none other will spell out what is written between the lines as surely as you will do.

So take it, dear child, your own book, and God bless you now and always.

# CONTENTS.

# MRS. BEAUCHAMP BROWN.

## CHAPTER I.

### MARGARET.

EIGHT persons were dining in a charming room of a charming house on Beacon Hill in Boston,—dining, not eating dinner, the latter being an animal necessity, the former an æsthetic enjoyment ; and Mrs. Beauchamp Brown, the hostess, was one of those people who discover æsthetics by the same subtile law of attraction that led Columbus to America, or Galileo to the revolution he so obstinately fought.

A very queer person was Mrs. Beauchamp Brown, and quite as much of a liberal education, if you studied her exhaustively, as Lady Mary Wortley Montagu, to those who loved her. A leader, you might say the leader, of her world for forty years ; as autocratic, as self-centred, as indomitable, as ever a Russian Catherine or an Elizabeth of them all. What is to be known of this world in its social aspect and history, she knew ; what never was known before she invented and fulminated, and, which is more remarkable, made other people accept in spite of themselves ; she endured none but ultramontanists near her throne, and if Pope Joan be, as they say, a myth, Mrs. Beauchamp Brown was the reality she prefigured. For the rest, she was a widow, childless, wealthy, and worldly.

Just now she was very cross, all the more so that the laws of hospitality prevented her giving vent to her feelings, except in sundry sharp satirical remarks and two or three quiet snubs to Belinda McVie and Joan.

And it *was* provoking, to be sure. Here was Mr. Forsythe, the Hon. Reginald Forsythe, newly appointed Minister to Spain, the handsomest, most elegant, thorough-bred gentleman of his day, distinguished as a poet, an authority in belles-lettres, everything in fact that a man need be to constitute a brilliant *parti*, and perfectly wild to marry Margaret. Now Margaret, although a widow, and independent of everybody so far as fortune goes, was not yet thirty years old, and when she was not playing moon among the stars of Washington or New York, lived with her aunt, Mrs. Beauchamp Brown, in Boston, and, partly from indolence, partly from love to her mother's sister, allowed that lady to manage·her in some ways so entirely that when, as in this Forsythe business, she quietly took and kept her own course, it was a source of absolute grievance to Pope Joan.

This was the matter now. Mr. Forsythe had rushed from Washington to Boston, with the ink yet wet upon his credentials, to lay them at Margaret's feet, and ask her to go with him to Madrid as *madame l'ambassadrice*. Margaret knew, when she read the appointment, that he would come, and also knew, having lived much abroad, that it is a good thing to be an ambassadress tó one of the first courts of Europe. She liked Mr. Forsythe too, and be-lieved that he loved her very honestly, but —

He arrived, found her charming and affable as always, found Mrs. Beauchamp Brown impressive and eager, found Belinda McVie always glued to Margaret's side and impossible to get rid of. Mrs. Beauchamp Brown asked him to dinner, and sternly demanded that Margaret should allow him a chance to speak during the evening.

To her great relief Mrs. Ufford answered quietly, " Yes, I intend to," and left the room before her aunt could ask any more questions.

Mrs. Beauchamp Brown gave a good deal of thought and diplomacy to that dinner ; not so much to the mate-rial portion, for her housekeeper and her cook were phœnixes, and Robert, her solemn old butler, ought to have been gold-stick-in-waiting at Buckingham Palace, but to the construction of the party, that there should be neither a rival attraction to disturb the current of sympathy between Forsythe and his coy lady-love, nor such isolation as to make them conspicuous ; neither a dinner so entirely *en famille* as to seem negligent of the dignities of the guest, or so general as to allow Margaret to devote herself to somebody else and lose herself in a crowd.

The result of several hours' severe cogitation was this : Leverett Beauchamp, Mrs. B. B.'s brother (pardon the negligence and the alliteration, but life is short), a gallant and courtly old bachelor living at the Tremont House, was invited to take the head of the table, and show due honor to the Spanish Minister. Belinda McVie, Margaret's companion, a small, sprightly, shrewd little person, would sit beside the host and keep up a general conversation without venturing to interrupt anything the bigger people might say. Then, to balance the party, and give an arm to his hostess, she would invite Larry Beauchamp, a nice young fellow just graduating from Harvard, sure to say only the thing one should say at a dinner-party, and not likely to devote himself to Margaret, whom he nevertheless admired in a cousinly and deferential style. This made six at table, and one of Pope Joan's most solemn edicts was against a dinner company of more than six, unless there were as many as twelve guests. "Let us be cosey, or let us be stately," said she. "Six persons may talk upon one topic, twelve persons may talk upon six ; but eight or ten persons are too many for a general conversation, too few to be divided. Why else is it one of the laws of nature that dinner services come in dozens?"

Imagine, then, the indignant wrath of the autocrat when Margaret, who had been driving all the morning, came home at six o'clock with Larry Beauchamp's sister Elspeth, and Joanna Jennifer, another of Mrs. B. B.'s grandnieces, packed into the coupé, whence Belinda McVie had been ejected to make room for them.

"The babes in the wood, aunt," announced she, pushing

them into the drawing-room in front of her. " I found them at Doll's, and brought them home to dinner. Larry can take them out to Brookline before he returns to Cambridge."

Mrs. Beauchamp Brown glared at her grand-nieces, who cowered like two young partridges at sight of a gunner; but Margaret, laughing gayly, swept them out of the room and up to her own bedroom, before anything could be said, and there decorated and trimmed them up so prettily that she whispered to her aunt, while Mr. Forsythe was making himself agreeable to them, " They will ornament the table like bouquets of lilies and roses."

" And draw all the honey-bees away from your own garden," retorted her aunt tartly.

" Only the butterflies, and nobody cares where they go," replied Margaret, in the careless, mocking tone she used so much, and which, as her aunt well knew, denoted a condition of mind proof against all coaxing, all driving, all influence from without.

" She 's made up her mind to refuse him again," said Mrs. Beauchamp Brown savagely to herself, but nevertheless took care to seat them side by side at table, selecting Elspeth, as the least showy of the two girls, to place opposite, between her brother and Belinda, and hiding Joan by putting her next beyond Margaret, whose stately person and magnificent draperies of sapphire silk and satin quite obscured the nineteen-year-old figure, and modest gray and brown walking dress.

But mischievous Joan revenged and amused herself by making eyes at her great-uncle Beauchamp, beside whom she sat, and who, being sensitive about his age, his bachelorhood, his wig, his teeth, his padding, and his powder, called himself the cousin of his nephews and nieces in the second generation, and was always open to any little coquettish advances from the latter, showing the wisdom of the serpent in rewarding such efforts in a substantial manner; as now, when he invited Joan and Elspeth to go and hear " Pinafore " after dinner, promising to drive them home afterward, evidently not intending Launcelot to be of the party.  Joan accepted, as she always accepted every amusement, with eager delight; Elspeth glanced at Margaret, at her hostess, at her brother, and reading no disapproval in their faces, accepted also; and as the dessert was already on the table, Mrs. Beauchamp Brown, not sorry to see the field cleared for the grand *coup* of the evening, graciously said, —

"And as it is a pity to lose the first of a new play, we will excuse you three young people as soon as you like."

Mr. Leverett Beauchamp did n't like to be called "young people" any better than he liked to be called old, and he did like his sister's Extra Dry Mumm, and was intending to have another bottle of it; but as Joan had already pushed back her chair, and Elsie was saying good-by to her brother, it could not be; and, consoling himself with visions of a little supper at Parker's after the play, he rose also, made his farewell speeches to Mr. Forsythe, and departed. Forsythe would not sit down again, being secretly anxious for his *tête-à-tête* with Margaret; and Mrs. Brown, nothing loth, led the way to the drawing-room and rang for coffee, while Margaret, with a slight excuse, followed the little cousins, of whom she was sincerely fond, to her dressing-room, and sent both away the richer by some pretty ornaments and the happier by some smiles and kisses, — for this Margaret was one of the few women whose charm is as great for women as for men, and she counted as many fervent lovers in the one sex as the other: girls especially adored her, and clung to her society; while she really seemed as well satisfied with the crude homage and innocent flatteries of these lovers as of the others. Indeed, one of Margaret's charms was a sort of universal sympathy, a grand sweetness of nature, that showed her something attractive in almost everybody and made her tolerant of almost everybody's faults; not that she was one of those tiresomely amiable people, whose indiscriminate praise of every person and thing they ever saw gives one the desire to contradict and abuse them, for she seldom praised and less seldom dispraised anything or anybody; in fact, I am afraid she was indolently careless as to characters or events except as they intersected the circle of her life.    A disappointed lover once said bitterly enough, —

" You are like the sun, madam ; one stands in its rays and his whole heart is filled with its gracious warmth, and feels new life throbbing within it ; one moves just a little into the shadow, and all is changed : the sun shines on just as warmly, just as pervasively, but it is on somebody else, and it is quite a matter of indifference to the sun whether it is A or B who is warmed.   The sun's nature is to shine ; that is all."

Margaret made no reply to this, except to slowly raise her great gray eyes and look at the speaker with a grieved and wondering look which made him feel as though he had behaved very badly, and go away remorseful and devoted instead of angry, while Margaret murmured sadly to herself, " They say now-a-days that the sun itself remains cold and dark, and all its light and heat are shed abroad."

# CHAPTER II.

## AS YOU LIKE IT.

"WILL you indulge me with a game of chess, Mrs. Ufford?" asked Mr. Forsythe, laying down his coffee-cup, and wondering whether chess or music were the best cover for a private interview. Margaret smilingly assented, and leading the way to the alcove, where stood the chess-table, felt a great wave of weariness surge over her spirit, and thought, O how I wish somebody would do something I never dreamed of! I am so tired of all this!

And yet, with the force of habit, — the force rather of her own pleasure-craving, pleasure-giving nature, — she looked at him from under her long lashes, and listened as if on his words hung all the interest of her life, and dropped her voice to the honey-sweet murmur that was itself a caress, and smiled into his eyes that wonderful, inscrutable smile of hers, innocent as a baby's, yet thrilling with some strange, indefinite promise, that set a man's heart beating, and tingled like little arrows of flame through all his veins.

"She will not refuse me to-night. At last she loves me, or she wishes to be *madame l'ambassadrice*," said Forsythe to himself, and planted his queen in range of a pawn.

"You must play more carefully at Madrid, Mr. Forsythe, or the countrymen of Ruy Lopez will laugh at American chess," said Margaret, taking the queen, and showing the edges of white teeth that seemed to smile with the lips.

"Yes, I have lost my queen, but I may take yours yet," said the minister slowly. "I would give not only this game, but myself and all that I possess, to call the fair white queen my own.   Do you think I shall?"

"Fight for her if you want her.   The brave not only deserve, but generally win, what they desire," said Margaret very softly, and without raising her eyes to those demanding them.

"That is all going on well, and it was a fortunate stupidity of Leverett's to ask those two girls to the theatre," said Mrs. Beauchamp Brown, settling herself in her own especial armchair at just the right distance from the fire, and preparing for a doze.   Suddenly, however, she straightened her back, opened her eyes, and demanded, "What are you going to do with your vacation, Launcelot?"

Larry started, and dropped the stereoscopic view Miss McVie had just placed in his hand, while that little person, coloring angrily, put the stereoscope to her eyes to hide her face.   Seeing her mistress deep in a flirtation, and her hostess equally deep in an armchair, she had naturally concluded the field to be her own, and made some quiet little preparations for utilizing it, in the direction of this fine-looking, debonair young fellow, whose youthful overflow of devotion to women, included in its gush even this poor little unlovely waif, and who would very amiably have seconded her plan of a half-hour's whispered nonsense over the photographs, had not the design been perceived and sternly frustrated by his aunt, who, pointing with her fan to a sort of stool of audience placed near her chair, demanded for the second time, —

"Where are you going this vacation, Launcelot?"

"I really don't know, aunt," replied the Class Poet, feeling very young as he seated himself upon the stool and watched his playmate going studiously through the views by herself.

"Don't know?" repeated his aunt sharply.   "Well, I advise you to go to Jericho and wait for your beard to grow."

Larry laughed.   He was not easily offended, and really liked Mrs. Beauchamp Brown, who had been very good to him in a substantial way, his father being a poor country clergyman.

"Oh! I have a plan," said he, "only I don't quite know where we shall carry it out. Two or three fellows and I are going on a walking and reading tour with old Moberley. I believe we are to do the St. Lawrence, Quebec, Montreal, and that sort of thing first, and then down through the White Mountains and Franconia, and settle somewhere about there for a few weeks of regular hard grinding before we get home. I'm going to enter the Law School, you know."

"Good gracious! That explains it!" exclaimed his aunt so vivaciously that Larry started, crying, —

"What! Explains what?"

"The stupidity and folly of the laws. It never occurred to me before who it is that makes them."

"Excuse me, aunt; but it is not the lawyers who make them, and I am in no danger of being a Congressman," replied Larry rather tartly, and quite forgetting that the Hon. Rufus Brown had represented his district at Washington with great satisfaction to his wife and himself, and had, so far as tradition goes, done no harm to his country or his constituents.

Mrs. Beauchamp Brown was silent for a moment, and then she asked, "Did you say Professor Moberley is going with you?"

"Yes, aunt. Do you know him?"

"I have seen him, and I know his family. Phillips Moberley is not a young man now."

"About forty, I should say, and a regular old brick. Knows no end, and is just as quiet and gentlemanly and patient, as a sub-tutor. The fellows think he's immense, and we were in great luck to secure him, especially as he don't care for money. He's a bachelor, you know, and don't go in for society or clothes, or anything but books, so that his salary as Ass. Prof. more than keeps him."

"Larry, you grow more slangy every day. 'Ass. Prof.' indeed! You can go home now, if you want to. I sha'n't go to Class Day, but Margaret will, and mind you have as good a spread as anybody. Jenkins will pay the bills, and give you a hundred dollars for your holiday. If you spend more you 'll have to earn it ; your father has n't got it to give.  Good-by, for I don't expect to see you again before we all leave town."

" Thank you very much, aunt ; you are always generous and good.  Good-by.  I suppose you are going to Newport, as usual ; " and Larry, rising, held out his hand, in which his aunt deposited two dry, chalky fingers, covered with diamonds, as she coldly replied to his last words.

" Do you indeed ?  Never mind thanking me.  Good-by.  Miss McVie, would you be so kind as to read to me for a while ?  If you sit quite close and speak low you will not disturb the chess-players."

" Nor overhear them," muttered Miss McVie, as she selected the novel just then in hand from the books upon the table, and resigned herself to her task.

At about eleven, Mr. Forsythe took leave, his manner as courteous and easy, his face as controlled, his voice as full and firm as when he came ; and yet he bore away a wound such as men have died from before now, or lived to wish that they had died first.  Perhaps it was one of the final touches of an education fitting him to deal as diplomat with the wiliest court of Europe.

As the door closed behind him, Margaret threw herself upon a sofa, her arms above her head.  She looked very handsome, with the light glancing from the curves of her red-gold hair, and her round white arms and lovely hands gleaming from the lace and silk of their open sleeves, — very handsome, and yet the shrewd eyes of the old worldling, who loved her as she loved nothing else in creation, took on a look of pain in gazing at her, she looked so hopeless and so weary.  Pale she could not be, for her complexion was of that wonderful luminous white, one sometimes sees, and only the lovely curving lips were red, — those marvellous lips, around which forever seemed to hover an inscrutable something, a just dawning expression never fully revealed, a mystery like that which men have studied for centuries in the sad, majestic beauty of the sphinx, — a promise never fulfilled, a lure to beckon the student on and on, until life is spent and heart gone, and he is no nearer the end than in the beginning.

If Monna Lisa's face is the despair of painters, Margaret Ufford's might be their hope, but a hope with no better fruition than despair.

So she lay with closed eyes and still, still mouth, until Belinda McVie glided across the room, and sank, a little black silk heap, upon the floor beside her. It made one think of a horrible little beetle threatening the heart of a magnolia.

"You are very tired, dear Mrs. Ufford," murmured she presently.

Margaret stirred, but did not open her eyes as she whispered, "So tired!" and Mrs. Beauchamp Brown's strident voice interposed with, —

"Too tired to talk about it, Miss McVie. If you will go up and see that Josephine is in her mistress's room, and her chocolate ready, it will be more to the purpose than anything else you can do."

"Shall I?" whispered Belinda, pointedly deferring to her employer for orders.

"Yes, if you will be so kind. I am sure you will be glad to get to your bed too, so good-night," said Margaret, rousing herself to smile and look kindly at her poor little dependent as she dismissed her.

"Thank you; good-night, dear Mrs. Ufford. Good-night, Mrs. Brown," said Belinda, making for the door, but not fast enough to escape.

"Mrs. Beauchamp Brown, if you please, Miss Belinda McVie; I must trouble you to remember that in future."

"I beg pardon, Mrs. Beauchamp Brown. Good-night."

"A very offensive person that, Margaret," said Mrs. B. B., as the door closed with an obtrusive softness. "Where did you pick her up?"

"In London, Aunt Phyllis. She went out with the Belknap Pinckneys as governess to the little girl that died. I saw her with them, and then she came and asked me to bring her home, offering her services for the passage-money. I rather liked her, and engaged her for a year as companion. She has a mother somewhere in Pennsylvania whom she supports. Poor thing, she is very forlorn! One can't be really vexed, although she is a little tiresome sometimes."

"Tiresome! I wish that was the worst of her. But, Meg, what 's the matter with you? Are you going to Spain?"

"No, auntie."

"You 've refused him?"

"Yes."

"Margaret, you 're a heartless coquette, and, what is worse, you 're a fool. There is not such another match in America, and you 've encouraged him shamefully."

"I know it, aunt. Both statements are quite correct."

"Well! Bless my soul, there you lie as calm and serene as a dish of cream, and acknowledge yourself a coquette and a fool, and don't care a brass button. Do show some life or spirit about something."

Thus adjured, Margaret rose, and slowly walking to the other end of the room, stood for some moments contemplating herself in the full-length mirror.

She had so many charms, this Margaret. Nature had lavished the dowry of a dozen beauties upon her, and one was always discovering some little extra touch that would have been another woman's chief boast. She walked so elegantly, she stood so statuesquely, she moved her head, hands, feet so harmoniously, her motion and her rest were each so perfect of their kind, and withal she understood herself so thoroughly and dressed so admirably. Dressed a good deal, I am afraid, but in such exquisite taste, that one must forgive a certain lavishness of lace, jewelry, costly fabrics, faint, pervasive odors, — all the half sensuous enhancements of beauty that this sumptuous sort of beauty loves, and will carry off. Few of the women who admired and studied Margaret tried to imitate her : they generally said they were not rich enough ; they secretly felt they were not imperial enough.

Awhile she looked, then came as slowly back, and sinking into an armchair, put out her feet to the fire, with a little shivering sigh.

"Well," demanded her aunt, "what did you see in the

glass?  An idiot who quarrels with her bread-and-butter?"

"I saw a very strong, healthy-looking young woman, not in the least likely to die at present, and what she should live for I can't imagine," replied Margaret drearily. "I went to see how a fool, a coquette, an idiot, a creature of no use to herself and of infinite harm to other people looked, and I saw."

"Come, Meg, what's the use of talking that way?" demanded Mrs. Brown, a little frightened.  "I did n't mean to vex you, child, only to rouse you up a bit.  You 're no fool, we both know, and as for being a coquette, why, you were born one, and can't help it."

"Can't I help being a wretched cheat and hypocrite, and making men think I am true and honest?  If I can't I had better die at once, or have small-pox, or turn imbecile, or be gotten rid of in some way."

"Nonsense, Meg.  All that means that you did n't refuse Reginald Forsythe before he asked you, or try to make yourself disagreeable to him ; and pray, why should you?  That 's all over, and next week we 'll get away from town.  Do you know, child, I have a plan.  You don't care much for Saratoga and Newport this year, do you?"

"I loathe them, and every other place like them.  I think I will take Belinda and go to Switzerland.  Tiring one's self to death up and down the Alps is more satisfactory than mooning round the piazzas or driving on the beaches, or playing ten-pins or billiards or croquet, or dancing, or listening to the stupid malice of the women and stupider admiration of the men, at those places."

"Margaret, what 's happened to you !  I don't know you !  You 've roused up to some purpose, and I don't admire your energy any more than I did your apathy. But stop, don't say another word until you hear my plan. You know my old friend, Myra Moberley?"

"She 's dead, is n't she?"

"Yes, died while you were in Paris last winter.  Did you ever hear of her housekeeper, Eunice Small?"

"No, indeed."

“Well, she is a personage, I assure you, and you may know her better than you expect.  Poor Myra was a little queer in her last years, you know.”

“ Insane, was she not ? ”

“ ’Sh, my dear ! Moberleys and Beauchamps never go insane ; they become eccentric, peculiar, queer if you will, but nothing so common as insane.  Well, when Myra got queer, this Eunice Small, who had lived in the family in one capacity or another for twenty-odd years, became her nurse and constant attendant.  She was very patient and good with her, and poor Myra felt it, and showed her gratitude by constantly making her presents of anything that happened to catch her eye at the moment.  I dare say Eunice occasionally suggested what would be most acceptable ; but in one way and another she accumulated the oddest collection of plunder that you can imagine.  One item was the Turkey carpet off the dining-room, and another was a set of Burke’s heraldic works, all bound in red Turkey with gilt edges, and the Moberley arms on the outside.  Then there were pictures and silver plate, and a whole set of India china, and quantities of damask, a set of chairs, and I don't know what all.  Eunice took everything, and stowed all away in an attic bedroom, under lock and key ; but every once in a while, when any of the Moberleys came to look after their aunt or cousin, — for she had no nearer relatives, — Eunice would say, in her hard, dry way, —

“ My mistress gave me the roasting-jack yesterday,” or whatever it might have been ; and Myra would always add, with her malicious little laugh, —

“ Yes, you need n’t think Eunice stole it.  Everything in that attic I gave her, and it ’s all right.”

So when poor Myra died, Eunice quietly carried off her possessions in two furniture wagons, and took away a good bit of money due her for wages too.  She always amused me so much that I kept track of her, and soon heard that she had gone down to her old home, Plum Island, on the coast of Maine, and bought back the little farm where she was born and bred, until she went as a young girl to the Moberleys. She repaired the old homestead, and bringing down her inherited possessions, placed them about the house, in company with the straight-backed settles, three-legged stools, wooden rocking-chairs, and patchwork bedquilts that had always lived there. Then she took her imbecile grandmother out of the poorhouse for company, and settled herself to her *otium cum*, like Cincinnatus; but like him she finds rural felicity a little slow after so many years of active city life, and has written to ask me if I could recommend some invalid lady, or quiet person of that sort, to board with her. I had not finished reading her letter before I resolved to go there myself, partly to refer to the ' Landed Gentry ' for our connection with the Lovells, partly to amuse myself in studying Eunice, and partly to see her grandmother. Besides, to tell the truth for once, Meg, I am a little tired of our world myself, and would like a variety; and as I have done and seen everything under the sun all my life, the only variety possible is to go where there is nothing to do and nothing to see, and Plum Island is precisely that spot. Not a human being except the aborigines is to be met there, and card-cases are unknown."

" And at the same time Burke's ' Landed Gentry ' and India china would gently remind one of civilization," suggested Margaret, smiling slyly.

" Yes, and Eunice is an admirable cook. She knows everything about the table, setting, serving, and providing it," replied her aunt with grave satisfaction.

" That is good, and after all one has to consider what one is to eat and drink, if one is ever so world-weary."

" Indeed one must, my dear. It is the first sensible remark you have made to-day. Well, will you go? "

" Yes, I will go, and let us start very soon, aunt."

" Next week. I was at first going all alone, and then I thought it would be awkward if I were to die down there, and perhaps in a fit of gratitude present all my portable property to Eunice before departing. I do not want a servant, and I thought of Elspeth Beauchamp as a nice, quiet little creature, not likely to bore me with girlish nonsense and chatter, but I have concluded now to carry Joan also, partly because Elspeth would be so lonely, and partly to keep her out of Larry's way."

" Larry !   Is he *épris* of Joan?"

" Oh, yes, of course.   Boys always begin with their cousins ; but it is not desirable that they should end with them.   He is going away with Phillips Moberley, — you remember him, Margaret?"

Margaret looked pained, and the rare flush mounted to her cheek.

" Yes," said she softly, " of course I remember him."

" Well, he 's at Harvard now, an assistant professor, and Launcelot and some other young men are going to Canada on a reading party ; but people can come home from Canada and people can correspond, and on the whole I had rather have Joan under my own eye, so I shall take her.   Then if you go, it is just a nice square party, and I shall have you to speak to when I feel like speaking."

" Yes," replied Margaret dreamily.

" And you won't carry the McVie, will you?"

" Why — no, not if you object."

" I do, most emphatically."

" Then she may go home to her mother for a while.   I suppose that will please her."

" Anywhere, so that she is n't where I am."

" Anywhere, anywhere out of the world ! " murmured Margaret, rising to say good-night ; but she did n't quote it apropos of Belinda McVie.

# CHAPTER III.



EARLY morn is not a universally becoming period, especially if one has spent the night in travelling, and is as yet breakfastless. Mrs. Beauchamp Brown knew this as well as anybody, and carefully adjusted a thick black lace veil over a very cross and wayworn face, before emerging from her state-room on the Cambridge, as that admirable boat stopped at Rockland, and passengers for Mount Desert and several other points were requested to transfer themselves to a smaller craft, commonly called the Useless, although originally named after the great General of these United States.

Margaret knew it, and cast one steady, inquisitorial look into her ivory-backed handglass before she put it in her bag. She had passed a sleepless night, and was obliged to rise just as she could have gone to rest ; but her limpid eyes were clear and serene, her forehead unlined, the rose-red of her lips unpaled, not a shadow upon the proud loveliness of her face.

" I wonder if I shall care when I see the first autumn leaf," said she, deftly packing her bag, for Margaret was not one of the persons who can travel the world around with only a toothbrush and a box of paper collars. " At least it will be a sensation. I wish I were seventy instead of nine-and-twenty next birthday."

As for Joan and Elspeth, neither of them had yet seen her twentieth birthday ; neither of them knew that summer roses turn to autumn leaves ; neither of them ever thought of such a thing as a favorable light or a becoming time of day. They were already on deck, watching the picturesque

Maine shore, and the approach to Rockland, which is not at all picturesque.

" Pie and cake, coffee and tea," read Elspeth upon a sign, as the Cambridge ground up against the pier. " How can people eat such stuff for breakfast ? "

" Pies-an'-things, nursie used to call them," replied Joan aloud, and then very softly, " Don't look behind, Elsie, but one of us has an admirer.  He does nothing but stare, and hovers around like a bird of prey."

" Does he ?  Oh, do see that pig running about loose, and the old man trying to catch him ! "  And Elsie laughed out in her pretty tinkling little way, like a tiny waterfall.

Joan laughed a little also, but her great dark eyes never lost sight of the young man who so undisguisedly watched, not the landscape and not the wharf, not the legend of pies and cake, and not the fugitive pig, but the two charming girls in the first flush of youth and beauty, — that beauty of the half-opened blossoms on the Tree of Life which we so oddly style *beauté du diable*. And as that same tree bears all manner of fruit, so does it all manner of blossoms, and none more diverse of hue and odor than these.  Joan was a brunette, vivid, bright, and rich of coloring as a humming-bird, with a delicious pulpiness and lusciousness about her warm brown flesh, like a sun-fed, full-ripe peach.  She was satirical, audacious, coquettish, wilful, irresistible, and provoking ; just out of school, and beginning to survey the world as the Spaniards did America, with a view to enslaving its denizens and appropriating its treasures.

Elspeth is not so easily outlined.  If her cousin suggested tropical birds and richly ripe fruit, Elsie made one think of fair springtide blossoms, of dewy dawns, of far reaches of the moonlit ocean, with all the possibilities that human eyesight is too gross to absolutely see.  Like moonlight, too, her coloring was ethereal, and hard to define, her pure skin, now white as a lily, now faintly flushed with a lovely bloom, —

> " Like a lily, which the sun
> Looks through in his sad decline,
> And a rosebush leans upon."

Her innocent, steadfast eyes were of the color of a placid lake before sunrise, a color without a name ; her hair, fine and soft as unspun silk, was not unlike it in color, and spite of its maidenly snood and careful tendance, broke into a million little riotous curls on brow and temples and in the nape of her white slender neck, catching the sunlight on their burnished curves, and dancing gleefully in the sweet, strong wind sweeping in with the morning tide.

"That girl looks like an embodied dawn," said the young man to his elder companion, and this one turned, and sharply surveyed both her and her cousin with eyes that seemed to comprehend everything in a glance.

"Yes," said he coldly. "And dawn always seemed to me a very raw and unsatisfactory state of existence. Nobody can tell what sort of day may come of it, or how you may long for night to end it."

"The other is pretty too," replied the young man irrelevantly. He was apt to be irrelevant, and it always annoyed his companion, who suddenly turned away, and began to pace up and down the deck, as if for exercise. Not much distressed at this, the young man moved a little nearer to the two girls, and was rewarded by the very slightest oblique glance of Joan's demure dark eyes. He colored with delight, and moving yet a little nearer, knocked over a stool, which happily touched in its fall the edge of Joan's pretty travelling dress. He lifted it in haste with one hand, touched his hat with the other, blushed yet deeper, and exclaimed in Londonese, — for really it is n't English like other English you know, —

"O ! Beg pardon, I 'm sure."

The girls both turned and looked at him. A very young man, not more than two-and-twenty, blond, good-looking, carefully groomed, as he would have called it, with an air and manner not so much of society as of the right to a place in any society, the air of birth and lineage, — a gentleman without peradventure, although it remained to be proved whether he were a silly or a wise, a clever or a dull, a good or a bad gentleman.

"O, it did n't touch me at all," replied Joan, smiling so

as to show a ravishing dimple and a set of brilliant little teeth.

" What an extraordinary place this is that we 're stopping at," ventured the stranger, putting a single glass in his eye, and surveying Rockland with an air of good-humored toleration.

" Is n't it lovely?  My own, my native land ! " exclaimed Joan, clasping her hands in mock rapture as she cast her eyes over the monotonous white wooden houses, the half dozen churches, the " stores " and engine-house and tavern, schoolhouses and town-hall that make up Rockland.

" O !  Beg pardon, I 'm sure, but I did n't suppose " —

" We will go to the other boat now if you are ready, girls," said a very, very haughty voice just behind the speaker, and turning sharply he found himself *vis-à-vis* with Mrs. Ufford, who looked through him at her cousins with as little recognition as if he had been a pane of glass.

Not a very wise or clever gentleman, but still a gentleman in every instinct, he raised his hat, bowed to the three ladies in whose society he found himself, and withdrew, Joan returning his salute with a demure bow and glance, Elsie not seeing it, and Margaret not noticing it.

Mrs. Beauchamp Brown, followed by a porter laden with hand-luggage, emerged at this moment from the cabin, and the whole party silently passed down the plank, across the wharf, and on board the Useless, where the first few moments were passed in settling themselves, and in questioning surly officials as to the possibility of breakfast on deck ; but when the aunt crossly retreated from the wind and sun to the fastnesses of the cabin, Margaret, comprehending her youthful cousins in one glance, said in the cold, sweet voice that always carried her reproofs much farther home than any scolding, —

" Pray, don't allow persons to make acquaintance with you in travelling, girls.  Aunt Phyllis would be extremely annoyed if she knew it, and I confess that I am very much astonished.  It never occurred to me that you two needed watching."

" Oh, but Cousin Margaret, he knocked over a stool and

fancied it hit Joan, and so he was apologizing," explained Elspeth, in all simplicity.

The woman of the world looked at her, at first with stern scrutiny, then with a half smile of sadness and pity, which faded as she turned to Joan, and quietly said, "Don't do it any more, Joan ; that 's all."

"If I had known he was going to tip over the stool I would n't have been in the way, cousin, but you see I did n't know," replied Joan pertly, and at that moment the two gentlemen came on board and walked forward. Margaret glanced at them but said nothing. Elspeth colored painfully, making herself look like an aurora borealis, and Joan, with a pout half comic, half mutinous, exclaimed, —

"There, Cousin Meg, I did n't ask him to come. I did n't, upon my word !"

"I would n't undertake to chaperon you at Long Branch or Saratoga, you monkey," replied Margaret, laughing. "At any rate, if they manage to speak with us, don't tell where we are going. Everybody on board this boat is supposed to be bound for Mount Desert, and no doubt these gentlemen are ; but as your aunt and I are especially seeking a lodge in a vast wilderness where we shall ·find nothing more human than Friday's footprint in the sand, don't expose our retreat."

"No, indeed, cousin," promised Elsie fervently, and Joan innocently inquired, —

"But how in the world could we tell them anything if we are not to speak to them ?"

Margaret looked at her attentively. She was beginning to be interested in this rebellious, handsome, self-asserting cousin, whom hitherto she had seldom seen, and was disposed to class among the youthful relations of whom she briefly disposed by saying,

"I don't much care for veal, thank you." But something in Joan reminded her of herself in her teens, — a something very early repressed and weeded out by good taste and culture, but whose reminiscences made her tolerant of a nature eager for admiration, impatient of control, and incapable of fear, so she suddenly laid her soft white hand over Joan's slender brown one, and said, "Come little girl, be good, and we will trust each other."

"That's the way to make me good, Cousin Meg, to trust me," replied Joan brightly; and just then Mrs. Beauchamp Brown looked out at the cabin door to say, "They have brought something they call breakfast up here, if you like to come and try it."

An hour later, matters had assumed a different aspect. Mrs. Brown, refreshed in spite of herself by the viands and beverage (a strict regard for truth will not allow us to call them steak, omelette, rolls, and coffee, although the waiter did) she had superciliously absorbed, was now seated in state in the best corner of the afterdeck, three armchairs serving as seat, footstool, and sofa-table, and divided her attention very affably between the coast of Maine and a little book called "One Summer," which she read here and now, as she explained to the girls, because the scene was laid in this vicinity, and she made it a point, whenever she travelled, to read works written by the natives, and, if possible, descriptive of the manners, customs, and scenery.

"That's what they call in the army living upon the country," suggested Joan demurely. Mrs. Beauchamp Brown did not like young girls to offer uncalled-for remarks, nor to jest too freely with herself, so she only said, "Humph!" and put on her eye-glass. She said she used glasses because she was near-sighted; but Joan had already quietly observed that she put them on for the book, and took them off for the scenery.

Margaret, seated quite at the stern of the boat, also held a book in her hand; what was between its covers I know not, nor did she; for her eyes, strong as an eagle's, were following the weltering sheen of the sunlit sea to the horizon line, and her thoughts, voyaging still farther, were picturing another summer morning long ago, when she, with her husband and her father, sailed merrily out upon the blue waters of the Mediterranean, and the bright, beautiful world was new to her, and life looked all too short to fulfil its promise of delight.

"He loved me — he loved me so much," whispered she, recalling the tender, stately, courteous gentleman whose wife she had been, yet never loved. And then she thought of Reginald Forsythe, and knew that there was a love as strong, as honorable, even more fervent than the first awaiting her, and for a little moment she doubted if she had done well to refuse it ; but then a cold repulsion filled her heart, and she shook her head, saying to herself, " Not unless I could put back the shadow on the dial and forget what all these years have taught. It was only a child's ignorance then, to marry without love : now it would be a woman's sin."

" There is only one morning in each day," said a voice behind her ; and turning in haughty surprise, Margaret discovered that the aphorism was not addressed to herself, but to her aunt, and that the speaker was a fine-looking man verging upon middle life, who, with a camp-stool and book in his hand, was aiming toward the steps ascending from the main to the upper deck, and, pausing for a moment at Mrs. Brown's side, to look at the lighthouse which the Useless seemed on the point of running down, had been by that lady accosted with a demand for its name ; to this naturally succeeded a few more remarks, ending with the one brought by a sudden flaw of wind to Margaret's ear.

" Ah ! Joan's friend's friend ! " remarked Mrs. Ufford to herself, and, looking about, soon discovered a blond head covered with a Glengarry cap, and holding a cigar between its lips, and wearing a general air of peace and mild ennui incompatible with the near vicinity of an object of admiration. As this apparition appeared above the edge of the hurricane deck, and Margaret knew her charges to be promenading the forward deck, she dismissed her responsibility for a moment, and carelessly watched the face of the elder gentleman, still talking to her aunt, although with one hand upon the rail of the steps as about to mount.

"Now where have I seen that man before?" asked Margaret of herself, watching the play of the clean-cut features, the square, resolute chin, and penetrating, but somewhat furtive, eyes which seemed to gather all that they desired of men or things in brief, unexpected glances, and when one looked at them were generally downcast or vaguely wandering over the distance. The tall, almost burly, figure was hidden in a long, loose travelling coat, buttoned to the chin, and although he touched his hat in replying to Mrs. Brown's first address he did not remove it.

"Where have I seen him?" pursued Margaret lazily, for she did not much care to know, after all. "In Paris, in London, in Rome, the Holy Land — where was it? Oh, I know — but no, it can't be the same — and I never knew that man's name. Can it be? That was four — five years ago — at the Madeleine. Of course, not the same ; but I would like to see that man again."

"Margaret!" called her aunt, in a pleased voice, and Margaret had nothing to do but rise and move toward her, sorely annoyed at being thus dragged into a conversation which she herself never would have begun.

"This gentleman has been at Dinan, dear old Dinan, and all up and down the Breton coast and the Channel Islands, and he agrees with me that this Maine scenery is wonderfully like it. Don't you think so?"

"I suppose all rocky coasts resemble each other more or less," said Margaret coldly. At sound of her voice the stranger, who had only glanced at her furtively and turned away his eyes, raised them suddenly, and shot a piercing look into her own eyes, — a look so searching and so imperious that it seemed to stab through all reserves and pretences as a Milan dagger through a silken doublet. The rare color flew to Margaret's face, and her eyes drooped, but the next moment a world's training came to her aid, and she raised them with a look whose haughty coldness might have frozen the most resolute intruder upon her acquaintance. It was, however, but one of the deadly arrows shot into the air and falling harmlessly wide of its aim, for the stranger was steadfastly regarding the deck, as he said in a singularly cultivated and musical voice, —

" Yes, they resemble each other just as human creatures do ; but one who studies either nature or humanity will always find individualities, and I seldom forget place or person that I have once seen."

And, with a most courteous and all-pervasive bow, he mounted the steps and joined his companion.

" A most gentlemanly person," said Mrs. Brown complacently.

" I don't like Jesuits," replied Margaret, going back to her chair, and resolutely opening her book.

3

# CHAPTER IV.



"ELSIE," said Joan, in a low voice, as the two girls, arm-in-arm, briskly promenaded the forward deck, where a keen salt breeze, following or facing them, swept aside their skirts, displaying Joan's slender ankles and proudly arched instep, and, snatching Elsie's golden locks from the ribbon and net that vainly bound them, threaded them into a thousand little spirals, glittering like an aureole in the morning sun. Both fresh young faces glowed with the bold kisses of the breeze, and Joan's hazel eyes and Elsie's gray ones were bright and dewy with exercise and the new wine of joyous youth.

"What is it, Joan?"

"I'll tell you something. Our blond admirer is in the hands of a dry nurse, who won't let him speak to us. I saw them when we came out here; the youth wanted to come too, and nurse would n't let him, but trotted him off somewhere, and now he's on this deck overhead, and has been trying to make us look up at him; but Cousin Margaret put me on honor, you know, and so I would n't see him, and after a while he turned sulky and walked off with a cigar, but every little while he strolls over to this end and peeps down, just like a squirrel out of a cage. You remember our poor old Bun, don't you?"

"Yes, the cat got him at last, did n't he? What a tail — "

"Elsie, you are such a provoking creature! I tell you of a charming beau, and you reply with the tale of a squirrel."

"Joan! That man heard you and turned to look at us."

"What man? That sailor?"

"I don't think he's a sailor, but never mind. O Joanie, is n't this wind and the sunlight and the sea and everything just splendid! I feel as if there were two Elspeths in my shoes."

"That's the reason you wear them so big, I suppose," remarked Joan, glancing from her own natty French boots to Elsie's vastly sensible country-made shoes, but at the next turn she contrived to lead her companion to the other side of the deck, that she might have a good look at the solitary individual, standing like a figure-head in the very peak of the bows, whom Elsie reported as having presumed to look disapprovingly on herself.

"Oh, no, not a sailor!" was her verdict at the first glance, and in half a dozen more turns, during which she had kept up an animated conversation upon shoes, shoemakers, Hastings the shoemaker, his wife, baby, elder daughter, scarlet fever, jelly, pony-carriage, and Fuss, Elsie's pony, she had so carefully catalogued this stranger's features, expression, figure, dress, that she afterwards made an admirable sketch of him, calling it the Lookout on the Palos; for Joan possessed two talents, — the one very usual for young ladies, the other very unusual: she was a capital draughtsman, and read the people she met, both physically and mentally, quickly and well.

"A great deal better worth while than the dry-nursed youth! I wish he would look round again ; I suppose I must n't make him. I wish Meg did n't trust me. I wish Elsie would be naughty for me."

Such and such like were the thoughts skurrying like mice through this reprehensible young woman's mind, and whimsical Dame Fortune, reading them, came to her aid by suddenly snatching the little sailor hat with its strip of blue veil from Elsie's head, and whirling it forward close past the Lookout, on its way to the Atlantic Ocean. But as the end of tissue brushed his shoulder, the Lookout launched a long arm upward, deftly caught the flying thing, gravely regarded it for a moment, then turned and looked for its owner. There she stood, the golden curls all broken loose and flying out like the glory around one of Fra Angelico's angel heads, the pure color mantling high, the sweet, innocent eyes wide open, a shy, delicious smile quivering upon the baby mouth, an indescribably charming air of virginal reserve, mingled with girlish amusement, expressed in every line of the face and form.

As for Joan, she laughed outright, clapped her hands, and only wished it had been her hat.

The gentleman — for none could look at him and doubt his position, in spite of the coarse simplicity of his attire — looked from one to the other, while a brief smile flashed across the gravity of his face, illuminating it as a passing gleam of sunlight does a sombre sea.

"It is yours," said he, handing the hat to Elsie, and raising his own with the other hand.

"Oh, thank you! I am ever so much obliged; it was very stupid of me to lose it," stammered Elsie.

"And very clever of you to catch it," suggested Joan, wishing to gain a full glance of those wonderful Irish eyes, —

"Greenest of all things blue, bluest of all things gray."

"Not at all; merely the habit of cricket," replied the Lookout, shooting one gleam of fun in her direction, and touching his hat again as he turned back to his position in the bows. Not even Joan could continue the conversation, or beg him to remain, but there was something in that one look of the powerful eyes, that one flashing smile, the modulations of the voice, the courteous indifference, and yet perfect appreciativeness of the manner, that stirred the little coquette's instincts, as the sight of the prince of mice might the princess-royal among kittens.

"He saw that we were pretty girls, he looked at every one of Elsie's lovely gold threads, he knew that I wanted to know him, and he politely turned his back and surveyed the seaweed!" so to her own ear murmured Joan, and followed Elsie into the cabin to readjust hat and hair, with a comic sense of slight and injury upon her, not unmingled with astonishment.

As the two girls entered the cabin by the forward door, Mrs. Beauchamp Brown and Margaret appeared from the afterdeck, and the elder lady, beckoning her nieces, announced, —

"We 're just arriving, girls, and you had better pick up your novels, handkerchiefs, umbrellas, and things now. I 'm not sure but we 'd better keep on to Mount Desert after all. I must say these barren little islands don't look very encouraging."

"Oh, we 're going to make the wilderness blossom like a rose, and the solitude is precisely what we 're seeking," said Margaret hastily. "I suppose Eunice Small has a delightful little lunch all ready for us."

"Well, a good lunch would be acceptable, I must say, for I could not eat a morsel of breakfast, if breakfast you can call it," said Mrs. Brown, and nobody contradicted her, although a suppressed smile lurked around Margaret's lips and danced in Joan's eyes.

"You have n't told anybody where we are going?" asked the elder cousin, as the two glanced at each other.

"I have n't spoken to any one but Elsie," hastily exclaimed Joan, a little injured. "Oh, yes, to the man who caught Elsie's hat, but I did n't tell him. I 'm afraid he would n't have cared if I had."

"Why, surely, I had a fan, — my black and gold fan. Have n't you seen it, Margaret? Elspeth, run out and look where I was sitting! Joan, is n't it among those shawls?"

Five minutes of active exertion upon everybody's part resulted in finding the fan in Mrs. Beauchamp Brown's own handbag, and by this time the brain-piercing whistle of the Useless announced that she was approaching Plum Island, at a rocky and nearly inaccessible point called White's Landing, invented for the use of the few families of *quasi* Whites living in that vicinity. The usual and commodious landing was some miles farther on, but Margaret, who seemed since morning to have acquired a morbid horror of sharing their solitude with any of their fellow-passengers, had persuaded her aunt that it would be far nicer to debark at White's Landing, and drive across the island, than to mix with the crowd at the common wharf.

"Passengers for Plum Island, White's Landing!" vociferated the steward, and the four ladies presenting themselves at the gangway, were handed into a large, flat-bottomed boat, called in those regions a gundalow, a corruption of gondola, and suggesting a curious antithesis of the Italian and New England forms of speech and modes of thought.

A long, lean, brown White managed the gundalow by means of a pole considerably longer and nearly as stout as himself, and applying this to the side of the Useless, so soon as his passengers were seated, sent his clumsy craft into the seething whirlpool between the steamboat and the shore, whose black and jagged rocks seemed to have rushed out into the water to meet the intruders, as the surly dogs of an inhospitable house fly to forestall the visitor whose carriage stops at their master's gate. Mrs. Beauchamp Brown was angrily scared at the seething waters and the grinning rocks; Elsie was delighted at them and smiled, as Una at the lion; Margaret felt vaguely annoyed at everything, and lowered her gray veil; and Joan looked back at the Useless.

The young Englishman, with the Glengarry cap and the single eyeglass, stood upon the upper deck, gazing upon the gundalow with an incredulous stare, very funny to behold, but whose full meaning Joan did not understand until later. Near him, with a book in his hand, sat his companion, his eyes furtively glancing in the same direction, and a smile of some mysterious meaning, Joan rather thought satire, playing about his firm, handsome lips.

On the forward deck the Lookout man paced slowly up and down, his arms folded, his head bowed upon his breast.

"He does n't know that we are leaving ; he would n't care if he did!" said Joan to herself, and bit her pouting lower lip till it glowed like the heart of a pomegranate.

"Man! This thing is full of water! My feet are almost in it!" shrieked Mrs. Beauchamp Brown, as the gundalow lurched and heaved shoreward. The White man looked over his shoulder, and slowly wrinkled his leathern cheeks into an encouraging smile.

"'Like ter, never killed a woggin,'" replied he sententiously. "We 'll be ashore in a brace o' shakes."

"We 've had more than a brace of shakes already," murmured Joan, as the gundalow banged against a big rock, and sheered off scathless in her usual style.

"I must say I mistook my vocation when I set out as a pioneer," exclaimed her aunt crossly, and Margaret, whose spirits had risen since she left the Useless, gayly exclaimed, —

"I really begin to hope for a new sensation, and the sight of men and things a little out of the old way. Aunt, we 'll write our travels, like Mme. Ida Pfeiffer, and earn for Plum Island and ourselves an undying fame."

"She got eaten by savages or something, did n't she ? and served her quite right too. I don't believe in strong-minded women," announced Mrs. Brown severely, the "women" coming out with a jerk, as the gundalow struck the beach, and grounded about three feet from a little pier of rudely piled rocks.

The White man looked, and coolly remarked, "I did n't p'sume the tide was so low, but I guess you can fetch it, can't ye ? Or, hold on, I 'll make a kind o' bridge for ye."

And holding the gundalow in position with the pole, he dragged up a thwart with the other hand, and flung it across the chasm with a bang that made Mrs. Brown start and utter a little shriek.

"Don't holler till you 're hurt," suggested the White man, so benevolently, and with so little idea of possible offence, that everybody smiled good-naturedly, and one by one the party tripped across the bridge, and landing safely on the rough wharf, passed up a rocky path to a plateau in the lee of a lobster factory, whose pronounced odors and heaps of scarlet shells answered instead of the fragrant posy-beds of the rural districts. Another White man, long, lean, brown, sententious as him of the gundalow, stood beside a large open wagon, and severely contemplated the distant scenery, as if remonstrating with its rugged and forbidding aspect. He was there in hopes of a possible passenger to be conveyed inland, but Yankee independence forbade his making any demonstrations of his wishes, or even looking wistfully at the prey which the gods had so manifestly driven ashore for his benefit.

"Do you know where a woman named Eunice Small lives?" inquired Mrs. Brown abruptly, after a brief consultation with Margaret, who suggested that this was probably the hackman of the station. At sound of the voice he slowly brought home his attention from the horizon, and, after contemplating the four ladies, one by one, inquired in a high-pitched, nasal voice, "Did you want to go to Eunice Small's?"

"Yes. Can you take us there?" demanded Mrs. Brown.

"Wa-al—yes—dunno but I kin," replied the White man, as hesitatingly and reflectively as if the idea of devoting himself and his horse to such a use now occurred to him for the first time, and then adding more briskly, "It 's quite a piece."

"What do you mean?" sternly demanded Mrs. Brown.

"Whaddoo I mean?" retorted White, "Why, its fo' five mild over to Eunice's from here."

"Very well, I suppose you can go four or five miles as well as one, if you 're paid for it, can't you?" asked Mrs. Brown, who was getting very cross with the heat, the fatigue, the poor breakfast, and want of her customary appliances.

"Yes, I s'pose I kin," replied White sulkily, for if hard cash is a rare article in the outlying settlements of a State not wealthy in its centres, and therefore a thing much to be desired and toiled for, the dignity and independence of man is a growth as vigorous as the pine trees, as pronounced as the rocks. The White man wanted money, and intended to get as much of it from these travellers as he could, but he would also have enjoyed jumping into his wagon and driving away without another word, leaving this supercilious old lady to find her way to her destination as she could. A Latin would have served her all the more readily for her scorn, an Englishman would have charged it in the bill, the American felt and resented it, weighed it against a five dollar gold-piece, and found it become an airy nothing.

"Jump right in, and we 'll be going," was his next remark. "The two girls kin sit forrod, and the others, bein' they 're a little heftier, 'll ride better back. I 'll go borry a chair for the old lady to climb in."

He strolled away to the lobster factory, and Mrs. Beauchamp Brown carefully raised her veil so as to give full scope to her vision, and looked at Margaret, who met her eyes gravely enough at first, then burst into a laugh.

"Excuse me, Aunt Phyllis, but it *is* all so funny," said she.

"Funny!" echoed Mrs. Brown majestically. "We cannot sit like Ariadne upon these rocks until the return of the steamboat, but if I live till to-morrow I shall return to Boston and put myself in the Asylum for Incurable Idiots. That 's where *I* belong."

But when the wagon was packed, and the sleepy horse, developing powers modestly concealed from the public gaze, had surmounted the first steep hill, Elsie uttered an exclamation of delight, and drew everybody's attention to the magnificent view of sea and shore, and blue,

blue sky, and lovely neighbor-isles and bold, isolated rocks, over which the sea broke in showers of glistening spray, and an eagle far overhead winging his silent way to the top of Green Mountain.  Everybody exclaimed in delight, and, at Joan's request, the White man halted his horse, and sat with his elbows on his knees, idly flicking the wheel with his whip, and wishing he had charged by time rather than distance; but it was not a long halt, for Mrs. Beauchamp Brown soon exclaimed, " Come, let us get on to our wigwam and roots.  I am far beyond scenery or romance of any sort."

A long hour of discomfort ensued, and even Joan had subsided into weary silence, when, after a steep ascent, the driver, pointing with his whip, briefly announced, " That's Eunice's, — that with the lalocs in the front yard.  'Pears strange she don't get it cleared up some."

Everybody eagerly looked along the whip, and saw the quaintest, queerest little house imaginable, composed, as is so often the case in this district, of two houses, the first built by the pioneers, simply according to their necessities, the rest added on by the more flourishing and ambitious children or grandchildren, who aspired to parlors, front doors, and spare bedrooms.  The elder portion of these houses has a sort of pathos about it, — a simple dignity quite wanting to the younger.  It tells of the brave struggle of two young hearts beginning the world together, the contempt of all those false needs that would keep them apart, the courage, independence, self-respect of a man and woman who dared be outwardly poor; and then, — ; but never mind, go into one of those old, brown, low-ceiled kitchens, with its great fireplace, sunken floor, worn stairs, little windows, perhaps still diamond-paned, great beams with old, old hooks along them, whence once hung the squashes, no, pumpkins, bundles of herbs, hams, strings of onions for the winter's food of those who seldom ate other than the produce of their own acres; and, standing there, bring back the people who first lived within those four walls, and the little bedroom beyond; the young wife, the young mother; yes, you will find it all there; all the romance, all the poetry, all that Whittier has written in "Snow Bound," and many a heart has dreamed but could not say. Try it and see.

The front yard was, as White had said, choked with lilacs, so that the glorious sea-view was quite hidden from the lower windows, and the front gate opened in a sort of bower or arcade of intermingled branches, growing so low that Margaret had to stoop her stately head in entering, and Joan suggested what a grand chance for Joab if he could have driven Absalom into it. In this bower, like a fate-lady at a fair, stood a gaunt, peculiar-looking woman, so shy and furtive of expression and manner as she waited to welcome her guests, that she reminded one of a newly-caged wildwood creature, only looking for an opening to spring away and lose itself in its native forest.

Mrs. Brown at once assailed her, even before the wagon stopped. "Well, Eunice, here we are, and I never was so disappointed in my life! If I had known what a God-forsaken place this was! — Why did n't you tell me, I should like to know? Racketing over these horrible roads!"

"If you 'd gone to the head o' the Island you 'd have done better. Jubal went up to fetch you."

"It would take more than Jubal to fetch harmony out of this crowd," murmured Joan to Elsie, who looked scared and said nothing.

"Give me your hands, girls, and I 'll jump you down," said the White man, quite unconscious of undue familiarity and holding up a pair of leathern paws, into which Joan without hesitation laid her slender gants de Suede, and leaped lightly to the ground, with a gush of girlish laughter; Elsie followed as simply as if it had been a wooden pole she leaned upon; Margaret meanwhile conveying herself out of the wagon as if she had been dismounting from a throne, and Mrs. Beauchamp Brown clambering down by means of a chair. The five dollars were handed over, Mrs. B. B. severely remarking that it was like paying a dentist's bill ; and the White man drove away with content upon his granitic features, and visions of a Jersey calf, sternly dashed to the ground but yesterday, again looming fair and rosy upon the horizon.

" There 's Jubal now," announced Eunice, as the rattle of coming wheels mingled with those departing. The new-comers instinctively turned to look at a being in whom their hostess was evidently so much interested, and beheld, not the inventor of stringed instruments, but first the head, then shoulders, body, and magnificent tail of a big chestnut horse coming round the angle of the house, then a great open wagon furnished with two seats, upon the first of which sat a shrewd, good-natured-looking man, impossible as a native of any place but northern New England, sandy of complexion, wiry of form, alert of expression.  His quick gray eyes took in and embraced the groups at the gate, and, checking his horse's rapid pace, he called out, —

" Your folkses baggage is over to the Head, I guess, Eunice."

" My gracious ! " gasped Mrs. Beauchamp Brown, — one of whose prerogatives was to utter an occasional expletive herself, but never to permit them to anybody else, — " Margaret, do you see ? "

" Yes," murmured Margaret, in a tone between amusement and dismay, while Joan, catching Elsie by the sleeve, shook all over in a fit of subdued merriment, and Elsie's innocent eyes opened wide and incredulous, while she, like the rest, beheld, seated comfortably on the back seat of Jubal's wagon the blond youth, with his mature companion, whom they had left on board the Useless, bound for Mount Desert.

" Do you want Jubal to bring your trunks, or did you speak to Barzillai ? " inquired Eunice, in the subdued and somewhat weary tone learned by years in a sick-room.

" Trunks ?  What ?  Who are those people ? " demanded Mrs. Brown, in angry confusion, while Margaret slightly and Joan cordially returned the salute of

the two gentlemen, of whom the elder looked blandly
unconscious ; the younger delighted, amused, and a little guilty.

"Oh, those are Mehitable's folks.  She said she was
going to have some.  Jubal will get the trunks if you
like."

"Very well, arrange it with him," replied Mrs. B. B.
haughtily, and, brushing past her hostess, walked up the
lilac bower and in at the open door, followed by her
party.

# CHAPTER V.



"OH, how pretty!" cried Elspeth, for once the first to express herself; and all the rest echoed her surprise and pleasure, each in her own way, for the scene was unique and charming, whether to a child of nature like Elsie, or world-wise and world-weary women like Margaret and her aunt. On either side of the little square entrance-hall lay a great, low-ceiled room, the windows overgrown with vines and shrubs, through which filtered a cool, green light, yet more softened by draperies of embroidered India mull depending from a fantastic cornice of old brocade. The floors were covered with matting, and in front of the fireplace in the parlor lay a great Turkey rug, its colors harmonizing with those of a silk shawl used as cover to the table in the centre of the room. At one side the table stood a sleepy-hollow reading-chair, covered in old Spanish leather, its rich gilding dim with age, and at the other a cane-seated ship-chair. In amicable contrast to these mute tokens of study and travel stood in one corner a great, square, chintz-covered easy-chair of the kind dear to our great-grandmothers, and never seen in houses of the *nouveaux*. Some wooden shelves of primitive construction supported a few books, the rich russet and gold bindings of the volumes of Burke shining out among the rest, while a pile of Thomas's "Farmer's Almanac" dating a quarter of a century back, the original "New England Primer," an old, old black-bound family Bible, and some venerable hymn-books, spoke of the "rude forefathers" who had built and dwelt in this home before ever Eunice or Miss Myra Moberley or Mrs.

Beauchamp Brown were thought of or needed in the world. Upon the walls of the parlor hung two or three good engravings, and one black expanse richly framed, wherein, by diligent study in a strong light, might be discerned a copper kettle, a tobacco-pipe with a stupid old man's face behind it, and a figure surmounted by a cap, bending over what might be a churn, possibly a child, perhaps a barrel or a wash-tub ; and this Mrs. Beauchamp Brown pronounced a genuine Teniers, and studied pensively and enviously during many hours of her sojourn at Plum Island. But it was none of these properties that had evoked the admiring exclamations of the guests as they entered ; it was the fragrant and verdant beauty of the great masses of wild-flowers, the bank of ferns filling the fireplace, the cornice, extending all around both rooms and the hall, of spice-breathing spruce boughs, framing the doorways, and fringing the great beams overhead. In a dark corner of the little vestibule stood a whole tree, its branches decorated with artificial flowers, half concealed beneath the leaves, and producing in the obscurity a glowing and startling effect. The room opposite the parlor was fitted for a bedroom, with a great four-posted bedstead of richly carved mahogany, hung with curtains of white linen, embroidered in crewels with the story of Absalom and David and Bathsheba, and the Queen of Sheba. The fireplace of this room, wide enough to take logs four feet in length, was hidden by an enormous oil-painting in a tarnished gilt frame, depicting the exodus of Hagar from her master's tent, the glowing beauty of the slave contrasting temptingly with Sarah's leathern and spiteful countenance. A cruel fracture of the canvas where Ishmael's head should have been injured the effect of the piece, and probably had brought it to Plum Island and its present " base use," but a good deal of interest and beauty remained. Peeping behind this, Joan was first to discover a pair of great iron andirons furnished with hooks, across which a spit might be laid, and meat duly roasted in the orthodox fashion. An artistic pile of drift-wood, surmounted by dry pine-branches and fir-cones, lay ready for the touch of a match ; and so cool and strong are the night airs of this coast that few evenings came in which it was not pleasant to sit by the flickering blaze, feeding it with now a handful of cones, and now a branch of spruce, at whose resinous twigs the fire would snap and dart like a wild beast.

From the parlor opened a dining-room, cool, fresh, quaint, and bowery as the rest, and here stood ready a luncheon-table, its heavy damask sweeping the floor, its garniture of old Nankin china, cut glass, and Sheffield steel, with an antique plated tea-urn giving dignity to the whole apartment.

"There !  That 's what I told you ! " exclaimed Mrs. Beauchamp Brown, marching straight through the parlor and up to this table, her triumph as an historian dispelling her irritation as an explorer.  "That 's what I knew we should find here.  And see, did n't I tell you Eunice knew what civilized creatures eat?  See that Dutch cheese, those Albert biscuit, that dried ginger, that dish of olives ! What did I tell you ? "

"Won't there be doughnuts and pie ? " asked Joan in a tone of dismay.  "I thought there always were pies and doughnuts in the country."

"I am sorry you should be disappointed, Joan Jennifer," replied Mrs. Brown sharply ; "but we come into the country to live like city people."

"What a horrible sarcasm ! " whispered Joan to Elsie, who looked mystified, and followed as Eunice led the way upstairs to two great, airy bedrooms, with a little bower, all green branches and white curtains, off one, and a connecting link between the two principal rooms, also giving access to the garret and to the back of the house, but fitted with a quaint little tent-bedstead and a washstand. This, half-passage, half-room, Joan immediately appropriated to herself, desiring that it should be known as "On-the-way," while the closet given to Elsie she called "Maiden's Bower ;" Mrs. Beauchamp Brown's apartment, with its hangings of green moreen and garniture of four funereal designs, " Grand-gloomy-and-peculiar" ; and Margaret's, "Kashmeer," from the perfume of an especial soap much affected just then by the occupant, and also from an Indian shawl with which she hid a great, clumsy armchair beside the bed.

"What about the room downstairs?" asked Mrs. Brown sharply. "That is fitted for a bedroom too, is n't it?"

"Yes 'm," replied Eunice in her discreet voice. "I thought perhaps the young ladies would take it, or you might like to ask some friends down. I could accommodate a couple more at the table."

"Eunice Small, I told you in the first place that I wished the house to myself," exclaimed Mrs. Brown indignantly; "and if I 'm not to have it I won't stay. As for these girls, they will remain under my own eye " ——

"Like the elephant's trunk in the conundrum," whispered Joan, and set Elsie to giggling, while the irate aunt continued, —

—— "So you may take the sheets off that bed and put them away as soon as you like, though I don't mind the bedstead, as it came from the Moberley's and is not musty, I suppose."

"Yes 'm," replied Eunice meekly, and went downstairs, whence presently drifted up the tones of a high-pitched nasal voice, with these words : —

—— "Never thought of such a thing as their coming to-day, and not a bit of victuals cooked up nor nothing, and Josiah he 's gone to the Cap'ns to kill his pig, and is a-going to bring home half on 't for us to have some to-morrer, and I let Semanthy and Matildy go off plumming, for I thought the rosbries would be kind o' handy for supper, and not cost nothing neither ; so that 's just how I 'm fixed, and here they be, and I knew you had a plenty ready, and your table 's big enough, and I thought they might just as well sit down and have something with your folks. Like enough they 're acquainted, all coming from Boston so, and I 'll pay you what 's right."

The voice paused, evidently for want of breath, and Eunice's subdued tones replied, with considerable hesitation, —

"I'd just as lieve as not, so far as I'm concerned, Mehitable, but I don't believe Mrs. Beauchamp Brown would listen to it.  She's very set in her ways, and not overly obliging"——

"Eunice Small, I can hear every word you say," remarked Mrs. B. B., out of the little lattice at the back of her bedroom, commanding the side door where the two women were standing.  Eunice looked up, and a gleam of humor passed across her impassible face.

"Excuse me, ma'am," said she, "then maybe you'll be so kind as to give your answer for yourself.  This is Mehitable Barnes, my cousin, that lives in the next house, and she's got two gentlemen come unexpected to stop with her, and was wanting to know if I could board them for to-day.  I don't suppose there's any use in asking"——

"It is very impertinent of you to suppose anything of the sort or to undertake to answer for me in any way, Eunice Small," replied Mrs. Brown majestically.  "You may tell your cousin to say to the gentlemen that Mrs. Beauchamp Brown will be happy to see them at lunch and dinner, or until their own accommodations are ready.  Do you understand?"

"Yes 'm," replied Eunice in the monotonous and utterly inexpressive voice she had acquired in six-and-twenty years of servitude, and Mrs. Brown closed the window and returned to the washhand-stand.  Joan, separated from Elsie by Margaret's Vale of Kashmeer, executed a noiseles *pas seul* of delight, and Margaret frowned into her mirror, and smiled languidly at noticing how well the frown became her.

"My dear aunt might even be got to heaven if some Mephistopheles would try to drag her to the other place," said she.

A silvery bell rang as the clock struck one, and Mrs. Brown silently led the way to the parlor, followed by her three beautiful nieces.  Two gentlemen stood at the bookcase, and the elder, turning to greet the ladies, displayed the peculiar dress and tonsured head of a Roman Catholic clergyman ; his companion, without his hat, looked more blond, more boyish, but yet more attractive, with his air of inborn refinement, and deference to women, than on board the boat.

"Allow me to offer our apologies and thanks, madame," said the priest, a slight accent betraying that his perfect English was acquired and not inherited, "and to present my friend and pupil, Mr. Smith."

Everybody bowed, and the younger man, in an oddly hesitating voice, said in turn, —

" Mr. Williams, Mrs. Beauchamp Brown."

The courtesy of a true *grande dame* is superior to fatigue, annoyance, or hunger, and Mrs. Beauchamp Brown was *grande dame* to the crest of her white puffs and the tips of her little hands ; so she greeted her guests as she well knew how, and marshalled them to the dining-room, seating them as she thought they would best like, the priest at her own right hand, and the youth between the two girls, while Margaret took the foot of the table and avoided everybody's conversation.

Joan quietly but very positively pounced upon the prey thus delivered into her hands, Elsie ate bread-and-butter and drank milk with an exceeding relish, and Mr. Williams, with the power of a man of the world, led the conversation into the channel he had found so navigable in the morning, speaking. so modestly yet so intelligently of France in general, and Brittany in particular, that Mrs. Beauchamp Brown, who rather considered this province as under her especial patronage, exclaimed, —

" Ah, Mr. Williams, it is easy to see that you are a Breton, or at least have lived there very much, as I have. It is only long experience that gives such familiarity."

. The priest bowed, with his subtle smile, replying, —

" Indeed, madame, our poor Brittany deserves no such stigma as to have fathered a poor vagabond like me. I have not lived there more than everywhere else. Last, in England."

" Yes, I perceived that Mr. Smith is English," said the hostess, with a smile toward the blond boy. Joan caught the smile, and was wickedly inspired thereby to betray her playmate into a dilemma.

"Oh, what do you think, Aunt Phyllis?" exclaimed she. "Mr. Smith is saying that we don't pronounce our name properly.   He says it is Beecham."

"Indeed!" exclaimed Mrs. Beauchamp Brown loftily, while a small pink mounted to her cheek.

"Why, you know," stammered poor Mr. Smith, his face bathed in blushes, but standing his ground manfully, "Beecham 's the way to pronounce it, though it 's spelled Beauchamp, of course."

"I was just saying that I perceived you to be an Englishman, Mr. Smith," replied Mrs. Beauchamp Brown, in a voice smooth and cold and keen as a razor.

Mr. Smith, being English, did not recognize the fact that he was beaten, and would have continued the topic, but Joan with compassionate haste drew his attention to herself by asking in a low voice, —

"But why, Mr. Smith, should the English choose to pronounce a French name in such a very un-French way? It is a purely French name, you know."

"Why, I suppose it is because when we English want a thing we have a fashion of annexing it, as you Americans say, and doing as we like with it," replied Mr. Smith, very willing to subside into a *tête-à-tête* with his charming neighbor, who tossed her head as she replied, —

"That fashion did n't work very well when you tried to annex thirteen colonies a century or so ago."

But Mrs. Beauchamp Brown's vexation soon evaporated, and she was able, as they returned to the parlor, to say, "It was a happy chance that procured us the pleasure of your company to-day, Mr. Williams.   We shall see you again at dinner time, I trust."

"Thanks.   We do not wish to abuse your hospitality, but the temptation is great," replied the priest, glancing with a smile at his pupil, who was laughing with the two girls at the window looking toward the sea.

"Here 's Jubal, Cousin Margaret," exclaimed Elspeth, who had eyes to spare for the outer world.

"Not with our luggage already?" said Mrs. Ufford, who had been unusually silent and depressed since their arrival.

"No, with a big empty wagon and two horses.  Here he is."

The tap of a whip-handle on the open door seconded her announcement, and on Mrs. Brown's exclaiming "Come in !" the door was pushed wider, and Jubal's keen, good-natured features and straw hat appeared in the room.

"O ! I did n't know but some of you might have a notion to go over to the Head just for the ride.  I should n't charge any more.  Maybe the girls could go."

"You are very kind, sir, but it is quite " — began Mrs. Brown haughtily, but Margaret interposed,

"I should like to go very much, Mr. —— "

"Keene, ma'am, Jubal Keene is what they call me.  Some folks get it Jubal Cain, after the old Bible worthy, but that ain't what 's intended."

"And may we go too ? " demanded Joan eagerly.

"Is there room for three of us ? " asked Margaret.

"Well, there ain't but one seat in, on account of the trunks ; but if you would n't mind setting on them coming back, I could put in another to go over."

"If I might go too ! " pleaded Mr. Smith, holding up hands of mock supplication to Margaret, who glanced at Mrs. Beauchamp Brown, and replied, —

"A merciful man is merciful to his beast, Mr. Smith, and I am sure Mr. Keene is too merciful to ask his beast to drag six persons and sixteen boxes over these roads "

Mr. Smith colored a little, and bowed somewhat stiffly.  Evidently he was not accustomed to having his requests refused, and as the wagon drove off with its merry freight, he and his tutor walked away in the opposite direction.

Mrs. Beauchamp Brown watched both parties out of sight, and then going back to the sleepy hollow and Burke, she remarked aloud,

"Very odd how things turn out sometimes.  I thought I was coming here to an absolute hermitage, above all to avoid men, and here are these two actually billeted upon us.  Two girls and a young man on my hands !  Well, I 'd rather Joan flirted with a stranger than wrote letters after Launcelot."

# CHAPTER VI.



THE drive to the Head o' the Island, as the point nearest the mainland was commonly called, was very pretty, passing through a thick-set spruce wood, over a wide creek, which all but cuts Plum Island in two, and along the coast, giving a constantly varying view of the pretty islets composing this archipelago, upon which man, exercising his proud prerogative as master of nature, has bestowed such names as Butter, Pudding, Sheep, Calf, and Bear Islands, and dignified the headlands and bays with the titles of Herring Point, Lobster Cove, and Clam Creek.

A cluster of houses, a lonesome looking meeting-house, a blacksmith's shop, and two or three "variety stores," with a shed called the post-office, constituted the town ; and here Jubal paused to converse for some moments with a gentleman, who having recently killed a cow, was anxious to dispose of part of the beef, and "thought like enough Eunice and Mehitable might like some, seeing as they had folks stopping with them."

"I suppose you eat beef, don't you?" asked Jubal of Joan, who shared the front seat with him.

"Sometimes," replied she demurely ; and Jubal promising to "name it" to the ladies in question, shook his reins as a signal to his friend to remove his foot from the shaft where he had planted it, and drove on.

"Some consid'able responsibility in taking boarders down here," said he, twisting himself so as to look at Margaret on the back seat.

"Yes? I dare say," replied she graciously.

"You see 't ain't as 't is with you to home, where if you have some one come in unexpected, you can sly out the back way and get a pound of sausages or a slice of steak to cook up quick, or maybe send down to the baker's for a pie or some doughnuts," pursued Jubal, a little proud of his experience in city ways. " I was up to Boston myself two year ago, and I admired the way my cousin got along."

" Oh, it is very convenient," replied Joan gravely. " You can send into the restaurant close by my aunt's house, and get a plate of baked beans any time, for six cents."

" I want to know! It must come awful handy," said Jubal thoughtfully.

" I did n't know there was a restaurant near Aunt Phyllis's house," said Elsie, with a puzzled air.

" Why, yes, dear, kept by a man named Parker, don't you know?" replied Joan, turning to cast a warning look at Elspeth, who exclaimed " Oh !" and burst out laughing.

" There used to be a school — school of good manners I think they called it — where his house now stands," remarked Margaret quietly, and Jubal cast a quick glance at Joan out of the corner of his little gray eye, and colored slightly. Presently he halted at a lonely farmhouse on the edge of a thick piece of woods, gave the reins to Joan, and ran into the house, returning in a moment with a gun in his hand.

" There," remarked he, jumping into the wagon, and laying the gun across his knees, the muzzle carefully pointed outward, " now we 're safe anyway, and it 's always better to be on the safe side. Go along, Gershom !"

" Safe from what, Mr. Keene?" asked Joan impetuously.

" Why, there was an Injun devil, as they call 'em, a specie of wildcat I believe it is really, seen in these woods, and though I don't presume it would attackt us in broad daylight so, it 's always better, as I say, to be on the safe side, and I just borrowed my brother's gun to carry through the woods. If you 'll keep a good lookout on your side the road, Miss, I 'll keep my eye on this, and drive too."

" But really, if there is danger, Mr. Keene," said Margaret, a little anxiously, "we had better not go at all.  I had no idea " —

"What 's that — away down that wood road?" interrupted Jubal, pointing with his whip, and as Joan eagerly bent forward to look, he twisted his head over his shoulder and bestowed a quizzical smile and unmistakable wink upon Margaret, who received it with an unaffected stare of astonishment and a flush of indignation; then murmuring, "Quand vous êtes à Rome," — she turned and looked into the woods like the rest.  Joan, a good deal excited, stared down the shadowy vistas of the wood roads, examined the tree tops, and narrowly watched each turn of the road, Jubal exciting her attention by frequent exclamations, and questions as to this or that appearance, until, as the road at length emerged upon a high bluff commanding the sea-view, he laid his gun in the bottom of the wagon, dryly remarking, —

"Well, I guess we need n't worry any more about the wildcat, seeing it was quite a number of years ago that he was shot, and there hain't been any mourners to his funeral as I 've heerd of.  I expect they feed on baked beans wuth about six cents a plate now."

"Oh!" cried Joan, turning an indignant scarlet face upon the perpetrator of the successful hoax.

"'T ain't owe, it 's pay, according to my reckoning," said he, grimly smiling, and turning toward Margaret, who, nodding assent, said meaningly, "Persons who don't like settling accounts, should n't open them, Joan."

"But is the gun loaded?" asked Elsie, her agony of silent terror giving way to quavering speech.

"No, Miss, nor hain't been since last winter.  There 's the Constitution coming in, Bangor boat."  And Jubal pointed to a tiny steamer just rounding up to the long wooden pier at the foot of the hill they were rapidly descending.  A number of wagons and quite a pile of merchandise, among which Mrs. Beauchamp Brown's and Margaret's English leather trunks shone with aristocratic distinctness, filled the end of the wharf; and here Jubal checked his horse, the ladies dismounting and wandering down towards the steamboat, which had thrown out a gang-plank, over which two or three persons had already passed.

As the three ladies drew near, a couple, very different of bearing from these, made their appearance, and stood for a moment waiting their turn. "Great heavens!" exclaimed Margaret behind her shut teeth, "are they coming here?"

"What a handsome man!" murmured Joan, squeezing Elsie's arm; while Elsie, unheeding her, was whispering, "Oh! what a beautiful lady!"

All three were correct. The man, tall, dark, distinguished in appearance, was certainly unusually handsome; the lady, resembling him very much, but several years younger, and with an air of fashion and habitual supremacy about her, might be styled beautiful by a girl of Elsie's age and experience; and they were certainly coming to Plum Island, for they were already there.

As the lady tripped over the plank, she caught sight of Margaret, and started so violently as nearly to fall into the water, had not her companion put out an arm to support her. As they reached the wharf he glanced up, and in turn saw the pale and distressed face, bent eagerly, yet shrinkingly, toward him.

"Margaret! Mrs. Ufford!" exclaimed he, turning very pale, and clinging to the arm he still held of his companion.

Margaret was the first of the three to regain self-possession. "How do you do, Mrs. Trevylyan! Captain Douglass!"

The new-comers stepped forward and shook hands, the lady nervously, the gentleman impressively, and Mrs. Trevylyan said,—

"Is it possible that you are staying here, Mrs. Ufford? I thought it was an absolutely uninhabited island."

"So did we," replied Margaret, a little laugh half concealing the point of her intimation. "I am here with Mrs. Beauchamp Brown and these young ladies, cousins of ours."

"Tom Beauchamp's daughter, I am sure," said the

lady, fixing her unbashful, beautiful brown eyes upon Joan.

"No," replied Margaret coldly. "This is Miss Jennifer, daughter of my cousin, Lucia Beauchamp, whom you may remember, and this is my cousin Edward Beauchamp's daughter. Mrs. Trevylyan and Captain Douglass, my dears."

"And now, Margaret, what sort of place is there for us here?" demanded Mrs. Trevylyan gayly as she shook hands with the girls, upon whom her beauty, grace, and elegance produced a visible effect.

"Why, there is no place at all, unless you have made arrangements," replied Margaret decisively. "Really, I cannot advise you to remain on a venture."

Mrs. Trevylyan looked a little scared and turned towards the boat; two men were hauling in the gang-plank, and the paddles were already revolving. She pointed at it with her finger, chanting gayly, —

"'Too late! Too late! Ye cannot enter now!' No, Mrs. Ufford, the Jonahs are never pulled in again; you will have to find a whale to give us lodgings. What sort of place have you?"

"My aunt has hired a house, and we are her guests," replied Margaret coldly, "and really I can offer no advice whatever."

"Perhaps your cavalier can," replied Mrs. Trevylyan, a certain air of effrontery hardening her face and voice. Margaret turned away and spoke to Elspeth, leaving the new-comer to introduce herself and her request to Jubal, who had come to ask Joan about a missing portmanteau.

"My friends tell me that you may know of a lodging for my brother and myself, sir," interposed the high-bred and sweet-toned voice, and Jubal, beaming appreciatively, replied in his blandest manner, —

"I should be very happy to accommodate you, ma'am, but there ain't a public house on the island, fur 's I know."

"But some kind fisherman or farmer might take us in," urged the lady; "some one living quite near the house where my friends are," and her voice rang maliciously. "Perhaps you, yourself."

"I? Wa-al — I d' know. We 've got a spare room, to be sure, maybe two ; and we calc'late to live pretty com-f'table, nothing extry, not city doings you know, but just good common farmer's living ; and my wife she was say-ing she did n't know but she 'd 'commodate some folks for a few weeks. I might ask her."

"She 'll be sure to say yes, if you consent," said Mrs. Trevylyan, actually expending one of her especial smiles on this unsophisticated Maine farmer ; but she wanted food and shelter, and even *grandes dames* will sometimes pay a good price of a personal nature for what they really want. At any rate, the price this time was effectual, for Jubal was routed, horse, foot, and dragoons, and pro-ceeded to make the rest of his arrangements with a speed and alacrity that showed he was only afraid of losing the opportunity of playing Good Samaritan himself.

"Ready for a start now, I guess," announced he pres-ently, coming up to the group, who were chatting in rather a constrained fashion, for Mrs. Ufford had not heard what arrangements the new-comers had effected, and would not inquire, nor did Mrs. Trevylyan inform her, while Capt. Douglass, seated upon a beam at the edge of the wharf, seemed either suffering or abstracted, and said nothing. .

"I 've got a man to take over all the baggage together," said Jubal contentedly, "and I 've borryed his seat and put it into my wagon, so six of us can ride, and I kind o' thought it would be pleasanter for you folks than to take some trunks and some passengers in two teams."

"Yes, indeed, it was very thoughtful of you, Mr. Keene," said Mrs. Trevylyan sweetly, and then turning to Mrs. Ufford, she carelessly announced, "We are to be at Mr. Keene's house for a few days, it seems, and I hope it is near you all." -

"I am sure I don't know," drawled Margaret, unable quite to conceal her annoyance ; and her friend smiled, scoring one to her own side in the long account opened some years since between these two potentates of society.

A little discussion about seats was raised by Mrs. Trevylyan, but was promptly checked by Margaret, who coldly said, —

"We will sit as we did coming over, and Mrs. Trevylyan and Capt. Douglass can take the extra seat behind. Get in, Joan and Elsie."

"You would not be so severe if you knew how ill I am, Margaret," said a hollow voice at her ear; and as she mechanically laid her hand in the thin and burning one James Douglass held out to help her into the wagon, Margaret looked into his eyes, and read there the terrible confirmation, and more, of his words. Pity and relenting shone in her own, and as she returned the pressure of his hand she softly said, "Indeed, I am very sorry, James."

# CHAPTER VII.

## A LITTLE COMPANY.

"IT is certainly a comfort to make one's self respectable once more," said Mrs. Beauchamp Brown, surveying in her only mirror, 12 × 9 instalments of her brocade and Byzantine dinner dress, with its garniture of point d'Alençon lace, and the diamond and cat's-eye ornaments in which her soul just then especially delighted. "Margaret, what are you going to wear?"

"I have not changed my dress," replied Margaret, appearing at the door of her room in the same gray travelling suit she had worn all day.

"Not change! Why, my dear, it is indecent not to dress for dinner, especially when one has guests."

"I have no guests, and desire none," replied Mrs. Ufford ungraciously; but, to do her justice, it was of the latest comers she was thinking; for Jubal, finding matters at home not quite as forward as he expected, had contrived that his lodgers should share in the invitation for dinner extended to Messrs. Williams and Smith. But Mrs. Beauchamp Brown took the slight at once to herself, and said such harsh and disagreeable things upon the text of whims and airs, and persons who thought nobody of consequence but themselves, and who found the common usages of society a constraint they were glad to throw off, that Margaret went quietly back into her own room and shut the door. Her aunt, much huffed, went downstairs; and Joan, looking like a carnation in her striped red and white tissue, stole into Elsie's room to help her put on her pretty green muslin and whisper comments on "Aunt Phyllis's tongue," to which Elsie only replied, "It was very kind of her to invite us here, Joan, and a great help to poor papa."

"O you little Bayard-ess!" exclaimed Joan. "Well, is n't this Capt. Douglass magnificent? I should like to see him in uniform! He belongs to the regular army, you know, and was wounded in Utah two or three years ago."

"Was he? Actually wounded!" exclaimed Elsie, with big eyes. "How strange it is to be a man and fight!"

"Yes, but I think I could too. I can quite fancy the rush and din of battle, and the savage desire of victory, and the enemy looking out of the smoke, and the sabre over one's head, and the answering blow, and the blood streaming down, and " ——

"O Joan! you 're murdering me!" cried poor Elsie, whose 'lint-white locks' were in Joan's hand just then, and in the heat of battle received a ferocious pull.

"Come, girls, are you ready?" demanded Margaret's voice, and pushing open the door she stood before them, dressed quietly, yet charmingly, in mauve silk, her fair, soft neck jealously veiled by a Marie Antoinette handkerchief crossed upon her breast. An amber necklace glimmered amidst its folds, and amber upon her wrists and in her hair harmonized with the faint odor clinging to her like an atmosphere.

"How nicely you look, Cousin Meg!" exclaimed Joan. "So you did change your dress," added she significantly.

"Yes," replied Margaret gravely, "it was a want of respect to Aunt Phyllis not to do so."

Elsie's shy eyes stole up to Margaret's in timid approval: the two souls, so diverse in most things, were one in the pride of loyalty.

"Come now, little maids, let us go down," cried Margaret gayly. "The banquet waits and the guests arrive."

"Yes, there is Captain Douglass," cried Joan, looking down through the clematis covering the window. "Is n't he splendid, Cousin Meg?"

"Not to be compared to Mr. Smith!" replied Margaret mockingly; and the three swept down the crooked stairway and into the dusky parlor, — a threefold vision of grace and beauty, such as that old house could never have known before.

The priest, his pupil, and Captain Douglass stood about the room in the usual forlorn style of men just before dinner, and Mrs. Trevylyan was making a dead set at Mrs. B. Brown, who received the advances warily and with a certain reservation of cordiality, as who should say, " This is all very well, you know, but then " ——

" Dinner is ready, Mrs. Beauchamp Brown," announced Eunice, with the dignity of a major-domo ; and the company filed out, Mrs. Brown taking considerable pleasure in assigning seats, and otherwise assuming the position of hostess, exactly as if she had been in her own house in Boston ; and in fact the present position of things rather drolly enforced a truth occasionally brought home to some of us, — that it is not easy for the bond-slaves of either the world, the flesh, or the devil, to escape their master simply by going to lonely islands, and saying, " I will be free for eight weeks, but do not care to permanently emancipate myself."

The dinner was good and abundant, for both Mehitable and Jubal had contributed what they considered a fair proportion of eatables, and Eunice, with her knowledge of the tastes and capacity of such persons as she had lived among, selected, adapted, and transformed her material in a manner truly astonishing.

" Now, this is what I call the perfection of rustication," said Mrs. Beauchamp Brown cheerfully, as she marshalled her guests again to the parlor. " One leaves the world behind, and yet retains a choice crumb of its pleasures. Sudden and entire change of diet is sometimes dangerous."

" Asceticism made easy, or a hermitage with all the modern conveniences," suggested the priest, with a little smile.

" Exactly," replied Mrs. Brown ; " and that's what modern religionists are looking for, I believe."

Mr. Williams bowed courteously, as he quietly retorted,

"Yes; it is but seldom that we find even a woman living quite up to the standard of the martyrs, and of course we, poor sons of Adam, only follow as they lead."

"It is so mean of you men to be always throwing that apple in our teeth!" exclaimed Mrs. Trevylyan, who had tried the edges of her own pearly teeth on Blondin, — as Joan had already nicknamed Charles Smith, — and finding the fruit rather crude and tasteless, had dropped it and turned to the ecclesiastic, who, not unwillingly, allowed her to develop a fund of humor, various information, and general conversational talent, making him a real acquisition to persons so far removed from their usual mental pabulum as these, our worldly eremites.

"O Joan, the full moon is rising over the water!" announced Elsie, putting her head in at the window, where her cousin and Blondin stood skirmishing, after the manner of youths and maidens at first acquaintance.

"Let us go out and look at it," suggested he; and the three crossed the road and, passing over and under some bars, stood in the field beyond, through which a footpath led sinuously down to the sea, skirting a grove of chestnuts and maples, amid whose dewy darkness a whole colony of little birds twittered and whispered themselves to sleep.

The priest presently rose, and strolled towards the door. Mrs. Trevylyan frankly followed, saying, —

"How does the world look by moonlight, I wonder?"

"Shall we go and see?   Mrs. Ufford, won't you step out into the moonlight?" replied the priest, not to be beguiled into a romantic ramble *tête-à-tête* with an obvious Circe.

Margaret hesitated; her aunt had disappeared to hold council in the dining-room with Eunice. If she remained, it was for Douglass, who hungrily watched for a word; if she went, it was with his sister, whom she disliked, and the priest, whom she dreaded; but she went, and so impaled herself upon both horns of the dilemma, for Douglass came too, and all four crossed over into the wooded field, waiting, however, to remove the bars their juniors had so lightly passed.

"I'm glad you have come, Cousir Margaret," cried

Elsie, running back from the edge of the wood; "we want to go down to the water. May we? will you come?"

"Yes, little Moonshine. Don't she look just like the moonlight, Camilla?"

Mrs. Trevylyan flushed perceptibly. She would have given a great deal to be restored to Margaret's good graces, and hailed with delight this use of her first name, not guessing how Margaret was at that moment nipping the end of her tongue between her teeth, in punishment for the careless tripping.

"Yes, indeed, she does, Margaret," cried she; and as Elsie laughingly sped away, Mrs. Ufford turned sharply from the flood of sentiment and effusion poured out upon her by her former friend, and addressed herself to the priest, who, nothing loth, replied, ranging himself beside her as they walked. Camilla, offended, seized her brother's arm, murmuring, —

"Margaret wants to flirt with the priest. Do come along and let her alone."

"She would flirt with the devil to get rid of me," replied Douglass so bitterly that his sister veered around, comforted, and petted him, and forgot herself in consoling him.

"You have been on the Mediterranean by moonlight, Mr. — Williams?" said Margaret, stammering; and then turning her sumptuous eyes full upon his, demanded, "Why are you called Mr.? All Catholic priests are Father, Père, Abbé, Padre, according to nationality, are they not? I suppose in Paris you were styled 'Père,' were n't you?"

"Yes. Did you learn my name there?"

"No, I never heard your name, of course. I do not know you, nor do you know me; but you spoke at dinner-time of having been in Paris, and I have been there enough to know the ways of French priests. My question, however, was not of Paris, but of your proper address. I never before met with a priest with a secular title."

"I quite confess the justice of your stricture," replied

the ecclesiastic, with dangerous frankness, "and not only throw myself upon your mercy, but beg your advice and counsel.   Shall I have it?"

"Ten years ago, I was as ready to assume the position of censor and adviser to my superiors as any other girl of nineteen," said Margaret bitterly.   "But those ten years have taught me, among other things, that when a man of the world, a priest, — a Jesuit, I believe, — asks counsel and censure at the hands of a woman younger and far less experienced in all ways than himself, he " ——

"Well?   He what?" demanded the priest, in a sharp, short tone, as a fencer feeling his adversary's steel.

"He either thinks her a fool, or wishes to make her so."

"Ah !   Well, madame, you are certainly sincere ; and if I had supposed you a fool, or wished you to become one, I should at once abandon the theory or the intention ; but I did neither, and so, comforting my bruised knuckles as best I may for their undeserved rap, I simply go back to my first proposition, and request your opinion upon a point you should surely understand better than I, and that is the prejudices of your countrymen."

"In the direction of Roman Catholic priests?"

"Exactly.   When I was coming to this country I was warned that to use my proper appellation, and to obtrude my proper character or profession, would subject me to great annoyance, and cause a good deal of disturbance wherever I might find myself outside the great cities, but more especially in the rural districts of New England.   It was in consequence of this advice that, since leaving Montreal, I have registered myself everywhere as simply 'F. Williams,' the 'F.' representing Father, if you will, and desired my young friend to address me in public as Mr. Williams.   It was not by my direction that he presented me by that title to Mrs. Beauchamp Brown and yourself, and I am now rather sorry that he did so.   Would you advise me to assume my own title here, and do you think honest Jacques Bonhomme will be outraged at the presence of a Catholic clergyman?"

"The whole state of mind is so essentially that of a foreigner," exclaimed Margaret laughing outright, "that I can forgive your asking counsel, even if you did it as a flattery to me, for you evidently stand in sore need of even such poor aid as I can give. In the first place, there is no Jacques Bonhomme in America. The stupid, ferocious animal so named in France, he whom even Voltaire describes as half-monkey, half-tiger, has no existence here. The farmers, fishermen, laborers even, of a place like this, of any place in the United States, unless it is given over to foreigners, are a class of thoughtful, law-observing, self-respecting men, each one of whom feels that he or his son may be President some day if he cares to take the trouble, and who believes in the largest liberty of conscience and opinion for himself and his neighbor. They don't admire Romanism, for they judge it by its results in other countries; but if you like to promenade this island from end to end in full canonicals with a cross-bearer going before to proclaim,

"'Behold Father Williams, a Roman Catholic priest!' you need apprehend nothing worse than a little grim laughter and a few rather caustic jests. Half the people would n't take the trouble to look at you at all. So, you see, the incognito is quite thrown away, and you had better simply return to your usual appearance and style, and submit to be taken very little notice of by anybody but your acquaintance."

"You heal the bruised knuckles with a bath of brine and vinegar, as they do the slaves' backs in the South," said the priest, trying to laugh.

Margaret looked at him, her eyes glittering in the moonlight. "Next time you ask my advice," said she, "you won't get it, for if you had honestly wanted it, you would take it good-humoredly. Besides, they don't have slaves in the South any more, and the North was not responsible for them while they had."

"I cry *peccavi*, and ask a truce. Even Goliath might fear so skilful a slingster; much more a poor, clumsy Englishman like myself. And will you be so very kind as to announce me to your friends as Father Williams, an un-worthy priest of the Catholic Church, and tutor to the young man you see with me, whose parents, with an honorable ambition, desire him to be educated for the priest-hood, and allow me to aid in the good work, by giving my poor services during the summer months.  We have been about two months in the country now, and came down through Canada to the White Mountains, and so to Boston, but were advised to go no farther south until cooler weather.  Oddly enough, we heard of this place on the passage from St. John's to Quebec ; the son of the woman we board with was a sailor on board, and spoke so much of his home in various interviews during the night watches I shared with him, that we were curious to see it, and thought it might be well to rest here for some weeks, and look at our books."

"I see.   It is very kind of you to devote yourself so completely to your young disciple," said Margaret soberly. "His parents are of inferior position, and poor, I think you said?"

"Oh, so-so," replied Father Williams carelessly.  "But before we join that gay group on the point, Mrs. Ufford, I should be very glad to resume for a moment a conversation held between us long ago, but as fresh in my mind to-day as if five years were but five minutes."

"My memory is not so good as yours, Father," replied Margaret, haughtily, "and the follies of five years ago are with me five years buried and gone."

"Ghosts five years and five times five years buried may come to haunt us unexpectedly," said the priest very gently, "and if such an one trouble you at any time during our neighborhood here, remember that it is part of my profession to lay such visitors, and soothe the consciences they trouble.  I intrude no more, remember, but I am always ready to help or counsel, if the need that once brought you to me should return again."

"I thank you, Father, and I believe you are as sincere as you are courteous.  But some ghosts are quietest if let alone, and some wounds do not bear handling."

"Oh, but this is really a glorious scene !   Last full moon we were on the St. Lawrence, Charles, and  it was nothing so fine as this, was it ?" exclaimed the priest as they joined the group on the point.

"Not to be compared," said Blondin, looking at Joan.

# CHAPTER VIII.



### AND A LITTLE MORE COMPANY.

THE bright summer days grew to weeks, and life in the little colony at Plum Island fell into its regular swing, as it always does if time is allowed for the process. Mrs. Beauchamp Brown, carrying out her whim of retirement from the world, was precisely the same Mrs. Beauchamp Brown who for half a .century had sought the world in its worldliest aspects, and had moulded it and moulded herself to it, until to become unworldly for her must have been to become other-worldly. If Plum Island had remained in its normal condition, she would never have remained on it ; but what with Mrs. Trevylyan, just from Washington, and only seeking auditors for a *chronique scandaleuse*, none the less virulent that it was charmingly disguised ; what with Captain Douglass, who, when he chose to talk, knew everybody and had been everywhere, and was always a gallant and courteous gentleman ; what with Father Williams, whose caustic wit and polished sarcasms were the delight of the worldly veteran of society, she did vastly well for companionship, without counting Blondin, whose good looks and aristocratic manners suited her ; or Margaret, who was always agreeable to her, even when she quarrelled with her ; or Joan and Elsie, at whom she laughed or scolded as the humor took her, and watched with Argus eyes when either Blondin or Captain Douglass was at hand.

As for Margaret, she had not so many resources. She hated scandal, and did not love Camilla Trevylyan. She avoided Douglass whenever she could, and was soon tired of being amiable to Blondin, who worshipped her at a distance, and constantly made Joan jealous by chanting her cousin's praises. She talked a good deal with the priest, but found it fatiguing to be always on guard, and was resolute never to allow him to penetrate the outermost circle of the defences she threw about her life, past and present.

After all, she enjoyed Elsie rather better than any other member of the party, and frequently stole away with her for a long walk through the odorous evergreen woods or upon the shingly shore, returning flushed and tired, but more than ever beautiful, with hands full of ferns, growing here in rare abundance; or pebbles and shells, with which they littered their rooms for a while, and then collected in a great hollow rock in the field, where a pool of rain-water kept them bright, and where they, as Joan remarked, "were just as happy as if you had n't loved them and left them."

"Go up to the house with the treasures, Elsie," said she, after one of these expeditions, "and if I am especially wanted, or lunch is ready, ring the big bell out of the window. I should like to stay here a little."

Elsie went, and Margaret, standing all alone under the great oak upon the shore, looked out across the sea, her eyes full of passionate longing, the woe of a hungry heart quivering upon her lips. Her white hands were wrung together, and stretched down as if in pain, her head was raised and eager as Diana's looking through the clouds for Endymion; she looked like the dryad of the oak, lamenting the decay of the old worship, listening for the steps of votaries who should come no more.

"Shall I never live?" whispered she. "Is there nothing in sky or sea or earth to fill my heart? Must it forever be this weariness, this craving, this void? Was I made for nothing? for nothing is all that I have found. Oh, the horrible, horrible weariness of living."

"Margaret!" said a timid yet passionate voice close behind her. She turned with a frown and saw Douglass.

"Don't look at me so!" cried he, seizing the hand she coldly withdrew. "Don't be vexed at my following you, dogging your footsteps, living upon the sight of you. You know, Margaret, oh, you know too well, how I love you!"

"So well that you make my life a burden with your persecutions," replied Margaret bitterly.

"And what have you made of my life?" flashed back Douglass, yet more bitterly. "A year ago you found me, a man in the fullest vigor of man's life, happy and proud in my profession, gay, careless, heart-free, afraid to look no man in the eye, glorying in the strength and life that God had given me, and glad to use them for His service. That was the man you found at Newport, the man you met again at Washington, and whom, four months ago, you dropped out of your white hands a crushed, worthless, dried husk, from which you had taken all the pith, all the value; taken and toyed with, and flung it aside. And now,—do you want to know what I am now, Margaret Ufford? Do you want to know what taskmaster has succeeded you, what is the name of my new slavery? Shall I tell you?"

"You shall tell me nothing, you shall insult me no longer!" cried Margaret, with blazing eyes. "You are a madman, and should be shut up in a Bedlam. If I had my will, you should go to one to-day. Let me pass, and do not presume to speak to me again as long as you live. If you have any decency you will leave this island, where your presence has always been an impertinence."

She swept past him and through the wood, superb in her unrighteous wrath; no longer the tender, longing, loving Diana waiting for Endymion, but Diana insulted by Actæon, Diana demanding vengeance and destruction.

Mrs. Beauchamp Brown was much displeased that Margaret should be too tired to appear at lunch, and deliberately weakened the tea she sent up to her, so as to make it almost undrinkable; but as Mrs. Ufford never so much as looked at it, the punishment did not avail, and by dinner-time all appeared as usual, and the presence of the priest and Blondin, who had arranged to dine every day at the Nunnery, as Joan called her new abode, diverted Mrs. Brown's attention from her niece.

The evening rather dragged, for neither Mrs. Trevylyan nor Captain Douglass appeared. Elsie read, Joan sat on the door-step with Blondin ; Margaret, buried in the great square armchair, looked steadfastly at the little fire upon the hearth, and said not a word ; and Father Williams, furtively watching her, played but a distracted game of chess with Mrs. Beauchamp Brown. The gentlemen retired early, and by ten o'clock the inmates of the Nunnery were already lighting their bedroom candles, and Mrs. Brown, with solemn precautions against explosion, was extinguishing the kerosene lamp, of which she stood in profound terror, mingled with aversion, when the sound of familiar melody came drifting in at the open windows, so startling that dignified dame that she gave a little convulsive puff down the chimney, and, as the flame rushed up into her face, jumped backward, exclaiming, "Ugh ! the nasty thing ! it will go off in spite of me. Who under the sun is singing Opera Bouffe down here ? "

"That's Larry's voice, I 'm positive ! " cried Elsie, running to the door, while Joan, taking up the refrain of "The Two Gendarmes," softly sang it out of the open window.

"Girls ! Elsie, come back ! Joan, keep quiet ! " cried Mrs. Beauchamp Brown in vain, for Elsie had already gladly cried out into the night, —

"O Larry, is that you ! " and Joan's rich contralto had made itself audible on the other side the lilacs.

"Elsie ! " cried her brother's voice in tones of incredulous surprise. "Wait a minute, fellows ! " and, striding up the dark little path, the handsome collegian sprang in at the door, seized Elsie by the shoulders, kissed her fervently, and looked about him in blank amazement ; for not only was he astonished to see his friends at all, but to see them in this strange abode, with its sylvan decorations and odors, while the dim light of the two candles, hastily set down by the girls on hearing the familiar melody, gave the whole thing so unreal and visionary an effect, that Larry may be pardoned for staring about him in the most unmannerly style, and exclaiming, —

"Why, it is n't really you though, Joan! And Cousin Margaret! No!"

"And my aunt, Mrs. Beauchamp Brown," suggested that lady, in a tone of awful severity.

"Beg pardon, aunt, but my feeble intellect could only embrace the objects directly before me," apologized Larry, with a twinkle of his merry brown eyes. "Allow me to embrace you in a more personal manner," and respectfully laying his hands upon his aunt's shoulders, he brushed first one cheek and then the other with his mustache.

It is very sad to think it, but actually Mrs. Beauchamp Brown was mollified by that caress, and it was in her very kindest tone that she demanded, —

"Well, and how came you here, young man?"

"Why, I hardly know, unless it was the attraction of gravitation," and Larry stole a small glance at Joan, who received it with demure appreciation. "We have been roaming to and fro through the earth for the last six weeks, and finally hit on Moosehead Lake, about the jolliest place you ever saw, but not at all good for grinding classics. So we came along down to Bangor, and, inquiring for a lodge in a vast wilderness where no attractions or distractions in the shape of society were to be found, heard that two gentlemen, pursuing the same studious quest, had passed through Bangor on their way to Plum Island, and were probably the only foreigners in the place. We immediately decided that if it was the place for two students it was the place for six, and although we desired no irresistible distractions in the shape I now see before me, it might be an advantage in our hours of relaxation to meet a couple of men with whom we could exchange ideas, tobacco, and dictionaries.  We arrived this afternoon, and have secured board and lodging with a charming young widow called Brown."

"Molly Brown, who has the pinks in her yard ?" demanded Elsie.

"Pinks, yes.  Molly, I don't know, as she has not yet requested us to call her by her first name ; but it is a pretty little cottage at the turn of the road going down to the shore."

"That's it.  Molly sings in the choir," announced Elsie, with interest, and Mrs. Beauchamp Brown demanded, —

"Who is 'we'?   How many of you?"

"Three fellows and Mr. Moberley, our tutor."

"Phillips Moberley !"

"Professor Moberley !" cried Margaret and Elsie together.

"Yes.   And he's standing in the road now.   May n't I ask him in for a moment?   Sneyd and La Branche are out there too.   May they come in ?"

"Oh, not to-night, pray !" cried Margaret impulsively, and her aunt, looking angrily at her, said, " I don't know why not.  *I* see no objection to allowing three gentlemen to make a short call, even if it is ten o'clock. We have not quite adopted the hours and fashions of Plum Island, I believe."

Margaret seated herself in the great armchair, whose projecting wings nearly concealed her, and made no reply.   Her aunt glanced at her, and stubbornly repeated, "*I* see no objection.   Ask them in, if you like, Larry."

Nothing loth, Larry obeyed, and in a moment three men entered in his wake, and seemed to fill the little room to overflowing.  The professor came first, and made his bow to Mrs. Brown, with a smiling apology for the intrusion at so late an hour.

"Oh, we don't call it late, Professor," replied she, a trifle sharply.  "At least, — Margaret, you know Professor Moberley."

Margaret half rose and bowed, without corresponding to the slight motion of the professor's hand.  He, not knowing that she was present, started and colored in hearing her name, but, recovering himself at once, passed on to greet the girls, both of whom he had met at class days and various college festivities.  The collegians comported themselves like other high-couraged, well-bred young fellows, and looked with much satisfaction upon the two pretty girls and the handsome young woman who represented the Mirandas of this savage isle.  Nor did the ladies fail to appreciate the good looks and manners, and the promise of agreeable intercourse, shown forth even in the ten minutes of their stay by the guests, — Margaret surveying and classing them with two or three quiet glances of her practised eye; Joan studying them with the fresh ardor of a student still thrilling with the delight of learning, not yet become routine; and Elspeth frankly interested in persons of whom her brother had so often spoken, and with whom he was now living.

Very different from each other, and from Launcelot Beauchamp, the two men were fair types of the South and West, as they were before the upheaval of the great earthquake, which, in shaking the structure of our country to its foundations, has, God willing, settled it upon a firmer basis.

Cyprian La Branche, the son of a Mississippi cotton planter of immense wealth, slight, nervous, elegant of figure, swarthy of coloring, with glowing dark eyes, and a voice almost too caressing and tender for a man, showed his mingled French and Spanish blood in every outline, and breathed the languid grace of his tropical birthplace in every tone, yet not without the mercurial energy and love of amusement of his age and surroundings.  Upon his father's plantation he might have appeared effeminate; after four years in a Northern university, and fellowship with Northern men, both his physical and mental muscle were well developed, and not only could he fence and ride like a Mississippian, but walk, run, and box like an Englishman or a Bostonian.

Tom Sneyd was a Kentuckian, — six feet two in height, shoulders and chest to correspond; with eyes like an eagle's, teeth and jaw that would break a bar of iron, curly brown hair, and a mustache like two great bird's-wings, a laugh that shook the house, and courage that would shake the world. Tom Sneyd was the gayest companion ever sat beside his friend at the feast, the most devoted comrade that ever threw himself between his friend and death in the fight, the bravest, simplest, sweetest nature that ever God put in a giant's frame.

A little older than his companions, for he had turned seven and twenty, Sneyd lingered at Cambridge in the law school, more because he could not bear to leave his *Alma Mater* and the pleasant Boston circle into which his genial manners, good introductions, and generous wealth had brought him, than from any expectation of finding his career in the devious paths of the law.

"Very well-behaved young men, very good companions for Launcelot," pronounced Mrs. Beauchamp Brown complacently, as she once more lighted her bedroom candle. "The Sneyds are one of the best families of Kentucky, and married with the Stuyvesants and Mavericks in the last generation. As for La Branche, I met his mother several times at Saratoga and Newport, and she was the most elegant woman I ever saw, and wore diamonds fit for a queen. It 's not at all a bad idea, their coming to Plum Island."

But Margaret, looking at her pale, pale face in the mirror, whispered, "This world is full of ghosts. Can the land of shadows be more fearful?"

# CHAPTER IX.

## BARBARA ALLEN.

A CLATTER of wheels and cheerful tumult of voices in front of the house called the ladies of the Nunnery to the door and windows, as they left the breakfast-table, there to behold two wagons, each drawn by two horses, Jubal driving the one and Larry the other, while the professor, La Branche, Sneyd, and Blondin leaped to the ground and shouted cheerful good-morrows to their friends.

"We have come to beg you to show us the island," cried Larry, fortunately remembering to address himself to his aunt, who graciously responded, —

" All of us ? "

" Yes. We found that Mr. Keene was in the habit of going out with you, so we engaged him and he got a second wagon, and we can take everybody. Mr. Smith was trying for the second wagon, so we persuaded him to join our party."

" Certainly. We are quite in the habit of making excursions with Mr. Smith," said Mrs. B. Brown, with a cordial smile at Blondin, who received it with a grateful gasp. " Let me see, there are nine of us.".

" 'Ten counting Jubal, who won't trust any of us with Gershom and Abijah, even if we knew the way ; but he says each wagon will hold five if we ' set snug,' and *I* don't mind setting snug at all, do you, Elsie ? "

" Oh no," replied Elsie, so simply that her brother roared, and Mrs. Beauchamp Brown reprovingly said, " See here, young man, remember we 're not all college boys, if you please."

"That's what made me so obliging, aunty dear," muttered Larry, in a tone not audible to his aunt, but quite so to Joan, whose little hand he squeezed unperceived.

"A note for Mrs. Ufford," said Eunice Small's mournful voice, as she appeared in the doorway.

Margaret took it in some surprise, and, frowning slightly at the oppressive perfume of the paper, read, —

"Margaret, you *must* come over here and try to quiet my poor brother. He will kill himself or me, or go raving mad if you don't. I can do nothing with him, and am utterly worn out. Come, for God's sake !

"CAMILLA TREVYLYAN."

"What is it, Meg? Good heavens, how pale you look!" exclaimed Mrs. Brown, who had watched the reading of the note with impatient curiosity.

"Mrs. Trevylyan has sent for me. Captain Douglass is very ill, and she is quite frightened and worn out," said Margaret, with the intense calmness of suppressed emotion.

"Dear me !" exclaimed her aunt fussily, "I hope he is n't going to die or anything, down here. You can't do anything about it, Margaret; you could n't nurse him, of course, and your advice is n't worth a *sou-marqué* in sickness. Send word that you deeply regret, and come with us."

"No, aunt ; I must go to Camilla. She wishes to see me for something especial. I must go." And Margaret's face took on the look nobody ever struggled against. Her aunt recognized and resented it.

"Go, then !" said she angrily. "It is just like Barbara Allen, for all the world. Of course, everybody knows that Jim Douglass is dead in love with you, and I suppose he 's taken to drink in consequence ; there 's something wrong about him, anybody can see, and his sister has no rational account to give of his sickness, although she 's always telling how ill he is. It 's not at all unlikely that he has an attack of del. tre. now, and a nice scene that it is for you to go into ! It 's actually indecent !"

"O Aunt Phyllis, don't, don't!" moaned Margaret, clenching her hands in each other, and glancing this way and that, like a hunted creature longing to escape. "I am desperate already in looking at the harm I have done, and you are making it worse."

"Hush, child! They'll hear you!" exclaimed her aunt, glancing through the window at the merry, noisy group outside. "Don't you fret like that, **dear**, don't! Of course you shall go if you must, but — certainly I can't leave you to walk over there alone, and I don't suppose you want a wagon-load of girls and boys to go with you. Good! There's Father Williams coming along the road, I suppose to see his nursling off. Now if you'll let him walk as far as Keene's with you, I won't say another word ; but really, as for leaving you to go alone on such an expedition, I never will consent ; and I don't think you'll absolutely defy your aunt, who has been like a mother to you all these years, will you, Meg?"

"I can't, when you ask like that, Aunt Phyllis," said Margaret, laying her cold lips upon the old woman's cheek. "But I am very sorry to have the priest with me."

"You must. I'll tell Larry to speak to him while you go and put your bonnet on. You can go out the side door and down the lane if you want to avoid that clanjamfray in front of the house."

Margaret silently submitted to whatever arrangement her aunt saw fit to make, and in ten minutes found herself walking beside the priest, down the lovely little lane, all dewy and odorous still with the breath of early morning, and vocal with the song of blackbird and bob-o'-link, while deep in the heart of the bordering wood, the solitary thrush poured forth the pathos of his love.

Margaret saw and heard nothing, but with her eyes steadily set forward, moved swiftly along, utterly regardless of her companion, who glanced shrewdly at her from time to time, but said nothing.

A distant bell rang out to announce nine o'clock and the beginning of school. Margaret raised her head, listened, and laughed bitterly.

> "'And as she went along the way,
>     She heard the bell a knellin',
>   And every stroke did seem to say,
>     Oh, cruel Barbara Allen!'"

repeated she, and turning a mocking glance upon the priest, inquired, —

"Do you know that ballad, Father Williams?"

"I do not know the myth, but I know the verity," replied the priest significantly.

"What verity?"

"The punishment sure to overtake a soul that has trifled with the life and death of another soul, simply for its own selfish amusement."

"Has Douglass made a confidant of you?"

"I watched with him last night. We called to see him in the afternoon, and his sister begged me to stay with him, for she was frightened at his state."

"And he talked of me?"

"Forgive me if I do not answer. A priest learns to be very discreet even when he is not officially bound to be so."

"Oh, I assure you I had no intention of intruding upon your private conversations with your penitents, if Captain Douglass is one. My exclamation was involuntary."

"Captain Douglass is no penitent of mine. He is not a Catholic," replied the priest, so serenely that Margaret felt ashamed of her petulance, and humbly said, —

"Pray excuse my ill-temper. I am very much troubled in several ways, and it makes me morose and disagreeable to everybody."

"Poor child! stumbling among the thorns and sharp stones, unable to find the way out, or to heal your wounds, or to undo the harm to yourself and others, and all the while a smooth, safe path close at hand, a guide, a physician, an adviser, yearning to help and comfort you."

He spoke very softly and without looking toward Margaret, who at first made as if she did not hear, but suddenly turning half scornfully, half yieldingly toward him, demanded, —

"You mean yourself, don't you, by the 'guide, physician, and adviser'?"

"God forbid such blasphemy!  I mean my Master," said the priest, crossing himself; and Margaret, more vexed at her blunder than impressed by the teaching, quickened her pace, and presently emerged from the wood into a fair, green pasture, where Jubal's pet cow and calf luxuriated in special timothy and clover, and drank at the bright brown brook dancing out of the wood close beside the bars which Father Williams deftly lowered for Margaret's passage.

"You learn quickly, Father," said she, waiting for him to put them up again.  "You never saw things like these in France."

"But I have not lived more in France than in several other countries.  I have no nationality and no home," said he, walking along beside her, with a quiet smile.

"Are you a Jesuit?" demanded Margaret, somewhat irrelevantly.

"I am an unworthy member of that society — yes," replied the priest coldly.

"Then Rome is your country and your home, I suppose," said Margaret, with a searching glance.

"Not more than of every Catholic.  The Papal See is the headquarters of the visible Church, of course. Here we are, and here is Mrs. Trevylyan coming to meet you.  Shall I walk home with you?"

"Not the least need in the world, thank you.  I do not know how long I shall stay, and won't detain you. Good morning."

"Oh!  I am so glad to see you both!  Please don't go, Father Williams!  I should like to speak with you about my poor brother.  Come in, Margaret.  It is so good of you, but I thought you would come ; I assure you I did not exaggerate the need.   This way."

It was Mrs. Trevylyan who spoke, and Margaret confessed, as she had seldom done, the exceeding charm of her rival's beauty, — softened, not dimmed, by watching and grief, and rather enhanced than diminished by the simplicity of her white wrapper, with its dusky crimson ribbons, and the plainness of her hair, simply coiled in the nape of her neck.   Partly the subtile influence of this beauty and grace, partly her own wounded conscience, softened Margaret's feelings and tone toward this woman, who had been both her dearest friend and deadliest enemy, and toward whom she now professed utter indifference ; so, as she held her hand, she softly said, —

"Poor Camilla! it is hard lines for you."

"O Margaret, if you only knew how hard!"   And the poor, tired child burst into tears and turned sobbing away.   But the world teaches a more powerful and tyrannical stoicism than did Zeno, and it was not a minute before Mrs. Trevylyan turned a composed face upon her guests, saying with a little laugh, —

"It is wretched to be such a nervous animal.   Pray sit down, Father Williams, and excuse me for a moment. Margaret, will you come with me?   No, wait here until I see if poor Jim is ready for company."   She crossed the passage to a room at the other side of the front door, but immediately returned, signing Margaret to come.

"I shall leave you with him, but we shall be in the room here with the door open if you want me," whispered she.

Margaret nodded, for she could not speak, and followed into the dark, breathless room, its atmosphere laden with a peculiar odor from which her healthy and sensitive organization instinctively shrank.   Douglass lay upon a sofa, his head bolstered high, and his hands nervously clutched upon a scarf made fast to a hook above his head   Camilla went up to him, and, laying her hand very gently upon his forehead, all furrowed with pain, said, —

"Here is Margaret come to sit with you a little. Don't tire yourself or trouble her, will you?"

"No," moaned a hollow voice, hardly to be recognized as that of the soldier whose shout of fierce delight had many a time led his men into the thickest of the fight.

Margaret took the chair placed for her close beside the couch, and Camilla, with a lingering, anxious look, left the room, closing the door behind her.

"I am very sorry to see you so, James," said Margaret vaguely, for, truth to tell, she found it hard to speak any but the words so persistently ringing in her brain, —

> "Then slowly, slowly got she up,
>   An' cam where he was lying;
> An' coldly, coldly looked she down,
>   'Young man, I think you 're dying.'"

Douglass's reply was more bitter than that of Barbara Allen's lover.

"You well may be sorry," said he, "and I sent for you to show you your own work."

"My work?" faltered Margaret, covering her face to shut out those burning, eager eyes.

"Yes.  Do you know what is the matter with me?"

"No, except that you say it is my fault."

"Your fault, yes; but the immediate physical cause, the agent that has scorched my blood to fever, and wrung my nerves until they are a mere system of torture, and vitiated my senses until I cannot bear God's daylight or the singing of the birds or the touch of my sister's soft hand; that drives sleep from my eyes until I am crazy with unrest, and makes all food loathsome, even while I sink from exhaustion: do you know the name of this fiend to whom you have delivered me?"

"Alcohol?" gasped Margaret, her dilated eyes fixed upon the face of the tortured man, which bore out the truth of his words in every ghastly lineament.

"Alcohol!" repeated he with a sneer. "Alcohol is an angel of mercy in its dealings compared with this. Opium, madam, opium, that is what it is called; and if the infernal regions hold a worse devil, I should like to know his name."

"O James, have you given yourself over to that awful slavery! Is it that which has made you like this?"

"Given myself over?" cried Douglass fiercely. "No, but been given over by you, Margaret Ufford! You meshed me with your beauty and your smiles, and your soft, sweet voice, and your thousand charms ; and when you had me bound hand and foot, a helpless slave, you turned and left me, and this fiend came to finish the work you had begun!"

"God forgive me! O God, forgive me!" moaned Margaret, sinking upon her knees and hiding her face.

The all but maniac gleam of the opium-eater's eyes softened as he watched her, and the look of weary pain, banished for the moment by strong excitement, returned upon his face.

"Poor Margaret," said he softly, "how could you help it, how could you but be the Lorelei of whom you used to sing? It was the way you were made ; and if the fools must wreck themselves at your feet, why all the worse for them. Don't cry, dear, don't feel badly! it is n't worth it, and can't mend what's done. After all, it's but one life gone to the bad out of millions of lives, and not worth the moan you have made already. See, child, if it is any comfort, I forgive you fully and freely, and I never will say or think such things again, — that is, when I am myself. O my God, how I suffer! Go, go, leave me while I can control myself. Such sights are not for you. Go, I say!"

His voice rose to a shriek, and Margaret, dreadfully frightened, fled out of the room, calling Camilla to come quickly. She obeyed without pausing to reply, and closed the door, but that slight barrier was not enough to hide the horror of the paroxysm torturing the unhappy creature, until his groans and cries brought the woman of the house to inquire what could be the matter. Margaret turned away without reply, but Father Williams quietly answered, —

"Poor Captain Douglass is in great pain, but it is nothing alarming. He has these attacks occasionally since his last campaign in the Indian country, where he was severely wounded. His sister quite understands the trouble, and the proper remedies, however. Yes, thank you, if she needs anything, we will let you know at once. Don't be alarmed, it is all right."

"It is not the effect of a wound received in the Indian campaign," said Margaret, almost fiercely, as Mrs. Keene withdrew contentedly to her own quarters.

"Did I say it was?" inquired the priest calmly. "Would it have been better to tell the whole dreadful truth, or to rouse her curiosity by refusing any explanation?"

"Oh, I don't know, — I don't care!" moaned Margaret, twisting her hands together and leaning her forehead against the open sash, through which floated the breath of the flower-garden, the song of a bob-o'-link in the meadow beyond, and the cheerful voices of children at play in the woodside.

Nature following God's law, man following his own. Which is the fairer, which the better content?

The groans died away in weary moans, then came stillness; and after a while, Mrs. Trevylyan softly opened the door and came out, her face ashen pale, her eyes strained and wild. Sinking into a chair, with her hands clenched upon the arms, she sat staring stonily in front of her, until the priest, sitting down beside her and taking one of the cold hands, said gently, —

"Courage, my daughter, courage! It is hard for you, but you are helping him, and must bear up for his sake."

"Oh, it is so horrible to see him in his agony!" moaned Camilla; then, turning upon Margaret, she demanded passionately, —

"What did you say to him that day by the shore? He came home and shut himself up in his room. I knew what that meant, and when I forced my way in, he was already almost senseless with opium. I made out from his mutterings that he had seen you, and that was all before he was gone.  He had taken so much already that I have had to give him more, to keep him from dying in convulsions, and it will be weeks before he is where he was when we came here.  This is the work I have been at for the last year, Margaret, and you know best what has occasioned it."

"I can bear no more, no more, no more!" cried Margaret wildly; and before any one could stop her, she darted out of the house and down the path to the wood, burying herself in the forest like the wounded doe who flies to greenwood solitude for healing and safety.

"She will be better alone," said the priest, watching her from the window, "and I will sit with your brother while you try to rest, Mrs. Trevylyan."

# CHAPTER X.



"NOW how are we to divide?" asked Larry, as the party assembled at the gate, and Jubal drew up his wagon to receive the first instalment.

"Elspeth may go with you, and Joan with me," announced his aunt decisively. "As Margaret is not here, you will chaperon your sister. The rest will suit themselves. Jump in, Joan."

"I shall sit in front with you, Mr. Keene," declared Joan, who in the dearth of material for genuine flirtation, often entertained herself by bewildering Jubal, who met her advances in a manner at once so wary and so admiring as to amuse her immensely.

"That's your seat most gen'ally, I believe," replied he on this occasion. "But I expect we'll have to take in another passenger to-day, for that heavy gentleman is going to set with your brother, and that 'll be heft enough on the front springs of Zip's old wagon."

"Take me in front!" exclaimed Blondin eagerly. "I'm not so very heavy."

"You ain't thistle-down, but you're lighter than some of 'em," remarked Jubal, while Blondin delightedly sprang up to the seat beside Joan, leaving a narrow strip of cushion for Jubal. Behind them sat Mrs. Beauchamp Brown in great glory, for handsome Tom Sneyd, without glancing at the younger ladies, had not only offered her his aid in clambering into the wagon, but seated himself at her side, with the evident intention of making himself agreeable; and Mrs. B. B., if asked, like the ancient French coquette, at what age a woman ceases to value the attentions of the other sex, might, like her, have replied, "Ask some one older than I."

In the other wagon, the professor sat beside Larry on the front seat, and Cyprian La Branche with Elsie on the back. Every one was suited, except Larry, who cast envious glances at Blondin, which Joan perceiving, immediately beamed full upon her neighbor, whom at first she had rather slighted.

Jubal's wagon took the lead, and with much noise of merry voices, laughter, communications shouted from one party to the other, and all the gay tumult of youth and happy health bound upon pleasuring, the four horses, two wagons, and nine souls with bodies to match, travelled rapidly along in the cloud of sun-gilded dust, which almost hid them from the curious gaze of "the town," as the cluster of houses before described was politely styled.

"Guess I'll show you Dow's P'int," remarked Jubal, turning to the left of the blacksmith's shop. "It's about as sightly a spot as I know of hereabout.'

"Dow's P'int?" repeated Joan saucily. "Was Dow the little husband that Mother Goose put in a pint pot, and is this the pint he was put in?"

"It's the pint he come out of," replied Jubal dryly. "But I reckon it would n't hold him now, seeing he's turned into mackerel."

"Into mackerel! Now what do you mean, Jubal?"

"Got capsized up to the Grand Banks in a squall, and it's reasonable to suppose the mackerel ate him."

"You horrible man! Is that the way you talk of your friends and neighbors?"

"Waal, you see, Miss Joan, I'm only a poor ignorant Plum Islander, and don't know a great deal anyway. I do suppose now up to Boston they always speak kind and charitable of their friends and neighbors, don't they?"

"Oh, yes, ma'am," said Tom Sneyd's great voice on the back seat, "we have a good many connections in and about Boston, and my father and mother often speak of the Beauchamps, very possibly your father and mother, as among their early and valued Boston friends."

"Yes, indeed, I am quite sure I remember Mr. and Mrs. Sneyd as among mamma's visitors while I was a little creature brought in with the dessert," said Mrs. B. B., as complacently as though she had been telling the truth. "Did n't they have a little boy in those days, an elder brother of yours?   I seem to remember a little boy."

"They lost two or three children when they were first married," said Tom simply, and not adding that he was quite sure his mother was a little younger than Mrs. Beauchamp Brown, whom, in his grand, single-hearted chivalry, he liked none the worse for pretending to be younger than she was, or for sundry little devices to extract compliments and attention from him.   To this sort of man a woman is always an object of reverence and protection; of attention if she speaks, of admiration if she asks for it, of honorable blindness and deafness if she insists upon making a fool of herself.

In the other wagon, the professor, who won the hearts of his pupils by invariably treating them as gentlemen and equals, discussed the last new wrinkle in English pronunciation with Larry, who rather affected purism in that direction; and La Branche told Elsie of the *Mardi Gras* in New Orleans, and the riotous pranks of his own especial clique of comrades, who went masked and disguised from house to house of their acquaintance, reciting nonsense verses of personal application, dancing to the music of a banjo played by one of themselves, making burlesque love to the young ladies, and telling fictitious news to the mammas, refreshing themselves wherever they were invited, and — but the end of the account was rather indefinite, as possibly the young man's remembrances also were, and Elsie, who had laughed until she was tired, quietly helped him with, "And when twelve o'clock brought Ash-Wednesday morning, you all went home and sobered down to sleep."

"Oh! oh, yes, of course," replied La Branche, with the slightest possible movement of shoulder and eyebrow,— the lingering trace of the French gesticulation he had brought North, and had, after two or three good bouts at fisticuffs with democratic schoolmates, repressed, until it became no more than the *soupçon* of garlic in a French cook's finest *ragout*.

"Are you an Episcopalian then?" asked he, snatching at the first opening of escape from the questioning he saw in Elsie's eyes.

"Oh yes, all of us," replied she, a little proudly. "My father is a clergyman, and pretty High Church, too. Are you?"

"I 'm a Catholic, Roman Catholic I believe you insist upon calling us," said La Branche, with his languid, mocking smile. "Almost everybody in New Orleans is Catholic."

"How strange! Nobody is here, that is, nobody nice," replied Elsie innocently, and then blushed all over, perceiving her rudeness. La Branche took his revenge in watching the lovely pink creep up and up and deepen to scarlet before he said, —

"I 'm sorry you don't find me nice, but so it is."

"I beg your pardon — I did n't mean — you ought to know I could n't mean " ——

The tears stood in her eyes, and La Branche hastened to reassure her.

"I am sure you meant nothing but what is kind and sweet and courteous. I was teasing you just a little bit, and really am the one to apologize. There now, we have had our first quarrel and reconciliation, and that you know is usually a long, long step toward friendship. Do you suppose it will be in this case?"

The shy, sweet eyes glanced up at him with a smile, and although the tremulous lips did not form a sound, La Branche was answered, and his own eyes said how well. He snatched a twig from an arbor vitæ tree just then brushing his shoulder, and giving it to her, said softly, —

"Do you know that arbor vitæ, the tree of life, is a symbol of undying friendship? Will you have it?"

Elsie took it without a word, and, perhaps luckily for both, Larry turned just then to ask his sister a question, and she eagerly bent forward to reply.

La Branche's long, sleepy, dark eyes watched her until a

soft fire began to glow in their depths, herald of a passion sudden and ardent as the sunrise of the tropics.

Elsie, to be sure, had never in her life looked so lovely. A vague excitement flushed her cheek and brightened her eyes and thrilled in her voice, and broke up the dreamy calm of her manner: it was the stirring of the pond-lily that all night long has slept fast folded in its calyx-leaves, upon the quiet water's breast, and now feels the imperious sun's heat summoning her to unfold, show him her golden heart and render him the incense of her breath.

"Hold on, back there!" shouted Jubal, halting Gershom and Abijah in front of a gate fitted with a long pole, raking back from the top like the mast of a felucca; a heavy weight attached to the lower end of this pole balanced the mass of the heavy gate, and prevented it dragging upon the ground as it opened and shut.

"How curious it is to see the uneducated mind applying the principles of mathematics to practical matters, by a sort of instinct," said the professor to Larry, as he contemplated this arrangement. "Archimedes could not more wisely have utilized the attraction of gravitation, the force of the lever, the " ——

"S'pose you could drive through this gateway without carrying away the posts *both* sides the road?" cheerfully inquired Jubal of Joan, to whom he had intrusted the reins, while he opened the gate. She, ambitious and rash as Phaeton, made no verbal reply, but applying a sharp cut of the whip to Gershom's flank, and shaking the reins with an encouraging cry, caused that valiant beast to dart so suddenly forward that Abijah, unprepared to second the exertion, dragged him sideways, and brought the wheel on his side against the post with a violence that would have shattered any delicate vehicle.

"Joan, what *are* you about! My gracious!" screamed Joan's aunt, while Joan herself, more angry than frightened, and utterly disclaiming Blondin's polite offers of assistance, tugged at the reins so sharply that Gershom, already wounded in his feelings, began to back viciously, while Abijah, rubbing his nose against the stone wall, showed a disposition to kick if he could only find room.

"It 's nothing ! Don't be scared !" said a voice in Joan's ear, and a strong hand, reaching over her shoulder, seized the reins, and in a moment backed the horses to a proper angle, then with a judicious touch of the whip sent them forward through the gate, Jubal meantime dancing about, and watching his opportunity to jump into the wagon again.

"That 's all right now, Miss Joan !" said Sneyd, as he drew the spirited creatures down to a walk. "You were n't frightened, were you?"

"Not in the least, but awfully provoked at myself," said Joan, turning a glowing face over her shoulder as she resigned the reins to Jubal. "I do hate not to know how to do things."

"I 'm afraid you 'll have to give in that hosses is one of the things you don't know how to do," remarked Jubal dryly, as he leaned over to look at the wheel.

"Very true," replied Joan frankly ; "but there 's nothing I can't learn to do, and I 'll learn horses before I 'm many months older."

"I 'd advise you to get a patienter beast than Gershom to practise on," said Jubal, who was unquestionably somewhat vexed. Joan turned upon him like a little cat.

"You need n't be so cross about it. I 'm quite ashamed of you to show such temper about an old wall. You 're a worse rebel than Stonewall Jackson, I declare."

Jubal and Tom Sneyd laughed. Mrs. Beauchamp Brown reproved, and Joan cleared up sunnier than ever. The road inside the gate was only a private wood-path, the spongy turf deadening the hoof-beats of the horses and rattle of the wheels, and the crushed herbage sending up a cool, fresh smell to mingle with the aromatic odors of the balsam-firs and spruce, the juniper and pine, whose sharp little fingers clutched at Elsie's floating hair and Dame Brown's fluttering veil, and Joan's brown little hand, thrust out to them in gay defiance.

"Declare for 't, I should think Hez would come out

here some morning, and wind all them scratchy twigs with cotton wool, so 's 't we could drive through pleasant," remarked Jubal, as a dry branch of arbor vitæ raked across his cheek, and would have served Mrs. Brown in the same way had not Sneyd dextrously caught and snapped it.

"Who 's Hez?" asked Joan, snatching at a tall aster.

"Cap'n Hez. Have n't you heard of him? Boothby his name is, but everybody calls him Hez and Cap'n Hez. He owns all the land round here, though it ain't much use to him, for he goes to sea, and so don't require land."

"But it 's Dow's Point, not Hez's Point," suggested Joan.

"Oh, Dow got disap-pointed, and sold out years ago. Here we be." And Jubal, modestly stifling his appreciation of his own joke, drove out of the woods upon a wide level of verdant pasture-land, jutting far out into the sea, and breaking off at the coast-line in a sharp bluff, below which lay a pretty, pebbly beach. The view was glorious, the fine salt breeze intoxicating, the sunlight cheery without being oppressive ; and everybody jumped down from the wagon with exclamations of delight, and streamed toward the edge of the cliff, where Jubal, after securing the horses to two of the trees scattered over the headland, showed them a path winding down its steep face to the beach, where the sea broke wooingly in curving lines of foam.

"Go down there !" cried Mrs. Beauchamp Brown, approaching, and peering over the edge, while Joan and Elsie ran down the path, light as chamois. "Not until I 'm one of the goats at the left hand, that have to go down whether they like it or not. I 'll wait here."

"Suppose we go and sit in the wagon under that druidical old oak," suggested Professor Moberley. "We shall have all the view and all the air, with the advantage of a back and a cushion."

Mrs. Brown agreed with alacrity, and the professor, gayly offering his arm, escorted her to the wagon, with hardly a sigh at resigning his plan of hunting the beach for echini and encrini to add to his collection.

But he was rewarded, for Mrs. Beauchamp Brown, who had her own ideas of gratitude, and moreover was old enough to be willing to make herself agreeable after the fancy of her companion rather than her own, spoke of nothing but Margaret, and especially of her recent refusal to become *madame l'ambassadrice.*

"I really think if Margaret marries again, — as I'm sure I hope she will, for her first marriage was a mere farce," pursued the crafty old lady, — "she will be more likely to accept some honest, simple gentleman, whose heart has been proved by years of constancy, and whose life has been with the stars and the sciences, rather than to burden herself with the responsibilities and fatigues of such a position as Forsythe offers, and many a man, abroad and at home, has offered before him. Margaret might be an English duchess to-day if she had chosen, — yes, or an Italian princess, or "——

"She might be anything that is noble and exalted in her own right," softly interrupted the professor, who would not hear of Margaret's affairs at second-hand.

Larry, meanwhile, hungry for a word with Joan, whom he had hardly seen since his arrival, was hasting after her down the beach when he was detained by Blondin, who, looking very pale and determined, stood waiting for him at the foot of the path.

"Mr. Beauchamp, may I have a word with you in confidence?" asked he, seating himself upon a rock, and nodding Larry to one close by.

"Certainly, Mr. Smith," replied poor Larry, casting an impatient glance at the group of four, disappearing round the neighboring point, La Branche clinging close to Elsie's side, and Sneyd stooping his lofty head to laugh into Joan's eyes.

"It's a little awkward, I know," began poor Blondin, and he need not have put in the adjective, "but you are the only gentleman I have seen in connection with the party; and we Englishmen, you know, don't think it honorable to go on as you Americans do, and never say anything to the men of the family till all's settled."

"Excuse me, Mr. Smith," interposed Launcelot with frigid politeness, " I don't quite follow you. In what respect are Englishmen more honorable than Americans?"

" Dear me ! I did n't say that, you know, not at all," explained Blondin, growing pink and warm, " but the truth is, I 'm awfully gone on your cousin, — cousin, is n't it?"

" Miss Jennifer, do you mean?"

"Yes, Miss Joanna Jennifer, though Joan is a prettier name, and goes beautifully with " ——

" Smith?" interposed Larry, his eyes glinting dangerously.

" Ah ! that 's just it, Mr. Beauchamp," cried Blondin eagerly, " that 's just what I want to tell you, as man to man, for I feel so cursedly like a cad going on this way. But, you see, Father Williams made it a point in coming over here that we were to travel *incognito,* and I was to study and not go into society. My mother was so afraid of my getting entangled, you know, and " ——

" Great heavens ! man, do speak out, or else leave it alone," burst out Larry, as the last flutter of Joan's skirt disappeared behind the cliff. " If your mother and your nurse — I really beg your pardon, your " ——

" Father Williams was my tutor until last year, when I came of age, and now is my chaplain. I am Roman Catholic," said Blondin, suddenly recovering self-command, and his inherited, but not as yet personal, dignity ; for this blond boy would have ridden gayly to his death with the Six Hundred, or fought De Bussy behind the Couvent des Carmes with a rose between his lips, or jumped into a boiling sea to save a little child, and thought nothing of either achievement. It was Joan who routed him so mercilessly, and for all his two-and-twenty years, this English lad was years younger than an American lad of twenty.

Larry looked at him, and standing up, said gravely, —

" I don't want to intrude on your confidence, Mr. Smith ; and if you feel that your chaplain or your mother has a right to insist upon your concealing your real name, it is not my business to interfere. At the same time, I must say that I agree with you that it would be highly ungentlemanly conduct to address a young lady, or even to associate familiarly in her family, under an assumed name and position.  What do you propose to do about it ? "

" That 's what I was going to ask you, as Miss Jennifer's relative.  I will, if you wish it, tell you all about myself, and you shall say whether Mrs. Beauchamp Brown ought to know, and " ——

" But, after all, what reason have you to suppose that Miss Jennifer is interested in you?  Have you ever spoken to her? " interrupted Larry.

" Not at all.  I have several times said I should not think it honorable."

" Well then, Mr. Smith, had n't you better wait until you have reason to suppose your identity a matter of interest to the young lady, and to make everything fair, I will mention to my aunt that you are travelling under an assumed name.  You may give me your real name, or not, as you like."

" My name is Egbert de Bracy, and I am called Lord Strathmore.  Here is my card."  He quietly handed it to Beauchamp, who as quietly took it, the gentleman of the republic nothing daunted at the title, the gentleman of the monarchy nothing presuming upon it.

" I will tell my aunt what you have said, Lord Strathmore," said Larry, rising, " and she will decide on the proper course with regard to her niece."

" Only," said Strathmore eagerly, " I should be so awfully glad if I might get Joan to care for me without knowing.  It 's a great thing for a fellow to make sure it 's himself, and not his name or possessions " ——

" Lord of Burleigh, eh ? " suggested Larry ; then, a little haughtily, " although my cousin is hardly in a position to be very much dazzled even by a title.  A well-born American girl does not call the queen her superior."

" By Jove ! I 'd like to see Joan at court — ' presented on her marriage by ' — let 's see — the Duchess of ——."

" You may have heard a homely proverb about counting chickens, my lord ; and since you have been so kindly confidential toward me, I will reciprocate by confessing that I have some reason to hope that Miss Jennifer's affections are already engaged. At any rate, you will please consider me an avowed rival, and determined to win the game if possible."

With which parting broadside Sir Launcelot walked rapidly away, snatching off his hat to let the salt sea wind cool his heated forehead and toss his tawny mane.

Close by the Point he met the returning party, and was saluted by Joan's gay voice, —

"Just fancy, Larry, Mr. Sneyd is going to teach me horses. He is going to send to Bangor for a saddle-horse and a light buggy, and we are going to ride and drive the whole continual time. Is n't it too altogether lovely?"

"No doubt Aunt Phyllis will consider it so," growled Larry, unable quite to stand up like a man to this second blow ; but Sneyd, with his thunderous laugh, replied, —

"O, I shall make it all right with Mrs. Beauchamp Brown, first of all. She is very kind to me."

"And what are you going to take up, Elsie?" inquired her brother, turning with a very poor assumption of carelessness to the other couple, who stood with heads close together, examining a bit of coralline sea-weed. "Are you going to set up a bicycle?"

"I?" replied Elsie, with a start and a lovely blush. "I am not going to do anything, except Mr. La Branche has promised to show me about all these sea-grasses and plants, and I am going to make a book of them."

"O!" said Larry. "Well, let 's go home."

# CHAPTER XI.



"**E**LSIE!"
    "Yes, Cousin Margaret."
The girl stood beside a clump of alder, plucking leaves, and weaving a garland for the little sailor hat lying in the grass at her feet, while the morning sun, darting his glory through the thick branches overhead, touched the pale gold of her hair to the aureole of a saint.  She softly sang, —

> "'T is a pilgrim, strange and kingly,
>    Never such was seen before!
> Ah, my soul, for such a wonder
>    Wilt thou not undo the door?'"

Margaret, never too preoccupied or too unhappy to admire any form of beauty, had stood for some moments contemplating the pretty picture, herself unconsciously making one of richer and more glowing loveliness, as she stood in the full sunlight, her boating dress of garnet colored and white striped stuff, falling straight and close about her shapely limbs, and her wide-leafed hat, with its sweeping white plume, casting a sharp shadow over the upper part of the face, and leaving the glowing lips and brilliant teeth smiling in the smiling sunshine. She held an oar in her hand, or rather leaned upon it, as Dian upon her bow.

"Do you feel like rowing, little Moppet?" asked she, as Elsie ran lightly up the path toward her.

"Yes, indeed, I feel like doing anything you will do with me, Cousin Meg."

"Then scamper up to the house and get the other oar, — I tried to bring both, but could n't manage them, — and I 'll go on to the boat.   I have the key."

Elsie set off like a deer up the path, and after her came the parting injunction, "And, Moppet, don't tell anybody, if you can help it."

"No.   It 's awfully jolly not to tell."

The little wretch knew that Cyprian La Branche would be looking for her within the hour, and exulted beforehand in his discomfiture.   Yes, even Elsie had so much of Eve in her, — of Eve, who, when there was but one man on earth, must coquette with the devil.

The pretty skiff, brought down from Bangor for the ladies' use, — for ornamental boats are not in the Plum Island way, — was perfectly manageable for two practised oarswomen like these.   The sea was like an inland lake; the wind, which but the day before had been furious and fitful, blew faintly and steadily from the west, and all things seemed harmonized for once to the fullest enjoyment of body and mind.   The channel between Plum and Eagle Islands was soon passed, and the little boat swept out into the more open sea, although several miles still lay between it and the outer islands of the archipelago.

"Have you your little compass on your watch-chain, Cousin Meg?" asked Elsie, turning on her thwart to cast a longing look across the shining waters to the shimmering line where sea and sky mingled in one dazzling radiance.

"Yes, dear ; why?"

"Oh nothing, only I was thinking how nice it would be to row out of sight of land, away, way out there, and lie, just one little speck, with only water around us and only sky overhead, — just we two, and nobody else."

"And lunch, Moppet?"

"O Cousin Meg, what a come-down !"

"My child, I have lived ten years longer than you, and in the course of that time have eaten — let me see, ten times three hundred and sixty-five — thirty-six hundred and fifty more lunches than you have, consequently, I am by all that amount more earthly, not to finish the quotation with 'sensual and devilish,' so you see I take good care not to leave my commissary wagons too far in the rear, even when voyaging with so romantic and ethereal a shipmate as my Moppet."

"Well, at any rate, let us take a good long row out toward the sea, ' the sea, the sea, the open sea!' Take the bearings, please, Cousin Meg, and point us due south, and then row until we're tired. O, I forgot! There is something to eat and a keg of water, a breaker, Jubal calls it, in the fore-cuddy. Don't you know, Aunt Phyllis told him to see that they were always there, —some biscuit and water?"

"So she did. Well, if we get carried out to sea by a current, or are shipwrecked on Butter Island, or stranded on a whale's back, we need not fear immediate starvation. There, I'll lay the compass on the thwart beside you, and you may regulate our course, since we have no steersman, and I am not competent for anything more than stolid, straightforward pulling."

"The bow oar is bound to do the steering," replied Elsie cheerfully, as she settled to her work ; and for about half an hour the little craft skimmed steadily southward under the even and methodical impulse of the two well-managed oars. Margaret was first to cry enough, and she did it so suddenly that Elsie's next stroke sent the boat swerving wildly from her course, and drew an exclamation of dismay from that young lady, at which Margaret laughed aloud.

"I could n't help it, my dear," cried she, laying her oar athwart ship, and resting her folded arms upon it. "I kept up to the very last minute, and probably shall never pull another stroke as long as I live. Certainly not until I have had some water. You see, Aunt Phyllis's precautions were wise. Must we drink out of the breaker, if that 's its name?"

"O no, there 's a dipper, a nice new tin dipper, so bright that it serves for mirror as well as goblet. Wait till you see!"

And Elsie, shipping her own oar, went down on her knees, and half diving into the cuddy, presently emerged with a pannikin of water, which she handed to Margaret, saying, "Did you ever drink out of a tin dipper before, cousin?"

Margaret did not reply until she had thirstily emptied the cup, then returning it, she said, "I don't remember that I ever did, Moppet, but I once drank Tokay at the czar's table, out of priceless old Venice glass, and it was n't to be compared with the draught I just swallowed."

"Nothing 's good unless you want it," replied Elsie sententiously, as she helped herself to some water.

"Moppet! What 's that?" demanded her cousin sharply, as the girl resumed her seat. .

"What, Cousin Meg?"

"That floating thing away over there, in the line of my finger. Don't you see?"

"Yes. Why, it can't be — O cousin, it looks like a man!"

"So I thought. Pick up your oar and row down."

"But cousin — if he 's dead!"

"Well, if he 's dead — what then?"

"Oh, but are n't you frightened? Do you want to go any nearer? Let us get away!"

"Why, Elspeth, I am astonished! Are you really a coward? I did n't know any of us were. If it is a man and he is dead, he must be buried and his friends told. If he is n't dead, he must be saved. Suppose it was Larry, and two women came within sight, and ran away and left him because they were *afraid!* Should you love those two women?"

"O cousin!"

"Well, put your oar into the water then, and row. Now!"

The oars fell, and if not as evenly as before, the skiff made its way with tolerable directness towards the floating mass, lifted now and again upon the wash of the tide, and showing more and more plainly as that repugnant object to living eyes,— a lifeless human body. Elsie, obliged to direct the course of the boat, glanced fearfully round from time to time, and dipped her oar so nervously and feebly that it needed a sharp word or two from Margaret to steady her, before the boat could be brought alongside, and secured by means of a boat-hook to the body. Margaret, who, with all her sensuous delight in the luxurious, and avoidance of pain, had nerves and resolution fit for Florence Nightingale when necessity developed them, leaned over and softly raised the head. As she did so, she bit her lip to restrain an exclamation of horror, for her fingers pressed upon a fresh, deep wound extending backward from the temple.

"He has been murdered!" thought she, and a sick horror for the moment almost overpowered her senses; but either the pain of her touch, or naturally returning consciousness, drew a low groan from the wounded man, and restored full self-command to his preserver.

"Elsie, he's alive!" cried she. "We shall save him. O child, are n't you glad?"

"Is he really alive? Oh, indeed, I am glad! I'm not a bit afraid now, Cousin Meg."

"Poor fellow! What can we do? We can't get him into the boat, and he ought to be taken out of the water directly, and his wound dressed," muttered Margaret, afraid to tell her timid assistant of the ghastly discovery she had made.

"Why! Why, Cousin Meg, it's the Lookout!" cried Elsie, for the first time seeing the white face floating close at her side. "The man on the steamboat, don't you know? and Joan has done such a nice picture of him. She calls it the 'Lookout on the Palos.'"

"Give me some water. Oh, if we had only a little wine or spirits, smelling salts — anything. You have n't anything, of course, Elsie?"

"No, cousin, nothing. Here is the water. Oh, here is a bottle of — rum, I think it is, that Mr. Moberley carried the other day to put some creatures in that he expected to find, and he left it on board because he was going again in the afternoon and did n't. It's got one thing in it — a sort of crab, I should think. Will that do?"

"Let me see? What a nasty little object! but I don't believe he's poisonous; it is a crab, I think. At any rate, we 'll risk it. He 'll die if he don't revive."

She poured a little of the alcohol into the pan, and holding up the wounded man's head with one hand, forced the liquid between his teeth with such good-will that he gasped, swallowed, coughed, and feebly opened his eyes.

"Thank God!" cried Margaret heartily. "He 's coming to his senses."

"He 's tied to that grating. That 's what kept him up," said Elsie, bending over the side, and touching the edge of the wooden grating, upon which one arm and shoulder with the head were partially buoyed up.

"There! Take a little more. Do!" said Margaret, coaxing a little more of the crab's bath into her patient's mouth.

"Where am I? It 's very wet!" muttered the Look-out, feebly raising his unfettered hand half-way to his head."

"You 're in the water, and we want to get you into our boat. Can you help yourself a little, do you think?"

"Oh — yes — I remember. Is that man drowned?"

"There 's no man here but yourself. Never mind him now," hastily cried Margaret, half afraid of hearing some horrible story of attempted murder, half anxious to keep the ghastly subject out of her patient's mind. "Swallow a little more of this, and rest your head back on my arm, so!" And Margaret, quite regardless of her sleeve wet to the shoulder, or of the strain of the position, curved her arm under the wounded head, and held it a little above the water, while she administered another draught of the fiery spirit. A faint color crept into the lips and cheek, and the eyes opened more intelligently.

"I met with an accident," whispered the Lookout, looking uneasily from side to side.

"Yes, I know. I would n't think of that now, but of getting into the boat," said Margaret gently.

"There 's some rope here in the cuddy, Cousin," said Elsie, pulling it out. "Could n't we make it fast over here in the tholepin holes of the further gunwale, and then pass it under him in two or three places, and so pull him in by degrees? It would n't careen the boat as much as if it was fastened to this side, would it?"

"Elsie, you 're too clever for anything! Quick, now, get it through the holes and pass it over here!"

"Elsie!" murmured the Lookout, fixing his eyes upon her and smiling feebly.

"He remembers us on board the Useless," whispered Elsie, coloring guiltily, as she rove the line with the deftness of a sailor boy. Margaret helped as she could, and when all was ready administered a last sip of the rum, and said encouragingly, "Now I 'm going to cut you loose from that grating, and then we shall pull with all our might on the free ends of these ropes, and if you at the same time lift yourself as much as you can by the gunwale, I think we shall manage to get you into the boat. Will you try?"

"Yes. I can help myself considerably, I think," said the Lookout, a certain resoluteness creeping into his eyes and settling around his mouth, that encouraged Margaret wonderfully. Placing themselves as much to starboard as possible, so that their weight should counteract that about to be raised over the larboard gunwale, and making sure that the knots held fast in the tholepin holes, the two heroines began to pull in on the lines, whose free ends passed under the body of the Lookout, held it in their bight, and, of course, lifted and rolled it over as they were gathered in. A hundred and fifty pounds or so is a good lift for girlish arms, but it was no dead weight, for the resolution of eye and lip found expression in the muscles of leg and arm, so that almost before anybody knew how it happened, the long, dripping body came tumbling over the gunwale and down into the bottom of the boat, where it lay for the moment quite motionless.

"He's stunned a bit, or faint," said Margaret, kneeling beside him and straightening the head. "Elsie, is n't there a big shawl in that cuddy?"

"Yes. Aunt Phyllis sent it down and said it was to stay here for emergencies."

"Well, this is one. Give it me."

She folded the shawl in a pillow, tenderly laid the head upon it, covered the long limbs as best she might with the light wraps she and Elsie had brought with them, and then seizing her oar, cried vivaciously, "Now my Elsie, let us row as we never rowed before. A man's life is at stake, and our diligence may save it."

Without reply, Elsie dipped her oar, and pulled so rapid and powerful a stroke that Margaret, after doing her very best for some moments, was forced to beg her to moderate her zeal.

Half an hour of silent exertion brought them to the channel of their own island, and Margaret, looking for the hundredth time at the white face so near her feet, saw that consciousness had again returned, and that the eyes were fixed contemplatively upon hers.

"You have saved my life," said a faint voice.

"I hope so. It was a great privilege for us," replied Margaret almost as faintly, for her breath came only in gasps, and her head seemed hooped with iron, and there was a singing in her ears, as if the disappointed mermaids were chorusing their anger at seeing their prey carried beyond their reach.

"You are killing yourself. There is no hurry now — stop and rest."

It was so strange to see that man, just rescued from the jaws of death, not yet able to sit up, assuming care and control of others, and to hear authority mingling with the tremor of his voice, that Margaret smiled, and without turning her head said, "Hold up a bit, Elsie. I must get my breath."

"Oh! Does n't it set one's heart going — such a pull as this!" panted Elsie, thankful for the moment's pause, although she would have died at the oar rather than ask for it, her tender conscience already beginning a long course of punishment for the momentary cowardice that would have left a fellow-creature to die, rather than face a grisly sight.

"I am so sorry — a pity it had n't been men," whispered the Lookout; and Margaret, even in that extremity, resented the slight to her charms.

"I think even women were of some little use in this case," said she coldly.

"I had rather men tired themselves than women," said the flickering voice; and the eyes closed, and a slight frown of utter weariness came upon the brow.

"Can you row again, Elsie? Very gently will do," said Margaret, taking up her own oar. The boat glided steadily forward, the little waves rippling musically along her sides, the sweet, faint air blew off shore, bringing the breath of the balsam-firs, and Margaret silently studied the face at her feet. A sad mouth, stern unless it smiled, and then inexpressibly sweet, clear-cut, noble outlines, straight, strong brows, a head shaped for brain-power. She could not see the eyes then, but learned them later, — wonderful eyes, long and narrow ordinarily, but occasionally opening wide to emit a flash of blue lightning, before which nothing mean or cruel, or impudent or vile, was ever known to stand; reading hearts and minds with a quick, quiet glance, hardly noted before it was gone; so capable of expression as often to convey their owner's meaning without words, stern and hard at times, and at times luminous with love, and a tenderness past speaking.

"Boat ahoy! Bound for Clam Cove?" hailed a merry nasal voice, and Elsie eagerly replied, —

"O Mr. Keene, I 'm so glad you were down here. We need help so much!"

"Sho! What 's the matter?" inquired Jubal, his jocular tone changing to one of real concern as he hastened along the top of the bluff to the landing, and stood ready to seize the bows of the boat as soon as she came within reach. Margaret, too exhausted to speak, pointed down at the white, silent face, and Jubal, peering over at it, again exclaimed, " Sho ! " and then meditatively added, " Picked up at sea, drownded."

"No, not drowned," said Margaret faintly. " Get some one to help you as quickly as you can, and carry him up to the house."

# CHAPTER XII.



"IF the boat is gone, they are sure to be out in it; they row a good deal together, and pull beautifully for women. We will go to the landing first, and if the boat is there we will keep along shore, and perhaps meet them."

So said Cyprian La Branche, leading the way through the wood skirting the field going down to the sea. His companion, a man considerably larger and several years older than himself, made no reply, being fully occupied with warding off the blows of the branches flying back from Cyprian's hand, and in securing his footing on the steep and slippery little path. Just at the last few steps, and when the salt air already smote sharply on his sense, the narrow path was blocked by an approaching body, and Jubal's nasal voice exclaimed, —

"You 're Mr. Right, this time, anyway, young man. The women folks have picked up a wreck, and want help."

"What do you mean?" demanded La Branche, whose Northern education had not been liberal enough to include the right of man to be familiar with his social superior, and who consequently did n't like Jubal and was n't liked by him, while Sneyd and he were sworn comrades.

"Come and see for yourself," replied Jubal, turning back across the little glade lying between the wood and the shore. La Branche and the other followed curiously. Margaret, still seated upon the thwart, had dipped her handkerchief in water, and was bathing the temples of the wounded man, who stirred and muttered faintly in his swoon.   The. sound of footsteps and voices roused her, and looking up she exclaimed in great astonishment, —

"Reginald Forsythe!"

"Yes.   Can I help you, Mrs. Ufford?"

"This man is to be carried to the house," suggested Margaret dubiously, for the idea of the diplomatist did not connect itself in her mind with physical exertion.   He, feeling the doubt, smiled a little bitterly.

"Nothing more than that?" exclaimed he.   "Let us see how we shall get at him best.   My good man, is there anything in the shape of a hand-barrow, a gate, or a shutter at hand?"

Jubal, who did n't like being called "my good man," and quite recognized the predominance Forsythe all unconsciously asserted, glanced at him carelessly, and stepping into the boat replied, "We 'll see first what 's wanted, and after that whether we can get it.   Say, brother, are you coming to?"

"You sha'n't drink any more!" muttered the wounded man, opening his eyes and staring fiercely at Jubal, who put his fingers on his pulse a moment, then said, —

"The fever of that wownd on his head is getting a-holt of him, but I guess he can hold up a little; no need of a litter this time.   If two of us put our hands together this way, — king's chair, the children call it, — and set him on, and t' other man goes behind and holds him up at the back, we 'll take him right up to the house, easy as fallin' off a log.   First of all, let 's lift him out on the grass.   You take his head, mister, and I 'll see to his legs.   There, now, Mr. La Branche, I guess you and me are nearest of a height; we 'll take him first, and this gentleman can be rear-guard. Many a man I 've helped carry off the field down South, this same way."

"You were in the Northern army, I suppose," exclaimed La Branche, glancing at him with strong disfavor.

"I wa'n't likely to be in any other," replied Jubal dryly, as his sinewy fingers gripped the Southerner's blue-veined wrist.

"I should like to have met you there!" muttered La Branche, placing his hands in position. Jubal laughed.

"You were a little boy when I was down South, I reckon," said he. "Ten or twelve years make a good deal of odds along about your age. Now then, mister, if you'll just lift him up stiddy, stiddy, and set him right on our hands — that's it. Now then — lift!"

They raised the helpless form, laid the heavy head upon Jubal's shoulder, and with Forsythe supporting the back, began their slow and painful journey, Margaret and Elsie following, until the former said, —

"Get past them, through the bushes, Elsie, and run up to the house. Tell Eunice who is coming, and have the great room downstairs made ready for him. How fortunate it is not in use! Then tell Aunt Phyllis, and try not to offend her. Say I sent to ask leave, but speak to Eunice first."

Elsie ran, slipping through the bushes like a bird, and when, ten minutes later, the little *cortége* reached the gate of the Nunnery, nearly all the family were assembled outside to greet it, while Eunice within hastily put the great curtained bed in readiness to receive its unexpected inmate.

"There's no doctor in this part of the island," announced Mrs. Beauchamp Brown, who fortunately had taken the unexpected event very pleasantly, "but Father Williams understands surgery; he was chaplain once in the French army you know, and helped in the hospital, and I have sent over to Mehitable's for him. Oh, poor fellow, how deathly white he is! Why, Margaret, what an adventure! I'm sure you can't feel bored this morning. There, Eunice, that's all right, stand away and let them put him down! Poor fellow! I think he's a gentleman, Meg, — see his hands."

Her aunt's busy chatter stung Margaret's excited nerves like the stab of an army of mosquitoes, and it was with a strange sensation of anger and jealousy that she watched Eunice settling the patient upon his bed, examining the wound, fulfilling with ease and skill all the initial duties of a nurse, so familiar to her, so unknown to Margaret, whose own perfect health and sensuous organization had given her a certain intolerance of suffering and weakness in others, a repugnance to sick-rooms, and, I am afraid, something of the same feeling that induces the herd of deer to drive the sick and wounded from their companionship. But now all this was merged in a certain feeling of proprietorship toward this, her prize, this flotsam that the great sea had brought to her — to her alone, not to all those who surrounded him — this something to do and to care for, and to help, in a good womanly fashion, free from all the weary affectations of fashionable charity ; it was the promise of an interest, a vocation, for a while at least, and she would not relinquish it ; so, after sitting for a while and watching Eunice and listening to her aunt, and hearing Father Williams's verdict that the young man had got a pretty deep cut on the head and lost a good deal of blood, but would be none the worse for it if the fever did n't run too high, she quietly said, —

"Very well, I shall nurse him, with what help I need from Eunice ; and unless you feel quite competent to undertake the case, fever and all, Father Williams, we must send to the Cove for a doctor."

"I really think, Mrs. Ufford, without being presumptuous," replied the priest, "that the patient would stand a better chance with me than with a country doctor. I have dressed scores of sabre-wounds and treated the subsequent fever under direction of the best army-surgeons in the world. This is nothing different, and if it were my own brother I would not hesitate to undertake the case."

"Very well then," repeated Margaret, "we will consider that you are the doctor, and I am the nurse, and everybody else is to keep out of the room unless requested to enter ; that is, of course, except my aunt, whose advice and experience I shall often claim."

The *amende* was barely in time to avert the storm gathering upon the brow of the august dame referred to, and it was very dubiously that she replied, —

"Of course I shall help if I 'm needed, it 's no more than a Christian duty, and this is quite a case of the Good

Samaritan, and I hope I'm neither a priest nor a Levite, but I don't think you're at all the person for nurse, Margaret, not at all. We could easily find some woman in the neighborhood, and Eunice knows all about nursing. I don't believe you'd better undertake it, had you?"

"It's something to do, auntie. It's an interest, and I sha'n't be half so dull as I have been lately," murmured Margaret in her aunt's ear; and as she had justly concluded, that clever old lady felt the force of a selfish argument when a purely benevolent one would have fallen powerless.

"Oh well, if it amuses you, child, and takes up your mind," said she, nodding; "it will do *pour passer le temps,* I suppose, and it's proper enough, for that matter, since you are a widow, and I am here. You can lay it up as a good work against next Lent, and not bother with that sewing-school this year. But here's Forsythe come down on purpose to see you."

"And I am very glad of something to keep me out of his way," replied Margaret, following her aunt out of the room, as the priest and Jubal prepared to undress the patient and lay him between the sheets, Father Williams having stalked home in haste and returned with some of Lord Strathmore's linen and toilet accessories.

"How came Mr. Forsythe here?" continued she, as they went upstairs, that Margaret might change her dress for one better fitting her new duties.

"God knows, and I should n't wonder if Camilla Trevylyan knew also," replied Mrs. B. B. irreverently. "All *I* know is, that he appeared an hour or so since, walking in as coolly as possible, and remarking that as his departure for Madrid was delayed for some weeks, he thought he would run down and see us again. He has found a room at Cap'n Hez's, and takes his meals at Jubal Keene's."

"Of course Camilla must have written to him," said Margaret indignantly, as she let all her bright hair fall over her shoulders and twisted it into a great coil at the top of her head. "It's really shocking the way that woman goes on, and her husband alive."

"If he *is* alive," replied Mrs. Brown nonchalantly. "The Sioux have corrected a good many mistaken marriages."

"I hope they won't hurt Colonel Trevylyan," replied Margaret, selecting a turquoise-blue neck-tie for her white wrapper, and taking a bottle of cologne from her box, "for if Camilla flirts as a wife, she would shame us all if she were a widow. Come, let us go down."

"There 's one thing to consider, Meg. If you shut yourself up with this sick man, you play right into Camilla's hands by leaving Forsythe at liberty. The thing you really ought to do, in the interests of propriety and Colonel Trevylyan, is to go to walk with Forsythe this evening, let him offer himself, refuse him, and tell him to leave the place by to-morrow's boat."

Margaret paused with her hand raised to tap upon the door of the sick-room, and turned upon her aunt one of the brilliant smiles so celebrated among her admirers, so rarely seen of late, —

"I care more for my new *métier* than for the interests of Colonel Trevylyan and his whole regiment, with propriety to boot," whispered she. "Could n't you tell Forsythe that I am too busy just now to refuse him, and ask if he can't send me a postal, after he gets to Madrid?"

"Incorrigible! But I must ask him to lunch, and you must appear."

"Can't in a wrapper, auntie. I 'll go first and take a biscuit and a glass of wine. Don't send for me, will you?"

"Not if you won't come. Let me see how he looks now." The room was too light, and the patient was but just released from the torment of having his wound dressed and his clothes changed, so the heavy brows were knitted in a frown, the lips pale and stern in their compression, and the eyes resolutely closed, although not asleep.

Mrs. Brown looked steadily at him for a few moments, then pulled Margaret to the door, where she whispered, —

"My dear, he 's the Corsair out of that volume of Byron

which Larry lost overboard t' other day. Somehow he has soaked out of the book, and materialized in the water. He 'll eat you, as soon as he 's a little better."

"I 'm not afraid," replied Margaret gayly; "but it 's evident he 's not sugar, or the sea would have melted him."

# CHAPTER XIII.



"OUR new inmate is named Paul Baruther," announced Father Williams, who, with Mr. Forsythe, Larry, and La Branche, had accepted Mrs. Brown's invitation to lunch. "The name was on his handkerchief, and when I asked him if it was his own, he said 'Yes.'"

"Baruther?" repeated Mrs. Brown. "I don't think I ever heard that name. Western, perhaps."

"When Aunt Phyllis thinks anything odd and uncouth, she always settles it as Western," whispered Joan to Larry, who for once had the field to himself, and was bending all his energies to improve the opportunity.

"Should you judge him to be a person of any position, Father Williams?" continued the hostess judicially.

"Why, I am hardly a judge of such matters," replied the priest, with a slight tremor of the lips. "But he is not a person accustomed to manual labor, and still has powerfully developed muscles. I suppose that argues leisure for athletic sports, does it not, Mr. La Branche?"

"I should say so, Father; and in fact this Baruther strikes me as quite that sort of person."

"What sort of person? Athletic sports, well-developed muscles, or absence-of-manual-labor person?" inquired Joan, who did n't wish to answer Larry's last murmur.

"The sort of person in whom all those combine, Miss Joan," replied the Southerner, with languid malice, "The Sneyd sort of person, for instance. Don't you like that style?"

" If Mr. Sneyd had taken a fancy to go floating round in the water with his head cut open, I fancy Cousin Margaret and Elsie would hardly have got him into the boat so nicely," replied Joan sharply. " Six foot two, with breadth of shoulder and weight of bones to match, are not so easily handled as this waif of theirs."

" He 's no stripling either, Miss Joan," replied the priest. " A good six foot in height, and, though a trifle gaunt and grayhoundy just now, he has the build for a good brawny fellow ; and not so very young either, — thirty if he 's a day."

" And thirty 's not three hundred, Father Williams," retorted Mrs. Beauchamp Brown with some asperity, as she pushed back her chair from the table.

" When I was thirty I think I felt older than I do now, at hard on fifty," replied the priest good-humoredly.

" Let us have a game at croquet, we four," proposed Joan, foreseeing a *tête-à-tête* with Larry, unless she averted it by some other arrangement ; and although La Branche murmured in Elsie's ear, " It would be a deal nicer to lie in the grass and hear you read Tennyson," and she assented with a little look, they obediently followed energetic Joan, who already was tossing the bright balls out on to the strip of somewhat shaggy turf which served as a croquet-ground.

" I am going over to see how Captain Douglass is to-day," said Father Williams to Mr. Forsythe. " Shall we walk along together ? "

Forsythe, who did not play croquet, knew that Mrs. Beauchamp Brown wished to retire for her afternoon nap, and felt there was no hope of Margaret for the present, so he assented ; and after an official visit to the sick-room, where he found the patient asleep and the nurse watching him as if he were a chrysalis, liable to open at any moment, Father Williams led the way down the pretty road, past Molly's bowery cottage, where a pair of heels in the window, and a jovial laugh issuing from it, told of Tom Sneyd's presence, to the low-browed, rambling farm-house where Douglass and his sister domiciled.

Camilla, dressed in a charming *négligée*, sat in the cool, shaded parlor, and after welcoming her guests, said to the priest, —

"My brother is lying on the couch in the other room, reading.  I know he wants to see you, to talk over that book you lent him.  Will you go in?"

"I came to see if he felt like a little talk," replied Father Williams, with the peculiar tremble of the corners of the mouth that bespoke his appreciation of some jest known only to himself, in this instance, perhaps, an appreciation of Mrs. Trevylyan's motive.  If this was to secure a *tête-à-tête* with Forsythe, who looked bored and out of temper, she did not improve the opportunity for some moments, but allowed the conversation to drag on in the lifeless and heavy fashion inevitable where both parties are thinking of something else, and have no motive for special exertion.  At last, turning half round and fixing her eyes upon his face with an appealing glance, she said, —

"Won't you be vexed if I ask you something, Mr. Forsythe?"

"Was I ever vexed at anything you said to me?"

"Perhaps not; but hardly any man can bear to have a woman see that he is being"——

"Well?"

"Ah, you won't like it.  I'm afraid to say it."

Mr. Forsythe changed his seat to one very near Mrs. Trevylyan, and, so to speak, waked up.

"What is it?" demanded he again.  "The idea of your pretending to be afraid to say anything!"

"Well, being made a fool of, is what I was going to say."  And Camilla fixed her eyes upon Forsythe's face with the look of a child that has set an engine in motion, and waits to see the result.  The diplomat slightly raised his eyebrows, slightly smiled, and asked, —

"And that is my position now, you would imply?"

"Yes."

"Let me, with the Eastern potentate, inquire, 'Who is she?'  For, since Adam, when a man is made a fool of, it is a woman who does it."

" Did n't you meet Belinda McVie in New York ? "

" Yes ; last week."

" I thought so.  And did n't she tell you where the Beauchamp Browns were, and all about it ? "

" My dear Mrs. Trevylyan " —

" You used to call me Camilla."

" May I ?  My dear Camilla, can you expect a hardened veteran like myself to repeat one lady's remarks to another ? "

" Thank you for placing me on the same footing with Miss McVie, but that is neither here nor there.  If you won't tell me, I will tell you, that Margaret Ufford's companion gave you to understand that her mistress was down here, and was not unwilling that you should know it, and come down.  Not as a message, — oh no ! Belinda is too well trained for that, — but as a disinterested expression of opinion on her part.  Very likely she begged you not to betray her breach of confidence to her mistress ; very likely she remarked, with tears in her eyes, that she knew dear Mrs. Ufford felt regret at having said No instead of Yes, and only wanted an opportunity to unsay it, but was too proud to do so.  Tell me, Reginald, am I not pretty near the truth ? "

" Perhaps first you will tell me what grounds you have for this charming little romance ; and also how, supposing it to be remotely founded on fact, it proves me a fool, or on the road to become one ? "

" I knew you would be vexed, and you are.  Your voice is cold and hard as ice, and you have put that look on, that horrid, sneering, Mephistopheles look, that I always told you I hated.  It 's too bad, when I only wanted to warn you, and not have you made a cat's paw of, and then thrown away again ; it 's always the way when I try to help any one I care about, and I never will again.  Let us talk of something else.  What 's all this story of a drowned man picked up by Mrs. Ufford and her cousin ? "

" Camilla, you would have been an inestimable treasure to Torquemada.  What lessons you could have given him in the art of refined torture!  Come now, I have confessed your power, I have thrown down my clumsy weapons, and humbly cry 'Quarter!'  Won't you be merciful and tell me what you are driving at?  Of course you ll tell me in the end, — the whole prologue leads up to it; but if you only would tell me at once, and put me out of agony!"

"Oh, when you coax, I never can resist, if it was to make out my own death-warrant," said Camilla, with the glance and a smile, on which she relied to do great execution.  "It is n't much, you know, but then —  Promise me, first of all, that you won't repeat it to Margaret. It is my secret, remember."

"I am not likely to betray any woman's secret."

"Ah, don't be stern!  You frighten me so, I don't know what I am saying."

"Nonsense!  Will you go on?"

"Well, how·do you suppose I knew that you had seen, or rather were going to see, Belinda McVie?"

"I suppose Belinda wrote you to that effect."

"And what motive should Belinda have for throwing herself in your way, and volunteering all that information?"

"I don't know; good-nature, or perhaps a woman's fondness for managing a love affair."

"Belinda McVie's good-nature!  Do you consider me a fool?  And do you suppose that thoroughly-trained *ame damnée* would dare to betray her mistress's lightest secret without her mistress's permission?"

"Permission?  Do you mean that Margaret told this woman to let me know her hiding-place, and bid me go to her?"

"O you clumsy man!  And you a diplomat!  Do people say things straight out in stupid Anglo-Saxon like that, and is that to be the style of your negotiations at Madrid?  I dare be sworn that if you put Margaret Ufford under oath, she could safely swear that she never gave any such instructions to her companion, and Belinda would be unable to produce any but the vaguest credentials; and yet Belinda knew well enough what she was wanted to do, and what she would be well paid for doing."

"Even so, I don't exactly see how I am made a fool," replied Forsythe, watching his companion's face from under his eyelids. "If Margaret wished me to come, and after some feminine fashion conveyed that wish to me without a direct message, surely I am no fool to obey the summons."

"Yes, but the trouble is here, my friend. She does not want you for yourself, she wants you to play off against Professor Moberley. She does n't mean to marry either of you; she likes a train of courtiers, but not a prince-consort, and Moberley's devotion is a little wearisome and exacting all by itself. It did well enough while poor Jim was to the fore, but he got knocked over very early in the engagement."

"Don't be ill-natured if you can help it, Camilla."

"I have enough to make me so, I think. My only brother, and the dearest thing in the world to me, just wrecked by that woman's coquetries; and now you, for whom I care a great deal more than you deserve "——

"What about Jim?"

"Why, I brought him down here on purpose to get away from society, and build him up if I could."

"If he will take opium, what can he expect?"

"And whose fault is it that he takes opium? Did he ever touch it before last summer, at Newport? But, for heaven's sake, Reginald, don't quarrel with me. You are so wound up in Margaret Ufford's meshes that you cannot see the truth if it blazes at you like noonday."

"About your brother. What did she do to him, down here?"

"Just what she did at Newport last year. Smiled at him and flattered him and led him on, until one fine day she tired of the game, and turned upon him with scorn and taunts and cold denial. It drove him mad, poor boy, all shattered as he is by the results of her former treatment; he came home here and took a dose of opium, enough to kill ten men ; it drove him wild, and that is what he is just creeping back to life from now. Then, as I say, she found Moberley tiresome without a rival, and Belinda McVie was ordered to meet you in New York, and artlessly send you down here. Do you see ? "

Forsythe made no reply, but, rising, went and looked out at the window for a moment, then took his hat, and, bowing ceremoniously, would have left the room, but Camilla was at his side, her hand upon his arm, her great, beautiful eyes, swimming in tears, upraised to his.

" Ah, Reginald, I only wanted to save you from harm, and you are so angry you do not speak to me."

He looked down at her a moment, then, stooping, kissed her quivering mouth, saying, —

" It does n't matter whether you are true or false ; you are very handsome, and you don't pretend to be good."

Then he went away.

# CHAPTER XIV.



"THERE is no reason why you should not join the family at lunch to-day, Mr. Baruther," said Father Williams, considering his patient attentively, as he sat in the sunshine near the open window, a little table beside him to hold his book, a plate of orange beautifully prepared, and a vase of flowers. Margaret, in her pretty cambric dress, with an apron tied round her waist, and a charming little cap upon her head, flitted around him, somewhat like an artist around a just-finished picture, somewhat like a bird around her hidden nest.

"To-day!" exclaimed she dubiously. "Oh, I hardly think to-day, Father Williams!"

She did not know it herself, but there was a little selfishness in her reluctance to see her invalid go forth as a well man. These three weeks had been to her such a delight, such a new opening of life; she had been so busy, so consciously useful, so taken out of herself, giving pleasure, innocent pleasure, to another by the use of her abounding graces, and laying up no regrets for the future, holding to his lips no Circe-cup, sweet as honey to the taste and with bitterness and death in the dregs, but the pure, cool draught of womanly tenderness and charity. To know for once that she had been to a man not only delight but use, and the gratitude and faith she had a right to receive in return, were sweeter far than all the passion and pursuit with which her lovers had sated her.

So she said, coming close to Baruther's chair, and looking wistfully down at him, "Not to-day. Do you want to go to-day?"

"It must be some day, you know, and why not to-day?" asked he, smiling up at her. She smiled too, although still a little sadly, and stood looking at him in silence for a moment, then said, —

"I wonder what they will think of you."

"Think I need upholstering, I fancy. Too much frame with too little padding and covering." And Paul complacently spread out two skeleton-like hands, and glanced at the gaunt limbs around which his clothes hung in folds. Never a handsome man, severe illness had so reduced him in flesh and blanched him in color, so sunken his eyes, and intensified the stern strength of the lower part of the face, as to make him almost repulsive in appearance unless the brilliant smile, which was his chief beauty, lightened the rugged outlines of his features, or the ever-changing eyes took on one of their softer or merrier looks. Then, indeed, few resisted the charm, or denied that, ugly or handsome, sick or well, seldom is a man found possessing the personal attraction that made Paul Baruther an almost irresistible power among his kind.

"I suppose it must be some day, and to-day as well as another. But still, I consider you under my care, mind, and you are by no means well, you know. You will do what I tell you for some days yet, won't you?"

"I will be very obedient."

Nurse and patient exchanged smiles, and Father Williams, who watched them both with curious interest, rose and said, —

"I shall expect to meet you at lunch then, Mr. Baruther, and introduce my ward, Mr. Smith, who is anxious to make your acquaintance. By the way, without being impertinent, may I remind you that we none of us know as yet the particulars of your accident, and although you have naturally avoided so disagreeable a subject during your illness, perhaps it will be as well if you empower Mrs. Ufford or myself to give an answer to the questions sure to be reopened on the occasion of your appearance in public. Hitherto I have simply said you were too ill to talk, and I did not know."

"An admirable answer," replied Baruther, in such a tone of annoyance, that the priest quietly rejoined, —

"And you wish I would continue to make it. Of course, that is for you to decide."

"Excuse me. I did not mean to be rude, but it is an intensely disagreeable subject to me, and one I had not made up my mind how to treat. However, as my nurse says, it must be some day, and to-day as well as another, and you two, at least, have the right to know, so if you will sit down again, and you take that pretty embroidery and your little chair, so, I will tell you all about it."

"A bit of orange, then, before you begin, — your lips look dry, — and I think a sip of sherry. Yes, it is eleven o'clock."

She flitted around the room for a few moments preparing the little lunch appropriate for the hour, and both men watched her with appreciation of the grace and beauty that made her presence like sunshine in the room; but the priest's regard was almost a sneer, and the invalid's was as candid and quiet as that of a child watching its beautiful young mother.

"Now, then!" said she, settling upon a low chair close beside her invalid, a whole lap-full of bright crewels illuminating her dress and apron.

"I am English, you know," began Paul, with a dubious glance at Margaret, who nodded assent, murmuring, "Oh yes, I knew that at once."

"And I came to this country to see if I did n't want to live here," continued Baruther, leaning back in his chair and looking out of the window, as if he read the story he was telling upon the patch of warm, still sky between the lilac bushes.

"It's no matter, just now, about my plans in life, I suppose, although there is nothing I might not tell, but

I wanted to be quiet and get away by myself — what are you laughing at, Mrs. Ufford?"

"Because that desire seems to have been epidemic this year," replied Margaret. "My aunt and I came here to get away from the world; Father Williams and Mr. Smith came here to get away from the snares of the American women; Professor Moberley and his three pupils came here to get away from croquet and the German; and Captain Douglass and Mrs. Trevylyan came here to get away from me; but all four of these parties have succeeded in finding the very thing they were running away from. How is it with you?"

"Just the same. I was running away from comfort and softness, and I never was so comfortable or luxurious in my life. However, I went to Mount Desert, having read of it in some American paper as a charming spot, and amused myself in rambling about the island, stopping in farmhouses, and carefully avoiding the hotels and fashionable resorts of which the place is full. The last night I spent at a queer little cottage in the woods near Green Mountain, where I did not tell my name, as they seemed quite content to call me Kunnel or Cap'n. In the morning I paid my score and walked toward the sea, not caring at what point I reached it. I found some boats anchored outside, with skiffs — dories they call them — on the beach, and a sailor-looking man throwing stones into the water. I spoke to him, and asked if one of those boats was his, and could he take me out for a sail. He said he was a stranger, but could sail a boat, and would go to a cluster of houses a little farther up the beach, and hire a craft. He was gone a while, and coming back nodded me to follow, and stepping into one of the dories pushed off. I asked if he had any difficulty in hiring the boat, and how much it was to cost. He muttered something in answer, but just then we reached one of the boats, and in getting aboard I lost the reply, and was so occupied in helping him get under weigh, fastening the dory to the buoy where the boat had lain, and the little bustle of starting, that I did not ask again.

"For an hour or so everything went well enough. I sat forward, looking out to sea and thinking very little of my immediate surroundings, until I noticed all at once how wildly the boat yawed from side to side, so that in the freshening breeze we really were in considerable danger of being taken aback, and capsizing. I looked at my sailor, and found him with a whiskey-flask at his lips, and evidently far gone in intoxication. I spoke, at first quietly, then sharply, ordering him to put the boat about, and make for land. He swore savagely at the interference, and shook the tiller this way and that, making the boat stagger as if she were drunken herself. I expected to be in the water in a moment, and the first thing I did was to cut loose the grating in the bottom of the boat to serve as a raft, as it actually did. Then I stepped aft, and ordered my boatman to lay aside the flask and sail his boat steadily shoreward, or give up the helm to me. He swore he would do neither, but would carry me with him to a place I need not mention, and to emphasize the threat gave the tiller a sweep that sent the gunwale dipping under the water, shipping a barrel full at least.

"That would n't do, you know, so I seized the tiller, and tried to force the maniac — for he was no better — away from it. He resisted, we struggled, I got him by the throat, and he dealt me a blow with the flask upon the head, breaking the bottle, and cutting me as you saw. At the same moment the wind, as I had foreseen, took our sails aback, and with the water aboard to help, over we went, all standing. My last thought was of the grating, and as I touched the water I grasped it, and clung tight until the chaos of the upset had subsided a little; then I managed with my neck-tie to bind my left arm securely to it, and then a horrible, sick faintness came over me as the blood streamed down into my eyes and mouth, and I knew nothing more until Mrs. Ufford and Elsie came to the rescue."

" And you don't know the name of the sailor or of the owner of the boat ? " asked the priest.

" Not in the least ; neither the name of the sailor, or the owner, or the boat, or the hamlet where I found them," replied Baruther earnestly. " The facts I have given you are absolutely the only ones I have of the affair. I should very much like to know what became of the man."

" Yes, to prosecute him," suggested Margaret vindictively.

" No," said Paul quietly. " To rescue him from a worse shipwreck."

" No doubt one could hear of the loss of the boat by going to Mount Desert," said Father Williams. " But I do not believe your man really hired the boat, or that anybody there saw him. He was very possibly already drunk when you first spoke to him, and hardly knew what he was about, although able to mechanically carry out his usual occupation."

" Yes," replied Baruther, " in recalling our first interview, I can see that there was something odd and repulsive about the man, which at the time I set down as merely a surly manner peculiar to Americans of that class, but which I now think was the doggedness of intoxication. I shall go to Mount Desert by and by and see after it all."

" Nothing annoys me more than the English misapprehension of Americans," said Margaret warmly. " What you just said, Paul, goes with your Jacques Bonhomme, Father Williams, and one is as absurdly untrue as the other. You come over here, looking for the fawning peasantry of the old countries, and because our free-born, self-respecting working class do not cap and bow to you, cringing with eye and lip, and hating you in their hearts, because such a man as Jubal Keene understands perfectly when little Mr. Smith tries to patronize him, and resents it after his own manner, you talk of the surly manner of Americans, just as in another class you talk of their nasal voices, awkward habits, and bad English, because you insist upon taking the petroleum princes and bonanza owners for our ladies and gentlemen."

Father Williams rose and took his hat, making a profound bow to Margaret as he passed her.

"Yes," said he, "America is a great country, the country of emancipation and freedom, especially for women, who, being emancipated from the restraints both of God and man, find themselves free to speak and act in a manner that God no doubt is good enough to excuse, although men find it hard to follow His example."

"Better too much freedom of thought and speech than the slavery of a Jesuit monarchy," retorted Margaret hotly, and with another bow the priest departed.

Margaret, who had risen from her chair, followed him to the door, saw that it was closed, took a turn through the room, glanced at Paul with a questioning and almost timid look, and finally came back to her seat beside him, and picked up the scattered crewels.

Paul sat perfectly still, his head against the back of his chair, his face very pale, his eyes closed.

"Don't you feel so well, Paul?" asked his nurse softly.

"No, I feel pained."

"By what?"

"To see one who has been so good to me degrade herself by ungentle and unwomanly sneers. You insulted that priest, Margaret, and I shall never think so well of you again until you have apologized to him."

"Apologize to him!" repeated Margaret slowly, while her head rose upon her neck, the color mounted to her creamy cheek, a blue fire flashed from her widely opened eyes. "Apologize! Pray what does that word mean, Mr. Baruther?"

"It expresses a process of civilization well known in England, although an American is, as it seems, ignorant of it."

A tap at the door, and as it softly opened, Mr. Smith's voice asking, "May I come in?"

# CHAPTER XV

NOBLESSE OBLIGE.

MARGARET opened the door, regarded the astonished Blondin with the air of Zenobia surveying a
Roman officer, and haughtily saying, —

"Certainly. Walk in, Mr. Smith," swept out of the
room, and went upstairs to her own.

Baruther leaned a little forward and looked at his visitor
in great astonishment, softly exclaiming, —

"Strathmore !  You here?"

"Yes.  Is n't it odd?"

And the youth sat down upon Margaret's little sewing
chair, deposited his hat upon the floor beside him, and
laughed like a school-boy in possession of a capital joke.

"But, my dear fellow, what does it mean?" pursued
Paul. "The last I heard of you was from my aunt, who said
you had gone away with a tutor to make up the little defi-
ciencies standing in the way of your degree at Oxford."

"Yes, that 's the neat way the Mater puts it, I believe,"
replied Blondin contentedly. "The fact is, you know,
that her heart is set upon seeing me an M.P., and after I
was so confoundedly plucked at my examination we both
felt it necessary that I should get up a little smattering at
least of the classics, history, and political economy, before
I offered myself to the free and independent voters of
Chiselhope.  So I promised her to give one solid year to
study before I went in for society and that sort of thing,
and as I could n't well keep out of it at home, after coming of age, and all that, I retreated to the wilds of America with Father Williams for guide, philosopher, and friend,
— Telemachus and Mentor, you know."

"Quite so. And Circe?" inquired Paul dryly.

Blondin laughed foolishly, and picked up his hat.

"Oh, there's no Circe in the case here," said he, "although I don't deny that I think I have found the future Lady Strathmore. The trouble is, I promised my mother I would preserve my incognito, and not entangle myself in any way; and I can't go back on my word, you know."

"Certainly not."

"And at the same time I can't behave like a cad and make love to a girl, and keep off other fellows, and never come to the point, don't you see?"

"I should think the happy medium is not to make love to the girl," suggested Paul.

"Ah, but I can't help it, don't you see?" exclaimed Blondin in a sort of triumph. "She's that stunning, I'd like to see the man that could resist her. Have n't you seen her? She's in this house; Joan, you know, Miss Jennifer."

"If!"——sententiously suggested Paul.

"What's the use of bothering with 'if'?" pettishly retorted Blondin. "Where's the American girl that would n't jump at a title, even if I can't get her without bringing up that heavy artillery? She likes me, I can't doubt that, lets me help her in and out of the wagon sometimes, gives me her shawl and basket to carry, laughs when I make a joke, oh, she encourages me a good deal; but the trouble is, there's Beauchamp has the inside track as cousin, and then Sneyd is forever taking her to ride and drive, and as they're his horses I can't get the start of him, and Father Williams won't let me send for horses of my own."

"Well, but, Egbert, if you promised my aunt that you would not engage yourself, or tell your real name "——

"Yes, I know, but then you remember there's a higher law than even a promise; *noblesse oblige*, eh, Paul?"

"That's rather a bull, is n't it? *Noblesse oblige* to tell lies? Where's the nobility of lying?"

"Oh, you always were full of crotchets. Why under

the sun did n't you marry Lady Sue when she threw herself at your head?" demanded Strathmore pettishly. Baruther frowned, and coldly replied, —

"That does not seem to me a matter necessary to discuss. I have told you several times that I do not intend to marry."

"Have n't you gotten over that craze yet?" asked Strathmore with his boyish laugh. "You will, depend upon it."

Baruther closed his mouth, but made no other reply. His cousin glanced at him uneasily, and hitching the sewing chair a little nearer, laid a persuasive hand upon his knee, saying, —

"Now look here, old fellow, that 's the worst kind of rubbish, you know, and it makes me feel badly, because I 'm to reap the benefit of it. Suppose your father did get the property that my father ought to have had, and perhaps played rather a sharp game on him," ——

"Defrauded his brother," muttered Baruther behind his clenched teeth.

"Well, well," returned Strathmore in a soothing tone, "it 's all over now, and my father retrieved himself by a good marriage, so I 've plenty and to spare. What 's the good of grinding away at the blots on a page that 's turned over? Let 's write our own fairly, and let it go at that. For you to live unmarried so that your property may come back to me, is, as I said at first, just Quixotism and nonsense, and nothing will give me greater pleasure than to dance at your wedding — with Joan for my partner. Besides, there 's our grandfather's twenty thousand pounds."

"To the first great-grandson."

"Yes. A sort of premium to us two to get married and raise up heirs to the old fellow's name. Are you going to leave me to walk over the course, and take the stakes without opposition?"

"It looks like it," and Paul smiled contentedly. "I am in deacon's orders already."

"Well, that 's nothing to do with it, has it? In fact,

the Bible says a deacon must be the husband of one wife, so it's all the better. You don't mean to be a celibate, I suppose?"

"Tell me something more about yourself. How far has your courtship progressed, and who knows of it?"

"Only Beauchamp. I felt it right to speak to him before going any further with Joan, and so I told him my real name, and that I was looking towards his cousin."

"And so broke the promise to your mother."

"It was a foolish promise. In fact, Father Williams absolved me from it."

"Nonsense!" ejaculated Paul indignantly.

"We won't begin on that," replied Egbert, with considerable dignity. "I am a Catholic, and you are not"——

"I beg your pardon. I believe the Anglican Church to have as good a right to the style 'Catholic' as the Roman."

"Well, I don't; so let's drop it, before we get into a row, as we 've done too often already. I told Beauchamp, and gave him leave to tell his aunt and Mrs. Ufford, if he thought best, and I asked him not to tell Joan until I had got her promise to marry plain Charles Smith. I have n't got it yet; and those three, her guardians in this place, are the only persons who know my name. Now, Paul, what do you say? You know I always took your advice when we were little chaps at Eton."

"You rather had to, as you were my fag," said Paul, with a laugh, "and I believe I generally advised honesty, did n't I?"

"I remember the tremendous licking you gave me once for lying, if that comes under the head of advice," replied Strathmore good-humoredly. "But, as I tell you, my confessor has absolved me from my promise to my mother, and is not at all unwilling to have me engage myself to Joan."

"Then I should say he 's abusing Lady Strathmore's trust in him," said Paul severely. "She selected him, did n't she, as your adviser and travelling companion?"

"Yes."

"Why should he wish to favor this marriage, against all

his patroness's wishes, then?" And Paul looked scrutinizingly at his cousin, who moved uneasily in his chair, and cleared his throat before he replied.

"Well, my mother has arranged a marriage in her own mind for me — a Miss Carricksford of Devonshire. Did you ever hear of her?"

Baruther shook his head.

"Well, they're Catholics like us, but hate the Jesuits, and they would make me tie up everything upon the girl and her younger children, and of course Father Williams wants me to help his Society, — he's a Jesuit, you know."

"Yes," said Paul, remembering Margaret's outburst.

"And I've promised him that, if I marry Joan, I'll give a good sum to founding a college and hospital at Glen Strathmore, and he'll be director and my domestic chaplain. Miss Carricksford would be under the control of the Dominicans, who hate the Jesuits."

Paul stared in astonishment at his cousin. A man come to man's estate, of average intellect and strong will, with quite sufficient appreciation of his own importance, and yet so completely in leading strings that his master did not even trouble to disguise from him the machinery by which his puppet was worked! This was indeed the power of Romanism, of Jesuitism, so completely to enslave will, intellect, pride, honor, that neither the slave himself desired freedom, nor could another force it upon him! Still Paul would try.

"Don't you see then, Egbert," cried he, "that this priest is using you simply as a tool to aggrandize his Order and give himself a position of influence and authority? Don't you see he is encouraging treachery and disobedience to your mother"——

"I owe obedience to only one Mother, and that's the Church," said Egbert, in a learned-by-rote voice.

"Does the Church do away with the fifth commandment? I've no patience with you, Strathmore! Can't you see that all this priest wants is to get your money and to marry you to a little nobody, who will neither understand nor oppose him, and whose children are to be trained

by him to become the puppets of future confessors, just
as you are his. Miss Carricksford has powerful relatives, and is, you say, under control of a rival order in the
Church, so that in marrying her you are lost to the Jesuits.
That 's Father Williams's game ; can't you see ? "

" Well, as long as I get Joan I don't care ; and I 'd
rather be bullied by my own confessor than by a whole
tribe of Carricksfords and some Dominican priest into the
bargain." And Egbert settled back in his chair, with the
look upon his face of stolid obstinacy that Paul remembered so well at school. The donkey that has once
planted his feet will be skinned rather than take them up,
and the fool who has set himself to a certain course will
not be stirred from it by another's wisdom or another's
indignation.

" Does your priest know who I am ? " asked Paul, after
silently revolving this theory for some moments. · Lord
Strathmore's face brightened visibly, and he laughed
aloud, while he replied, —

" No ! Good joke, is n't it ? Come now, you talk of my
being under his thumb and all that. See if this looks like it.
I knew, of course, the minute I heard your name, who it
was, and I knew *le père* had never seen you, and only
heard of you, if at all, as Paul de Bracy, for my mother is
not fond enough of you to talk more than need be, and I
don't remember speaking of you, unless in a general way,
as my cousin of the younger branch ; so when I heard of
Paul Baruther, and remembered your last letter, where you
said you were going to spend some years in travel, and
then decide your future course, I thought I 'd just keep
quiet until I 'd seen you myself and found out what your
plans were. I knew if the father got hold of it, he 'd just
manage the whole after his own fashion, and take it all
out of our hands before we fairly knew that he understood
it. Besides, I rather fancied keeping something to myself that he 'd like to get hold of."

" Treachery, deceit, and concealment are the vices of
the slave," said Baruther quietly ; and Strathmore started
indignantly to his feet, exclaiming, —

"That's enough, — quite enough, Paul Baruther ! I was a fool to give you the chance. Now I 'll be off."

" Hold on, Strathmore ! Give us your hand, old fellow, and don't bear malice. I wish I was half as good-natured as you. You must n't mind my growls ; I 'd no business to speak in that way, though I can't take back the gist of what I said. Friends ? "

" Always friends, old Paul ! I should n't know you if you were decently civil. And don't let on that we know each other till my affair with Joan is settled."

# CHAPTER XVI.

## THE NAUGHTY FIGS.

IT was an ideal afternoon, — the sun's too ardent rays
screened off by the great white cumuli floating like
continents in the limitless blue sea of the summer sky ;
a gay little breeze playing bo-peep with the marigolds and
hollyhocks of Eunice's posy-bed, and bringing delicious
wafts from the neighboring field, where the hay was down,
and men and oxen at work among it.   Joan, Elsie, Larry,
La Branche, Sneyd, and Blondin played six-handed croquet, the men brown and handsome in their flannel shirts
and trousers, — a costume voted strictly *en regle* for boating, croquet, or lawn-tennis, — the girls flushed and brilliant with warmth and exercise, and, when the sun shone
out too brightly, darting for shelter under the great apple-
tree close to the croquet-ground, beneath whose ample
shelter Paul lay upon rugs and cushions.  Mrs. Beauchamp
Brown sat in a camp-chair, Margaret posed like a sultana
upon a gayly striped Indian shawl, and Professor Moberley
lay at her feet, reading aloud, and glancing up at her, occasionally meeting a shy answering glance that made his
deep, musical voice falter over the rounded periods of the
" New Republic."

The rattle of passing wheels made everybody look up ;
it was Jubal in his wagon, with Captain Douglass on the
seat behind him, and Mrs. Trevylyan and Mr. Forsythe
behind.  Everybody bowed, smiled, shouted greetings,
and raised their hats.

" Where are they going, do you suppose ? " asked Mrs.
Beauchamp Brown, a little indignant that she had not
been consulted.

"Only to drive," replied Margaret carelessly. "There are so many of us that Jubal has to take us in detachments, unless he hires other horses."

"Captain Douglass has quite recovered from his attack, has he not?" asked the professor, watching Margaret's face.

"Yes," replied she, steadily meeting his eyes. "He was here last night."

"I saw him at the gate, as I went by," said he, still watching the soft, perfectly guarded face.

"Yes, I noticed you. I was there too," replied Margaret; and Moberley opened his book again, then glanced at his watch, and rising suddenly, said, —

"Five o'clock! I must go home to do a little work before dark. Good afternoon."

"You will come in this evening?" asked Margaret, raising a pair of reproachful eyes to his. He faltered, smiled uneasily and answered doubtfully, "I suppose I shall. I always do."

"Five o'clock!" echoed Mrs. Beauchamp Brown. "Almost time to be dressing for dinner. I believe I will go in and rest a little in a dark room, before my toilet. This glare makes me quite dizzy. Meg, you won't be late?"

"No, aunt."

"And tell Larry to bring in my chair."

"Yes, aunt."

"And, Paul, don't you stay out much longer. You know how early the dew begins to fall.

"I'll be careful, Mrs. Beauchamp Brown."

She was gone, and Margaret resumed her crewels. Paul lay quite still, looking at the sky. Margaret glanced uneasily at him from time to time, colored a little, turned whiter than usual, and at last softly said, —

"Paul!"

"Yes?" replied he, without looking toward her.

"Won't you tell me —— I can't think of any reason, but surely you are not the same that you were?"

"No, thank God!" replied Paul heartily, and glancing

toward her, " I was very ill and very troublesome, and now I am getting so well that I shall soon be off your hands altogether."

" I did n't mean that.  You know how glad I was to take care of you.  It is very unkind to speak as if I thought it trouble."

" Oh, I don't.  You were exceedingly devoted and untiring.  I shall never forget your kindness or cease to be grateful for it.  I only wish I could repay it."

Margaret was silent, with a curious sense of being baffled and restrained, of not getting on, of powerlessness. Baruther's voice, as she already had learned, was one of wonderful expression, so flexible in its tones as hardly to need articulate words to convey its meaning, and ranging through a great many shades of indifference, anger, pleasure, emotion, and reproof.  The especial tone in which he now spoke, and in which he had spoken to her for several days, was one that always reminded her of snow, — so soft, so quiet, so chill, so repellent, yet so gentle. But Margaret had the habit of success, and it is a wonderfully powerful weapon, as well as capital armor.  She sat quiet for a moment, pricking her needle through and through the flower she had just finished ; then, looking suddenly full into Baruther's face, she softly said, —

" It is mean and unmanly for you to speak to me like that.  If what I have done for you is really as commonplace as your words and manner imply, it is not worth mentioning at all ; if it is —— what I hoped, it gives me a right to something beyond the cold courtesy you might offer to a Sister of Charity, whom you were dismissing."

Baruther turned, and, leaning his head upon his hand, looked steadfastly into the fair face bent toward him, and at last slowly said, —

" 'The service was among the greatest one of us can render to another ; you saved my life, certainly once, perhaps twice ; for the careful nursing of my fever was as important as the rescuing me from drowning.  You have, as it were, bought a place in the life so saved, and so long as I live I must feel not only lively gratitude, but a very especial interest."

Still Margaret stabbed at the heart of the rose, with an unsatisfied expression upon her downcast face.

"That is very well," said she.  "But —— you are different."

"Since when?"

"Three days.  The day you left your room."

"And what happened that morning that might account for a change, however slight, in my tone?"

"You said I insulted Father Williams."

"Yes; you insulted with a personal taunt a priest, a good man, and your own guest."

"But he was very rude to me first."

"And the high-bred courtesy of your reply made him ashamed of his own discourtesy, I suppose."

"Please don't be sarcastic; I hate sarcasm.  And have you been vexed with me about nothing more than that?"

"I have not been vexed with you at all.  See, you have cut some of the threads of that rose by thrusting your needle through and through it as you talked.  Suppose you say to me, Don't be vexed with the poor rose, but look upon it as perfect, just as you did a little while ago! I should have to say, Of course I am not vexed at the rose, but it would be absurd to pretend it is as perfect as it was or that I like it as well.  Do you see?"

"The rose can be mended," said Margaret softly, as she began to pull out the frayed threads.  Paul smiled. "Yes, and when it is mended I shall like it even better than I did at first, for it shows courage and resolution to repair what we have carelessly injured."

A pause, until Margaret, threading her needle with crimson crewel, said, in half-comic resolution, —

"I 'll tell him I 'm sorry he is a Jesuit.  Won't that do as well as if I say I 'm sorry I called him one?"

"Will it do as well to put some blue stitches into the rose as crimson ones?"

"I don't know —— it might be effective; but on the whole I think I won't."  And Margaret's eyes sought Paul's with the half-rebellious submissiveness of a proud nature confessing for the first time a conqueror.  His eyes replied with the smile she had not been able to evoke from them in three long days, and again a happy silence fell.

Paul was the first to break it, and he did it hesitatingly.

"Margot, there is something else,—something I have not even a shadow of right to interfere with, and still "——

"You can't be content to let it alone?" suggested Margaret, upon whose face and voice had passed a change like sunshine. "Well, what is it?"

"Do you think it is nice for a woman to be a coquette?"

"No, it is very naughty." And Margaret's mocking smile flashed into her Mentor's face like summer lightning. This time there was no answering smile, and it was very soberly that Paul went on.

"You use English very precisely. A coquette is just that."

"Just what?"

"Naughty. What a good old Saxon word that is,—a thing of naught, worthless, valueless, empty, impertinent. Jeremiah tells of a basket of naughty figs so unattractive that nobody cared to eat them."

"Well, if you are going to scold, please do it and have it over, without any quibbles about the Saxons and Jeremiah," said Margaret pettishly. "It is nearly time to go in."

"Quite time," replied Paul, rising from his lair. "And since we agree that a coquette is a thing of naught, as uncomely and valueless as the naughty figs, there is no need of saying anything more about her."

Margaret's face was flushed, and she picked up her work, her book, her shawl, in a vivacious manner, very unusual to her ordinarily dignified and leisurely motions.

"Going in? Hold on, and let me help you, Baruther," cried Larry, dropping his mallet and running to give his arm to the invalid, while Sneyd, following, relieved Margaret of her light burdens, and with the other hand gathered up Paul's rugs and cushions in a giantesque fashion peculiar to himself. As the two young men deposited their burdens and left the bedroom, Margaret lingered, asking rather coldly,—

"Shall I get you a glass of wine or anything before dinner?"

“Thanks very much, but I want nothing.”  Still she lingered, and at the door suddenly turned and asked, —

“Do you mean Professor Moberley or Captain Douglass?”  Baruther raised his eyebrows significantly.

“If conscience stings in two distinct places, it argues conscience has received two distinct wounds, does n’t it?”

Margaret went out, and closed the door.

That evening, as on most evenings, the little colony assembled at the Nunnery, and although Mrs. Beauchamp Brown would never allow the party of thirteen to sit down at table together, a good many merry little suppers were enjoyed, a great many games of cards, chess, and back-gammon were played, a great many couples sat upon the doorstep or quietly strayed up and down the road, as lonely as a woodpath after sunset ; in fact, the world went on much after its dear, old, ever-new, ever-delightful fashion, when youth, beauty, leisure, and men and women are factors of the inevitable result.

Margaret, who had through dinner been unusually silent and thoughtful, went out directly after, and, crossing the road, stood leaning upon the bars and watching the sun setting across the water, and illuminating it into a Fra Angelica background for the graceful little islands set like emeralds upon it.

“Pensive, my queen?” said a voice at her side.  She turned her eyes without moving her head, and coldly replied, —

“Yes, Captain Douglass.  It makes me pensive to think what fools we are, and allow ourselves to be made, and make others.  Knaves, fools, dupes, villains, — that is mankind.”

“Good heavens ! Margaret ”——

“Don’t be hurt if I ask you to say ‘ Mrs. Ufford,’ in future, Captain Douglass.”

“I beg your pardon ”——

“No, don’t take it that way ; don’t be vexed.  I never was more truly your friend ”——

“O Margaret, do you mean ”——

“Never more truly your friend than in saying, once for

all, that I shall never be more than your friend, and asking you to be content in that conviction."

"You did n't talk so last night, Margaret."

"Last night I was amusing myself in utter indifference to your welfare. To-night I humiliate myself by confessing it, and tell you the truth in your own interests."

"Is this another form of coquetry, or is it the truth at last?" demanded Douglass savagely. "Ever since I was so ill you have been more than gracious to me, and last night you gave me fair reason to suppose you were relenting altogether. What does it all mean? If you have any real, honest feeling under your fatal fascination, speak the truth, once for all."

· "You have a right to upbraid me, Jim," said Margaret, humbly yet bitterly. "Everybody has with whom I have had anything to do, I think."

"No, no ; I won't have you talk so !" interrupted Douglass passionately. "The queen can do no wrong, and though madmen like myself may rave, and reproach and insult her, it is because they *are* madmen ; and she goes on, ever a queen, ever throned above all obloquy or remorse."

"O Jim, don't talk like that ! There is one of the troubles, — one of my excuses, if I have excuses. You and the rest tell me I am a queen, I can do no wrong, it is not my fault, and the rest ; and I, poor fool, believe you, and play the part you set me, as if it were a reality."

"Dear, you are ill to-night, — morbid, unlike yourself," said Douglass tenderly. "Take my arm, and walk a little way toward that glorious West. Never mind what we were talking of ; let us talk of something else."

"I will walk a little way, if you will wait until I fetch a wrap," said Margaret. "But I must talk of what is in my heart."

"Anything, so that you walk and talk with me," murmured Douglass passionately, and Margaret left him without reply.

As she came downstairs, enveloped in a cream-white

Chudda wrap, falling like moonlight about her statuesque head and figure, she met Baruther, who, standing aside to let her pass, shot into her eyes one glance of stern disdain, then went silently on.  A pang like a knife shot through her heart, and her very lips went white, but the next moment curved into a haughty smile as she said to herself, —

"He thinks I 'm flirting again with Douglass.  Let him find out his mistake for himself."

Under the lilacs she met Father Williams, who bowed coldly and would have passed, but a hand whiter than the Chudda was extended from its folds, and a voice the sirens might have envied, softly said, —

"I was rude to you the other day in Mr. Baruther's room.  Pray excuse me."

"Most gladly and most fully.  I am afraid I was a little discourteous myself in speaking as I did of the rule for American women without specifying the charming exceptions."

"Then we are friends," said Margaret, acknowledging the gallantry by a careless nod and smile, "and I may ask a favor of you."

"I am grateful for such a proof of your sincerity.  What is it ?"

"I am going to walk with Captain Douglass, and I am afraid of the result.  It is a real proof of confidence in you, Father, to place myself in so absurd a position, and imply such importance to my movements, but I am afraid that poor fellow will resort to his enemy again to-night."

The priest nodded a grave appreciation of her meaning, and she went in a still lower voice, —

"Can't you be in the way, as we return, and quite carelessly join him, and walk home with him?  Perhaps he will tell you his trouble.  If he speaks of me, tell him that you are confident I shall never listen to him, — tell him," and the soft voice vibrated with self-contempt, "tell him, if you like, that I am a coquette, and not worth caring for.  Don't spare me, if you can disenchant him."

She was gone, and the priest, looking after her as she and Douglass passed out of sight, murmured, —

"Now what does this mean ?  I must look into it."

# CHAPTER XVII.

## THE CHOWDER PARTY.

"EF it 's clams you say, there ain't a place like Blue-b'ry Neck for 'em, nowheres about," said Jubal; and a chorus of merry voices exclaimed, —

"Then let us go to Blueberry Neck without delay."

"It 'll be an all-day job, I guess," pursued Jubal cautiously; "five mild or so over there, and part of the road among the bushes, taking down fences and all that " ——

"How perfectly lovely!" interposed Joan.

"And then I 'll have to dig the clams, got to calc'late 'bout low water, — you 've heard of ' happy as a clam at high water ' hain't you, Miss Joan?  That means 'cause they can't be got at, at high water.  Then there 'll be a fire to make down among the rocks, and corn to roast, — s'pose you want some green corn roasted, don't ye?"

"Life without green corn roasted is but an idle farce," remarked Larry; and Jubal, with a malicious grin, retorted, "Reckon, then, you young fellers don't get much green corn down to Cambridge College.  Well, I 'll see that there 's corn and Cap'n's biscuit and salt and pepper and onions along, and Nance will let me have potatoes and milk and salt-pork and a kettle."

"Who 's Nance?" demanded Mrs. Beauchamp Brown suspiciously.

"Miss Judkins, wife of the man that lives over to Blue-b'ry; ain't but one house handy to the p'int, and that 's his'n," replied Jubal in the sort of reading-made-easy style he often adopted in answering local questions of this style.

"And she will sell the materials for the chowder, you think?" pursued Mrs. Brown majestically.

"Oh, I 'll fix all that, and let you know what it cost when we get through," said Jubal easily. "I 'll get Hez's big wagon, and we 'll all go together if you say so."

"I will drive one of the ladies in my buggy. Miss Jennifer, will you do me the honor?" inquired Sneyd with elaborate carelessness.

"Oh no, it will be more social for us all to go together if Keene can find a wagon large enough," said Mrs. B. B. a trifle sharply. Joan said nothing, but raised her eyebrows with a little smile at Sneyd, who nodded securely, as who should say, "I 'll talk her over. Wait and see !"

"Well, let 's count noses," continued Jubal. "There 's fourteen of you, all told, ain't there? that is, if all hands are going."

All hands signified their intention of joining, and Jubal was proceeding, "Then I make fifteen "—when Baruther, who had been talking with Elsie on the sofa said,—

"Please count me out. I am afraid I am hardly strong enough for a whole day's exercise and dissipation."

"Oh, that 's too bad, Mr. Baruther ! It will be so forlorn for you all alone," said Joan eagerly.

"And then Margaret won't go," added Mrs. Trevylyan, in simplicity or malice, who shall say? Margaret took it in the latter way, and replied in a supercilious drawl,—

"I don't see how that follows. I have n't your devoted nature, Camilla, and don't give up everything to my friends."

"But then you allow them to give up everything to you," suggested Forsythe aside ; and Margaret, with a fine smile, murmured under cover of the general conversation,—

"No indeed, I will not allow you to give up Mrs. Trevylyan's society for mine, not for a moment."

"Can she be jealous?" asked the diplomat of himself, and felt a new wave of hope and resolution surge over his spirit.

So, with much chatter and laughter, and good-humored yielding of private opinions to the general wish, and universal deference to Jubal's decisions, the plan was at length quite settled, and the party separated early, that every one might, as Blondin phrased it, feel "fit" the next morning.

At eight o'clock the big wagon was at the gate, and also the pretty open buggy and spirited little horse brought down from Bangor by Sneyd for the use of his pupil, who was or was not permitted to use it as the wind blew fair or stormy from Mrs. Beauchamp Brown's quarter. On this occasion her bland and smiling face betokened such calm within that both Joan and Sneyd considered the matter as settled without saying, and whispered that conviction merrily to each other.

"Go and ask her, though, and give her a fascinating smile to make all sure," murmured Joan, and Sneyd only paused to whisper, "Show me one for a pattern; you have so many that you can spare one surely."

At that instant, the lightning out of a clear sky — of which we all should stand more in terror than of honest storms — fell; for as Sneyd, with a complacent smile, approached Mrs. Beauchamp Brown, Father Williams dexterously interposed, and said loud enough for both to hear, —

"Mr. Sneyd, I wonder if you will be so kind as to take me in your little buggy this morning. My sciatica is threatening an attack, and ten miles in that rude wagon would settle it. The buggy looks very easy."

"Oh — well — yes — I — the truth is, I was just going to tell Mrs. Beauchamp Brown that I had asked Miss Joan to go with me," stammered Sneyd; and Father Williams, with a look of disappointment rather over-adequate for the occasion, stepped back, saying, —

"Oh certainly, excuse me, I beg. It is no matter at all. I can stay at home of course, and I dare say I should only be in the way among all you young people."

"Why 'of course'?" exclaimed Mrs. B. B. peremptorily. "Of course, Sneyd, you will take Father Williams, if it is a matter of his going or staying at home. I'm astonished you should hesitate. As for Joan, she is going with me."

" I 'll tell you how we 'll fix it," exclaimed Sneyd, far too big and brave to resent the old lady's tutelage. "Smith can drive as well as I, and I 'll lend you and him the buggy, and I 'll go in the wagon.  How will that do?"

" Oh, not in the least, I could n't think of such a thing!" exclaimed the priest, spreading his hands and bowing in a style supporting the theory of his French extraction.  " I could n't for a moment think of depriving you of the equipage you enjoy so much.  No, I want your company quite as much as I do your carriage, and unless you will bestow both on the poor infirm old man, he will stay at home and study the Georgics instead of acting them."

O wily harpist on the thousand strings, how well you knew the tones of this great kindly nature!  Sneyd fairly colored with eagerness as he replied, —

" Don't put it that way, Father Williams!  If I. or my horse or my buggy can do any good to anybody, I 'm more than pleased to give up my own pl — plans " (he was going to say pleasure), "and I dare say Miss Joan will have just as good a time in the big wagon."

He looked toward her rather ruefully, just in time to catch the most withering glance her young eyes could bestow, and to see her turn with her brightest smile to Blondin, who was offering to take charge of her wraps and basket.

" She 's mad with me, and will flirt like thunder with that fellow or Larry all day, to pay me off," meditated Sneyd.  " But if a man says he 's sick and old, and asks you to help him, I 'd like to know how you could refuse."

" Now, my son," muttered the priest in the ear of his pupil, a little later, " I have given you an opportunity ; see that you improve it."

And to Mrs. Beauchamp Brown he found occasion to say, " I thought over what we were speaking of last night, and if you still think it best to let Miss Jennifer know," —

" I told her before I went to bed," interrupted Mrs. Brown rather defiantly.  The priest looked astonished, dubious, resigned, doing each expression carefully and a little broadly, that they might take full effect. Then he replied very meekly, —

"Of course you are the best judge, and I cannot presume to comment. I promised Lady Strathmore that the incognito should be preserved, and that her son should not engage himself; but the matter has been taken entirely out of my hands, by Lord Strathmore's own action, and then of course you were the one to decide as to telling Miss Joan. When it comes to matters of social *finesse* like this, a poor bookworm like me has no chance, and is fortunate to find such an ally as yourself."

"Don't be alarmed, not in the least, my good friend," replied his ally, with a little series of patronizing nods. "If you are at sea, it's in my boat, and I understand the helm perfectly, per–fect–ly! As you justly say, it was my right to inform my niece of the identity of her suitor, and I did so, contrary to your advice and wish, I admit; but as you again truly say, I must be, in the nature of things, a better judge of these matters than you, and so I shall tell Lady Strathmore when I see her. She can't but be satisfied with my niece when she knows her; Joan will make a very handsome countess, and I shall go over with her to see her properly started."

"Now then, Aunt Phyllis, if you will get in," said Larry, coming to offer his arm; and as Father Williams turned away toward the buggy, he indulged himself in a small smile of infinite humor.

Margaret, exquisitely dressed, somewhat in the Watteau style of Marie Antoinette at the Little Trianon, and with a dangerous light glinting in her half-closed eyes, stepped back into the house as her aunt climbed into the wagon. Paul stood in the doorway, watching the departure of the party, his finger in the volume of Shakspeare which was to be the solace of his loneliness.

"I hope you'll have a happy day, Margot, and a good day to recollect," said he gently as she passed.

"Thanks," replied she coldly. "I have managed to entertain myself tolerably so far through life, and suppose I shall continue to do so."

She passed on into the parlor and returned with a book. I am afraid she did not know the title of it. As she drew back her skirt to pass Paul, still standing in the doorway, he compelled her eyes to meet his own, and said, —

"How much kinder you were to me while I was ill than you are to yourself now. What is it that you resent?"

"I!" exclaimed Margaret in bitter mockery, "I resent! I unkind! I changed! How like a man, how like you! You accuse me of all sorts of folly and wickedness, you misjudge my most innocent actions, you treat me with that hateful cold kindness in which you excel, and then you wonder that I should be at all different! The truth is, Mr. Baruther, that I have too long been accustomed to giving the law to be able to receive it gracefully."

"The truth is that you are spoiled, and more's the pity!" replied Baruther hotly; then, with sudden self-control, "I beg your pardon. It is quite true that I have no right to dictate to you. It arose from a mistaken zeal for your real happiness, but of course you are the best judge how that is to be reached. I won't interfere again; good-morning."

He stepped aside, and stood looking over her head at the persons outside, removed from her by perhaps three feet of space outwardly, but all at once radiating such an atmosphere of impenetrable reserve and coldness as to place himself utterly out of reach in any real sense, and yet remaining the courteous and high-bred gentleman, which was all that nine tenths of the world ever found in him.

Margaret glanced at him, shivered a little in spite of herself, and passed on. Her keen senses and imperious, pleasure-loving nature felt that coldness like a blow. As she mounted to her seat between Forsythe and the professor, Baruther's eyes slowly rose to the level of her queenly head, and watched her until their depths grew dark with trouble, and a frown as of physical pain contracted his brow.

"If I could give her life for life!" muttered he, "If I could make her as happy and as perfect, as she is beautiful and charming!"——

"A kind of a pretty day for 'em, is n't it?" said a monotonous voice at his elbow; and turning, he found himself face to face with an old, old woman, her figure bent and leaning on a stick, her face all seamed and puckered with wrinkles, her eyes blinking and uncanny, — old and ugly, and poor and uneducated; but the frown and the look of pain died out of Paul Baruther's face, and he answered, with a kindly smile, —

"Yes, indeed. And for all of us. Are you going out?"

"Well, I don't know. Out and me hain't had much to say to each other for a good many years. I 'm kind o' crippled with rheumatiz, and need a sight o' help getting up and down steps. Eunice she 's awful busy and don't think, I suppose; young folks mostly looks arter their own selves, I 've noticed."

Paul gravely pondered the question of Eunice's youth for a moment, but no smile reached the surface, and then he asked, —

"And are you Eunice's grandmother of whom I have heard?"

"Yes, I be. My husband was son of the old folks that built the back end of the house. When we was married we put on the front. That was my bedroom oncet."

She lifted her cane and pointed into Paul's own room, and a curious quaver of regret and pride and reminiscence struck through the cracked old voice, giving it such pathos and dignity as the straying breeze may sometimes draw from the broken and forgotten instrument, tossed aside with the lumber of the garret. The young man looked at her attentively, and the expression that made his rugged features beautiful passed upon them.

"Let me help you down the steps," said he, "and I think by leaning on my arm you can manage to walk a little way. Stop, I must take some medicine first, and let me give you a little too. It is called port wine, and is good for feeble folk like us."

And when Eunice, in mingled alarm and anger, came to look for her charge in the quarter of the house where she was strictly forbidden to intrude, she found her seated in

Paul's comfortable chair, looking fresher and younger than she had done in ten years, and describing in the quaint language of her age the troubles and privations of the early settlers on Plum Island, and how her father had shot a bear "right out in that very chip-yard, and ma'am she smoked the hams."

"Well, grandmother, I do say!"—began Eunice, but Paul lifted a face whose authority was not all concealed by its kindliness and genuine interest, and said,—

"Your grandmother has been so kind as to accept my invitation to rest a little after our walk. I have been extremely interested in her stories of this place in the old times, and hope I shall hear some more of them some other day. Good-by for the present, Mrs. Small."

"Good-by, young man. I 'm obleeged for your politeness." And with a funny little courtesy the old lady hobbled out of the room, Eunice following, with a face of undisguised astonishment.

# CHAPTER XVIII.

## THE CHOWDER.

PLUM ISLAND is in its topography a land of sur-
prises and sudden delights, for it is shaped not unlike the sheet of dough from whose circumference the
cook has cut many tops and bottoms for her tarts, leaving
a succession of deeply indented bays and irregular prom-
ontories, while here and there the bays so nearly meet
those of the opposite side as to leave only a strip of connecting land, occasionally so narrow and so low as to be
submerged at high tide. It was one of these hyphens of
land that connected Blueb'ry P'int with the main island,
and Joan and Elsie found singular satisfaction in the
thought that some sudden high tide like that of Lincoln-
shire, some eygre rearing its deadly crest across this isth-
mus, might forever cut them off from what for the moment
they called home, and perhaps sweep them from the surface of the earth.

"You would not mind so much if ? " — whispered La
Branche in Elsie's ear.

" If what? " asked that artless maid, not half so artless
now as she had been a month before.

" If we all went together? "

" Well, but should we go together? You said the other
day that it is only Roman Catholics who go to heaven, and
I don't see any pleasure in bidding good-by forever to
one's friends at the golden gate."

" Then believe as I do, and all will go well."

" I 'm not very fond of pottage."

" Pottage? I am too much in earnest, Elsie, to play
with words. What do you mean? "

"Esau sold his birthright for a mess of pottage, but the pottage in this case is not enough of a temptation."

Silly Elsie, to put on armor and use weapons she had not proved !  She loved La Branche in the very depths of her virginal heart, and she was so terrified lest any eyes, his especially, should discover the secret at which she had never herself steadfastly dared to look, that she borrowed Joan's lance of badinage and coquetry to defend it, and having borrowed, knew not how to use it.  Worse than her own awkwardness was the error into which she led her lover ; for La Branche, like many men of his jealous and suspicious temperament, lawless passions, and experience of his own power, valued more than all else the unsunned purity and crystalline truthfulness, the want of artifice and innocent betrayal of affection, so perfectly developed in this fair northern maiden ; and when of a sudden she appeared in a new character, when she met his passionate glance with a mocking smile, his intimation of future hopes with a sarcastic denial of value for the gift he was about to offer, when, in a word, the idea flashed across the imperious self-consciousness of the young Southerner that he had been trifled with, that this girl, like so many others, knew how to assume the exterior of an angel, and was at heart as vain, false, self-seeking as the rest, his angry disappointment knew no bounds.  Not that either he or she distinctly set forth in their own minds the mood or the belief which, in our clumsy human language, it takes so many words to formulate, but she was disposed to affect an indifference she did not feel, and he blindly resented the assumption without proving its reality.

"Certainly you had better not accept pottage  you don't value, — even supposing it has been offered to you," muttered La Branche angrily ; and as the heavy wagon halted at the foot of a steep hill, he jumped out, crying, "Come, fellows, let us walk up !"

All the men complied with the invitation, and Elsie, as the slow ascent opened reach after reach of glorious scenery, — first, woodlands still redolent with the perfumes of early morning, and vocal with the matins of the birds; then distant hill-tops, wooded to the lovely crest, where eagle and sea-gull made their nests; and at last the broad, glorious sea glinting in the morning light, a great sapphire sparkling back the golden sunlight, — Elsie watched the whole with wide-open, unseeing eyes, a sharp new pain burning at her heart, a bewildered daze upon her mind, a sort of chaos through which only loomed one shape, — the horrible shape of a first despair!

"Supposing it has been offered to you," so echoed the words of this ugly phantom. "He meant I was refusing his love before it had been offered — was bold, forward, unmaidenly — oh — and he knows I love him — oh — and now he will never love me any more — I have lost him, and for what? Yes, I do love him, — I do, I do! — and I will be cut all in little bits and burned in a fire before he shall know it! If he came this moment, and knelt before me, and asked me to marry him, I would laugh in his face, and say, 'How perfectly absurd!' Yes, I can be proud, I can hold my own as well as Joan, as well as Margaret herself, if I try, and won't I try! Oh, if Larry knew I had been taunted with loving a man that did n't love me! He won't know — nobody ever will know. I will bury the secret so deep out of sight that nobody can ever find it, and it will be buried with me. I never shall marry at all, and I probably shall die young; I always thought I should, and when I am dead, perhaps "——

A rather violent poke in the back from the point of Mrs. Beauchamp Brown's parasol prevented the sequel of this tragedy, and the strident voice of that lady startled back the prophet to real life by demanding, —

"Did you tell Eunice Small to put in a can of condensed milk for the coffee, I say?"

"Yes, aunt, I did."

"That 's right. This country cream is all very pastoral and that sort of thing, but for my part I like condensed milk a great deal better; and, besides, when one is used to a thing nine months in the year, it is too much trouble to form another habit for the three months. Elsie, what 's the matter? You look as white as a sheet and as dragged as a stick of cream candy. It 's too much for a growing girl like you to sit bolt upright on a board over such roads as these. We shall have you with a spine next. Come over here, and sit with me on the back seat; it is very comfortable, — no, not very, but comparatively, — and Phil Moberley can take your seat when he gets in again."

Elsie, too miserable to reply, too miserable to care, rather glad indeed to escape La Branche's neighborhood, made her way over the intervening benches, and sat down with her aunt upon the well-padded and high-backed seat from Jubal's wagon arranged for the elder lady's benefit. La Branche, whose anger had a little cooled with the ascent of the hill, and who was wavering between a desire for reconciliation and his first indignation, saw the movement, concluded that it was a coquettish one, and hardened himself in his anger.

The hill topped, and the passengers picked up, the wagon descended the other side at a rattling rate, rounded handsomely a curve at the foot, and drew up with a flourish at the door of a little farmhouse, which, with its dependencies, looked out of place and impertinent in presence of the grand combination of cliff and ocean, storm-tormented cedars, and wildly-heaped rocks and bushes, among which it was set down.

" Now then, here we be !" joyously announced Jubal, as he leaped to the ground, the reins in his hand. " Hallo ! sis, is your ma'am to home?"

Sis, a tow-headed damsel of about seven years old, stuck a finger in her mouth, and shambled away, perhaps to ascertain whether her mother was " to home," in the conventional use of the phrase; but before even the young men had dismounted from the wagon the door opened, and a tall, angular woman, thin-haired, yellow-skinned, weary-eyed, — the typical rural New-England woman, — stood surveying the party with a smile, pleasant of intention, but not agreeable of execution, owing to the defective teeth it exposed. Jubal immediately stepped up to the door, changed his whip to his left hand, and cordially extended the right to this lady, who accepted and used it as if it had been a pump-handle.

"Pleased to see you, Mr. Keene. How's your folks?" inquired she cordially ; and Jubal as cordially replied, —

"First rate. I hope I see you well."

"Well, I ain't more than middlin'. The dispepsy follers me pretty bad, and I 've had a season of tic ; but I keep raound. Come in, won't ye, all of yer?"

"I guess we won't just now, if you 'll excuse us." And Jubal looked dubiously at his thirteen companions, as if wondering if they *could* come into the little house, if they wanted to. "The fact is," continued he, in the sort of deprecatory way in which one might mention a participation in the sports of children, "we 're going to have a chowder down on the rocks here, — kind o' camp out, you know ; and if you could 'commodate us with a kittle and a few things, it would help along wonderfully."

"Lor, yes, I 'll give you a kittle and welcome," replied Mrs. Judkins, while an indulgent and amiable if toothless smile overspread her countenance. "But you 'd a sight better come into the house and set to a table comfortable with your chowder. You 'd be just as welcome as could be, and I never had no opinion of setting round on rocks and logs. I 'm one of them kind that likes to be comf't-able when I can, and I guess that old lady is of the same way of thinking, ain't she?"

Jubal smiled a crafty smile of sympathy with these Epicurean sentiments, but replied in a lower voice, —

"They 're city folks, you see, just boarding down here for a spell, and all they want is something different from what they 're used to. Up to Boston the sofys and chairs can't be padded too soft, and down here the rocks can't be too hard. I 'll take 'em down on the p'int and get 'em started, and then I 'll come up and tell you 'bout my chowder. S'pose Ephr'm can put up my horses?"

"Well, Eph he 's gone over to the Cove to get some groceries, but there 's the barn, and Sammy he can help any way you tell him to. He can dig clams first-rate."

"That 's clever.   We 'll get along, I guess."   And turning from the door, Jubal went to help his passengers alight, and escorted them through the clothes-yard, where Mrs. Judkins's household linen lay bleaching, anchored by great sea-pebbles at the corners of each article, and down a little hill and across a wild, heathy headland to a path descending steeply to the sea.

"Now if you young men are a mind to gether drift-wood for a fire and stack it alongside that rock, and if the ladies will make themselves comft'able, or set out the croquet and try a game," suggested he in the tone of an indulgent parent, "I 'll go and dig some clams."

"And as you drag them from their depths exclaim, 'De profundis clam-av-i,'" suggested Father Williams, in a tone intended only for Professor Moberley's ear ; but Larry and Mrs. Trevylyan, standing near, heard it as well, and as the priest moved away the young man remarked in a slightly disgusted tone, —

"Did you ever notice how irreverent the Roman Catholic clergy generally are?   It seems as if they had materialized everything that should remain spiritual, until they had lost all awe, or sense of mysterious beauty."

"Somewhat so," replied Camilla lightly.   "You have heard of 'the priest who received a present of a fine fowl on the morning of a fast-day, and calling for a bucket of water dipped it in, saying, 'Go down fowl, come up fish,' and then bade his cook 'Dress this excellent little cod for my dinner.'   True story, I assure you, Larry ; the ex-cook told it me herself.   However, do you know, I am strongly inclining to Romanism myself?   Jim 's gone over, horse, foot, and dragoons, already."

"Are you in earnest?"

"Never more so.   You need n't talk about it while we are down here, for I should want a suit of fire-proof armor and a set of brass knuckles before I met Mrs. B. B. again, but Father Williams talked poor Jim right over while he was so sick ; and I 'm just tottering on the edge."

"It seems very strange to me.   Can you tell me just what are the attractions which you and the Captain have found so irresistible?"

"Oh, in Jim's case it's a sort of *dernier ressort;* he's pretty well used up, poor fellow, and — it sounds like rubbish, but if ever anybody's heart was broken, it is Jim Douglass's. She's left him nothing in this world, and I believe a positive, material paradise seems to him the nearest thing in happiness that he has to look for. If we'd happened to go to Turkey, he'd have turned Mussulman, and it would have been still more consoling."

"And you, Mrs. Trevylyan, if you will allow me to question, are you also accepting Romanism as the best substitute for Islamism?"

"No, I —— Larry, I feel a sort of foolish confidence in you that the other fellows don't somehow seem to inspire. You're such an honorable, clever sort of boy. I wish I'd had the luck to be your sister."

"If I can help you in any way, dear Mrs. Trevylyan, or if it is any comfort to you to talk, I beg you will consider me a brother for the time, and trust me. At any rate, I can promise that no brother could be more discreet."

"I know it, Larry, I know it, but — oh dear, oh dear, it's no use! I've got to go on, on to the bitter end."

She stopped suddenly, as they paced along the beach, and stood gazing out upon the sea, her hands twisted together, her eyes so full of a strange, woful terror that Larry, half frightened, laid a hand upon her arm, saying, —

"For God's sake, Mrs. Trevylyan, what do you mean? What are you going to do?"

She started, and turned upon him with a laugh, —

"Don't mind me, Larry; it's only that I'm a little hipped and blue, and hardly know what I'm saying. And don't mention about the Catholic departure, will you? Perhaps I shall never do it; but, do you know, there is something very tempting to me in the idea of penance: to go and make your confession and do your penance and have absolution, seems to settle things so much more definitely than any of our Protestant systems. I never should have done half the things I am sorry for, if I had gone to confession in the beginning."

"I suppose it may be a safeguard for impulsive persons,"

said Larry reluctantly, and then with a sudden thought of what she had previously said, he added, —

"But not even a Roman priest would, or at any rate should, give an indulgence for a sin not yet committed. There would be no soporific for conscience in saying to a confessor, 'I am going to do something very wrong, and I know it is wrong, and still I mean to do it.'  Penance is only good for penitents."

"I dare say.  Really, Larry, you ought to become a priest yourself; especially if Joan concludes to take Sneyd or Smith instead of you.  All really manly priests are disappointed men.  Come, let us get back to dear Mrs. Beauchamp Brown ;  I am pining for her society."

Meantime the croquet was set out, and Sneyd was trying hard to snatch a few moments aside with Joan, feeling that he deserved a little reward for his good-nature in the matter of Father Williams, whom, by the way, he had found, in spite of himself, a most attractive and amusing companion.  But Joan was more wilful and capricious than ever, laughing and jeering at every approach to sentiment, contradicting every assertion or suggestion, flying hither and thither, handsomer and brighter than she ever had been before, — at once too fascinating to be avoided, and too perverse to be any satisfaction to the most devoted lover.  Blondin, very pale and anxious, and yet with a sort of uneasy hope in his eyes, hovered silently around her, and got now and then a word or a glance, cast at him like a bone to a dog, and which he snapped up very like the said dog.

Yes, Joan knew that she might be a peeress of Great Britain, might live in a castle, and wear a coronet and hereditary diamonds.  And Joan loved rank and diamonds and soft living and the respect of men ; she loved these well.  But she loved a certain noble, honorable gentleman also ; and she did not love Egbert de Bracy, Lord Strathmore.  And among all these loves and want of love, no wonder her eyes blazed like stars, and her cheeks and lips glowed like a salamander's in the heat of a furnace fire ; and she jested and jibed and laughed, and lashed with her sharp tongue at everything and everybody.

And Elsie, poor little Elsie, whose wind-flower nature succumbed at 'once to the storm that only roused her fiery-hearted cousin to eager life, went and sat down close to her aunt, under the group of balm-o'-Gileads, which "united stood" against the never-weary wind upon the brow of the cliff, and meekly took her bit of lace knitting from her pocket, and worked away at it as if she had been in her father's parlor.

"What's the matter, child?" asked the aunt sharply, after one or two shrewd glances at the downcast face ; and Elsie, not untruly, said how tired she was, and how her head was aching, and that she did not feel like croquet or walking. Just then it was that she heard, floating up from under the cliff on whose brow they sat, —

"What! Do you talk Spanish, Mrs. Ufford?"

"Yes, indeed, Mr. La Branche. I wintered once in Havana and afterward spent three months in Spain, and quite resolved in those days that I never would speak anything but Spanish."

"A lady's resolutions are not immutable," said another voice significantly ; and Margaret coldly answered, —

"Not always. Some of mine will prove so, I trust, Mr. Forsythe."

"Mine always prove so, Mrs. Ufford."

"I never encountered any resolution absolutely immutable except in a donkey on which I wished to ride up Vesuvius, and which positively would n't go, and did n't," replied Margaret quietly.

"Four-legged donkeys are not so ingenious as biped," retorted Forsythe. "If I had been that Neddy, I would have started on a run, and carried you not only to the crater, but over the edge and into it. We never should have had another difference of opinion."

"Brute force does occasionally get the better of reason," said Margaret coldly. "And do you talk Spanish, Mr. La Branche?"

"It was my mother's language. She was a Habanese, and my first memories are of her beautiful eyes, and the soft diminutives she lavished upon me."

"Then it will bring pleasant memories to your mind if I talk to you in Spanish," lisped Margaret in her pure Castilian; for she had adopted that, rather than the Cuban pronunciation. La Branche turned his glowing, dark eyes upon her, and as the two walked down toward the sea, the musical periods of their talk came drifting back to Elsie's ears, mingled with the plash of the little waves breaking far down the beach, and the melancholy cry of the loon sailing high overhead.

"O aunt," moaned she, pressing both hands over her eyes, "I cannot bear it, I cannot stay! May I go up to that house and ask the woman to let me lie down?"

"Yes, child. The glare of this sun is really intolerable, and I don't wonder your head aches. Go, and I will come up and see you by and by." And so Elsie, with only a murmured "Thank you," sped away like a poor little white dove, fleeing to hide its death-wound in its own nest.

"Perfectly abominable of Meg!" muttered Mrs. Beauchamp Brown, rubbing the end of her nose irritably. "If she wants a steel to sharpen up Forsythe on, — and really he is rather gone on Camilla Trevylyan, — she need n't pick up La Branche that way, and trundle him off under poor little Elsie's very nose. Horribly selfish Meg is, but how neatly she takes what she wants, and how nobody can stand against her!" And the old lady chuckled with pride in her darling pupil, and rubbed her nose again.

"Now then, folks," exclaimed Jubal's merry voice, as he appeared coming from the house, carrying a huge iron kettle in one hand and a tin pan in the other, while Sammy trotted at his heels, laden with a basket of sundries, "who wants to learn how to make a clam-chowder?"

"I do. There is nothing at this moment so near to my heart as the desire to make clam-chowder," announced Joan, throwing down her mallet. Her court, of course, followed suit, the priest and Douglass wandered after, and Jubal disappeared over the edge of the cliff, with a train after him like that of the Pied Piper of Hamelin. The fire, for whose support an ample supply of drift-wood had been collected by the young men, was soon built in a convenient angle of the rocks, the slices of pork delicately fried in the bottom of the kettle, and then the clams, already coaxed out of their shells, the sliced potatoes, hard biscuit, onions, milk, and spices were added, and mingled in the harmonious and just proportion on which the perfect tone of the whole composition depends.

At another fire, kindled at a short distance, a great tin coffee-pot of such coffee as never before had diffused its fragrance on Blueb'ry P'int was brewed, and ears of corn were laid to roast in their sheathing leaves.

Another basket, brought by Jubal from his own house, was unpacked, and displayed an array of little bowls and mugs, " loaned by the store," as he complacently explained, and such provision of doughnuts, cheese, pickles, and loaf-cake as made one wonder if " dyspepsy " would n't " foller pretty bad " on the visitors as well as the denizens of Blueb'ry Pint.

Joan, glad of the opportunity to work off some of the nervous excitement tingling all over her, flew about, setting tables on the tops of flat rocks, peeping over Jubal's shoulder into the bubbling caldron which he so jealously guarded, poking sticks into the fire, dragging out the corn and investigating its progress, and ordering her satellites about in the most peremptory and charming manner.

Mrs. Beauchamp Brown, carefully conducted by the professor, crept down the steep little cliff-path, and was duly installed in what Joan pronounced a Siege Perilous constructed of rocks.

The chowder was lifted off the fire, the bowls filled and handed round, spoons appeared from the depths of Jubal's basket, bread-and-butter was cut, everybody laughed, jested, said they never were so hungry in their lives, pronounced the chowder delicious, bowls and iron spoons the most charming table equipage in the world ; in fact, the whole thing was the broadest and plainest possible success.

Margaret, sitting a little apart with La Branche, talked Spanish, and said such things in it as one cannot say in dear, clumsy, inflexible, honest English. She, too, like Joan, like Elsie, had her little restless asp hidden in her bosom, and stinging her to spasmodic action, and, as with Joan, the effect was most becoming. La Branche, fancying that Elsie avoided him, either honestly to quench his hopes, or through coquetry, did his best to banish her from his thoughts ; and, manlike, found it easy enough to absorb himself in the new object of admiration to which he turned.

Let us pause for one moment to admire ingenuous human nature. Margaret, struggling against the highest, purest, and most ennobling emotion that ever had offered to enter her life, a humble and self-distrusting love, assumed an absolutely hollow mask of absorbed interest in La Branche and desire to cultivate his regard.

La Branche, truly and deeply in love with Elsie, played at love-making to Margaret, and both saw through the other's pretence, and both deceived everybody around, and tried to deceive themselves. It is said that Grimaldi was a very melancholy man, and frequently streaked the paint upon his cheeks with tears.

"You see," said Father Williams aside to Douglass, "how utterly hopeless your pursuit has become. Not only has she forgotten you, but she is absorbed in a new flirtation. Turn to the Church, my son, with all your heart ! She is a mistress who will never disappoint you."

"You see," whispered Camilla Trevylyan to Forsythe, who gloomily reclined at her elbow, and covertly watched the beautiful face now turned in profile toward him, and now raised in a long, eloquent look to meet the Southerner's glowing gaze, now drooped timidly before it, — "You see," whispered the bitter, jealous voice, "Margaret has not only thrown you and Moberley and Douglass over, but she has descended to capturing little Elsie's lover. It is a sign that a flirt is growing old when she takes to boys ! Reginald, there is some one who has never changed from her first feeling toward you " ——

Her voice broke off in a passionate tremble, and he moved a little nearer, and, unseen by the rest, pressed a hasty kiss upon the hand laid ready for it.

Margaret! Margaret! When the Recording Angel makes up thy account, will not that unholy kiss be laid to thy charge? "It cannot be but that offences shall come, but woe to him by whom they come."

Lunch over, Mrs. Beauchamp Brown felt the soft seductions of sleep stealing over her full-fed senses, and condescendingly declared her intention of going to have a little chat with that good woman up at the house. Sneyd, somewhat disgusted with the marked preference shown during the last hour to Lord Strathmore, started up, and offered to escort his elderly flame upon this errand of benevolence, and was complacently accepted.

Arrived at the house, they met Elsie at the door, who eagerly demanded, —

"Are we going home now? O Mr. Sneyd, would you be so kind —— Aunt, may I go with Mr. Sneyd, if he will take me? I can't — I really can't go in the wagon. I am too ill to talk and laugh, and it shakes my head so."

"Why not let me take Miss Elsie home now, and return?" suggested Sneyd eagerly; for, poor fellow, he had not quite relinquished the hope of escorting his fickle mistress, and at the same time was anxious to be of use to Elsie. Mrs. Beauchamp Brown hesitated, looked at the girl's swollen eyelids, pallid cheeks, and trembling lips, and significantly replied, —

"Very well, you may go, Elsie; but remember you are not to talk and tire yourself."

# CHAPTER XIX.

VINCENT DE PAUL.

NO doubt Paul Baruther would have cordially indorsed the taste of the individual who once informed us that "Shakspeare is a real nice writer, — so improving!" But for some cause his mood upon this day was not Shakspearian, and half through the Midsummer Night's Dream, he threw it aside, and took up a volume of Buckle. This lasted a little while, and then he found his wishes and his eyes straying out across the brown field, where now the grasshopper and the "Shrill cicadœ, people of the pine," had begun their latter-summer song, down to the shores of the sounding sea ; and thither he strayed, to lie for hours upon the slippery turf, shaded by a thicket of thorny bushes, and gazing out to sea, dreaming a young man's dreams, but of what ? Did a Vision of Fair Women rise for him in the quivering noontide air between sea and shore ? Did he see Titania and her troop far down the depths of the odorous wood ? Did he dream of Margaret's lovely face, her "sweetest eyes were ever seen," her luminous pallor, and mouth of passionate promise ? Did he, as she was doing, remember the misunderstanding between them, and long to have it done away ? Did he dream of the happy hours of the past month, and the possible happier ones of the future ? Alas, that we must say it! he dreamed of none of these, but by some strange perversion of fancy, some sense of the unfitness of most human dispositions, Paul Baruther, lying there in all the softness and beauty of the summer noon, recalled the story of Vincent de Paul in the slave market of Tangiers, moved to profoundest pity by the misery and homesick despair of a Christian captive, about to be led away from any hope of release or ransom, into the interior, and the saint, unable to pay his ransom, unable to help him in any other manner, offered to assume his chain, and serve in his place, until the released captive should, if ever, send ransom to his substitute. The offer was accepted, and for weary months the scholar who had been tutor to the sons of the house of Condé, toiled cheerfully and faithfully in the field, and to his dying day bore upon his wrists and ankles the mark of the galling chains he wore, until the promised ransom came, and he was brought home in triumph.

"And if the ransom had never come, and he had died in his chains, fallen at his labors, still he would have been brought home in triumph, — a whole legion of angels — a *fanfare* of trumpets such as no man has ever heard unless it was John in Patmos! If one had such a path as that opened before one's feet, it does not seem as if one could hesitate. Well, the nineteenth century calls for saints and martyrs too, soldiers of the cross, though without the prestige of the crusades. A brave man will always find a place to fight; and sin, the world, and the devil are as real enemies as Turks and Algerians."

"Mr. Baruther, sir! Dinner is ready. You said you'd take it early, you know, and have tea with the rest, and it's one o'clock."

So spoke Eunice, standing under the shelter of the great pine tree, as dark and gaunt and motionless as if she grew there, a middle-aged maiden dryad. And Paul came home from Tangiers and the clouds, and accompanied Eunice to the house, moving aside the boughs for her to pass and helping her over the wall, quite unconsciously it is true, but as carefully as if it had been Margaret. The delicately roasted little chicken, the feather-light batter pudding with creamy sauce, and the tiny mold of wine-jelly, were all silent tokens of Eunice's thought for her invalid hero; and as she deftly removed all, and put a pretty little dessert upon the table, she hoped, in a voice wonderfully softened from its usual arid tones, that he had "contrived to make out a dinner."

"An admirable one, — too good, I am afraid," replied Paul heartily. "You and my other kind friends are spoiling me for the rough-and-tumble of life."

"Sick folks and them that's been sick hain't no call to rough-and-tumble it," replied Eunice, brushing a microscopic crumb into her hand. "And I've been thinking to say to you, if you'll excuse the liberty, that I'd like first-rate to have you stop here right along all the season if you're suited, and say nothing about charging. Mrs. Ufford and Miss Elsie they picked you up, and Mrs. Beauchamp Brown she pays for the whole house, and I'd like to do my share, and give you board if you'll accept of it. I was thinking of it anyway, and then you was real kind to grammarm, and I sha'n't forget it."

Baruther pushed back his chair, got up and shook hands with his hostess, then, still holding her hand and smiling down into her face, said, "You are a very kind and good woman, and I thank you heartily. It is as much for you as Vincent's was for him, and teaches me a lesson of humility. Never mind what I mean. I am very grateful for your kindness, and will not refuse you the pleasure of doing it, for I know it is a pleasure to a good heart; so consider me under obligation to you, not for this nice dinner only, but all the dinners I have eaten and am going to eat."  .

"Thank you, Mr. Baruther, sir, thank you hearty," said Eunice with beaming face, and went away, quite persuaded, somehow, that it was she who had received the favor, and Baruther who had conferred it.

He, smiling a little at his own half-formed plan of compensating Eunice after his departure, strolled into the lonely parlor, where scattered books and fancy work, the open piano littered with music, and Joan's water-colors on a little table, all spoke of the absent

ones, who generally filled the quaint chamber with life
and mirth. Paul began to feel lonely, and wandering
round the room took up, now one and then another
familiar object. A little lace handkerchief lay upon a
chair, and taking it up he inhaled the sandal-wood perfume which Margaret passionately loved, and always
used, although never in excess. Baruther breathed it
in, and a light flush mounted to his cheek and a softness to his eyes very different from the glow and the
flash with which he had contemplated the triumph of
the soldier of the cross.

"Rare, pale Margaret! fair, pale Margaret!" murmured
he, and, still holding the bit of lace, sank into the Spanish leather reading-chair and a reverie. He was roused
by the rattle of light wheels, the pace of a fast trotter,
and Tom Sneyd's voice crying "Whoa!" Paul raised
his eyes in pleased surprise, and made two strides to
the door. Under the lilac bower slowly came Elsie,
looking like a very woful little ghost, while Sneyd's
hearty voice called after her, —

"Sha'n't I tie this beast, and come in to find Miss
Small for you?"

"No, thank you," replied Elsie's wee little voice.
"Here is Mr. Baruther, and I really don't need anybody."

"Well, good-by then, for Centaur won't stand and
it's a goodish drive back. We'll be at home by six or
seven."

"Good-by, and thank you ever so much;" and Elsie,
meeting Paul's astonished gaze, smiled a little, and
said, —

"I have a dreadful headache and did n't want to
stay, so Mr. Sneyd kindly brought me home by myself."

"I am so sorry. Come into the parlor where it is
cool and shady and sit in the sleepy hollow. Or had
you better go upstairs and lie down regularly?"

"Oh, I don't know. I am so glad to be at home!"
And most unexpectedly to herself, little Elsie, sinking
upon the sofa and hiding her face on the arm, gave

way to the passion of tears so manfully restrained during the drive home.  She could help crying while driving in an open buggy, with jovial Tom Sneyd as companion, but she could not help it in this quiet, secluded room, with only Paul, not yet recovered from his illness, to see her.

He sat down near her, and did not speak, until she, hastily mopping her eyes with a saturated handkerchief, looked up to say, with a watery smile, —

"Oh, what do you think of me, Mr. Baruther?"

"I was thinking, Elsie, that I had never properly and formally expressed my gratitude to you for helping to rescue me from a watery death, and I was wishing that I might in some measure repay the obligation now, by rescuing you from the same danger."

"What danger?" asked Elsie tremulously.

"Why, a watery death," and Paul smiled winningly; but Elsie was too much in earnest to be coaxed out of her grief with a small joke, and burst out again in uncontrolled sobs, moaning, —

"Oh, I wish I were dead any way!  I wish when they came home they could find me dead!"

"Why, Elsie, little Elsie, what is this?  Tell me, child, what has happened, and let me see if it can be helped; that is, tell me if it will be any comfort, not, of course, if you should keep it to yourself."

"I don't know — I don't care — I am very silly, but I do think Margaret might let him alone!  He never meant it, I know, and if she had n't stepped in, he would have come and made it up!"  Sobs choked the plaintive voice, and Paul, softly repeating, "Margaret!" laid the little handkerchief upon the table, and grew grave. Then presently, Elsie, finding, as poor women so often do, that a grief shared is a grief half removed, went on, amid sobs and tears and interruptions, to pour out all her story of doubts and fears and short-lived anger, and the strong, fierce jealousy burning in her gentle nature with a strange and terrible fire; and Paul, leaning an elbow on his knee, and his forehead on his hand, listened with pale face and knitted brows, and a look of stern anger settling about his mouth.

It was told at length, — all the poor, pitiful little tale, so sadly, sadly common to those who know the world, so exquisitely keen in its novelty and untried pain to the child's heart, rebelling against its first real sorrow.

Then Paul spoke in the gentle and controlled voice that showed he was binding down some angry or impulsive mood. "I think this can all be set right, Elsie," said he. "I am sure La Branche is very fond of you. I have noticed it for some time, and your cousin would not of course interfere to separate you if she had known. But even if it were not made up, Elsie, even if you had, like some of the rest of us, to go through life with one chamber of your soul locked up and *Hic jacet* on the door, had not you rather be the wronged one than she who did the wrong? Would not you rather be Rosamond than Queen Ellinor?"

Perhaps Elsie did not quite understand, but she caught the lofty mood and, moonlike, reflected a little of the fire and strength beaming from the eyes of the speaker, and so answered heartily enough, "Indeed I would," and thought she meant it, although I'm afraid she did n't, and was consoled and strengthened accordingly. Then Paul, knowing well how, even in the most delicate nature, soul and body are dependent upon each other, suggested to Eunice a little tray which presently appeared, and of whose contents he gravely and busily administered, first tea to moisten the parched lips and throat, then a spoonful or two of jelly, and finally dainty bits of cold chicken, flavored with a *soupçon* of cayenne pepper, and delicate bread-and-butter. With the last morsel of chicken, Elsie smiled; with the last sweet crust of bread, she laughed outright. Paul smiled gravely enough in hearing her, and carried away the tray, stooping his lofty crest as he went through the doorway.

"You promised to teach me cribbage," said he, coming back. "Won't you do it now, unless your head aches too much?"

"Oh, my head does n't ache at all now, thank you," cried Elsie, jumping up to fetch the board. "The tea has quite cured it."

"May you never have an ache that tea will not reach!" said Paul gently, and Elsie turned on him two innocent gray eyes full of tears, and softly answered,—

"I believe you would cure it if I had, you are so kind."

So they played cribbage, and chatted of Elsie's home and father and mother, and the cunning little bantams, and Topsy, a black kitten, until the sun rested upon the far mountain peaks, and the birds sang vespers instead of matins, and the great wagon, full of tired and silent folk, and the buggy with Sneyd and Joan came rattling to the door, and the famous chowder-party was a thing of the past.

# CHAPTER XX.

## THE FRIENDLY SMITING OF A FRIEND.

IT would have been amusing to one behind the scenes to note how, through that evening and the next day, Margaret avoided, without the least appearance of doing so, any opportunity for private conversation with Paul, and the gay and careless manner in which she addressed him in public.

Elsie, pale and silent, sat beside her aunt, and knitted, Joan played lawn-tennis with Sneyd, Blondin, and Larry.

La Branche looked gloomily on at the game for a while, and then, muttering something about grinding, walked away down the road, and presently encountered Baruther, returning from a solitary walk. He was passing with a depressed salutation, when Paul, turning, linked his arm in his, saying,—

"I will go over with you and get that Euripides, if you please. I have a little Grecian fever to-day."

"All right. Glad to lend it," replied La Branche rather morosely; and then Paul said,—

"Will you excuse a great impertinence in one to whom you have been very kind, Mr. La Branche?"

The Southerner's face brightened, and he answered heartily, —

"I can't imagine you impertinent, Mr. Baruther, and I am quite sure I shall be pleased at whatever you choose to say to me."

"I had confidence that you would take it in that way, but still it is a matter in which I have no possible concern, except a desire to see a very good and loving little girl and a kind friend of mine made happy in their own way."

“Ah!” said La Branche.  “That’s beyond you.”

“I hope not.  So many persons let their whole lives go to wreck on a mere misunderstanding.  If a man thinks the woman he counted true is untrue, don’t you think he should at least prove his suspicions before he acts upon them?  And if a girl thinks her lover is flirting with another woman, has n’t she a right to resent it?”

“Ay, but I did n’t flirt — if ‘flirt’ you can call it — until Elsie had snubbed me and jeered at me, and gone away and left me.  She went off riding with Sneyd, she did,” exclaimed La Branche, careless of concealment.

“She asked him to bring her home because she felt too ill to remain,” replied Baruther, almost sternly.  “I was at home when she arrived, and the poor, innocent, wounded heart could not conceal its grief.  She is a very simple, very loving, very earnest child, and what would be no more than a jest to her cousin Joan, is life and death to her.”

“But she all the same as refused me yesterday.”

“The very most innocent, most artless girl will fence a little with her first offer,” said Baruther, smiling somewhat sadly, as one who knew of what he was speaking.  “Now, La Branche, I won’t interfere any further, and you are very good to have borne with me so far, but let me give one bit of advice, in the hope you will follow it.  Find an opportunity before the sun goes down, and talk this matter out plainly with Elsie herself.  Be reasonable and just, and, above all, honest with her, and I don’t believe you will be disappointed in the result.”

“I ’ll do it, Baruther, and thank you for the plain speaking that seems to clear away the fog from my eyes.  I ’ll believe I have been a suspicious and stupid ass all through.”

“And one word more.  Don’t talk with anybody else beforehand.”

“What!  Mrs. Ufford or the priest?”

“Well, either.  I was not thinking of the priest, however.”

"You know a Catholic priest always feels he has a right to manage the affairs of all Catholic people he comes across, and I have n't been charmed with Father Williams's finger in my pie of late," said La Branche discontentedly. "I don't know, but it seems to me, it's as well for even a priest to show some delicacy" ——

"And not meddle uninvited in other people's affairs?" asked Baruther good-naturedly.

"Come now, you know I did n't mean that," exclaimed La Branche eagerly. "You came to me as a friend, and spoke man-fashion, honestly and openly, for my own good ; but the priest —— Well, I 'm a good Catholic, at least I want to be, but I don't want to have to swear to bring up my children Catholics, before I 'm even engaged to be married, and I don't want advice as to whether I 'll take this or that girl, nor to tell just what property I have, and how much I 'll give to the Church, and promise to build a chapel, and support a chaplain on my place, and all that. You see, priests don't meddle in your interests, they meddle in their own or the Church's, and one feels that one is only a tool in their hands."

"I 'm a priest, or going to be one," said Baruther, with a glance and smile of comic expostulation.

"Not Roman Catholic?"

"No, indeed. Anglican. Episcopal, if you prefer."

"High Church?"

"Yes, I suppose you 'd call it so, although the Church herself recognizes no such distinctions."

"By Jove, then, Baruther, you 're the man I 'd like to have for my clergyman! I could get some good out of manly, strong, honest teaching like what you 'd be sure to give. I 've more than half a mind to put myself in your hands. Suppose you tell me a little about the differences between the two. You 're sure to have thought it all out, and what's convinced a fellow that could teach Euclid mathematics, and Homer Greek is likely to be enough for me."

"I 'll talk theology to you with all my heart, if you like," said Baruther, laughing. "But don't fancy you

renounce Romanism, when you are only renouncing
Father Williams. His errors of practice are not half
so bad as his pontiff's errors of precept, on which he
acts."

"I tell you what, Baruther, I'm going to look into
this matter. I've been uneasy a long time, and I never
did fancy being led by the nose, and I never knew any
priest who understood any other way of handling one.
Then, little Elsie's faith, and the pure, sweet life it has
nurtured, and the old clergyman, her father, all seem to
me so much more honest and straightforward, and really
godly, than anything I ever knew. We'll have a talk,
say, to-morrow morning, shall we? I must settle matters with my little girl first."

"Quite so. The heart before the head in matters of
this sort," laughed Baruther, and went his way, neither
of them remembering the Euripides.

Swinging along home, for he did not know how to
walk slowly, and was getting strong enough now to
resume his old athletic habits, why should Paul Baruther
knit his brows so heavily, and mutter, "Physician, heal
thyself!"

Reaching the house, he turned suddenly aside, hearing the click of croquet mallets, and merry voices un-
suited to his mood, and leaping the bars strode down the
field and through the pine wood to the sea. His half-
formed plan was to find the same spot of thymy turf on
which he had lain the day before, and perhaps another
vision of Vincent de Paul or Huc, or Bressante or
Jorge, or some other hero and martyr who had wooed
torture and weariness and death, as other men woo a
fair young bride. If so, he was disappointed, for close
beside the brown, fragrant bit of turf sat Margaret, an
open book upon her lap, her face bowed in her two
hands. An air of desolation, of hopeless surrender,
clung about her drooping figure and beautiful, bowed
head, inexpressibly touching to one who knew her well.
It should not be, perhaps, but it is inevitable to human
nature to be more deeply moved by Zenobia in chains

or Medea desolate or Dido mourning, than by the tears of Martha Smith or Elizabeth Jones, good women and honest though they be. Their heights of power or of pleasure were not so lofty, and the fall therefrom could not have been so grievous.

She started as Paul trod upon a crackling twig, and raised a pale and haggard face. She did not often cry, this Margaret of ours: her wounds bled inwardly.

Baruther stood quite still and looked at her. She pointed silently and imperiously to a seat beside her. He shook his head, and was turning to go away, when she detained him, in a harsh, almost insulting tone.

"Yes, stay, since you are here, stay and have it out! I am tired of this grand, gloomy, and peculiar style that you have assumed of late, and I won't bear it another minute. If you have any fault to find with me, say it out in words, and let me answer. I won't be treated like an excommunicated creature, whom virtuous persons like you are bound to ignore and set aside, any longer."

He moved nearer and stood towering far above her. She, quick to feel even this disadvantage, rose and confronted him, superb in her sumptuous beauty. He looked at her, and then away across the shimmering noontide sea, as he slowly said, —

"You are so like a child, who, when things go wrong with him, beats his own head upon the floor, and inflicts far more pain than any one would upon him."

"Always some insulting and humiliating comparison!" exclaimed Margaret passionately. "Why do you alone, of all the world, see so many faults and weaknesses in me? Why do you hate me so?"

"Be honest with yourself. You know that I do not hate you. If I did I should certainly let you alone."

"Do you mean that you" ——

The words sprang from her lips, but died away as she saw their import, and for the first time a wave of rosiest red mounted to her cheeks and brow and "the nape of her white neck." Baruther looked at her, and for one instant a passionate admiration glowed in his eyes;

then, as if by an absolute physical effort, he wrenched them away, and such a look of pain settled on his white face as Vincent de Paul's corroding chain may have brought. When he spoke his voice was hard and controlled.

"It is perfectly true, as you have several times said, that I have no right to reprove or advise you, and I dare say my disapproving silence may be nearly as annoying as my words. Still, you saved my life. This spot, where by your care I was brought ashore all but dead, recalls the great debt of gratitude I owe you. I can never acquit myself of it, perhaps I do not dislike the obligation, but at any rate it gives me a right to try to do something, — a very little perhaps, but something — to give you back to life, to real life, true life, the life God gave you in the beginning, and which you are drowning and stifling and burying alive by every means in your power. I am not going to speak again. These constant dissensions do no good to either of us, and besides, I must very soon leave this place, this life of idleness and softness, and go about my work; so Margaret, my brave rescuer from death, my tender, faithful nurse, my dear life-long friend, if you will have it so, let me speak out for once, and do you listen as to the last words of a dying friend, for in very truth I would gladly give for you the life you saved for me."

She looked at him eagerly, questioningly, with her whole soul in her eyes, but he looked only at the sea.

"I will listen, Paul," said she softly.

"Then, Margaret, look at yourself, look at your life, fairly and honestly. Look, if you can, out of other eyes than your own; look at yourself as I see you. Endowed by God with a most marvellous combination of his best gifts, — beauty, grace, and a winning manner, that you may attract all who come near you; a clear, keen, and carefully cultured mind, that you may hold those whom you have attracted; wealth and position, that you may reach those of the loftiest as well as of the lowliest station, — a veritable fisher of men so far as a woman may hold that commission, a power in the world, a vital influence for those who come fully under your sway.  That is what God has done for you, and what he has given you, — yes, and more than all these, a heart capable of the noblest, strongest, bravest love human heart can know. Now consider what you have done to show your gratitude for these lavish gifts, what use you have made of them !"

But Margaret, writhing as if that hidden asp had struck his fangs into a vital part, covered her face with one hand, and extended the other with outspread palm toward him, moaning, " No! No! Spare me !"

" Have you spared yourself? have you spared others ? For all evil is double-edged, — we cannot harm others wilfully without deadly harm to ourselves.  Think of how you have soiled and wounded and crippled your own soul, while you have been torturing others.  Are you as good or as happy a woman to-day as if Captain Douglass were not a hopeless opium-drunkard, and preparing to become the slave of a religion he neither understands nor loves?  Is it not a stain upon your own purity that Mr. Forsythe, stung by your coquetries, has turned to another woman, a married woman, who for his sake is forgetting all restraints, all duties "——

"O Paul, Paul, that is not my sin surely !"

" Whose else ?  If you had treated him honestly and fairly when he first came, he would have gone away at once : but you could not bear to absolutely resign his homage ; you fed him with now a word, and now a glance, and again a half promise ; and while he lingered to discover your real meaning, the devil stepped in with work for idle hands to do, and you will see the result. Then Professor Moberley, that honest, honorable, simple-hearted gentleman, whose life you have made a wreck, not caring for it yourself, not releasing it that it might find comfort and healing in some truer woman's love ; and last of all, — yes, and meanest of all, — to turn your witcheries upon that boy yesterday, almost breaking poor Elsie's heart, and perhaps ruining the happiness of two lives merely to amuse your own idle forenoon."

"It was because you were vexed with me. I was unhappy. I did n't think of Elsie," moaned Margaret.

"What a way to prove my vexation unjust, and how like you to say you did n't think of Elsie! How this vice of coquetry has warped all sense of justice, all generosity, all nobility in your soul! How the grand and lofty nature with which God endowed you is dwarfing and distorting to the standard you have set up for yourself. It is like those monsters of whom Victor Hugo tells, who are, while infants, placed in grotesque earthen moulds, and compelled to live in them until the body has conformed to their horrible shape. Yes, and worse than that, Margaret, infinitely worse than that, for the corroding effect of coquetry eats into the heart of a woman's purity. I have seen scores of poor creatures haunting the streets of London and Paris, who will, at the last, be judged more leniently than the refined, cold-hearted coquette, who, preserving her own virtue intact, as she thinks, drives men to debauchery and despair, and death of soul and body too. The one slays her thousands, but the other her ten thousands."

"O man, have you no mercy, no pity!" And, unable to stand, Margaret sank upon the ground, and hid her face upon her knees. Paul looked at her, at first in abstraction, for he had not so much spoken to her, as of her class; and then an infinite, wistful pity dawned in his eyes, and he stooped a little, as if yearning to gather that crushed, sob-shaken, beautiful figure to his heart; but before she could have guessed the softening, it was gone, and he said, very gently and very calmly, —

"I am sorry to have distressed you, Margaret, but I cannot take back what I have said, not a word; for it is the truth, hard and stern and unlovely, perhaps, but after all the only true beauty of this world. You may, perhaps, never forgive me, and that will be a great sorrow for me to carry away from this place; but as God will judge us both, Margaret, I meant it all in truest, tenderest kindness. God bless you, Margot!" He lightly laid a hand upon her head, and was gone.

# CHAPTER XXI.

## MARGARET'S MADMAN.

"I DON'T know that I ever heard the idea suggested of a maritime heaven, but it strikes me as very attractive," said Joan, trailing her fingers along in the water, and complacently noting how her little brown hand shone white in the moonlight.

"I 'm afraid you 'll be disappointed then," said Larry, likewise watching this effect of the moonlight, "for we 're expressly told ' and there shall be no more sea.' "

"What a pity !" replied Joan dreamily. "I can imagine nothing more lovely in heaven or earth than such a night as this, — a sky without a cloud, a harvest moon at the full, this sweet soft air, and the musical sound of the little waves rippling along the side of the boat. It is absolutely perfect."

"Not perfect for me without the certainty of Joan," whispered Larry, desperately making an opportunity, since he could not find one. Joan, all her reckless gayety and saucy independence gone, sighed deeply, and leaning far over the side of the boat, whispered, as if to the little mermaids whose golden hair glittered through the waves, —

"Joan is not worth the wanting. Want something better and you may get it."

"What ! Do you mean I shall never win you ? " and poor Larry's clear-toned and somewhat cold voice faltered piteously, as he tried to read the mignonne face so resolutely down-drooped ; but it was Jubal's voice that broke the momentary silence that had fallen upon the party, each member of which found food for thought or longing or reverie in his own heart.

"Guess our wind is kind o' 'peterin' out," said he, "and we 'll have to raise a white-ash breeze. Miss Joan, s'pose you come and take the hellum, and me and some of the young gents 'll row. Mr. Beauchamp," he pronounced the last syllable as of the verb "to champ," "and Mr. Sneyd and Mr. La Branche and me; that 's a good team, and many hands make light work."

The new arrangement involved a good many changes of seat, and Baruther, relinquishing his place to the rowers, stepped up on the little forward deck, and found Elsie sitting at the foot of the mast, a snug corner hitherto sheltered by the foresail, and whence La Branche had quietly emerged when summoned to the oar. She looked brightly up as Paul took the vacant place, and he thought what a fair, spirit-like face it was, with its great limpid eyes so full of sweet content, the gentle smile upon the lips, the setting of glinting golden hair, the little thready spirals breaking away in a thousand careless curls, and the look of maiden purity and delicacy over all.

"*Wie geht's*, my child?" said he involuntarily. "How goes it with you?"

"Oh, so well, Mr. Baruther, and all thanks to you," replied Elsie eagerly. "If you had not set him right, Cyprian would never have asked an explanation, and of course I never would have spoken till he did, no, not if I died, as I dare say I should. People have died of grief, Mr. Baruther; you need n't smile."

"I smile with pleasure that you have escaped such a fate, little one. So all is right now?"

"Yes, indeed, and it is quite right that you should be the first one to know it, for it was you that made it right, and Cyprian and I both say so. He is going to speak to Aunt Phyllis and Larry to-morrow, and we don't think they will object, and papa and mamma always do exactly as Aunt Phyllis wishes. But, Mr. Baruther, there is one thing I 'm afraid of still, and you must see to that, won't you, please?"

"My powers are very limited, but if I can "——

"Oh, you can, for you can persuade anybody to do

anything, even Aunt Phyllis ; but this time it is n't she, it 's Margaret."

"Why Margaret, dear child?"

"What I 'm afraid of?—I will tell you. You know I love Margaret dearly, and I would n't say anything against her on any account ; but she 's so used to having every one devoted to her, and is so beautiful and every way charming, that it seems only natural every one should be so, and I don't think she likes very much that people should think about anything else when she 's by, and when she knows that Cyprian cares more for me than for her, I 'm so afraid she 'll take him away again, and can't you speak to her, and ask her not, please?"

Baruther smiled. Somehow the simple child's assumption of his power over Margaret gave him pleasure, but he answered jestingly,—

"Oh, I could n't be so impertinent. Besides, if La Branche loves you better than anybody else, there can be no danger, don't you see?"

"Oh, you don't know Margaret," said Elsie with a sagacious shake of her head, and opening her eyes very wide. "Nobody can stand against Margaret for a minute. If she cares to have anybody like her, she just looks at them and smiles, and says a few words, and they forget everything else. Why, it 's so with me myself. I was feeling ever so vexed with her about the picnic, you know, and kept out of her way all yesterday, and in the evening she came quietly, and put her arm round my waist, and kissed me, and whispered, 'Dear little Elsie ! I love my little Elsie ; does she love me?' and I loved her directly, and felt quite guilty, as if I had done her some wrong. It 's very strange."

"Yes, very strange," murmured Baruther absently, and turning a little, he lay, shading his face with one hand, and looking over the heads of the rowers into the stern of the boat, where sat Margaret, her white shawl carelessly draped about her head and shoulders, with an effect an artist would have given his best brush to capture, her fair jewelled hands clasped lightly on her knee, her face

raised toward the moon, in whose vivid light each separate marvel of her beauty shone out clear and distinct,
yet softened by the glamour of that tender radiance, in
which even an ugly woman may look beautiful to her
lover's eyes.   But beyond the beauty of the face was its
wistful and tender, yet sad expression.   Surely those were
tears which glittered in the upraised eyes, and the curve
of the soft mouth was one of fathomless melancholy.
Margaret sad !   Margaret mourning !   When had such a
sight as this been seen?   Margaret proudly contemptuous
of her triumphs, Margaret discontented, and demanding,
Alexander-like, new worlds to conquer, was no such rare
sight ; but in all her thousand changes of fascination this
change had never before passed on Margaret's face, this
look of wistful tenderness and humility never before had
rested there.

"Do you, Mr. Baruther?" asked Elsie impatiently, and
Paul starting said, —

"I beg your pardon !   What did you ask?"

"If you thought Aunt Phyllis would object?"

And as the child prattled on, Baruther turned his back
on that fair image, and gave all his attention to Elsie and
Elsie's hopes and fears and projects ; yet, rule his mind
sternly as he might, he could not shut out the "feeling
deeper than all thought," which sent his blood stinging
through his veins, and sung like a whole rose-garden of
nightingales at his heart.

Steadily sweeping on under its white-ash breeze, the
boat passed from moonlight into the dense shadow of towering cliffs ; and Jubal, taking the helm, guided it cleverly
to the little jetty made for the accommodation of the officials who sometimes visited the lighthouse on Burnt
Cub Island, whither our friends were bound, in spite of
Jubal's assurance that "lighthouses, like some folks, make
a great deal better show a little way off than when you 're
clost a-board of 'em."

The path lay steeply up the cliff, and through a dense
wood, mostly of evergreen, in whose depths the shadows
seemed to lie all the more darkly for the brilliancy of the

moonlight without; but youth and gayety can make sunshine in a shady place, and did so now, as the merry party streamed up along the narrow path, Jubal leading the way, and Professor Moberley silently and assiduously helping Margaret, who talked with him gently, but abstractedly.

Only a few persons could be admitted at once to the lantern, and Margaret was among the first. Returning downstairs she stepped out of the dark and oil-scented lower room, where the rest noisily waited, and stood for a moment in the moonlight lying so white and still without, then wandered aimlessly on, following the little path as it wound away from the promontory where the Pharos was set, and into the denser wood. The professor was detained for the moment in some talk with Forsythe about lighthouses and a new principle in their construction, and only Larry called after her, —

"Shall I go with you, Cousin Margaret?" And she, smiling back with the moonlight on her face, replied in that new, sad, and gentle tone that rang so thrillingly through her voice to-day, "No, thank you, Larry. I am only strolling about a little. Go up and see the light."

Winding capriciously in and out of the wood, the little path ceased abruptly on a rocky plateau overlooking the sea, where was set a signal pole. Margaret, approaching this, and putting an arm about it, stood looking out over the sea, where a broad path of glory led on and on, — leading whither? promising what?

"If it led to some other world, some other life, where one might begin again, and forget the defeat of this," said Margaret softly, and again that look of tender yearning grew upon her face, and her eyes shone full of tears. A noise in the undergrowth, close at hand, startled her, — a noise like an animal breaking and plunging forth from his lair; and indeed it was an animal more ferocious and more dreadful than any brute; for, as Margaret, clinging to the signal post, looked shrinkingly round it, a man whose bare, unkempt head, glaring eyes, inflamed features, and ferocious aspect proclaimed him either insane or drunken, burst from the bushes, muttering in sullen fury, and strode toward her, a thick stick brandished wildly above his head.

Margaret was courageous beyond her sex, but there was something in the aspect of the madman, in the lonely place, and her own helplessness, that smote her very soul with terror ; and, uttering a wild cry for help, she sprang toward the path, some ten feet distant. The cry probably irritated the maniac yet further, for, echoing it in a howl of fury, he rushed after, swinging his stick, and aiming a blow at Margaret's head that, had it reached, would no doubt have solved this world's hard problem at once ; but the extremity of terror was her safety, for, as she heard the pursuing steps, her own feet failed her, and she fell prone to earth, gasping once more, " Help ! Help ! "

Something rushed past her as she lay, there was the sound of a savage oath in the coarse voice of the maniac, a heavy blow as of a man's fist on a man's face, a whimper of craven pain and fear, rushing steps retreating into the wood, and presently steps returning to her side, two arms raising her strongly and gently to her feet, and a voice, trembling with tenderness, crying, " Margaret ! Margaret ! You are not hurt ! "

" O Paul ! "     And not knowing what she did, she clung about his neck, weeping out not her terror only, but all the pent passion of her heart. He held her close in one arm, caressing the beautiful head as it lay upon his breast, and murmuring again and again, —

" Margaret, my Margaret ! " while his face was radiant with the love that grows so strongly in a strong man's nature. She was first to recollect herself, and standing upright, while hot blushes burned the tears from off her face, she said, half apologetically, —

" I was so frightened, Paul ! "

" I should think so, Margot. And what do you think? It is my man, — my boatman, you know ! I recognized him in a minute. I was strolling up this path, not knowing you were here, and heard your first cry. You may fancy I sprang forward, and reached the place just as you fell. I gave the villain one tolerable blow on the jaw, and he ran away. Are you faint? You have turned so white ! Here, sit down a minute on this rock, and lean against the tree. I wish I had something to give you, even a crab's bath would be better than nothing."

She smiled faintly ; for they had often jested over the potion which she had so resolutely administered to him in the first moments of their acquaintance, and then he knelt beside her, and watched eagerly as the life and color came back to her face, until her own eyes met his in a long, eloquent look, and she said, —

"He had better have killed me, if I am as you described me, Paul."

"Margot, I was too harsh in my words and manner, and I wanted to tell you so. I am afraid it was all true ; but I might have been more gentle."

"It was true, it was true, — and that was the sting of it," moaned Margaret, covering her face with her hands, and then in a sudden, uncontrollable impulse she turned and threw her arms again about his neck, crying, —.

"There is no hope for me but in you. O Paul, take me and make me good. I will be so submissive !"

A heavy shudder shook that strong man's frame from head to foot, while through the inner being — the unseen, real man — passed such a throe as those with which Enceladus, prisoned beneath Etna's fires, shook all Sicily. His arms, eagerly raised to embrace that sumptuous, yielding form, dropped heavily at his side, and the mouth, parted in passionate tenderness for one instant, hardened and whitened with anguish, as it said in a voice so restrained as to seem icy cold, —

"Indeed, I will help you all I can, Margaret ; your welfare is very near to me, but you must do the most for yourself ; I can only help."

As he spoke, she shrank and seemed to wither away from him ; then gathering herself together, as it were, she slowly rose, steadied herself for a moment against the tree, then moved toward the path, saying in a voice far clearer, far colder than his own, —

"Shall we rejoin our friends? My momentary weakness has quite passed."

She walked steadily on, and he followed, silent and with drooping head, a sense of defeat and humiliation upon him, while yet his conscience indignantly repeated, I was right, I did my duty : why this unmerited shame, why this sense of loss?

" Margaret," exclaimed he suddenly, and making one of his great strides to overtake her, " I wish to explain my position to you. Perhaps I should have done so before ; but I am naturally reticent, and it did not seem well to speak of things not yet decided " ——

"There is one point absolutely decided, Mr. Baruther, and it is the only point concerning you in which I feel able to interest myself to-night," said Margaret, in the tone of insolent superiority she never before had assumed toward him. " Pray excuse me if I seem rude, but really the terror and fatigue and nervous upset of the last few moments have perfectly used me up. If you want some advice or help, had n't you better talk with my aunt, Mrs. Beauchamp Brown? She does the goody-goody sort of thing occasionally. As for me, I amuse myself; and when persons cease to be amusing, I* say, — good-by." She nodded her head as if dismissing an importunate beggar, and hastened over the few last steps of the path to join a little group standing outside the lighthouse door.

Paul remained where she left him, his hands hanging stiffly at his sides, his teeth locked, his eyes half-closed and blazing with suppressed fire. Nature had given to this man a haughty and overbearing spirit, a quick and violent temper, a keen sense of honor, and in each one of these rankled such a wound as it never had felt before. Nature had given him ready words and a tremendous power of sarcasm, and he had not, must not, open his mouth to reply. Etna shook, Sicily shook, as Enceladus writhed in torment. What unseen volcanoes and earths trembled as that mighty soul silently struggled and overcame !

When everybody had left the lighthouse, Baruther quietly stepped in, and found the keeper standing under the flaring kerosene lamp looking at some money in his hand. In few and calm words, Paul informed him that he had met a drunken or crazy man on the hill above, and suggested that as there was no house but this on the island, the keeper should be on the lookout for him.

"My old woman said she saw some one round in the bushes early this morning, and was kind o' scared," replied the custodian eagerly. "We 'll look out as you say. Much obleeged to you, sir."

# CHAPTER XXII.



"ALL aboard?" cried Jubal inquiringly, as he cast his eyes over his boat's company before pushing off.

Yes, there were La Branche and Elsie on the peak, "jest sp'iling the boat's way, but I suppose that ain't no matter," as Jubal muttered to himself; there was Joan, with Sneyd and Blondin at either side, while, just beyond, the professor and Baruther eagerly discussed the appearance of Aldebaran as betokening storm; there was Margaret, talking gayly to Forsythe, and including Douglass in the conversation by a look and smile; there was Larry, rather abstractedly listening to Camilla, whose eager eyes shot sparks of venom at Margaret, as she complained of her airs and graces.

"Coming over, you would have taken her for Ophelia," muttered she; "not a look or a word for anybody except the moon, and so meek and mild that she seemed ready to put herself for a warm rug under my feet, — and now look at her!  She'll hold those two men as if she had them impaled on corking pins, struggling and writhing and unable to get away, just so long as it amuses her to watch them dancing to her music, and when she's tired —— ugh!"

She waved her hand with a gesture of careless contempt, and Larry said good-humoredly, —

"You forget that Margaret is a dear cousin of mine. How do you get on in your Roman education?"

"I am learning the rule of silence at present," replied Camilla sulkily, for she felt snubbed, and also the necessity of being disagreeable to somebody.

"That's right," answered Larry carelessly. "Let us practise it a little in Margaret's direction."

So the sail home was not a brilliant success except to two whispering on the bows, for even Joan was a little weary of *l'embarrass de richesse*, and still could not make up her mind where the superfluity lay; and everybody except Elsie and her lover were glad when the boat touched land and every man was free to go his own way.

The Nunnery people, with the professor and his pupils, walked home together, Margaret leaning on Mr. Moberley's arm, and delighting him with low-voiced, quiet talk of the time when they first knew each other, especially of the Class Day when she, a lovely *débutante* of eighteen, and he Orator of the day, had met, and he loved her at once and for life.

"Who is that outside our gate?" asked Joan, as the merry party breasted the hill and came in sight of the house.

> "Now when they came to the castle yett,
> Oh, Christ you save and see!
> A proud porter there reared himself thereat
> Says, 'None may pass by me.'"

quoted Larry, in a low voice close to her ear, for the motionless figure was now at hand, and steadfastly regarding one after another in the clear moonlight. as if searching for a familiar face. His own appearance was striking, if hardly prepossessing. About forty years old, — that is, at the beginning of a powerful man's maturity, — tall, straight, and heavily built, the first impression his figure made was of strength and steadfastness. Standing motionless and dark against the blue sky, he looked as though he had been left there by some pre-Adamite deluge, and had allowed the present scene to shape itself around him. His head was bare and showed close-clipped sandy hair, turning gray already, and thin upon the temples, leaving a dome-like and somewhat projecting forehead, predominating heavily over deep-set gray eyes, cold, keen, and penetrating as icicles. The square jaw was full of strength, the mouth stern and close-lipped, the whole face wore that dull coloring which is not pallor, and betokens rather an ascetic habit than the habit of ill health. One might have called him a Scot from his complexion, but his inflexible and unmusical voice betrayed no accent warranting such surmise; and whether he dropped from the clouds, or sprang from the earth, or had been hewn from the primeval sandstone by some forgotten Pygmalion, and miraculously endowed with life, no man ever knew, although many guessed.

Such as I have described him, he stood; and the ladies, at whom he never glanced, passed him and entered the gate, lingering just out of sight to learn the sequel. Sneyd and Baruther came last, and, as the latter caught sight of the strange sentinel, he uttered an exclamation, — perhaps of delight, perhaps of dismay, — and, pressing forward, held out his hand, saying, —

"Rockfort! You here?"

"Yes," replied the other, in his dry, hard voice. "You did n't write, so I came after you."

"I have been ill, very ill for a while," replied Baruther hastily. "How did you find me out?"

"Were you hiding then?" inquired Rockfort calmly.

"Hiding, no!" returned Paul indignantly. "But I did not suppose it would be easy to trace me, for "——

"It was not easy," dropped icily from Rockfort's hardly opened lips. "If you are ill, you had better come somewhere and sit down, for I have a good deal to say to you, and no long time to say it in."

"Certainly, I ask no better than a long talk with you," replied Paul, grasping at composure with both hands. "But first of all come into the house, and see the people I am staying with. They saved my life."

"Indeed?" asked Rockfort composedly. "I suppose they meant it well. How did it happen?"

"I will tell you by and by, if you care to hear. You will stay with us to-night? There is a sofa in my room, if nothing better may be had."

"It will do perfectly," replied the visitor carelessly.

"A sofa or a chair, anything, only let us get to it at once. I have no time for ceremonious fal-lals."

"It is only decent to speak to the lady whose guest I am and you are to be," replied Paul. "This is not a public house of any sort."

"Lodgings, I thought," said Rockfort, casting a cold and comprehensive glance over the moonlit façade of the Nunnery. "Who are all those people?"

"Guests of Mrs. Beauchamp Brown, who hires the whole house and invites some of her relatives to spend the summer."

"Are you a relative of Mrs. Beauchamp Brown?" quietly asked Rockfort.

"No, but I was brought into the house insensible, after some people had pulled me out of the water, wounded and half-dead." And Paul's voice grew a little indignant.

"I see," replied Rockfort phlegmatically. "Well, if it is necessary, introduce me to this person, and then let us get away to your room and our talk."

The parlor was lighted brilliantly, for beside the kerosene lamp, which was the terror of dear Mrs. B. Brown's life, all the bedroom candles were lighted and ranged upon the mantle-shelf. It was Joan that did it, for, as she explained in answer to Margaret's feeble remonstrance, "These pre-Raphaelite things need a deal of light upon them, and I, for one, wish to study our guest intelligently. Here they come!"

She posed instantaneously upon the chair which she had pushed into the becoming corner under the candles, and sat, the image of unconscious grace, as Baruther entered, followed by his friend, the stalwart proportions and iron uprightness of the latter's figure forming an admirable offset to Baruther's powerful yet elegant and high-bred characteristics.

"My friend, Mr. Rockfort, Mrs. Beauchamp Brown," said Paul a little nervously. Mrs. Brown, always disposed to consider favorably a new acquaintance of the sterner sex, smiled graciously and extended her hand.

The new-comer received it with a hearty English pressure, which printed off each one of the rings Mrs. B. B. wore in dubious profusion, upon its neighbor fingers, and sent a flush of pain to that lady's withered cheek, but winking away the accompanying tears, she bravely said, —

"I am delighted to welcome any friend of Mr. Baruther. When did you arrive at Plum Island?"

"By boat about noon," succinctly replied Rockfort, and having answered the question truthfully, remained silent and immovable, his face lapsing into its ordinary stony calm, and his whole air suggesting that he might very probably remain standing upon that spot for the rest of his life, as indifferent to all outward events as the glacier-borne bowlder before referred to.

"Mrs. Ufford, Miss Jennifer, Miss Beauchamp," pursued Baruther desperately. Rockfort fixed a glance of stern scrutiny upon each of the daughters of Eve thus named, and perhaps slightly moved his head in combination with his muttered "Good-evening."

"Sit down, won't you, Rockfort?" pursued Baruther, having hastily named the gentlemen present; and perhaps to astonish Paul, perhaps in a desperate desire to do or say something to divert her thoughts from herself, Margaret pushed forward a chair close to her own, saying sweetly, —

"Take this chair, Mr. Rockfort."

Rockfort glanced at her, and moved his lips, but no sound issued forth, and doubling his long limbs in a wooden fashion all his own, he took the chair and sat upon it, facing directly forward, as though he had been in a street-car, and afraid of seeing some acquaintance.

Baruther, looking thoroughly uncomfortable, took the only other vacant seat at some distance, and Larry, always the ready gentleman, and in a manner the host, threw himself into the abyss of silence suddenly yawning in that pleasant parlor, demanding of the new-comer if any news were stirring, adding pleasantly, —

"For we of Plum Island are altogether out of the world."

"And yet copy the Athenians, whose whole occupation was to hear and tell some new thing," replied Rockfort, with a sour smile. "The last news I heard that interested me, was that the powers of hell are prevailing in Bulgaria."

"That's a word not mentioned to ears polite, Mr. Rockfort," said Mrs. Beauchamp Brown smartly; for she had swayed a social sceptre too long to hesitate in using it for anybody's offending knuckles. Rockfort fixed his cold gray eyes upon her in some surprise, then, with a smile a little sourer than the first, said, —

"Ears polite, I suppose, require a tongue polite to address them. Mine is only honest."

"You are a young man compared with me, Mr. Rockfort," calmly replied his hostess. "When you have lived some years longer and seen more of the world, you will perhaps learn that honesty and courtesy make admirable yoke-fellows." Then, too hospitable and too well-bred to leave her guest with a reproof, she added, —

"I am very glad you have found Mr. Baruther. He has been a little lonely now and then, while still not strong enough to share the amusements of the other young men, and I am afraid Father Williams and I have not entertained him very satisfactorily."

Something in these words seemed to displease the new-comer, for he drew his heavy reddish brows quite over his eyes, and from beneath shot a glance at Baruther, who, looking very much annoyed, was trying to talk to La Branche, who was distrait, and watching Elsie and Sneyd.

Again Margaret came to the rescue, and pointedly addressing Rockfort, began a discussion of the Turco-Russian question, venturing opinions under correction, and asking for information, in a manner charmingly feminine and still entirely honest, for as Margaret candidly confessed, when accused of ignorance in such matters, —

"I like to be ignorant of them; it does give clever men such delight to enlighten my ignorance."

Rockfort listened attentively to her remarks, replying to direct questions, but never helping out her half-formed sentences or correcting erroneous statements, until she said, with a deprecatory glance and smile, —

"I 'm afraid I don't know much about it all," when he replied in a sort of final manner, —

"No, you don't, but it is not important that you should.  Women are not called upon to busy themselves in these matters."

"We will bid you good-night, gentlemen," said Mrs. Beauchamp Brown, rising and making a little formal courtesy to the company as she took her candlestick from the mantle-shelf.

Those who had studied Mrs. Beauchamp Brown and her ways were familiar with the fact that certain emotions, noticeably that of anger, caused a slight paralytic action of the head, profanely called by Joan, "Auntie's niddle-noddle of indignation," and it was that disrespectful young person who now whispered to Elsie, —

"Hush and you 'll hear Aunt Phyllis's cap-ribbons rustling like dry leaves in October.  I pity that man to-morrow."

"'Sh! Don't!" whispered Elsie, glancing in terror at the broad but dignified back of her relative, as she led the way out of the parlor, and marshalled her little flock upstairs in severe silence.

"Now take me to your room," muttered Rockfort in Baruther's ear as the last petticoat disappeared, and Paul, nothing loth, obeyed.  Eunice, whom nobody had thought to warn, but who, like a good housekeeper, had eyes and ears everywhere, had prepared the sofa for the new guest, and lighted a little fire upon the cavernous hearth, lest some chill should linger in the densely shaded and ground-set room.

Baruther rather sullenly threw himself into his accustomed chair, and looked into the blaze, while Rockfort, standing in the middle of the room, glanced around it, his eyes seeming to chill everything they passed over.

"Not much asceticism visible here," said he, as he

finally seated himself upon a wooden chair, and looked keenly at his companion.

"I have been ill, I told you, and am not well yet. I did not arrange the room nor order the fire," said Paul in the moody tone he had used ever since his friend's arrival, or was it ever since his interview with Margaret? "However," continued he, rousing himself a little, "the real asceticism is to live above the consideration of these things. When St. Bernard went to visit a brother prior, and the latter accused him of luxury in using a gold-embroidered saddle and housings, the saint looked at it in astonishment and simply said that it was borrowed, and he had never noticed it."

"Oh well, if you are copying St. Bernard, all is well, and I must ask forgiveness for my own worldliness," said Rockfort, with his grim smile. "Now, then, what have you decided?"

"Nothing. Except indeed that I will be a priest."

"You might as well leave your answer 'Nothing,' for I suppose your mind was fixed when you took deacon's orders. What you were to decide before we met again was what sort of priest you will be, — regular or secular, celibate or married, choosing the higher or the lower life."

"On all these questions, or this one question, rather, I have decided nothing," said Paul briefly.

Rockfort got up and paced the room, his penthouse brows drawn down until only a spark, glittering beneath, told of the coldly angry eyes.

"You have thought of the curse upon him who putteth his hand to the plough and draws back?" asked he, pausing before Baruther, and looking down at him, while a strange, yearning gleam shot athwart the gloom of his face.

"I have not turned back," said Baruther, proudly raising his head, and steadfastly meeting the other's look. "I have offered my life to God once for all, but I am not clear yet in what way he will have me to use it. A married clergy is one of the great features of the Anglican Church, and they, in some instances, prove themselves more useful and acceptable than celibates."

Rockfort uttered a strange sound, somewhere between a groan and a growl, and strode at least a dozen times up and down the room before he came to stand again beside Paul's chair, and bitterly say, —

"You do well to say again and again 'I have been ill;' you are ill now, so ill that I can hardly recognize you. Is it physical weakness or spiritual decay that has so emasculated your will and enfeebled your purpose? When we parted at Oxford you were ready to go out, like Peter the Hermit, preaching a crusade against the world, the flesh, and the devil, and calling on all men to renounce them as you had done; and to-night, — God forgive me if I wrong you! — I find you the very humble servant of all three."

Baruther sprang to his feet, and confronted the speaker with eyes whose blue flame quenched the sullen glow of the other's.

"You have need to ask God to forgive you if you wrong me," cried he passionately, "for you do wrong me foully. Who set you to judge of me, pray tell me? How dare you decide my vocation or try to take the responsibility of my life? How can you, who quote Scripture so glibly, forget that it is to his own Master that every man must stand or fall? and what right have you to call one way of serving Him higher or lower than another?"

"Your anger is a pretty sure sign that you are in the wrong," quietly replied Rockfort, growing more granitic as the other became excited. "Also I think you are arguing more against yourself than me. Do you choose to tell me which of these women has been selected by Satan as your especial Eve?"

"I choose to answer no question asked in that tone," replied Baruther haughtily; and Rockfort replied, with the calmness of one so secure of being in the main right, as to willingly concede a little to him who is in the wrong, —

"I beg your pardon. I should not have spoken in that tone. Had we not better postpone our discussion until to-morrow? and I will not leave here until the day after. I can see that you are not yet strong enough to do without rest. Go to your bed."

"Yes, we will wait until morning," said Baruther wearily. "I am not fit to talk to-night, and like other sick children quarrel with my best friend for offering me medicine."

# CHAPTER XXIII.



A MILE or so from the Nunnery Cove rose a high and sharply overhanging cliff, from whose recesses trickled a tiny stream of ice-cold spring water. A great clam-shell lay beside it, and hither our friends often rambled, to refresh themselves by drinking of the spring after the toil and heat of reaching it, — curious epitome, if you will, of life's toils and gains, and the little circle in which they move.

In the shadow of the cliff, sheltered from the noontide sun, lay Baruther, a little weary with the three hours' walk which had made no impression upon Rockfort, sitting bolt upright upon a rock, the sun streaming over him, and his brows drawn shaggily down, to protect his eyes from the glare.

"Will you go with me to-morrow then?" asked he after some moments' silence, in which Paul abstractedly arranged the pebbles in the channel of the little brook into a mosaic of contrasting colors.

"I hardly think so," replied he, considering. "I have mentioned the first of September as my day, and there seems no good reason for changing. Mrs. Beauchamp Brown has been most kind to me, and I would not in any way slight her hospitality. Besides, I hardly feel fit for regular study and work while this heat lasts. It is so new to us, this arid American heat. Don't you feel it?"

"You 're sure you 're not deceiving yourself, I hope," said Rockfort, disdaining the weather question.

"Deceiving myself how?"

"In your motives. You have not told me, and it is no business of mine to inquire, but I suppose it is some of these women who have so shaken your purpose. Is it wise to linger near them?"

Baruther was silent, and re-arranged his mosaic in another pattern, then suddenly shaking the water from his fingers, and leaning upon his elbow, he said, —

"I should n't have expected you to counsel flight from any danger, Rockfort. I thought you liked it."

"There are dangers a man is bound to encounter and conquer; and there are dangers a man is bound to flee as soon as he recognizes them," said Rockfort sententiously. Again a silence, and then Paul said, in a voice discouraging further argument, —

"As I have already told you, I shall go at once to New York, and then decide whether I remain in this country and receive priest's orders in the American Church, or at once return to England."

"How you waste words!" exclaimed Rockfort dryly. "We have talked for four or five hours, and your ultimatum, delivered as if it were a Medean fiat, amounts to just what you said at first, — 'I shall choose God or Baal, and I don't know which.'"

"Don't it strike you, sometimes, Rockfort, that the faithful friend of the Proverbs may have overdone his business a little?"

"I dare say he made himself disagreeable," replied Rockfort calmly, "but if he was a faithful friend indeed, he did n't care at all for that."

Baruther rolled half petulantly upon his other side, and by that motion perhaps saved his life, for at the same instant a mass of rock, hurled from the crag above, whistled past his head, and crashed upon the sand where he had lain. So close was the aim, that the coat was torn from his back, and a small wound inflicted by a corner of the bowlder, and the noise and shock left it for a minute doubtful to Paul's own mind whether he were injured or not.

"Hullo, what 's that?" exclaimed Rockfort, springing to his feet, and glaring at the brow of the cliff, over which appeared the shaggy black head and gleaming eyes of the maniac of Burnt Cub Island.

Rockfort's jaw closed with a snap like that of a bull-dog, and, mute and determined as that other product of the British Isles, he sprang up the cliff at the first possible point, dragging himself by sheer strength of arm over the perpendicular brow, and warding off with his left arm the blow delivered at his head, before he could rise to his feet.

"Out of the way, you!" howled the madman, struggling to detach another great mass of rock, with the obvious purpose of hurling it down at Paul. "I've nothing to say to you! It's that fellow I want, that fellow that hit me! Tried to get away my liquor too! I'll pay him off, — I'll settle him!"

Still mute, still with iron jaw close-set, and small gray eyes warily watching each movement of his opponent, Rockfort sprang forward, seized the stick wildly brandished toward his head, twisted it out of the madman's hand, and then flinging both arms around his waist bore him heavily to the ground, falling with and upon him in a manner that would have rendered him utterly powerless, but for an unforeseen event; this was the sudden crumbling away of a large mass of the edge of the cliff, loosened by the upheaval of the rocks intended for Paul; the violent fall of the two men finished what this began, and the result was, that Paul, just rising to his feet after the half-stun of the first assault, found himself enveloped in a cloud of dust, gravel, earth, and stones, with the flying arms, legs, and heads of two men piercing it in every direction. Out from this chaos, as it settled, rose Rockfort, straight, stony, and calm as if nothing had occurred, who, looking down at the writhing mass at his feet, said, —

"The man is hurt."

"Are n't you?" demanded Paul, glancing over his friend's stalwart figure, and, receiving no answer, knelt down to examine the other sufferer, silent enough now, and lying in an unnatural position, suggesting that his leg must be broken, as a slight examination proved to be the case.

"We must get help and take him away," said Paul, rising to his feet and looking about him.

"Hospital in the place?" inquired Rockfort, trying to subdue the natural impulse to pant after his violent exertion.

"I should n't think so; no, of course there is n't," replied Paul, recollecting suddenly where he was. "If you will stay here, I 'll go and find somebody. Keene's house is n't far off."

Rockfort nodded, and seated himself beside the wounded man, while Paul sprang up the cliff and out of sight. In twenty minutes or so, he returned, followed not only by Jubal and two farm laborers, but by Mrs. Trevylyan and her brother. The men carried a hand-barrow used for transporting hay or grain, on which a board and straw-bed had been placed.

"Sho!" exclaimed Jubal, bending over the injured man, who had returned to consciousness, and lay glaring about him with the mute and helpless savagery of a wild beast caught in the iron jaws of a trap.

"Why, it 's Mehitable's Mose."

"Don't say! So 't is!" corroborated one of the men. "I heard a piece back that he 'd quit the Sary Ann, and was off on the queer up to Halifax."

"Drinked some, did n't he?" asked the other.

"Waal, some did say so, but I dunno," cautiously replied the first, while Jubal made vain attempts to gain a recognition or reply from the wounded man, whose blood-shot eyes ranged restlessly over all the faces grouped around, and settled persistently on Paul's with a glare of silent rage and revenge.

"Poor man! Let me give him some of this brandy. I snatched the flask directly I heard of the accident, and my smelling-salts. I was sure one or other would be useful. Let me speak to him. I 'm used to such scenes, you know, — a soldier's wife."

And Camilla — kind-hearted, fond of scenes, really anxious to help any one in distress, especially a man, and under somewhat romantic circumstances — knelt down, and was about placing the silver cup from the bottom of the brandy-flask to the lips of the sufferer, when Rockfort interposed, saying, in his dry, hard tone of authority, —

"You 're not to give him brandy. He 's brandy-mad already. It 's drink that ails him."

"Oh well, he needs it now to revive him. Of course it 's the thing," persisted Camilla angrily, and was placing the cup to the lips of the *maniac-à potu*, when Rockfort, with a quick motion of the back of his hand, upset it on the sand, repeating coldly, —

"He is not to have liquor."

"Really, sir," interposed Captain Douglass, "that is extremely rude, do you know! This lady is my sister."

"Pray, what has that to do with the matter?" replied Rockfort, always as calm as a block of ice. "This man is crazy with drink already, and if anybody tries to give him more while I am by I shall prevent it. You had better take your sister away from here."

"Children and fools speak the truth, and you are no child, Mr. Rockfort. Camilla, come with me." And Douglass, giving his arm to his sister, who was laughing immoderately, led her away.

The men, guided by Jubal, whose army experiences gave him a certainty of action and a decision of speech not ordinarily found in the rural character, now laid the wounded man upon the litter, and carefully bearing it over the stony beach to a point where the level ground ran down to the water, they gained the road, and, sending Jubal forward to prepare the mother for this sad home-coming of her son, carried him into the house and up to the hastily prepared bed in his old bedroom. Father Williams, who seemed to have become the accepted medical authority, was summoned, but declined to take the responsibility of the broken leg while a regular practitioner was within reach, and a messenger was despatched to the Cove, for the village Esculapius, who there filled the triple post of surgeon, physician, and apothecary. The leg was set, but not without great difficulty, for this Moses was by no means the meekest of men at any time, and now, hovering on the borders of the terrible delirium of intoxication, wild with pain, and a sort of aimless, brutal rage, he was almost impossible to control. Four strong men, besides the doctor, barely held him quiet during the operation, and when it was finished, and the patient for the moment quiet from exhaustion, the doctor, wiping his forehead, and looking dubiously round on his assistants, said, —

"I expect two men won't be any too many to handle him most of the time. Josiah he's at home, as far forth as that goes, but he's kind o' peaked, and Mose could tie him up in a hard knot and fling him up chimney, if he had a mind to. But there's a good many men of you, and you might take turns watching for a few nights any way."

"Ah, really, I'm afraid, you know, I should n't be of very much use myself, not knowing about illness and that sort of thing, but so far as money goes —— ah ! I shall be very happy to contribute, you know." And Blondin, upon whom the doctor had happened to fix his eyes while making this suggestion, twirled his yellow mustache, and looked supercilious and silly.

"There is no occasion for anybody here to-night. I shall stay," said Rockfort, in the sullen and monotonous voice that always seemed to grudge its betrayal of its master's thoughts.

"And I will either stay with you, or may be called at any moment," said Father Williams. "I sleep just across the passage."

Rockfort's small, cold eyes glanced sideways at the speaker, traversing the handsome, material face, well-fleshed figure, and garb of a Roman priest with evident disfavor, but in words he replied not at all ; and a slight curve at the corners of the mouth, a slight elevation of the eyebrows and movement of the hand betokened the French priest's appreciation of the discourtesy.

Baruther, pale, silent, and abstracted, stood beside the sick man's bed and looked down upon him. Suddenly Moses opened his red and angry eyes, and met that full, calm gaze. The first emotion was one of anger, and, scowling heavily, he muttered some incoherent phrases, of which a savage oath and the word "bottle" alone were audible. Next, he began to stir impatiently, his move-

ments threatening to disarrange the position of the splinted
and bandaged leg.  Then Paul, bending over that angry
and ferocious face, fixed his eyes yet more earnestly upon
his, with an expression of mingled power and benignity
impossible to describe.

"Be quiet!" said he in a low voice; and, as if the
words had been a charm, the scowl subsided, the nervous
motions ceased, the clenched hands relaxed, and the giant
lay motionless and subdued, staring up into the face bent
over him, its ivory pallor, high-bred lineaments, and clear,
resolute eyes contrasting so strongly with the brutal, inflamed features and animal red eyes they controlled.

"He's quiet now," said the doctor complacently.  "I
thought that draught would fix him.  "Well, I'll look in.
to-morrow, though I expect this gentleman is competent
for the case, and I don't suppose Barnes is anxious to run
up a big doctor's bill, especially as he owes me nigh on
fifty dollars already."

"Suppose we try to get along by ourselves, then," suggested Father Williams smoothly.  "Of course, in any
difficulty we should send at once for you; but if, as you
say, Barnes is unable to pay a regular surgeon, and I am
more than ready to give my poor services, perhaps you
had better not come again, unless we send for you."

"You're not a regular practitioner, thinking of settling
here?" demanded the doctor, with sudden suspicion.

"Dear me, no," replied the priest, smiling broadly.  "I
am a poor clergyman, here for a few days, at the ends
of the earth to-morrow."

"O well, I didn't know.  Yes, I guess we'd better fix it
so.  If I'm needed, you'll send; and if I'm riding this
way, I'll look in, and not charge anything.  Might as well
make a virtue of necessity."

"As well, and a great deal better," replied the Jesuit,
nodding.  "Good-night, then, my dear doctor;" and as
the doctor left the room, "Good-night, dear ass!"

While this conversation was going on, Blondin, finding
the air of the little garret stifling, had withdrawn, and
started for the Nunnery, charmed with the importance of

the news he carried, and hoping to interest Joan, who was a bit of a gossip, therewith. Rockfort, who alone perceived Baruther's conquest, silently pushed a chair behind his friend, and then stood perfectly motionless and blank as to expression, in his usual rocky fashion, his eyes fixed on the opposite wall.

Paul accepted the chair without removing his eyes, and some ten minutes passed before he quietly raised his head, looked at Rockfort with a smile, and said, " He is asleep."

" 'Then go and leave him with me. The air is better outside, I should think," replied Rockfort, himself despising comfort too much to know certainly whether pure or stifled air were around him, but careful of Paul, whose worn and pallid face troubled him.

" Go out, you," replied the latter decisively. " I shall wait to see if he awakes quiet or violent."

For his only answer, Rockfort silently took a book of devotions from his pocket, and seated himself near the window, looking like an image of Rameses the Great, carved upon the living rock of the Egyptian tombs.

# CHAPTER XXIV.



## CAMILLA'S CONFESSION.

IT would not have seemed probable that the fortunes of
Moses Barnes could affect those of the wealthy, aristocratic, or learned individuals so strangely collected on
Plum Island, and yet they did; for, by one of those
fluctuations of human fancy so impossible to predict,
Mrs. Beauchamp Brown took an intense interest in the
case, and was never weary of exclaiming at the eccentricity of fate which had led " Paul's murderer," as she chose to
call him, to turn up at Burnt Cub Island, alarm Margaret,
and then, in seeking to revenge himself upon Paul, " to get
his leg broken by that Rockman," as she always phrased it.

Mingling with this love of the marvellous, Mrs. Beauchamp Brown was suddenly seized with a fancy for playing
Lady Bountiful, — a little out of season, to be sure, she
generally reserving all active benevolence for Lent, — and
sent over to Mehitable's cottage such a collection of air-
cushions, hot-water bottles, warm wraps, cologne, smelling-salts, books, flowers, and pictures, as would have fitly
furnished a young lady's ward in a hospital. Several of
these articles she imported for the purpose from Boston,
and some she had with her ; but, besides these, she made
poor Eunice's life a burden to her with constant demands
for jellies, blanc mange, custards, and other delicacies, as
foreign to poor Moses's experience as to his necessities,
since, in his furious fever, he was unable to take any nour-
ishment save of the simplest nature.

Once Mrs. Beauchamp Brown went herself, with much
flourish of trumpets, to visit the sick man, but at the door
of his room was met by Rockfort, who, stepping outside
and closing the door, succinctly said, —

"You can't go in."

"And why not, pray?" inquired Mrs. Beauchamp Brown, a little at disadvantage, for the stairs had put her out of breath, the heat had made her red, and she could not assume a dignified position without falling downstairs.

"The man is raving with delirium tremens, and is n't a fit sight for any woman," replied Rockfort.

"Good Lord, man, what sort of a thing is that to say to me!" demanded the lady indignantly; but Rockfort, steadfastly regarding her for a moment from the summit of his stony indifference, opened the door, letting out a stream of howls and curses which fully verified his words, went in and shut it after him.

"The worst-mannered man I ever saw in my life!" indignantly exclaimed Mrs. B. B., her head violently agitated. "I don't doubt he makes poor Moses a great deal worse. What Paul can see in him —— I won't let him come over here again."

But when the autocrat attempted to enforce this decree, she discovered that the Rockman himself did not possess so immovable a will as lay beneath her favorite's gentle and polished exterior. He quietly explained that the sick man had taken a fancy to his presence, and sometimes could be quieted by nothing else, and that it was of the greatest importance to his life that he should be kept calm and still until the broken limb had knitted in some degree.

"But, Paul," interrupted the old lady at this point, "that 's all very well for those the poor fellow belongs to, and I 'm sure I 'm willing to send him everything under the sun, — why, I sent up to Pierce's for some boxes of gelatine for a snow-pudding, only yesterday, — but as for going and staying with him, it 's quite another thing; all very well for that Rockman and Father Williams, — it 's their *métier*, but you — why, Paul, the creature tried to kill you twice, and came mighty near doing it, too. You 'd better keep away from him."

"I 'm trying the heroic treatment on him, — actual cautery, — coals of fire," said Paul laughing, and turning away into his own room.

" Nonsense — stuff — rubbish ! " ejaculated the old lady, a good deal after the manner of a cat spitting.   " The child is as mad as Moses himself."

Yes, everybody was interested, everybody offered service, or at least inquiries ; but after a little it settled down to Peter Rockfort as chief attendant, Father Williams as physician, and Baruther as anodyne and regulator ; for when the patient was in any measure accessible to anything but simple force, Paul's eyes, Paul's touch, Paul's voice would quiet and control him as no drug had power to.   When the frightful attacks of mania came on, he gave place to Rockfort, whose quiet, ponderous strength, untiring determination, and iron nerves just fitted him for the position.   Others came and went, Sneyd occasionally offering his splendid muscles to serve in Rockfort's place when nature demanded a little rest and refreshment, and Larry and La Branche volunteering services they knew very little how to render ; but these three men were the regular inhabitants of his room, and gradually the matter seemed to become their affair and responsibility.

It was about ten days from the first attack, and Paul, wearied with a whole day's attendance, had gone home to bed, leaving Rockfort to watch alone, Father Williams being in readiness to come at once, if summoned.

The clock below struck ten, and the watcher, shading the light carefully from the eyes of the sleeping man, pulled a little, worn volume of Tertullian from his pocket, and settled himself for a quiet hour of study.

A light step upon the stair, a gentle tap at the door, and Rockfort, with an ungracious scowl upon his brow, softly rose, and opened it.   A slight figure stood upon the threshold, draped from head to foot in some glistering white raiment that enveloped the head and face, leaving visible only two starry, dark eyes, and a finger's breadth of white forehead, with dark hair rippling away in classic outlines.   Rockfort stood mute, contemplating this apparition, which he did not in the least recognize, even when Camilla, dropping the wrap from her head, swept past him into the room.

"You don't know me," said she softly, as he, closing the door, came back, and stood severely questioning her with his eyes. "I am Mrs. Trevylyan, the woman who wanted to give some brandy to that man when he was first hurt, and I have a great deal of knowledge of nursing, and am a capital watcher, and I have come to help you to-night. You can lie down and sleep, and I will sit by him and call you if you are needed. Is he asleep now?"

"Yes. I do not need you. I do not want anybody."

"But I want to stay. I have a special reason for wishing to be away from home to-night."

"And so made a pretence of charity?"

"No, I am really glad to do something for this poor fellow, and also to let you rest, for you need it."

"I am the best judge of that."

"What's the use of being so cross? To tell the truth, I want to see you."

"To see me! What for?"

"That will appear by and by. Women never go straight to the point. You don't know much about women though, do you?"

"As much as I want to. I don't like them."

"I dare say. That's the reason they will be apt to run after you. You're a clergyman of the Church of England, — the Episcopal Church, we call it, — are n't you?"

"Yes."

"Well, then, you are bound to listen to me, for I am a lamb of that flock, and may call upon one of its shepherds to help me."

"What help do you need?"

"I am tempted to become a pervert to Romanism."

"I wish the Romanists joy."

"That's not a shepherd-like speech."

"I am not your shepherd. Go or write to your own clergyman."

"I can't write to him, and I am sorely afraid I never shall go to him, for he was a very saintly man."

"Dead?"

"Dead."

Rockfort drew down his brows until only an undershot gleam of gray told that he had eyes at all, and went to look at his patient, who slept heavily in a half-comatose condition ; evidently, no ordinary conversation would disturb him, and he needed no present attention.  He slowly returned to his visitor, who had laid aside her wrap, and stood, tall, lithe, and beautiful, in a clinging dress of white *barège*, with only a knot of golden coreopsis in her hair and at her throat, — her dark, vivid beauty gleaming out in that sordid chamber like a jewel dropped in mire.

Rockfort, not an imaginative man, looked at her and thought of St. Anthony, then of Martin Luther, and wished he had a leaden inkstand at hand.  Then he grimly smiled ; it was the smile of conscious strength, of self-assurance, of the pride that is so dangerous footing to those who hold their heads aloft.

Seating himself and taking up Tertullian, he shot a side glance at the Lamia beside him, and said, —

"If you call upon me as a priest of the Church, to give you aid or counsel, I am, as you say, bound to listen. But be brief, and then return home.  You are not needed or wanted here."

Camilla found a chair, placed it opposite that of the priest, so that he could not raise his eyes without looking at her, and, taking a book from her own pocket, said, —

"I don't feel like talking just now.  Let us both be quiet for a while.  Don't interrupt your studies."

Rockfort glanced at her with a scowl.  She was already buried in her book and did not see him.  The yellow light of the oil-lamp fell softly upon the drooped head, showing its classic outline and graceful poise, the rich masses of hair rippling away from the brow and coiled heavily at the nape of the neck ; the dusky, peachy coloring, the pencilled brows and sweeping eyelashes, the eager, passionate lips and wide, soft chin, — the sort of chin that one longs to fit like a ball into the cup of his own palm ; the white draperies and golden-gleaming flowers finished the picture fitly, and few men could have steadfastly contemplated it without admiration and somewhat more.

Peter Rockfort read Tertullian.

The clock upon the chimney ticked steadily on; the sleeping man moaned and muttered in his heavy dreams; a death-watch in the wall at his head uttered its ominous alarm.  Camilla moved not a hair's breadth, except to turn page after page of her book and read it steadily through.

Rockfort knit his brows into one dense line, and scowled down upon honest old Tertullian, as if he had been Arius or Calvin.  Then he darted an impatient glance over the top of the volume at the absolutely motionless figure before him, and wondered what study so completely absorbed her; then, scorning himself for the curiosity, said in his heart, " Fashions or love ditties or a trashy novel, of course ; I only wish she would read it somewhere else."

He went to look at his patient, he glanced at the clock, he strode to the window, and cast black looks at the black night; then, returning to his chair, fixed cold, angry eyes upon the statue which had never stirred through all his restlessness, and said, —

" Really, you cannot stay here any longer."  I need no help whatever, and had rather be alone."

She slowly raised her eyes, and met his, full and unflinchingly.  Great, sad, soft eyes, such as Rockfort unwillingly remembered in a fawn that he once had owned and loved and petted.

" Don't be so hard with me !" said Camilla softly; and putting the book upon the table, she laid her face in her hands, with such a gesture of submissive sorrow as reached the little soft spot somewhere in the depths of Rockfort's indurated heart, and he said, not harshly or unkindly, —

" I don't mean to be hard, at least unduly so.  Tell me how I can help you, if you honestly need help, but don't expect pretty speeches and flatteries from me, for I don't deal in such rubbish."

" I wish nobody did ; I wish all men were as honest and true as you," murmured Camilla, bowing her head still lower, and pressing her fingers closer over her eyes.  Rockfort frowned, and smiled contemptuously, as he replied, —

"I don't want to receive, any more than to give, flatteries. Speak out like a simple, honest woman, talking to a priest, and say what you have to say."

"How can I speak out the things I have to say, if you treat me so forbiddingly?" cried Camilla passionately, and sliding down upon her knees, she raised her beautiful, agitated face toward him, an appeal for sympathy and pity and gentle dealing in every tremulous line, in the swimming eyes, upon the parted, quivering lips, in the clasped hands.

Rockfort looked, and turned away his eyes, slid his hand into his breast and grasped something there, looked steadily and coldly down at the appealing face, and said, —

"Get up, if you please, and sit upon a chair. I don't care for that sort of thing."

Had Margaret, could Margaret, have been in Camilla's place, she would have sprung up and gone away, stung to the quick, forgetting all else in an agony of self-contempt, but Camilla was at once less sensitive and more resolute. She felt the thrust sharply enough, and the angry blood rushed over her face and neck, but though shrewdly wounded, she had no mind to relinquish the combat, and cowering down as if beneath a blow, she moaned, —

"How can you, how can you! I came needing help and counsel, — yes, needing to be pulled out of the snare Satan has laid about my feet; I came to you, a priest sworn to help just such as I am, and you repulse me, you sneer at me, you drive me away with taunts and insult! Well, I will go, and when you hear bad news of me, say to yourself, 'She came to me in her extremity, and I refused help, I gave her the last push over the precipice. It is on my soul!'"

She gathered herself up like a broken, wounded thing, trailing itself away to die. Rockfort rose too; his iron features were agitated, his face flushed, his voice shaken as he said, —

"Stop! You have no right to say I refuse you help. I don't. Tell me your need in an honest, simple way, and such help as I can give is ready for you."

She was quick enough to know that, small as the concession was, it was much for him, and all she should obtain, and, turning, stood mute and tremulous, her face down-drooped, her hands twisted together. He looked, waited a moment, then, in a troubled, one might say querulous voice, demanded, —

" Well ? "

" Ah, please let me kneel ! See, just here, — I won't come any nearer you, if you are afraid of me," and with a faint little smile through her tears, she sank upon her knees, and looked beseechingly at him. Without reply he seated himself, and leaning an elbow on the table, shaded his face with his hand.

" You see," began she abruptly, " I don't really want to be bad, but everybody urges me on, and nobody holds me back. That 's the only thing that tempts me to Romanism : I want a confessor."

" You may find one in your own church," said the priest, " if you sincerely wish to relieve a troubled conscience."

" Can I ? Are you one ? "

" Every priest who follows the instructions of the Prayer Book, and believes in his own ordination, is one."

" But Father Williams says you are only shams, that you have no Orders in the English Church."

" Of course he does. I don't care to hear a re-hash of the threadbare attacks of Rome upon the Anglican Church."

" But I am doubting whether I can find peace and safety, except in that Communion."

" If you have sinned, you can find peace and safety only in true repentance, in humiliation and prayer. All these good gifts you may have in your present Communion."

" Repentance ! Oh, I do, I do repent ! but I cannot help it, I am so weak, and everything bad is so strong. I wish I were dead, I wish I might die this minute ? "

" Are you mad ? Wish to die with your conscience so choked with unrepented sin that it cannot even cry out ?

A person dying in the state you represent yourself has but one possibility before her."

"And that is "——

"Hell."

"There is no such place. I don't believe it. You talk in that way to frighten me. You don't believe it yourself."

And Camilla, honestly frightened and angry, sprang to her feet, took a turn through the room, and coming back to the table tapped upon the book she had thrown there, saying, —

"Do you know what this is?"

"No," replied Rockfort, glancing with disfavor at the gilded vellum cover of the little volume.

"It is Dante's Inferno," continued Camilla, the angry glow upon her face illuminated by a mocking smile, "and I was just reading of Francesca and Paolo floating through that gloomy air, folded in each other's arms. Do you know, it struck me that if I had the right Paolo, I might fancy that sort of thing more than a milk-and-honey Paradiso?"

"I should think there could be no doubt of your having the opportunity to prove it," said Rockfort, rising to his stoniest attitude. "And now I insist upon your leaving this place. Your appeal for help and wish for counsel is, as I suspected all along, a cloak for levity and wantonness.— Phryne masquerading as Magdalene, and doing it very poorly. Please don't try any more effects of that sort on me. I have not time to waste on bad acting. I had rather go to the theatre and see good."

He strode to the door and set it open. Camilla, choked with rage and mortification, swept past him, yet turned on the threshold, and steadfastly regarding him, flung out her hand in a wild Neapolitan gesture, and muttered between her clenched teeth, —

"On your head be it! You might have saved me!"

Then she fled like Vivien into the darkness, like her muttering, —

"Fool! Fool! And thrice fool I, to think I could escape! It is my fate, and fate is stronger than I."

Rockfort took up his Tertullian again, but could not read it, for always over the crabbed Latin text danced the fiery letters, "On your head be it !  You might have saved me !" until, flinging down the book, he sat, each hand grasping the wrist of the other, his brows gathered into one heavy frown, his iron jaw set, while again and again he asked himself the question, —

Could I ?  Was it my fault that she went away hardened rather than softened ?

# CHAPTER XXV.

## THOU ART THE MAN.

TO say that Margaret was unhappy is very little: she was miserable to the very depths of her being, shaken to the foundations of her existence; she felt as that same Sicily may have done while the throes of imprisoned Enceladus shook the everlasting rocks of Etna; as David felt when he moaned, "All thy storms and floods have gone over me!"

The great cry of her soul was answered; the hunger of years was, not satisfied but tantalized, with sight of the unknown food, the manna it had craved so madly. For the first time in all her eight and twenty years of sovereignty she found her peer, nay, more, her king; one to whom she could say, "You are my head. Guide my life, for it is yours;" for the first time in all her life she gave freely and royally of her heart's best treasure, "as a king unto a king," — not as a king bestows an alms upon his subject, and disdains return. She loved, and all the depths of her great nature, all the force that, like a kraken, slumbered under the fathomless mid-ocean of her soul, rose rebellious and protesting against this other force that claimed to be its conqueror.

Had it been a happy love, it would have been a formidable crisis for such a soul as Margaret's. Ten years of undisputed dominion over not only her own, but every life that had come in connection with her own; ten years of adulation, of humble confession of her powers of life and death; ten years of education in the divine right of such as she to reign; ten years in which, sitting unmoved upon her throne, she had seen men die, go mad, ruin themselves body and soul for her sweet sake, and die saying, as Douglass had, "The queen can do no wrong,"—all this had not fitted her to bow her imperial neck to Love's rose-wreathed yet most real yoke, had not schooled her heart or her tongue to say, in glad humility, "I will love thee and serve thee, honor and obey thee, till death do us part." Nay, even had all gone well, it must have been a troubled and perilous time in Margaret's life, when first she truly, honestly, and grandly loved; but now! She loved, she had told her love, she had confessed her subjugation and her weakness, and she had been repelled; he whom she, the queen, had elected as her king, had refused the throne, put aside the crown, told her that he needed not her love, sought not her fellowship, preferred his own life to a share of hers.

Over and over and over again in weary iteration Margaret told herself these things, thrusting the knife into her own heart up to the hilt, and turning the blade in the wound, until the tortured nerves grew numb with excess of anguish, and remained for hours in dumb apathy, to be roused again to keenest torture by some chance word or look. Sometimes she would go away into her own room, and, with bolted door, stand and stare at her reflection in the mirror, jeering and pointing at it, and taunting herself with words of scorn and doubt:—

"You, Margaret Ufford, do they call you handsome, do they flatter and court you? Oh, do they so easily make a fool of you? Poor thing, poor idiot, poor dupe! They only laugh at you, they only play upon your credulity to make sport for an idle hour! When a man, a real man, comes, he despises you, and will none of you! Take a lesson once for all—understand your own worthlessness, your own folly!" And so she would go on, until over-wrought nature gave way and she sank upon her knees, stifling the sobs that tore her heart to pieces, and sometimes setting her own teeth in her own white flesh, that bodily pain might for the moment dull the keener agony of her soul. O Torquemada, master of tortures, how puerile your most subtle inventions, your most devilish devices become, when compared with the self-inflicted agonies of a sensitive, proud, self-centred soul, which has humbled itself in vain to a fellow-mortal; which loves, has confessed its love, and finds itself disdained!

After one of these paroxysms, Margaret would dress herself a little more exquisitely than usual, carefully erase the slightest trace of agitation from her face, resorting sometimes to the cosmetics with which her toilet-case was furnished, but which she ordinarily despised, and go among other people, just a little gayer, a little more talkative, a little more charming than usual. If Baruther was present, her manner toward him was so nicely adjusted between careless friendliness and polite indifference that Machiavelli himself could not have decided how she really regarded him, — never avoiding, never seeking his presence, addressing him, if he came before her, just as she did Sneyd or La Branche, but never turning her eyes in mute appeal to his, that subtle mode of speech so dear to those who love. She addressed him always as Mr. Baruther, and once, when he called her Margot, although they were quite alone, cast such a glance of haughty astonishment upon him that he turned white to his lips, and said, —

"I beg your pardon, Mrs. Ufford. The habits of my illness cling to me. My happy illness!"

"You shouldn't let yourself become the slave of habit, Mr. Baruther," replied Margaret mockingly. "I never remember anything beyond the hour." And she went away. Paul stood where she left him, looking out upon the sunset sea, the three great headlands of the perspective already bathed in purple, the water weltering in gold and crimson as it glimmered out to the horizon line, the clouds gathering, like courtiers in their gorgeous robes, about the couch of their king.

He stood as she had left him, and looked out upon the glory, so far beyond him that no reflection of it illuminated his stern, sad face, until his eyes were dark with anguish, and his lips closed in one straight white line. When they opened it was to whisper, —

"God forbid that I should offer unto Him of that which costs me nothing!"

Stung by an intolerable pain, Margaret, as she left him, snatched a hat from the pine-tree in the vestibule, and went out of the side-door where he could not see her, flying from him, flying from herself, flying from life could she have escaped it.

"I will put an end to this!" muttered she fiercely, as she turned down the wood-lane leading to Jubal's farm. "I will accept Forsythe to-night; I will marry at once and go to Spain next month. After that, the deluge!"

She knew not how she reached it, but presently she stood in the vine-covered porch, her hand raised to the half-opened door, a sudden spasm of doubt and repentance withholding her from pushing it open. She was going to visit Camilla, to be sure, but had not she come with the silent expectation of meeting Forsythe? Did not she intend to give him the opportunity he had so long sought, and she so persistently evaded? Was she not, in fact, putting herself in the way of an offer? She! And as the full consciousness of her own act came over her, a blush of burning shame scorched her very brow, and her hand fell heavily by her side as the bitter thought shaped itself in her mind, —

I have fallen so low that I cannot guard myself from falling lower yet!

She was moving to withdraw, when a slight sound within the half-open door attracted her attention. Had she been seen? If so, she must go in, for at least a moment, not to seem peculiar. Bending a little, she peered into the shadowy room, to see if Camilla was there.

Yes, she was there; standing in the middle of the room, her arms round Forsythe's neck, his arms around her waist, his lips on hers, as she murmured, —

" O Love, love me!  Love me better than ever you did Margaret! "

She did not know she uttered a sound, as she turned to fly that loathsome sight; but she must have done so, for before she had gone ten steps he was at her side, eagerly apologizing, explaining, protesting, saying he knew not what, she cared not what.  Looking neither right nor left, answering not a word, Margaret hurried on, her face white and cold as marble, only her eyes blazing like two stars, only her lips quivering a little, as with a great disdain.

Half-way through the wood, he caught her by the dress and peremptorily exclaimed : —

" Stop!  You shall listen to me, you shall reply!  It is my right.  You have brought me to this place to serve as a tool in your torture of another man, and it is a tool that cuts two ways.  It is your fault, yours only, if I have fallen into an intrigue with Camilla.  You are responsible, — do you hear ? — and you have no right to assume this air of virtuous indignation and scorn !  It is your fault more than hers !  It is the fruit of your own treachery, and you are not to make wry mouths if it is a little bitter.  Come now, Margaret, be reasonable, be just, — if a woman can be just, — look at this matter calmly and dispassionately.  You have trifled cruelly with me, played with my love, led me on and cast me off to amuse your leisure hours ; even now, sent for me by your companion, when I had no idea of following you, and when I was here, treated me with such capricious coldness, such icy indifference, as fairly to drive me into another woman's arms, and then you turn round and fling me aside as if I were a creature below contempt ; as if I had been false to a faithful wife ; as if I had wronged you by giving some trifle of the love you disdain to a woman who adores me.  Come, Margaret, confess that I have something to complain of, and let us cry quits, and mutually forgive each other.  Promise to be my wife, and I will give you all the honest love of my nature, all the love that has been yours for so many

years, and which only in this last despair has given place
to an ignoble passion for another woman. Be my wife,
and never wife has had so true, so devoted, so loving a
husband as I will be."

He stopped and looked at her. She smiled, not at him,
or anything he had said, but at the grotesque thought intruding itself into her mind. It was, —

" So the shameless woman who runs round after offers
has succeeded in getting one ; and now ? " ——

The little bitter smile passed, and Margaret gravely
met the eyes so passionately fixed on her.

" First, let go my dress, if you please," said she, " and
then, before we part forever, tell me what you mean by
saying that I brought you down here by a message, or in
any manner."

" I received a message from you, or an intimation —
a diplomatic hint, if you will — that my presence here
would be agreeable to you. It came through Miss
McVie."

" Well, it was an utter fabrication, an absolute falsehood, do you understand? I never gave the faintest
hint that I wished your presence, for I did not ; I was
equally surprised and sorry to see you here."

" You speak plainly at least."

" And truly."

" H'm ! I will not contradict a lady."

" What ! Do you mean —— can you suppose, you
who have known me from a child, can you think that I,
Margaret Ufford, would tell — a lie ? "

The word seemed to choke her as it passed her lips,
and Forsythe knew, none better, how utterly impossible
falsehood was to her grand, free nature. But he was
very angry, very sore, and he replied with a hateful,
sneering smile, —

" We don't call it that, we diplomatists, and you are a
finished diplomatist. You would have been invaluable
to me at Madrid."

" Oh ! " And wrenching away the dress by which he
would have detained her, Margaret fled away through

the wood, her whole heart and brain on fire with rage and grief and self-reproach. Forsythe, whose anger already gave way to the love which had indeed been the absorbing passion of his life, pursued her; and she, hearing his footsteps and voice, and seized with a sudden unreasoning terror, began to run, sobbing and panting like a doe with the hunters hard upon her.

"What is this?" exclaimed an indignant voice, and Baruther, springing from the rock where he had moodily thrown himself down, apparently to study the growth of vivid lichens upon its face, placed himself in the path, and held out a hand to arrest Margaret's flight. She, brought to reason by the presence of a protector, stopped, glanced in his face with mute appeal, and, passing him a few steps, leaned her arm with her face upon it against the grim trunk of an old beech-tree, silently weeping out the passion that almost rent her heart asunder.

"What is this, Mr. Forsythe?" demanded Paul, as the pursuer halted before him with rather a shamefaced expression, giving way at this question to haughty resentment.

"Does it really concern you to understand all the little differences arising between Mrs. Ufford and myself?" inquired he with a sneer. "We were old friends long before either of us enjoyed the honor of your acquaintance, and very possibly may get on just as successfully now as we did then. Perhaps you will kindly pursue your walk, and leave us to ourselves."

"That will be as Mrs. Ufford decides," replied Paul as haughtily. "If she desires me to withdraw I will do so, and if she desires me to remain, I certainly shall do so."

"I do desire it, Mr. Baruther," said Margaret, turning round and speaking, not like the fugitive of a moment before, but like a queen surrounded by her guards. "It is Mr. Forsythe who will please to retire from my presence, and never, when he can avoid it, enter it again."

"Margaret, you are angry now, and speak rashly.

When you are cooler "——began Forsythe; but she interrupted him with a superb gesture of dismissal.

"Do not flatter yourself that I am angry. I am not. I am simply revolted and disgusted. Go back to the companionship in which I found you; the taint of it hangs about you still, and unfits you for my society. Go!"

"I go, but please to remember, in all time to come, that it was your fault that I first sought it, and it is you who send me back to it. It is more your guilt than any one's else."

And with a bow of exaggerated politeness to Baruther, who stood sternly and steadfastly regarding him, Forsythe strolled down the woodland path, returning to Camilla.

"My fault, my fault! You said it first, and now every creature echoes it!" exclaimed Margaret bitterly, as she turned her face again to the beech-tree bole.

"When I showed you how you had spoiled the rose, you said it could be amended to be better than new," said Paul gently.

"Yes, but this can't," cried Margaret, starting up, and facing him. "Here is a woman, a man's wife, a girl as well born and educated and married as myself, a friend of my earliest years, and she —— that man says, ' It is your fault.' O Paul, it is not, say it is not !"

"Not your fault that she goes wrong in her own nature, of course," replied Baruther, with a look of pain. "But your fault that Mr. Forsythe, worn out with your coquetries, has turned to her for the solace she has no right to give."

"She has pursued him for a great while. We almost quarrelled about it, she and I, last winter in Washington, and now she has brought him down here by some jugglery of a message coming from my companion, as if from me."

"And being here, you encouraged him and checked him, and kept him off and on in reach of the danger, until both he and she fell into it. Two souls ruined perhaps for eternity, that might have been saved had you seriously and honestly told that man, in the first days of his being here, that you should never at any time listen to his proposals."

Margaret stood with drooping head, and listless hands folded before her, like a child receiving a merited reproof from confessed authority, and Baruther found this mood of unwonted humility the most charming of all proud Margaret's varied charms.  He forgot what he was saying, he forgot all the world, he forgot himself, he remembered nothing, saw nothing in all the universe but one stately figure drooping before his rebuke, one glorious head bowed in silent submission to his displeasure, one beautiful, grand, loving woman whose heart he knew was all his own.   His voice faltered and fell into silence; she looked up, their eyes met, he made a step toward her, and held out his arms, whispering, —

"Margaret!   I will give up all else for you!"

And Margaret!   Standing there mute and motionless before him, — Michael and Satan fought out in her heart their never-ending, still-beginning fight, fought in one brief instant the battle of her life, and it was not the archangel that conquered.  She knew that all the love she had in her was his; she knew that to be his wife meant bliss and safety and delight; she knew that as she never had loved before, and never should love again, she ever must love this man; and raising her head, she looked in his face with a mocking smile, and said, —

"We are quits now.  I can forgive you, and part friends."

She actually held out her hand, but he did not take it, only stood and looked at her, with a look that she never forgot, — a look that stung like a steel lash.   Then he quietly said, —

"I was sane on that occasion.  Just now I was mad. Thank you for curing me forever of my madness." And turning, he left her, yet presently returned to say, "Will you please to go home?  I shall follow and see that nothing further molests you."  And she silently obeyed.

# CHAPTER XXVI.

## FATHER WILLIAMS SETS HIS HOUSE IN ORDER.

AND now, of a sudden, various matters drew to a crisis, and the colony at Plum Island seemed likely to disintegrate and scatter as suddenly as it had come together.

Blondin, indignant at the favor shown to his rival, pressed matters to an issue with Joan, who flatly and definitely refused his heart, hand, and even his title, her aunt's advice to the contrary notwithstanding.

The same day with this defeat, Lord Strathmore announced to his chaplain, with much more authority than he had ever before assumed, that he should leave Plum Island the next day, and not stopping to listen to any discussion of the matter, went to seek Paul, to whom he confided his disappointment, concluding by saying, —

"And now I advise you more than ever to give up your crotchet of celibacy, Paul, for I shall never marry at any rate, and you are my heir-at-law. Only you don't seem to care for girls as I do. Come and travel over this beastly country with me a bit, and then we 'll go home, and find some nice English girl who will brush all these cobwebs out of your head. American women are too coquettish for me. I like our honest, simple-minded girls a deal better."

Paul smiled, and said rather sadly, —

"It is good advice — for you, not for me. Take it. I do not say I never shall marry, for I have not yet decided my future course in various ways. But I am quite sure you should marry, and will do so."

"Well, come and travel with me."

"Thank you, no.  Rockfort and I have plans, and he is only waiting for this poor fellow to die before we go. It is a question of days now, perhaps only hours, and Rockfort won't leave him.  Did you ever see such a devoted fellow?"

"I suppose so, but why need he always be so excessively disagreeable?  Not more than one man in a thousand dies of a bad leg, but every one of us is the better for a pleasant word, and that is what Rockfort never gives."

"He believes in the *fortiter in re*, and no man has more of it," said Paul, smiling, but looking a little troubled, for he felt a good deal about the Rockman that he would not say.

Father Williams, who found his cautious and intricate policy a good deal upset by this hurried departure, spent the last twenty-four hours in finishing up all that he could of his summer's work, but not always satisfactorily, notably in the case of Camilla Trevylyan, with whom he held a long conversation to no effect, except to convince him that she was desperately resolved to follow her own evil inclinations, and had quite outgrown the spasmodic penitence and doubts that had led her to toy with the refuge of religion.

"No, Father," said she, rising to finish the interview, "I have tried religion in the balance, and found it wanting.  Your style is too full of shams and pretences, too plausible and unreal, to convince a woman who has seen through and gone through so many sorts of shams and pretences.  The other style, — oh yes, I talked once with that great bear of a Rockfort ; his style is quite too peremptory and, 'd——d if you do, and d——d if you don't,' for me.  Neither the honey-pot nor the whip-lash convince me of any way better than my own, so by your leave I will follow it"——

"'To the bitter end!'" ejaculated the priest.  Camilla laughed with effrontery and held out her hand, saying, —

"'That sounded honest for once.  Good-by, and don't bear malice.  I abandon Jim to your tender mercies."

And in fact, Captain Douglass was a convert quite after the orthodox Roman pattern, and a great source of satisfaction to his director, whom he consulted upon every conceivable subject, and without whom he did not carry an umbrella if it rained, or eat if he was hungry. As a reward for his docility, he already had the promise of entering a convent of Trappist monks about to be established in Pennsylvania, and took much satisfaction in contemplating the anguish that would fill Margaret's heart in hearing of this immolation.

One or two other converts remained to be visited and strengthened in their new faith, which they were directed not to promulgate, until Father Williams succeeded in having a Mission established on the island ; and then the really zealous and devoted priest returned home, and went up to the sick-room. Rockfort, even his iron strength shaken by long-continued imprisonment in the stifled little room, sat wearily beside the bed, watching the ashen face of the sleeper.

Father Williams came and stood beside him.

" He is going fast," whispered he.

Rockfort nodded.

" Go now and get a walk and some refreshment while I stay here," continued Father Williams. " You need it."

" You will stay until my return ? "

" Yes. Two or three hours at least."

Rockfort, who knew that he needed the change, cast a scrutinizing look at his patient, whose heavy sleep was now broken by the moanings of delirium, and went out, saying, " I will take an hour."

At the end of the hour he quietly opened the door and re-entered the chamber. Father Williams knelt beside the bed, and a small table stood near, covered with a white cloth. Rockfort stared at it, and the priest, rising and coming toward him, said, with a smile of gentle satisfaction, —

" I think the man is dying. I doubt if he sees morning. I have baptized him, and administered the Viaticum. He dies in peace and hope."

"He was already baptized. I baptized him myself while he was in full possession of his faculties and desirous of that grace," said Rockfort indignantly.

"I know it, my dear friend," replied the priest smoothly. "But you know that was at the best only a lay baptism, and perhaps no baptism at all; at any rate, it was not a Catholic sacrament, and I could not have given the Viaticum to one no better fitted to receive it"——

"And who asked you to give it to him at all?" interrupted Rockfort harshly. "No one could have been less fitted to receive it than this delirious, impenitent sinner. I was waiting for the lucid interval that probably will intervene before death, to try to awaken his conscience, and rouse some true contrition. He never has showed the slightest, so far, and at present he is perfectly delirious. I consider that you have done a very unwarrantable and presumptuous thing, and taken a fearful responsibility on your own soul."

"Say that I have interfered with you, brother, and you will come nearer to the true grievance," said the Jesuit, smiling more blandly than ever. "But if a man with his eyes wide open sees the blind leading the blind toward the ditch, and puts out a hand to drag back the led from its brink, he must resign himself to be scolded by the leader. I had to hasten the matter more than I intended, for we leave this place early in the morning, and I might not have had another opportunity."

"You will leave him to die without medical assistance, will you?"

"Nothing could save him now, and so long as his soul is saved, a little more or less suffering to the body does not signify. I will leave you an anodyne, but my work is done in this place for the present. Good-by." Rockfort took no notice of the good-by or of the hand extended to emphasize it. He was standing and looking gloomily down at the moaning and muttering man, and wondering how much he had known of what had been done to him.

Early the next morning Lord Strathmore and his chaplain made their adieus to whoever was visible at the Nunnery, and were driven by Jubal to the head of the island, there to take the boat.

The mail of that day brought one of many invitations to Margaret to join some friends at Saratoga, and she made hasty preparations to accept and start at once upon the journey.

That night Moses Barnes died, his hand in Paul's, his eyes on his, peace and hope lightening the haggard lineaments of his face. His last words were,—

"I 'm but a poor, ignorant sinner, sir, but I believe whatever you believe, for you 've forgiven me who tried to murder you, and no brother could have done more for me. I believe in any religion that makes such men as you are. I 'll say whatever you tell me."

Rockfort had done ten times as much for the poor wretch, had lavished his own health and strength without stint or thought upon him, but he said no such thing to him. Few persons love another for doing his duty, even if it be a most heroic and self-sacrificing duty ; but the godlike quality of love is, that it begets love in those upon whom it shines, and wins hearts and souls to itself, as the sun draws up the moisture which the frost hardens like iron.

Two days after this, Rockfort and Baruther left the island, and Forsythe with them. Camilla and her brother followed next day ; and Mrs. Beauchamp Brown, after indignantly saying that she did not in the least care if everybody deserted her, and that she should stay at least through September, one day abruptly ordered Joan and Elsie to pack their trunks, and Larry to telegraph to Rockland for state-room tickets.

"When I said I would stay at Plum Island, Eunice Small," said she, with crushing severity, "I did not suppose I should be as lonely as Robinson Crusoe, or the fog so thick that you could cut it with a knife. I shall go home at once."

# CHAPTER XXVII.

## AT THE FIFTH AVENUE HOTEL.

"MY dear," said Mrs. Beauchamp Brown, "you might have knocked me down with a feather!"

Margaret smiled, arched her beautiful eyebrows a little, and slightly raising her dress, put her feet, chilly in silk and satin that December morning, to the fire.

"She came and told you herself, did n't she?" asked she languidly.

"Yes, the impudent hussy, and enjoyed it, too, — at least she enjoyed coming, but I fancy she was glad to get away. It was the same morning I got your letter from Saratoga, saying that you had concluded to run over to Paris with the Woosters and get your winter toilettes yourself; and I was sitting over the fire in the breakfast-room at home, feeling rather cross, for I knew how I should miss you, Meg, when the door opened, and in she walked.

"'O, Miss McVie!' said I. 'So your mistress is going abroad, and has sent you to pack her trunks, I suppose.'

"'Dear me, no, Mrs. Brown,' said she, smiling like a hyena, and seating herself without invitation. 'I have only stepped in to give you a bit of family news, and never knew until now that Mrs. Ufford — for I suppose it is she to whom you so gracefully allude as my mistress — was going abroad at all. To Madrid, I suppose. Mr. Forsythe will, no doubt, try to make it pleasant for her.'

"'I never discuss my friends with their servants,' said I, taking up the paper and putting on my glasses.

"'Dear me, no, I would n't if I were you,' said she, in the most impertinent voice you can imagine. 'Do be careful, now, about Leverett and me, won't you? There will be such a temptation for you to talk.'"

" Aunt Phyllis ! "

" Yes, upon my word, that was just what she said.  I laid down the Advertiser, took off my glasses, turned round and looked at her, — just looked at her.  I fancy I got through even her brazen armor, for her hypocritical lips turned white as ashes, and she nestled on her chair. Then I said, —

" ' If you are crazy, go to Somerville ; if you are intoxicated, go to bed ; in any case, go out of this house.'

" She half rose, as if to sneak out of the room, but impudence got the better of shame, and settling herself back, she stared me full in the face, and said, —

" ' That was n't at all sisterly on your part, Phyllis ; but then you have n't heard my news yet, and don't know that I am your sister.  You called me Miss McVie just now ; but that was another of your mistakes.  My name is Belinda Beauchamp, and I am wife of Leverett Beauchamp, Esq., your own and only brother.  Here is my card.'

" She took out a card, and laid it upon my knee.  I flicked it off into the fire, and calmly said, ' I merely repeat my last words.  If you don't go, I shall call my servants to put you out.'

" ' How it would sound to say, Put Mrs. Leverett Beauchamp out of the door ! ' replied she, but she got up to go, for I had my hand on the bell.  She said a good deal more, trying to prove that I might as well accept her with a good grace, but I made no more answer than I should to the cat's mewing, and finally she went.

" Later in the day, Leverett himself came, and I indulged myself in the free expression of my feelings ; but, dear me, what was the use?  The poor fellow could n't make any sort of fight, even if he had felt sure of his own cause, and he did n't feel at all so.  From what he said, however, I gathered that the creature followed him to Richmond Springs, pretending to us, you know, that she was going to her people in Pennsylvania, and then just went to work and bagged him, stalked him as they do a deer, — poor silly dear that it is ! — and finally accompanied

him to New York, and was quietly married at the Little
Church round the Corner.  He showed me the certificate
and all, so there 's no doubt of it."

"And where are they now?" asked Margaret, who
could not but feel more amused than indignant.

" In Boston, at the Tremont House, if you please, and
going to stay there all winter, just to annoy me, I suppose.
I hear that a good many persons have called upon her,
although none of our intimates ; and, I dare say, she will
make a place for herself in time.  She knows how to
dress from studying you " ——

" I don't think my style would just suit her," said Margaret, enjoying the image of Belinda's *pétite* figure and
sharp little face lost in the magnificence she loved and
could carry off.

"No, you vain peacock ! it would n't," retorted her
aunt, half laughing, half cross.  "But she knows that, as
well as you do, and will adapt rather than adopt your
ideas.  Then Leverett has money and position and a circle
of his own, and the creature has a sort of rat-like cunning
that will show her how to utilize these materials in the best
possible manner ; so that I should say, on the whole, she
has succeeded admirably in what she undertook."

" Yes, and that is all one wants," said Margaret, with a
sigh.  " I wish I could say as much for myself in the last
three months."

" Why, what did you undertake, except to get some
new dresses?  You did that, did n't you?"

"Oh, yes.  Worth informed me that the new era in
America would date from my appearance in a certain
white, gold, and turquoise evening costume with which he
was inspired on my behalf.  I spent a little fortune with
him, at any rate."

"Then, what is it you did n't succeed in?"

" In amusing myself," said Margaret, carelessly, putting
a fire-screen between her own face and her aunt's eyes.
"Well, tell me some more about yourself. You asked the
girls to spend the winter with you."

"Yes, I did n't know how long you might stay on the

other side, and I won't let Leverett visit me ; so, seeing myself likely to be a little lonely, I wrote to the fathers and mothers that if the girls were not engaged to be married, and would go into society like rational creatures, they might come and stay with me until after Easter, and I would dress them suitably for the winter.  But I wanted no billing and cooing, no turtle-doves, nor cases of spoons ; no crying, no poetry, no mooning, nor sitting in corners. In fact, if I could have two bright young girls to carry about with me, I 'd have 'em ; and when they were going home, if they liked to finish up the season with an engagement, I would give a party to celebrate it, and present them with their trousseaux."

"And the parents agreed ? "

" I should think so," replied Aunt Phyllis dryly.  " I imagine, too, that Joan was very glad of a peep at the world before she makes up her mind.  That stupid little lordling is still fluttering after her."

" Blondin ? "

" Yes.  They call him Mr. De Bracy here in New York, and pursue him unremittingly.  He says he is coming to Boston after Christmas."

" And splendid Tom Sneyd ? "

" Oh, he 's at Cambridge still, and so is La Branche, and so is the professor.  Larry has gone into Gilbert's law office in Boston."

" A good many of the Plum Island set seem gathering in Boston this winter," said Margaret, sighing.

" Yes, and one you would n't dream of.  That Rockman is there."

Margaret's silken dress rustled sharply, and the fire-screen dropped from her hand almost into the fire.  Probably it was stooping to regain it that brought such a color to her usually colorless face, as she carelessly replied, —

" Indeed ?  Have you seen him ? "

" Seen him !  Well, you shall judge.  It was Advent Sunday, and you know I am very particular in being at church all through Advent and Lent, if at no other time. So I went, and noticed in a minute how full church was, and numbers of persons one never saw before.  I leaned over to Mrs. Blenkinsop, — by the way, I really do wish the wardens would have those high pew-walls cut down ; it is really difficult to communicate with your next neighbor unless you stand up, and that old red upholstery is so stuffy and inartistic.  Why not have one of those lovely new fabrics in conventional patterns, angels and cherubs, and things in mediæval tints, or perhaps mummy-cloth would be more appropriate to a conservative old church like ours." ᛫

"And Mr. Rockfort was there?" interposed Margaret, who could not sit through one of her aunt's digressive monologues just now.

"Wait and you shall hear.  I leaned over to Mrs. Blenkinsop, and, after the usual amenities, asking when they got home, and how Ethel was, and when she heard from Georgina, and telling her a little about ourselves, I asked, —

"'What's happened to bring all the world to St. Iamblichus this morning?'

"'Don't you know?' replied she.  'Why, it's the new preacher, Mr. Rockfort, the great English revivalist.  He's perfectly crushing, they say, and tells you the most awful things straight to your face — a regular John Knox, you know.  Our rector did n't want to invite him, for he's tremendously High and very strong, but we all brought such pressure to bear on the dear old man that he finally said, "Well, well, just as you like !  The voice of the people is the Voice of God, I suppose."  So sweet of him, was n't it?'

"Well, my dear, she had n't got any farther than that, when in came the Rockman himself, and, if you will believe me, instead of a decent black gown, he was dressed in a cassock and white surplice and purple stole.  How Dr. Stone ever consented to all that I don't know, but so it was, and so he began to preach.  The text was 'It is high time to awake out of sleep,' and the first sentence of the sermon was, —

"'My friends, why do you suppose I have chosen these

words as a text from which to address you to-day?  It is because your church is the Church of the Seven Sleepers, and even their sleep came to an end at last.  Iamblichus and his six brethren slept for two hundred years, but then they awoke, and glorified God for the wider and fuller and higher truth disclosed to men while they slept.  Awake ye, and do likewise ! '

"Well, my dear, that 's the style of the whole, and you can judge how steady-going, comfortable people, like the Midases and Crœsuses and Riches, liked it.  They did n't get their usual Sunday nap, at any rate, and old Peter Blackstone actually got up and went out, thumping his gold-headed cane all the way down the broad aisle.  The Rockman looked after him, just like an eagle making ready for a swoop on some poor little runaway rabbit, — and Peter *is* very white as to the head, and very pink as to the eyes, — but he did n't say anything, only laid it on a little heavier to those that remained.

"I liked it, you know ; it was something new in sermons, and made one think of one's French history, and how Bossuet woke up the court of Louis Quatorze, and how the great ladies soaked their lace handkerchiefs with tears and crowded to his confessional, and did all sorts of penance ; although Bossuet was very courteous, I believe, and the charm of the Rockman is that he is such a bear.  Before the sermon was over, I had seen my opportunity, and resolved to seize it.  I would make this man the fashion, and give Boston a new sensation, a religious lion !  We have done everything else to death.  Art and artists, acting and actors, lectures and lecturers, culture and culturists, science and scientists, — we have had them all, in public and private, until Bostonians actually escape from Boston every year, to get something different from the high æsthetic entertainment that they know will be provided for them.  You remember the story of the little girl whose mother was describing the spiritual joys of her own pet heaven, until the child, pale with dismay, inquired, —

" ' But if I 'm good all the week, ma, can 't I go down to — somewhere on Saturday afternoon and play ? '

"So I resolved that this winter there should be a mild flavor of fire and brimstone infused into the *caviare* of our usual entertainments, and that its name should be Rockman."

"O Aunt Phyllis! The idea of Mr. Rockfort as a social attraction!"

"Why not? Something new is just as much in request in the modern as the ancient Athens; but wait and see how I succeeded. Of course, the moment service was over, all the world began discussing the sermon, and wondering whether they had been insulted or converted, or a little of both. I walked up to the senior warden, — John Leroy, you know, one of my oldest friends, — and publicly thanked him for the treat he and the rector had provided for us, and asked him to escort me to the vestry, that I might invite Mr. Rockfort to dinner.

"I don't wish to blow my own trumpet, Meg, but you know and I know that such a demonstration as that on the part of Mrs. Beauchamp Brown would have its effect on Boston, especially at St. Iamblichus, and it did. If Peter Rockfort makes a success in Boston he may thank me for launching him. One of the vestry of St. Pancras, who had been shaking his head and mumbling 'Too high, too high for me,' declared his intention of getting him invited to preach for them; and Mrs. Featherstonehaugh declared they must have him at the Church of the Holy Frescoes, and I just hope they will: he 'll scare them to death. Well, to cut a long story short, John Leroy gave me his arm, and up I marched to the vestry, where we found the poor man looking like a fox with the hounds upon him, for about forty thousand persons were round him, all talking, all saying different things, all badgering him for an answer, an opinion, an explanation, an apology, — the Lord alone knows what all. I went straight up to him and held out my hand, saying very cordially, 'Charmed to meet you again, Mr. Rockfort, and in such a delightful manner. What a powerful discourse you have treated us to! I for one am really very much obliged to you.'

"Margaret, that man looked me full in the face, and without a bow or a smile or the slightest recognition, simply said, —

"'Don't talk about it then, but try to profit by it.'"

"Just like him!" exclaimed Margaret, laughing.

"Like him! of course it is like him, and I was not in the least offended, for it only proved how correct my judgment had been.  Nothing so original has been seen in Boston since Maelzel's Chess Player, and I was more than ever resolved to secure it for my own drawing-rooms; so, without noticing the impertinence, I forced my hand into his, and got it nearly jammed off in his bear's grasp, and said, —

"'Now, Mr. Rockfort, I am going to take you home to dinner, and won't have No for an answer.  I always dine early on Sunday, because of the servants, and I like, of all things, to have a clergyman that day, to show them how much I think of the Church.  A good example, you know.  Come right along, the carriage is at the door, and all these dear people must wait for another time to pay you their compliments.'  Now, Meg, was n't that all I could have said to Bossuet himself?"

"And what did he reply?" asked Margaret, wiping her eyes and stifling her laughter.

"Meg, he looked me full in the face, and said, 'I don't dine out.'"

"Was that all?"

"Every word.  I stood and looked at him a moment, and then I said, —

"'Three months have not changed you at all, Mr. Rockfort, have they?  Well, I sha'n't give up coaxing you to come and see me another time.  Good-by for the moment.'

"He may have said good-by, or it may have been a growl.  He made some sort of sound at any rate, and I went away "——

"Discouraged in your lion-hunt, poor auntie?"

"Discouraged!  Not in the least.  If we are to have a lion, let him be a full-grown black-maned man-eater, not one of your menagerie beasts, who nibble seed-cakes out of little boys' fingers.  No.  I have amplified my original plan, and intend fully to make my Rockman one of the great sensations of the season."

" Whether he will or no ? "

" Oh, he will.  The rector of St. Polycarp's has gone abroad for a year, and I induced two or three of the leading men there to engage Rockfort to supply that pulpit for the year.  I told them I would help pay off their debt, and engage to fill the church with people who never put anything but bank-notes into the alms-basin."

" And he has consented ? "  demanded Margaret breathlessly, for a sudden thought darted into her mind and usurped dominion there.

" Yes, he has consented.  He preaches his first sermon on Christmas Eve, which falls on a Sunday, you know, this year.  I believe he 's in New York this week, making arrangements.  What a nice hotel this is, is n't it ? "

And Mrs. Beauchamp Brown, raising her eye-glass, looked patronizingly around the room.  It was fortunate that she looked that day, for no man ever saw those dainty frescoes, that sumptuous furniture, those rich draperies and Moquette carpet again, never.

Margaret opened her lips, — and closed them ; opened them again, turned her face quite away, and at last asked, in a voice so carefully guarded that it sounded mechanical, " Have you heard anything of Mr. Rockfort's friend, Mr. Baruther ? "

" Not a word.  Why, he went home to England, did n't he ? "

" I don't know."

" I think he did.  Is n't it time for lunch?  Where are the girls?  I promised to take them to Tiffany's this morning.  Will you go out with us, Meg ? "

" Thank you, no, I believe not, aunt.  I have n't fairly rested yet from my voyage, and think I will try to sleep a little.  My head rather aches.  If you will send me some tea and a biscuit I won't go down to lunch."

And rising, she lightly kissed her aunt's withered cheek and trailed her draperies out of the room.

" Splendid creature ! "  said Mrs. Beauchamp Brown, looking after her.

# CHAPTER XXVIII.



JUST about twelve hours from the time that Mrs. Beauchamp Brown approvingly commented on the plenishing of her private parlor at the Fifth Avenue Hotel, a new ornament was added to the elaborate mouldings around one of the doorways. It was in . colors, a rich shade of Vesuvian artistically combined with a sort of dun or smoke color, and the design was more after the old school of nature than the modern improvements of conventionalism, — very pretty, but a little strong perhaps, for it really seemed to consume the fabric upon which it wrought, and was laid on in pigments of so pungent an odor that even a sleepy and weary servant sitting in the hall below perceived it, and after hazily wondering for a while if he had better go and see about it, or if it would all come right in the morning, and if — if — well — and then he dropped over head and ears into a dream of the great Christmas fire in the kitchen of Castle O'Brian where he had served as a gossoon in his youth, and ——

"Fire! Fire! Fire!" shouted some one from up-stairs, and Terence jumped from his chair with a whoop and a yell, and ever after recounted how he himself was the first to discover the conflagration and give the alarm, and save the lives and guard the property, and generally act as hero of the burning of the Fifth Avenue Hotel.

No cry, not even that of murder, produces such instant attention and excitement as that of fire. The deepest instinct of life is its own preservation, and whether it is the bivalve closing his shell and burrowing in the mud at sound of an approaching footstep, or the martyr giving his body to the flames that his soul may be saved alive, the motive is still to guard that subtile, mysterious principle which we call life, that indefinable link between the created and the Creator, that spark of divinity without which man were but a cunning combination of earths and gases, and the clam a bit of disagreeable gelatine.

Now, when you hear murder cried, instinct tells you that the danger threatens somebody else, and not yourself, and you run away from it or toward it, according to your sex, temperament, and position ; but at the cry of fire there is but one impulse in the mind of him who hears, and that is, escape from the vicinity of the subtle, sudden, treacherous foe. Men in general are not at all afraid of the devil, and do not recognize his approach, even if warned of it, but the bravest shrink from contact with the fire that may be quenched.

So when the shriek of that one shrill voice was heard in the upper corridors of the sleeping house, it awoke of a sudden to frantic excitement. Doors flew open, men, women, and children, with several little dogs, rushed hither and thither, each adding something to the noise and confusion, nobody doing anything to quiet it, poor human nature showing its seamy side without disguise, its selfishness, its folly, its unreasonableness, its brutality ; for strong men pushed past women and children to assure their own escape, women risked their lives to save their jewels or their poodles, other men and women lost even such reason as these first displayed, and sat upon the stairs lacing on tight boots, threw vases and glasses out of the windows, or clamored for porters to carry Saratoga trunks down the burning and crowded staircase. For some ten minutes Bedlam broken loose, — Pandemonium, — the end of all things, — are mild terms to express the frightful anarchy which reigned throughout that house ; but at the end of that time, the firemen arrived, and at once introduced two soothing elements, cold water and presence of mind, both applied with a positive authority to which every one gladly submitted. Resolute men in waterproof suits and hats pervaded every part of the house, haling away crazy persons who insisted upon "staying by the stuff" which was their life; pointing out the stairway to those who ran past and could not see it; carrying women and children, helpless through terror; saving property when it could be saved, and promptly sacrificing it to human life when the choice presented itself.

All honor to the brave brigade of Hook and Ladder, Helmet and Hose, for by their personal bravery, year by year, they save almost as many lives as an equal number of our other defenders slay, of men, women, and children, among the hereditary owners of this land, and wards of our paternal government.

Mrs. Beauchamp Brown, *prima donna* among the shriekers, alternated this exercise with giving orders to everybody for the instantaneous extinction of the fire, the calling of a carriage and removing her luggage to some better-conducted house, and for the immediate summoning of her party, who were lodged upon an upper floor, Margaret occupying one room, and the two girls another opening into it. Her orders given, Mrs. Beauchamp Brown, hurriedly, but still methodically, proceeded to arrange her hair, don her morning cap, get on her prunella half-boots, and exchange her gray flannel wrapper for a walking dress. This done, she began packing her trunks, and had nearly finished when a man dashed in at the open door, and before Mrs. Beauchamp Brown at all knew what was happening to her, had her down the burning stairs and out in the street, when he breathlessly bade a policeman, —

"Have an eye on that lunatic, or she 'll be back after her feather fan!"

Margaret, who had of late discovered that there were nerves under the hitherto perfect poise of her organization, had retired early that she might be alone, and spent hours in wandering up and down her room, trying to tire herself out that she might sleep, until, abandoning the effort, she took a dose of bromide of potassium, and finally succumbed to its effects, and slept heavily.

The girls, roused by the outcry, rushed into her room, but were unable to waken her at once, and Joan darted away, exclaiming, "I'll go and see if Aunt Phyllis is safe, and be back by the time you have roused her. I'll bring somebody to help save the trunks."

"Oh don't go, Joan!" screamed Elsie, her timid nature succumbing at once to terror; and as Joan, wild as a hawk with excitement, dashed out into the corridor, took a wrong turn, ran into the thickest of the danger, and was peremptorily driven downstairs, and into the street, Elsie sank down upon the floor at Margaret's bedside, sobbing and wringing her hands, while the smoke, rolling along the corridor in great, dun-colored billows, filled the room, lighted by the red glare of the flames without; for Margaret, dreading the darkness of her sleepless nights, had left her windows unshaded, that she might catch the first glimpse of morning light.

"Meg, Meg, Cousin Meg!" wailed Elsie, dragging at the white hand under the sleeper's cheek; and Margaret, opening her eyes, dim with the narcotic, drowsily murmured, —

"Don't cry, little Elsie! it will all be right."

"But there's a fire, cousin! The house is on fire, and we shall be burned to death!"

"What! Fire!" exclaimed Margaret, all alive in a moment and springing to her feet. "What are you doing there, child? Get on some clothes as fast as you can. Where is Joan?"

"Gone to find Aunt Phyllis, and get some one to carry out the trunks," replied Elsie, getting to her feet, and steadied all at once by finding some one to take the lead.

"Trunks!" echoed Margaret contemptuously. "Put your money and jewels, and Joan's, into your bosom, get on some shoes, and as many clothes as you can, take anything you can carry safely in your arms, and leave the rest.   Hurry for your life, child!"

Elsie made a step in the direction of her own room, but at that moment an explosion in a neighboring apartment rocked the burning house to its foundations and threw both women to the floor.   Somebody, in the first frenzy of alarm, had blown out his gas, and now the flames had reached the room.

"Margaret!  Elsie!" called a voice from the corridor, so filled now with smoke and flashes of flame as to make respiration dangerous and almost impossible.

"Paul!" exclaimed Margaret joyously; and in at the door they dashed, the two stalwart Englishmen, the two heroes who had that night wrought such marvels of courage and strength as only those men do who hold their own lives lightly when weighed against lives given them to save; men of that splendid courage whose growth is within.

"Where are you?  Speak!" cried Rockfort's voice, for they had entered through the girls' bedroom, and found no one there.

"Here!" exclaimed Margaret, rushing forward; and, as a sudden flame flashed out and lighted the room like noonday, they saw her, pale but glorious, her gleaming hair falling about her, her eyes flashing with the light of love that forgot all danger and all pride, her bare feet rosy-white, her dainty dress of lace and cambric falling open, and instinctively gathered together with one hand, while the other outran her feet and reached toward him. It was but an instant, a second, — a flash of sight and sensation; but until he dies Paul Baruther will never forget that ravishing image of love and joy and beauty. He caught his breath, as the swimmer all but strangled with the waves that have gone over him, and rushed toward her, then swerved aside, and snatching a blanket from the bed, threw it over Elsie, and lifted her in his arms, exclaiming, —

"Rockfort, save her!"

"I will save myself!" exclaimed proud Margaret, as Rockfort dashed toward her, blanket in hand.

"No, you won't! No time for folly now!" responded he, enveloping her in the blanket, and raising her as easily as if she had been a baby.

Through the fiery waves of smoke and gas and flame itself they rushed, the two St. Georges, while the dragon, raging for his fair prey, pursued them, and when he could not reach, all but slew them with his mephitic breath; for when they reached the open air even Rockfort's cast-iron lungs tore at it with great sobs, and Paul, thrusting his lifeless burden into the arms of a policeman, sank exhausted upon the ground.

Joan was waiting for them, — Joan, whose quick eyes and quick wits had seen them in the crowd, and knew that they, if any men, would give their lives for life, had reached them, even in all that press, and given the clear directions without which they could never have found that secluded room, and then found her aunt, and by a tremendous bribe secured a carriage and placed her in it, with a policeman to guard the door.

In this carriage Margaret and Elsie were placed, and Mrs. Beauchamp Brown, thrusting a very funny-looking head out of the window, exclaimed, —

"Come in, you two! Paul, come this minute! Rockman, I forgive everything, and I will be the making of you and St. Polycarp.  Come in!"

Rockfort, still gasping for breath like a great engine, looked at her, and made no more reply than the engine would.  Baruther, lividly pale, but with shining eyes, held out his hand and, smiling, said, —

"So glad you are all safe!  There is more to do here. We will see you to-morrow — where?"

"At the Hoffman House or the Gilsey, as we find room.  Be sure, sure now, to come, especially Mr. Rockman."

And the carriage drove away.

# CHAPTER XXIX.



MRS. BEAUCHAMP BROWN entertained certain convictions, far more thoroughly settled in her mind than the theory that two and two make four, or that the earth revolves about the sun, and takes a year in doing it.

Chief of these convictions was, that what she had determined to do was an inevitable event : the laws of the Medes and Persians might be annulled, two and two might make five, or the sun go round the earth ; but when Mrs. Beauchamp Brown had declared to Beacon Hill, " Thus and thus is to be believed and admired and pursued," so Beacon Hill would believe and admire and pursue. Probably the sincerity of this conviction was one of the secrets of Mrs. Beauchamp Brown's success, for it is a threadbare axiom that the world is prone to take men at their own valuation, and there is great depth in the Divine assertion, that if a man orders this mountain to remove and cast itself into the sea, *believing that it will obey him*, the miracle shall be worked.

Of course, to Mrs. Beauchamp Brown's faith in her own powers, we must add the habit of success, vast wealth, eminent social position, a great concourse of friends, acquaintance (clients, as the old Romans called them), and parasites of every degree ; and again, perfect health and strength, vast energy, a ready tongue, and a shrewd dogmatism that answered admirably instead of logic or reason.

With all these levers, if Mrs. Beauchamp Brown could not remove mountains, she could very easily move Beacon Hill, and she did it, inclining that stately eminence in any direction she heartily desired. Just now this direction was due east, toward the grim granite edifice known as the Church of St. Polycarp, and so zealously did she ply the levers, and so unscrupulously exert authority, influence, and cajolery, that the scant congregation of quiet folk who had sleepily worshipped at St. Polycarp's ever since it was a church, were astonished, and rather annoyed than gratified, to find themselves crowded from their seats and smothered in the velvets, furs, feathers, and laces of a new congregation, whose equipages blocked the street, and spattered the quiet old ladies as they crept along the sidewalk ; whose silken trains rustled impertinently over the coir matting of the aisles, and whose gold and bank-notes, though doubtless acceptable to St. Polycarp's empty coffers, contrasted ostentatiously with the quarters, dimes, and coppers slipped into the alms-basin from the black-cotton-gloved fingers that had earned, or at least laboriously saved, those poor little coins.

" It don't seem as if our dear old church belonged to us any more, since these fine folk have taken possession of it," complained Miss Julia Pennfeather to Miss Lavinia Murgatroyd, who all her life had sung second to Miss Julia. " Why, last Sunday, when I went to our own old pew, — the pew where my father and mother sat fifty years and more, — there it was, filled up with five ladies, wearing silk, satin, velvet, and fur enough for fifty, not to mention a stupid-looking man, who went to sleep on top of his cane all through the service. One of the women, my dear, looked so like a mastiff in a velvet coat, that she made me quite uncomfortable."

" I know, Julia," responded Miss Lavinia, with a sigh as eloquent as Lord Burleigh's nod. " But when you consider what an attraction St. Polycarp's contains now, you cannot wonder that all the world flocks toward it."

" What do you mean ? The surpliced choir ? " asked Miss Pennfeather, who loved to mildly badger her second, and who steadily discouraged the sentimentality which had been that virgin's characteristic for fifty years or so.

" No, Julia," replied she now, with a sigh yet more tender, " I did n't mean the choir. I meant the clergy."

"Well, I value Mr. Rockfort as much as any one ; but I don't know that he's an attraction to that extent," said Julia dryly. "Not for his beauty, at any rate."

"Oh, I was n't thinking of Mr. Rockfort," innocently replied Lavinia. "It is Mr. Baruther, his assistant."

"Now, Lavinia Murgatroyd," began Miss Pennfeather, taking off and laying down her glasses, in solemn preparation for solemn words, "don't, I beg of you, begin that sort of thing about Mr. Baruther !  There's nothing so fatal to any healthy life in a parish as to have a string of women always running after the clergy, — especially unmarried clergy ; that was what made all the trouble with Mr. Wilson, and I said then, and say now, that his death lies at the door of the girls and women of St. Polycarp's ; for, if they had n't got him into such hot water that he had to leave here, he never would have gone among those horrid Indians and been shot and scalped.  So now, you just cry Hands off ! yourself, and tell the other girls to do the same, if you want to keep Mr. Baruther here."

By this time, Lavinia, being of a weak and watery habit, was dissolved in tears, and Julia, satisfied with the impression she had produced, unbent from her sterner mood into one of pleasantry, and peace was restored.

The visitors, on their side, had their fling at the sober denizens of St. Polycarp's, commenting upon their dress, manners, and style of worship, sometimes contemptuously, sometimes good-naturedly ; but, from Mrs. Beauchamp Brown, who was affable to the wardens, down to long-legged Bessie Quinsigamond, who, from the height of fourteen summers, jeered at Miss Murgatroyd's bonnet and ecstatic expression, each and every one felt and behaved like explorers, who, in some *terra incognita*, have come upon a settlement of natives, and are at once curious to study their absurdities and willing to instruct them in the arts of civilization.

Even Joan, good-natured and unassuming Joan, was a little bitten with the patronizing mania, and kindly shared her velvet prayer-book with a pale young girl, meekly sitting beside her, pointing out the responses with the tip of her cream-colored glove, and rather astonished, when she could not herself immediately find her place in the Psalter, to hear her companion repeating the Psalm from memory. The young girl was dressed in drab alpaca, a cheap felt hat, trimmed with cotton velvet and a scanty feather; she wore dark gloves, too large for her hands, and great india-rubber shoes, which squeaked as she rose and sat down. She may have been teacher in a primary school, or perhaps only helped her mother with the housework and the shirts and socks for six boys and their father; but as Joan, standing beside her in a blue velvet dress, a toque of the same, with a bird-of-paradise plume, nattily perched upon her wealth of dark braids, perfect boots, gloves, and all minor appointments, looked askance at the pale, quiet face, noted the air of rapt devotion, and the atmosphere of purity and joyous content exhaling from this young girl's presence, she began to dimly wonder whether, after all, it was she who conferred the favor in this companionship, or if the happiness of the St. Polycarps was necessarily so much enhanced by the irruption of Beacon Hill.

An odd sort of companionship had meantime sprung up between Mrs. Beauchamp Brown and Peter Rockfort. Perhaps her steady determination to look upon his utmost rudeness as eccentricity, and her persistence in friendly overtures and hospitable entreaties in face of every denial, had its effect, as the dropping of water upon rocks, and Rockmen, always will have, given time enough. Perhaps, too, the wisdom of the serpent suggested, even to Rockfort's straightforward nature, that Mrs. Brown's ample resources and pleasure in splendid benevolence would be useful adjuncts in building up a decayed and impoverished parish, and as by one of the queer caprices of that queer old lady's nature, she chose to be extremely docile with her new rector, — for she had removed altogether from St. Iamblichus to St. Polycarp, — he was enabled to direct the golden streams of her bounty very much as he desired. With this substantial aid at his back, Rockfort found it much easier than he had expected to carry out certain radical reforms in the ordering of his new domain ; and before very long the grim old church put on an appearance of sober, mediæval comeliness, contrasting very favorably with the ugly dinginess of its former character. The altar was quietly mounted upon three steps (in order that everybody might see distinctly, as Mrs. Brown explained to the senior warden), and provided with cloths of various colors, a pair of brazen candlesticks, and a plain cross. The mixed choir was superseded by a little flock of white-robed boys and men, who were accommodated on benches in the chancel instead of the curtained gallery, whence the dulcet tones of the former had issued for thirty or forty years, while the wheezy little organ that had accompanied it was superseded by a first-class instrument, cunningly inclosed at the north end of the chancel, a handsome stone font occupying the southern extremity. The pulpit, hitherto rather the prominent feature at St. Polycarp's, was lowered, deprived of its sounding-board, and removed to one side of the aisle, while the old reading-desk made way for a simple lectern at the other side. The cassock and surplice which had so startled the seven sleepers became so constant a sight at St. Polycarp's as to excite no comment, even though supplemented by stoles matching in color the hangings of the altar ; and the daily Eucharist was offered in vestments, of which some startled Polycarpians whispered that they were perilously Catholic of appearance. A feeble-kneed vestryman carried this objection to the rector, who replied by picking up a prayer-book and pointing to certain words in the creed : —

"Read that, if you please," demanded he.

"I believe in one Catholic and Apostolic Church "——stammered the vestryman.

"Of course you do," replied Rockfort, closing the book with a snap, "and if you do, why don't you believe in Catholic and Apostolic vestments and practices?"

"Well, but it 's just like the Papists," persisted the vestryman vaguely.

" Not at all," replied the rector, launching his long arm toward a bookcase some four feet distant from his chair, and dragging down a great folio of engravings. " See, here are plates of the vestments worn in the Catholic and Apostolic Church when it worshipped in the Catacombs of Rome, and left sculptures of its life and ceremonies to instruct those who should come after. Not much popery in those days, was there, when Christians were daubed with pitch and set on fire to illuminate the sports of the rulers of Rome? Well, don't those vestments look very much like these ? "

And again launching out that tremendous arm, Rockfort pulled wide the door of a press where hung cassock, surplice, and alb, and opened some drawers beneath, where lay chasubles, stoles, and maniples of silk.

" Well — yes, I don't know but it is so," replied the vestryman, comparing the plates with the vestments as carefully and intelligently as, in his daily avocation, he studied samples of corn and grain.

" Now, then," continued the rector, whirling over the leaves, " here are plates of modern Roman vestments, really Popish because invented or sanctioned by successive Bishops of Rome. Do you see the difference? "

" Yes, anybody can see that ; this thing now " ——

" A fiddle-backed chasuble."

" Well, it 's neither like yours nor the sample from the Catacombs ; and this lace thing " ——

" An alb."

" But you and the parties in the Catacombs don't seem to hold to lace on your albs."

" We don't hold to anything differing from what the primitive church established as Catholic and Apostolic, and so far as Rome retains the usages and the ' faith once delivered to the saints,' so far we hold with Rome ; but the trouble is, that Rome is not content with the faith once delivered to the saints, nor with their vestments, but has added Mariolatry, papal infallibility, and several other dogmas to the faith, and lace and gewgaws to the vestments, and with all those additions we refuse to hold.

However, of the two I think Roman additions are less pernicious than Protestant subtractions, don't you? "

"Protestant subtractions?" repeated the vestryman, puzzled.

"Why, yes, it's better to celebrate the Holy Mysteries in a fiddle-backed chasuble and a lace alb than in no vestments at all ; and no addition to the Faith can so insult it as the denying His Wisdom and His Truth who says, 'Except ye eat the Flesh of the Son of Man, and drink His Blood, ye have no life in you.'"

"That's a pretty weighty text, sir," said the vestryman, nodding his head. "Where might it be found?"

"Saint John, vi. 53," replied the rector briefly as he closed and replaced the great folio. "No, my friend, you must n't suppose that vestments, even colored ones, are always tokens of Rome's corruptions, but you may be certain that all irreverent and indevout practices are symptoms of Protestant denial of Christ before men, and I suppose you remember the warning he gave to those who do that."

"Yes, sir. He 'll deny them before God," replied the vestryman thoughtfully, and went his way with three convictions warm at his heart : first, that he was a profound theological and archæological student and authority ; second, that his rector was nearly as good an one ; third, that he was resolved to aid, abet, and uphold said rector in whatsoever he undertook.

# CHAPTER XXX.



THE daily papers announced that the Hon. Reginald Forsythe and suite had sailed for Madrid, and in due time copied from the Diario of that city the official announcement of his arrival and assumption of his duties. Margaret read both these items, and to the first said, "Thank the Lord he's gone!" and to the last, "I wonder if he thinks of me. I wonder what has become of Camilla."

The latter wonder was resolved within a few hours, for, as Margaret stood contemplating a piece of turquoise-blue brocade at Hovey's, a voice close beside her asked for crimson velvet, and with a swift side-glance she saw Camilla, and knew that the latter saw her.

"Thank you. I don't think I care for it," said Mrs. Ufford graciously to the salesman who held the fabric up for her inspection, and, quietly gathering up the gloves and parasol lying directly in front of her neighbor, she moved away as serenely and slowly as if from the side of an utter stranger.

"O my dear, would n't I like to put you down in the dirt and walk on you!" muttered Mrs. Trevylyan behind her close-set teeth, as she bent over the velvet whose color was darkly reflected in her face.

"Six dollars a yard, ma'am," said the shopman blandly, and was rather startled at the black frown and wrathful tone in which his customer waved aside the rich fabric, saying sharply, —

"Do you call that crimson? It's brick-red, and very poor in quality. I will look elsewhere!"

She flung away from the counter, and the shopman, ruefully refolding his brocade and his velvet, solaced himself by muttering under his breath, —

" Well, you need n't go off mad in that way, if it is."

At the door, as Camilla left the shop, stood Mrs. Beauchamp Brown's *coupé*, and framed in the window, like one of Greuze's pictures, she perceived Elsie's cherubic head bent eagerly over a book on her lap. An evil thought darted into the heart where evil thoughts, alas ! had come to dwell as in their home.

" I will get hold of that little fool, and teach her something of life. That will hurt my lady more than anything I could do to her." And, with a smile upon her lips, she went up to the window, saying, —

" How do you do, little one ? It's a long time since I saw you. Are you with Mrs. Beauchamp Brown still ? "

Elsie looked up with a startled smile, and responded cordially. Margaret had carefully avoided sullying the minds of the two girls with any intimation of Camilla's depravity ; nor had she, indeed, told her aunt, in other than the most general terms, of the confirmation of their suspicions which she had received at Plum Island ; so that, although Joan — shrewder in worldly ways than her cousin — had a vague idea that Mrs. Trevylyan was not a desirable acquaintance for any young girl, and would probably never be received again at her aunt's, Elsie was unconscious as a daisy of the whole affair, and responded frankly and cordially to the greetings of the beautiful and fascinating woman who, standing at the window, was hurriedly saying, —

" Elsie dear, I want especially to see you, and get you to speak to Mr. La Branche about something, but I have reasons for not wanting Margaret to know where I am, so I shall ask you not to mention meeting me. Will you promise ? "

" Yes, indeed, if you desire it," said Elsie, astonished.

" Well then, come and see me at the Tremont, where I am staying. Just go into the public parlor, and tell a servant to call me."

"Oh! I could n't, Mrs. Trevylyan," exclaimed Elsie, aghast. "I never was in a hotel alone in my life, and I should n't know how at all. I could n't, indeed!"

"Idiot!" said Mrs. Trevylyan's heart, while her smiling lips replied, —

"Oh well, I will meet you somewhere. Don't you ever go out by yourself?"

"I always go to Evensong at St. Polycarp's at five o'clock, and almost always alone," said Elsie doubtfully.

"Well, I will see you there to-night, and we will take a little walk after service," replied Camilla hastily, — for through the window she saw Margaret's stately head bent over some laces, — and hurriedly repeating, —

"Don't mention to any one that you have seen me," hastened away just in time to escape detection.

"Let me see now, what shall I do with her?" thought she, walking rapidly up Summer Street; and had not decided the question, when, in turning into the parlor of the Tremont House, she met Mrs. Belinda McVie Beauchamp, who, after a rapid mental process of inquiry into her own interests as connected with Mrs. Trevylyan, gave her an impertinent little nod, and would have passed on, had not the other, with a smile as insolent as Belinda's was impertinent, said, —

"No, you had better not take that tone, Belinda McVie. I can do you a good deal of harm if you make an enemy of me, and a good deal of good if I am your friend. I can do something here in Boston, and everything in New York or Washington; so take wisdom, and be my ally."

"I 'm sure, Mrs. Trevylyan, I never thought of such a thing as being your enemy! We have always been good friends."

"Well, hardly that, you know," interrupted Camilla, with an insufferable smile, "but you have done several rather disagreeable things for me, and although I paid you well at the time —— let me see, I gave you fifty dollars for persuading Mr. Forsythe to go to Plum Island, did n't I?"

"I believe so. But I suppose, in the end, Mr. Forsythe gave you a good deal more than fifty dollars, did n't he?"

"That does n't strike me as a subject necessary for us to discuss," replied Camilla coolly, "although I dare say I could make it interesting to your husband. I have several letters of yours which I might show him; one, for instance, acknowledging the receipt of the fifty dollars, and saying you would have been glad to do the job for nothing if it was going to annoy Margaret Ufford."

"You can't show them without ruining yourself," gasped Belinda, turning green.

"Pooh! Do you think I 'm a fool? Besides, if I set out to ruin you, my poor little woman, I would n't mind burning my own fingers a little, and there are so many ways in which I can do it!"

"Perhaps I could do you a good turn with Colonel Trevylyan, if it comes to that," hissed Belinda, whose eyes had taken on an unpleasant greenish glare, like a cat's.

Camilla laughed contemptuously, and contemplated the sweep of her train in the long mirror.

"There, my dear, is one of my great advantages over you," said she airily; "nobody would believe a word you said without proof, and I made you return all my letters as fast as I wrote them."

"But I copied them first, my lady!"

"Oh, I suppose so; but who is going to believe that your copies are not originals out of your own little brain? If you tried to make a fuss with my husband, I should simply say that you were an ex-servant of Mrs. Ufford's, whom I had found it necessary to report for impudence, and so you were trying to revenge yourself in a very ex-servanty fashion. Colonel Trevylyan would not hesitate long which to believe."

Belinda made an heroic effort, swallowed something so unpalatable that it made her very pale, and, holding out her fishy little hand, said, —

"Oh well! There's no use in recriminations; I'm not a bit afraid of any harm you could do me, but I'm quite willing to be friends, if you like."

"Call it friends, if you please; at any rate, we will form an alliance, offensive and defensive, for the present, against all the world, and especially against Margaret Ufford, whom we both cordially detest."

"And Mrs. B. Brown, whom I detest still more."

"Do you? I don't, but I'll give her up to you, and I am going to stab at both of them through their pet lamb."

"Who?"

"Elsie Beauchamp."

"How? Come up to my room and tell me all about it."

The conspirators walked away together, and a country mother and daughter, who were waiting for friends at the other end of the room, exchanged admiring comments on the beauty and grace of one, and the elegant clothes and air of fashion of both of them.

"They must be very happy," sighed the daughter moodily, and the mother, thinking the same, smiled uneasily.

# CHAPTER XXXI.



IT was two days later, and Mrs. Trevylyan, rising late and breakfasting in her own room, wondered what made her feel so very queer, so chilled and burning hot by turns, so parched with thirst and unable to eat, with such a heavy languor in her head and such darting pains in all her bones. She rose from the table and went to look at herself critically in the mirror.

"There is nothing amiss that I can see," said she aloud. "My cheeks are a little too pink and my lips too red and my eyes too bright for this early hour, but I don't look ill. I wonder how it feels to be ill?" She went and sat down again, meditating this query in a wandering and hazy state of mind not at all like her own. Presently she sighed, and, pushing the heavy hair off her temples, muttered again, —

"Let me see. What was I going to do to-day? Oh, that little fool of an Elsie is coming again, and I 've got to tell her this wonderful secret about her brother, — I wonder what I shall invent? — and then McVie is to come in with Morris Beals and we 'll send him to escort her home and make his style of love to her. What was it I was to tell her? Oh my head, my head, why won't it stand still!"

A servant knocked, and presented a card. She rallied her reeling senses and looked at it.

"Rev. Vincent Williams," murmured she. "Oh, yes, yes, show him up, John, show him up here." And as the man departed, she rambled on, —

"What does he want? Could n't I get him to help about Elsie? She 'd make a dear little pervert to the True

Church, and nothing would torment them all more, especially as La Branche has just come out of it with such a flourish of trumpets. We could scare her into a convent, I dare say. Ah, how do you do, Father Williams? You have n't quite given up this wandering sheep, then?"

"My daughter, I wish indeed that sorrow and loss may do for you the work I failed to do in your prosperity," and the priest, taking her hand, looked mournfully into her feverish and unsteady eyes.

"Sorrow and loss! What do you mean?" demanded she imperiously. "Have you come like a raven to croak of death at my door? What sorrow, what loss?"

"Your brother, Brother Ambrose, as he was called."

"Was called, *was!* Do you mean that you have already murdered him? Is he dead, — is Jim dead?"

She seized him by the arm and shook it violently; her eyes glittered, her cheeks burned, her breath came hot and fast; she looked like a maniac, and Father Williams gazed at her in astonishment.

"Is this the way to receive a visitation of God?" demanded he sternly. "Your brother died a holy and good death, at peace with God and man. You mourn him as a heathen might, and resent his quick reward as a robbery of yourself. Sit down and I will tell you the details."

"What have you to do with it, at any rate? I thought he escaped out of your clutches and went — where?"

"He went to a monastery in Pennsylvania, as you very well know, Mrs. Trevylyan," replied the priest coldly. "And while I was in Philadelphia I received a letter from the Superior of that convent, informing me of his sudden death from pulmonary congestion, and requesting me to inform his friends. I went to the house myself, saw his grave, and gathered all the sad details of his illness for you. I came to Boston principally to give them to you."

"How good of you!" sneered Mrs. Trevylyan. "You take advantage of my poor brother's weakened condition of body and mind to juggle and deceive him, to blind his eyes and cheat his understanding, until you get him completely into your own hands" ——

"Pray, what motive but his own salvation could I have for doing what you say?" demanded the priest angrily.

"How should I know?" replied Camilla as angrily. "Some superstitious notion of buying your own soul by paying in to the treasury of heaven as many more as possible, or perhaps some honors in the Church. I neither know nor care for your motive, — a selfish one no doubt ; but what I do know and care for is that you have stolen away my brother, my only safeguard, all I had to love, and shut him up away from me, away from life and liberty and everything that could help him back to health, and he has pined away and died, and it is you that have killed him, yes, and killed me too ; for I might have tried, if he had been left to me, to keep straight for his sake, and now I will go to the devil as fast as I can, and it is you that have sent me, — yes, you, you false, bad priest, you stealer and murderer of men's souls " ——

She was pacing the room up and down in a frenzy of excitement and anger ; and Father Williams, who had listened to her reproaches with a livid face and blazing eyes, rose and took his hat, saying coldly, —

"It is useless for me to try to talk with you, madam, and you seem in no mood to listen to the details of your brother's illness which I have collected for you. I came, not only to bring this sad news, which I might have written, but hoping to find you so softened by affliction that I might lead you at least one step on the way from death to life ; but you are of those who, having eyes, see not, and ears, hear not, and will not listen " ——

A knock upon the door interrupted what seemed likely to be a yet more angry rejoinder from Camilla, and as a man entered with one of the ominous yellow envelopes of the Telegraph Company upon his tray, the priest abruptly took his leave, almost unnoticed by his hostess, who, snatching the telegram from the tray, walked away to a window to open it.

It was very brief : —

"Colonel Everard Trevylyan was shot at the head of his troops in a chance encounter with Sioux this morning."

She read it through, carefully refolded it in the envelope and placed it upon the mantel-shelf, then went and seated herself on a chair in the corner of the room, her hands quietly laid in her lap, her eyes fixed upon the opposite wall. An hour went by in utter silence and stillness ; then a servant entered to put up the room, but never noticed that quiet figure in the corner until she almost tumbled over it, and started back with an apology. Mrs. Trevylyan neither looked at her nor replied, and something in the stony face and rigid air so disturbed the woman that she said, —

"I beg your pardon, ma'am, but do you feel bad any way ?"

The wild, strange eyes turned upon her and then away, but no answer came ; the hard, white lips did not stir.

"You 're sick, ma'am. ain't you ?" persisted the woman. "Let me help you into the bedroom, and lay down a little, won't you ?  Supposing I send for a doctor ?"

No reply, and laying down her duster, Norah put a sturdy arm around the slender, rigid figure, meaning to raise it and carry it bodily into the bedroom ; but the contact of another humanity, as is often the case, roused the torpid nerves and powers of motion in the stunned organization, and pushing away the servant's arm, Mrs. Trevylyan rose to her feet, and pressing both hands upon her temples looked wildly about her, whispering, —

"Jim, dear old Jim, did n't they say he was dead ? Killed by the Indians, — no — a monk — a priest, — what was it that they said ?"

"It 's bad news you 've had then, ma'am ?" asked Norah, catching the muttered words, and giving way to the mingled curiosity and sympathy of her kind.  Something in the tone jarred upon the excited brain of the sufferer, and pushing aside the arm again enfolding her, she pettishly exclaimed, —

"There, there, it 's nothing you need trouble about. Go away and leave me.  I am going to sleep."

"And the best thing you can do, ma'am," replied the chambermaid heartily.  "You 'll excuse me bothering, I hope, but I was really afraid you was sick."

"There go, just go!   Never mind the chairs — go!"

And fairly pushing her out of the room, Camilla locked the door behind her, ran and secured the bedroom door in the same manner, and then snatching the telegram from the mantel, tore it open and read it through and through until the words seemed burned in upon her brain.

Then she dropped upon her knees, and raising a white, scared face and deprecating hands to heaven, she cried, —

"Mercy, mercy!   Thou art stronger than I!   Punish, but do not slay me outright!"

# CHAPTER XXXII.



THE night fell with a small, chill rain, drifting in from seaward on the bitter breath of an east wind, — such an east wind as has given Boston an ill name through all the land. A tall and powerful woman in the dress of a Sister of Charity, walking rapidly in from Cambridgeport, where she had been to visit a sick woman, drew her gray cloak more closely around her as she emerged from the shelter of the houses, and met the whole force of the storm sweeping down the length of the bridge. The clock upon the jail struck seven as the Sister reached the middle pier, and stopped a moment to turn her back upon the storm, and gather cloak and veil more compactly about her.

"God help the houseless poor to-night!" was her unspoken aspiration, and it seemed as if the thought had evoked its subject; for as she turned her face again toward the city, a figure glided by her more as if helplessly driven by the storm than with voluntary motion, and in passing turned a white, woful face not so much upon the Sister as past her, toward the angry, leaping water, sullen and dark except where the faint light caught upon the foam-wreaths flecking it here and there. Swift and noiseless as the wind itself she passed, and the Sister made some steps onward; but there was that in the face she had so briefly seen not to be forgotten or set aside by one vowed to the relief of suffering and sinful humanity, and presently she turned and looked back. The slight figure was just perceptible through the darkness, not moving now, but standing

against the rail, and leaning over toward the water.
The Sister quietly moved toward her, but had not yet
reached her side, when, with an inarticulate, dreary cry
of despair and recklessness, the figure lithely climbed to
the top rail, and for one instant reared itself, proud and
defiant, against the sky; the next moment it would have
plunged madly over to death and doom, but in that one
instant it was caught in the powerful grasp of two strong
arms, which set it upon its feet and held it there.

"What were you going to do?" gravely demanded
one of those voices which are seldom disobeyed.

"Die!" replied Camilla fiercely. "What right have
you to prevent me?"

"The right of God's commands in the first place; of
common sense in the second," replied the Sister. "It is
such a stupid thing to quench the fire by throwing coals
upon it! There is nothing that can't be either cured or
endured."

"Yes, there is. My life."

"Your voice don't sound like that of a coward."

"A coward! I am a soldier's wife, and as ready to
meet death as he was. Is that cowardly?"

"Did he meet his death in running away from the
enemy?"

"He! run away!"

"It is what you want to do, and to run from an
enemy that might be conquered into the arms of one
that no man has ever overcome."

"I can't think, I can't talk. My head is on fire —
the water will cool it — let me go!" And with a sudden
wrench the poor, delirious wretch tore herself away and
sprang upon the rail; but again the quiet strength of
the Sister arrested her determination, and throwing a
vigorous arm around Camilla's slender waist she led her
away, saying quietly and firmly, —

"You are ill, and do not see matters clearly. Come
home with me and we will talk them over quietly. Or
will you let me take you to your own home?"

"I have none; that was the reason I came here."

"Well, come to mine, and I will care for you."

Camilla murmured some reply ending in an inarticulate moan, and suffered herself to be led along so quietly that presently the Sister released her hold and contented herself with keeping a wary eye upon her motions.

Passing up Cambridge Street, they turned into one of the quiet, old-fashioned streets running up the hill, — streets bearing that air of better days and dignified decadence which is nearly as pathetic on the faces of streets as of people. Most of the great, roomy houses, inhabited fifty years ago by the aristocrats of Boston, are now lodging or boarding houses,. and not infrequently some forlorn little widow in rusty black, or some wife of a clerk upon a moderate salary, or some dowager, stately in the obsolete finery and manners of her youth, will say, —

" My father, or my uncle, or my husband owned this house, and his father was one of the richest men in Boston, and lived in a great house, with a big garden extending half down this street."

And the prosperous dry-goods man or grocer, sitting beside, and listening to the plaintive boast, retorts, aloud or in his heart, " A live dog is better than a dead lion," and congratulates himself and his wife that the proceeds of their "store" would buy the dead man's property over and over. Yes, all but his stately resting-place in King's Chapel or Mount Auburn, for the law will not allow even a decayed gentleman to be dispossessed of his bones.

Before one of these quiet, old, memorial houses the Sister stopped, and opening the door with one of the keys at her girdle, ushered Camilla into a hall, bare of furniture, except for a rich purple *portière* over one of the doorways, with an illuminated text upon its architrave. An atmosphere serene, quiet, and peaceful pervaded this house even to its entrance, and fell upon Camilla's heated brain and turbulent despair as the cool, damp air of a summer night upon the flushed face of a reveller escaping from the glare of some late debauch.

"Ah, this is good!" murmured she, drawing a long breath as the inner door closed behind her.

The Sister turned and looked at her under the hall-light, with a keen yet kindly glance.

"You are very wet," said she. "Come upstairs, and take off those dripping clothes; then you shall have some tea and go to bed."

But the allusion to physical comfort seemed to repel the quiet mood stealing over the excited brain, and with a gesture of abhorrence, Camilla turned sharply toward the outside door, when, from behind the *portière*, came a sudden swell of silvery voices singing a vesper hymn.

> "Lighten mine eyes, O Saviour,
>  Or sleep in death shall I,
> And he, my wakeful tempter,
>  Triumphantly shall cry,
> 'Against Him I have now prevailed,
>  Rejoice! The child of God has failed.'"

The gentle harmony wrought as it once did when Saul's fury sank down, quelled by the harp of the shepherd boy, and without a motion of resistance, Camilla suffered herself to be led upstairs to a quiet infirmary, warm, airy, and cheerful, where she presently found herself comfortably in bed, with a sweet-faced novice sitting and reading by a shaded lamp at the other end of the room.

"I have been asleep," said she aloud. The novice at once came toward her, and, arranging the bed covering, gently said, —

"Yes, for some time. Do you want anything?"

"I don't know. Am I sick?"

"You took cold, perhaps, in the rain. Sister said that in the morning she should send for the doctor. How do you feel?"

"Feel!" and Camilla laughed so elfishly that the young girl started and colored painfully.

"Well, where is this? Who are you? Who was the tall, strong nun who could hold me so firmly? I don't like gentle little pale things like you. Elsie is one, and

I don't like her.   Ha! when they see her on the street with Morris Beals, won't they howl? — Poor Beals, everybody knows his reputation, and for a girl to be once seen with him will be enough for a lifetime.   La Branche shall hear of it too."

" I would n't talk any more," interrupted the novice, in a sort of fright at what she heard and saw.   " Try to sleep.   Shall I read to you?"

" I don't know.   Have you Swinburne's Poems or the Decameron or something of De Kock's at hand?   That's my style of book."

" No.   I was reading 'The Spiritual Combat,'" said the young girl, bewildered.   Camilla laughed out in the horrible, harsh tones of delirium.

" Spiritual Combat!" echoed she.   " I fought one, too, but the devil got the better of me, and since that I can't fight.   No, I don't want to hear about that.   Take the light away, and go yourself.   I want to be alone and in the dark.   Then perhaps I shall sleep."

She insisted so strongly upon this that after a while the novice complied so far as to turn down the gas to a mere spark, and lie down upon one of the other beds, where presently she fell asleep.

In the gray twilight she awoke with a start, and a feeling that something was wrong.   Jumping up, she ran to the patient's bed ; it was empty, and the clothes, dried and folded upon a chair last night, were gone also : evidently she had quietly risen, dressed, and left the house, disturbing no one.   The poor little remorseful novice was not to blame, for she had not been bidden to watch ; but when the Sister heard of the escape of her charge she looked very grave, for she remembered that the bridge and the river still lay where they did the night before, and she hastily dressed herself and went out.

# CHAPTER XXXIII.

## CAMILLA'S REVENGE.

"COUSIN MEG," said Joan, coming into her cousin's bedroom, and finding her deep in the contemplation of a white satin dress arranged upon a dummy; while Josephine, upon her knees, her mouth full of pins, draped a lace overskirt upon it with bunches of Nile-green ribbon.

"Yes, dear," replied Margaret abstractedly. "A little higher, Josephine, and make those bows longer. I am going to wear this at Mrs. Jack's to-night, Joan. What shall you wear?"

"My old-gold tissue, I think, with the Roman ornaments. Can I speak with you by and by?"

"Yes, now. That will do very well, Josephine. You can take it to your own room and finish it."

Tenderly embracing the dummy, Josephine bore it away, the trail of the white satin turned up over its shoulder; and Margaret, lying back in her chair, wearily said, —

"Well, Joan, what is it? Does that silly little lordling still trouble you, or is Sneyd jealous?"

"Well — yes, both of those are true, and I have nearly concluded to have nothing more to say to either of them; but that isn't the matter. I want to tell you something, but I don't like telling tales, and it seems like it."

"No danger of your doing anything mean, my child. If you think it right to tell, no doubt it is right."

"Thank you, Cousin Meg. Well, it's about Elsie."

"I thought she looked worn and harassed of late. What is it?"

"I don't know, and that's the reason I told you ; but there's something going on, underhand, and I think her conscience troubles her for keeping it secret.   It began about a week ago, one evening when I met her going out by herself, and asked if she was going to St. Polycarp's to Evensong, and said I would go too.   She colored and stammered, and so evidently did n't want me that I turned it off, and decided to go and see Molly Lovering instead.   She seemed quite relieved, and I parted from her at our own door, and went to the Loverings.   Molly was n't at home, so I went and trotted round the Common for exercise, and was just rushing up Park Street, on the home-stretch, when I saw Elsie and Mrs. Trevylyan coming down Mount Vernon Street and turning up Beacon.   They did n't see me, and I was so astonished that I followed at a little distance to see where in the world they could be going.   It was n't very far, for they turned into Tremont Place, and disappeared ; I ran after, and was just in time to see them enter the Tremont House by the back entrance, Elsie casting a frightened look all about before she went in, but not being able to see me round the corner.   That evening I asked casually whom she saw at church and if she went anywhere afterward.   She looked scared, and made an equivocal reply ; but she is so fond of little mysteries that I thought nothing of it, until the next morning, when she slipped out by herself, so slyly that I *had* to go after her, and tracked her straight to the Tremont House again.   That afternoon, instead of going to church, she met Mrs. Trevylyan and Belinda McVie at Doll & Richards', and went out with them ; and ever since she has been creeping in and out, writing notes, getting answers, crying, moping, and carrying on generally in a fashion that really needs looking after.   I tried once or twice to get her to confide in me, but she was either so scared or so huffy at my advances that I gave them up, and concluded to put it into your hands and wash my own."

"It sounds rather badly, Joan, does n't it ? "

"Yes, and that's the reason I came to you."

"Still, I can't think anything very serious is involved. Elsie is innocent and simple and she is very timid. She might be made to believe almost anything and could be frightened into secrecy, although nothing would tempt her to tell a lie. I think those two mischievous women have got up a plot to vex us, especially me, by harming or compromising poor little Elsie, and have, in some cunning manner, persuaded her to keep her visits to them secret."

"I dare say that is it, Cousin Meg, but what shall we do about it. She has, I think, gone down there this morning. Ought Aunt Phyllis to be told?"

"Not if it can be helped," replied Margaret hastily. "I will speak to Mrs. Trevylyan myself. I think I can settle it without troubling Aunt Phyllis."

"You may meet Belinda McVie," suggested Joan.

"Mrs. Leverett Beauchamp," quietly corrected Margaret. "Well, it would not alarm me particularly if I did."

So it came about, that as the Sisters were saying their noonday office in the quiet chapel behind the purple *portière* of the house on Beacon Hill, that Mrs. Ufford, trailing her soft, rich silks along the corridors of the Tremont House, met a woman as tall as herself, by nature as imperial of port and bearing, but whose figure was hidden by loose robes of coarse gray stuff, while her head and face were shaded by a black drapery, from beneath which shone a pair of steadfast eyes, set in a face whose peace was of that assured sort which is conquered from an enemy who has sorely tried one's strength, but is utterly overcome at last.

Margaret bowed in graceful humility, murmuring, —

"Good-morning, my Sister," and was passing on, when the Sister, addressing the servant conducting her, inquired, —

"Can you tell me which room is Mrs. or Miss Trevylyan's?"

"This, if you please, Sister," replied the man respectfully.

Margaret looked at the nun in some curiosity, but as the door was already opened, she stood aside, allowing her to enter first, and followed into the room.

Camilla lay in bed, her face blazing, her eyes glittering in fever, her right hand tightly clutching that of Elspeth Beauchamp, who sat beside her, her face drooping in guilty confusion, her fingers feebly struggling in the iron grasp that held them. In her other hand the sick woman held Margaret's card, and, as she appeared, filliped it toward her.

" I could n't really believe that meant you, my rare, pale Margaret, my pure, pale Margaret!" mocked she. " I was waiting to see who Mrs. Ufford could possibly be who wished to be received by a Bohemian like me."

" I came for Elspeth," said Margaret coldly. " Will you please release her and let her go into the next room to wait a moment for me ?"

" Belinda is in there, she ran away when she heard you coming. You would n't thrust this lamb into the jaws of such a wolf as that, would you ?"

" Let her go, if you please!" And Margaret, with her eyes growing very bright, stepped forward, and laid her gloved hand upon that in which the girl's slender fingers were writhing in pain. Camilla tossed both aside, with a gesture of airy contempt.

" Take her, if you like," exclaimed she. " The mischief is done, I hope, physically and mentally. Don't forget, Elsie, those pretty stories I told you about the way in which girls like you live in Paris, and the gay, happy times they enjoy with their lovers, — not moped up like you, poor child ! and don't forget the little anecdotes of Mrs. Ufford's career in Paris and Rome, five or six years ago."

" Elspeth, go out of this room directly, and wait for me in the corridor !" commanded Margaret, in a tone before which Elsie quailed as if she had been struck. " And remember, I forbid you to speak one word, good or bad, to anybody until I come out."

" Afraid she 'll blab about the Count Montefiasco or

the Duc de Nemours!" sneered Camilla. "Don't forget their names, dear; and if Margaret undertakes to scold you, just remind her of them. And remember that every other woman you meet is just as bad, or worse, no matter how proud and pale they may look."

The door closed behind Elspeth, and Margaret, returning to the bedside, indignantly exclaimed, —

"I did not suppose anybody in the world was bad enough to do such work as that! Deliberately corrupting the mind of a young girl, and teaching her the grossest exaggerations, if not direct lies, about her own friends."

"Not lies, Meg. You can't say Montefiasco and the duke did n't fight for you, and poor Monte was killed, and his mother cursed you as his murderess."

"Silence!" exclaimed Margaret sternly. "Let my name alone, if you would have me keep silence upon matters that I can prove true, — matters for the law to handle, if your husband chooses " ——

"My husband!" shrieked the half-delirious woman, starting upright in her bed, and wildly extending her arms. "My husband! He 's dead, you monster! He 's dead, and Jim is dead, — poor Jim, who loved you so dearly, and has died for love of you, — he 's dead! They all are dead; yes, all! And pretty soon we shall all be dead too; yes, all, all of us, for I 've taken care that Elsie should have a present to carry home to you, murderess! Do you know why I held her hand so tight? Do you know why I have breathed into your face, my lady? Do you know what is the matter with me?"

"The matter?" exclaimed Margaret, shrinking back from the bedside where she had been standing; while the Sister, hitherto patiently waiting beside the door, crossed herself, silently moved her lips for a moment, and then, coming close to the sick woman, stooped and examined her face narrowly. A look of horror and repulsion shadowed her own as she did so, but presently disappeared, leaving only its usual recollected and steady strength of expression.

" Have you seen a physician ? " asked she ?

" Oh ! is it you, Sister ?   How did you find me out ? I came away because I knew that child would be here this morning, and I wanted, before I died, to finish the revenge I had begun upon this woman."

" Some articles, taken out of your pocket when your clothes were dried, were given to me to keep," quietly explained the Sister.   " Among them was a card with your name and address."

" Yes, I put it there, so that all the world should know whose body was fished out of the oyster-beds in the morning.   There was a letter, addressed to the coroner : did you read that ? "

" No.   I only looked for your name and address, that I might see if you were safe, and restore these things." And the Sister quietly laid them upon the table.

" You should have read the letter.   It was to say that I was driven to suicide by the death of my husband and brother, the latter owing to the plots of Mrs. Ufford and a Roman Catholic priest named Williams."

" I will burn it now, then, since you did not die," said the Sister, in a half-questioning voice ; and, as Camilla made no reply, she took up the letter again, and laid it upon the fire, saying, —

" And now tell me for what physician to send."

" I won't have any," replied the sick woman shortly.

" Then I must tell the landlord what I suspect to be your complaint.   It is not right to allow you to remain here in this manner."   There was a decision and a quiet force about the Sister's voice that reached even Camilla's disordered brain, and, turning her head away, she peevishly exclaimed, —

" Well, do what you like, I don't care.   Elsie has got it and Margaret too, and that hateful little McVie.   I don't care now what they do with me."

" Got what ?   What is the disease, Sister ? " asked Margaret, who had stood, pale and silent, looking from one to the other, as if dreading to ask confirmation of her fears.

The Sister raised her steady and resolute eyes to those half-shrinking, half-anxious ones, and replied in a low voice, —

" I think she has small-pox."

" And I know she has," exclaimed Camilla, with an elfish, shrieking laugh. " She's got it, and she's given it to all of you, proud Margaret and all."

# CHAPTER XXXIV

### THE YELLOW FLAG.

"OF course she must go to the Hospital," said the doctor. "They won't keep her here unless they 're fools, and she can have a private room and every comfort if she has money to pay for it."

"There will be money to pay for whatever she needs," said Margaret quietly.

"Margaret, Margaret Ufford, come here!" called the sick woman from the next room, in so strained and shrill a voice that the doctor, the Sister, and Mrs. Ufford looked at each other in dismay.

"Growing delirious," said the doctor. "Better go and see what she wants before it is too late."

Margaret was already gone. She found Camilla sitting up in bed, her long, dark hair streaming wildly about her, her arms outstretched toward the door, her eyes glaring with terror and anguish.

"O Margaret, Margaret," cried she, "save me, don't let them take me to the hospital! I heard the doctor say it, but oh, don't, don't let him do it! Meg, you used to love me, we were such dear friends in the old days, and Jim loved you so, poor Jim! For his sake, Meg! And I am sorry I did you any harm, I am indeed, but I was so jealous of Forsythe, and he always loved you best " ——

"Hush, hush, Camilla! Don't talk of that."

"Then promise me, promise!" and snatching at Margaret's sleeve, the poor creature wound her arms around her waist and clung close to her bosom.

"You really must n't allow that, Mrs. Ufford!" exclaimed the physician, an old family friend and adviser of the Beauchamps. "There 'll be no chance of escape from contagion if you don't keep your distance."

"O Margaret, Margaret, don't mind him!" wailed the sufferer. "You won't take it, you are too strong and perfect to be in any danger, and I have n't a friend in the world but you, not one, not one, Meg. Don't desert me! You won't, will you? You 're so brave, so strong, you 're not afraid! Stay with me, Meg, oh, stay with me, or I shall die in the beginning; and don't let them take me to the hospital,— promise me that, Meg, promise me!"

"But you can have a room quite to yourself, Camilla, and "—— began Margaret; but Camilla interrupted her with a loud and bitter cry.

"I have no friend, not one, not one! And they will carry me to die all alone in a hospital — all alone — no friend, not one! My husband dead, my brother dead, Margaret turned against me, not one left, not one!" The wail ended in a wild burst of tears, and slipping from Margaret's grasp, she fell flat upon the bed on her face, her hair streaming over the edge, her arms extended in an attitude of hopeless misery. Margaret looked down at her, and her face turned to the bluish pallor of marble. Then she laid a hand upon that fallen head, and quietly said,—

"You shall not go to the hospital, and I will not leave you, Camilla. Life for life, and James Douglass might have been alive to-day. I will stay with you, Camilla."

"But you can't stay here, they won't let you," exclaimed the physician impatiently.

"There is a small, unoccupied house on Spring Street, where we have one room hired for a girl in diphtheria," said the Sister. "She is better now and may be removed "——

"I will hire the whole house," exclaimed Margaret; "and if you can find some one to stay there with us "——

"Sister Ursula has had small-pox and will come to nurse Mrs. Trevylyan, and I know a woman who will go to do the housework; she has also had the disease," said the Sister quietly. "It will be necessary to buy some articles of furniture or send them from your own house."

"I will go down town and buy them at once," said Margaret eagerly; but the doctor interposed,—

"You must not go anywhere among people, or speak to anybody you can avoid, after coming into contact with the patient as you have, nor should Miss Beauchamp.  If you will write a list of the articles required, Sister, I will send my man to order them as soon as the house is secured, and that I will see to myself, if you like."

"Then Elsie had better be put in quarantine too," said Margaret, "for she has been more exposed than I.  Must we take her with us to Spring Street, doctor?"

"Hardly, I think, for she may not have taken it; the pustules are not perfected," and the doctor bent to examine Camilla's face, covered with livid crimson blotches.

"The young lady may come to our house, if she will remain in the infirmary until the doctor knows whether she has the disease or not," said the Sister.  "I must not idly risk the lives of the community, but she is welcome under those conditions."

"Thanks, Sister, and as soon as the disease is declared, she shall be removed to the house in Spring Street," said Margaret.  "There now, all that is arranged, and, doctor, I shall ask you to go round and tell Mrs. Beauchamp Brown.  I won't frighten her by going home or letting Elsie go, but will just write a note in the next room to ask for some clothes and things."

"You will have to do without a maid," said the doctor, who knew Margaret's ways from a child.

"Yes," said she quietly.  "I did without a maid last summer, and I nursed a sick person, too, and was none the worse for it."

"You won't have much nursing to do if you secure one of the Sisters," said the doctor, with a little bow toward the Religious, about whom hung an atmosphere of silence and recollectedness that seemed to deprecate even a sincere compliment.  "I have seen their work among the sick poor, and it is wonderful.  You can't hire nurses to take hold as they do."

"You can't hire conscience and true devotion," said Margaret graciously, and both physician and lady glanced with smiling approval at the tall, quiet, gray-clad figure, but turned their eyes away again with much the feeling of a man who has tried to compliment the Egyptian Sphinx.

Money and ready wit can achieve large and rapid results, and so it came about that before night Margaret was quietly settled in her own hired house in Spring Street, and looking with considerable satisfaction at the pretty little room, to whose embellishment she had contributed with her own hands, while on the floor below, Camilla was comfortably settled in a quiet back room, Sister Ursula in charge, and a buxom colored dame, called Phenice, busy in the kitchen.

"Was it only this morning that I was talking with Joan, yes, and looking at Josephine preparing my white satin for to-night," said she aloud. "I doubt if they see me at Mrs. Jack's, but I dare say they'll do as well without me, and I a great deal better without them. How odd, how very odd! I, nursing Camilla Trevylyan! Paul would say it was fitting expiation. No doubt it is, and if I die it is no more than just — but to die, to die of a loathsome and disfiguring disease! O my God, don't let me die, don't! I am not afraid, but — I have not lived yet, dear God! Don't let me die before — no, I won't say it even to myself! Will he care if I die? He is a priest now, I might send for him if I were dying — but no! He can live without me, and I can die without him."

She leaned her folded arms upon the table, and bowed her head upon them for a few moments, then raising it with a superb gesture, rose, and, walking to the little mirror, contemplated herself with a proud and contemptuous smile.

"Does small-pox first attack the brain, and turn its victims idiotic?" asked she of her own reflection, and, getting no answer, went to bed.

The days and nights went by, monotonous, yet charged with a current of subdued excitement, which at once kept

up the nervous energies and sapped the vital force of the
unaccustomed watcher.

"Do try to take more sleep, Mrs. Ufford," Sister Ursula
would say, again and again.  "I do not need you here,
and you had far better be resting, ready for the time when
I do need you."

"I can't rest, Sister," replied Margaret once.  "I dare
say I am a descendant of the Wandering Jew or his sister."

"He rested when his Lord came, did n't he?" asked
the Sister quietly.

"Margaret!" suddenly exclaimed the sick woman,
whom they had thought asleep.

"Yes, dear," said Margaret tenderly; for, in offering
her life for this her enemy, she had come to love her
again with more than the love of their early days.  Is it
not more blessed to give than to receive?

"I am going to die, Margaret!"

"Oh no, Camilla; indeed, I don't think it."

"Well, I am.  I feel differently to-day, and worse.  I
am going to die, and I want to see a priest!"

"Father Williams?  He is in town, I think."

"No —— never, never, never!  He is n't honest, he
is n't true; he taught me to make reservations, as he
called it: you 'd call it lying.  No, I don't want reservations and half truths and expediencies, now.  I want
the whole truth, — I want an honest man!"

"You became a Roman Catholic, did you not, dear, at
the time James did?"

"No, I did n't; I grew more like an atheist under
the teaching that converted poor Jim.  I was too well up
in all those crooked ways not to recognize them.  No,
Meg, I want to see Paul Baruther.  He 's the only man I
ever knew, — I believe he 's the only man alive — who says
what he means and does what he says.  He 's as courteous and gentle as Father Williams, and as strong and
true as Rockfort.  I 've tried them all, and I know.  If
my poor, tired soul can yet be saved, it will be by Paul
Baruther.  May I see him?"

"Why, certainly, dear, if he will come.  We cannot

send until the man comes for orders in the morning, or, perhaps, we 'd better wait for the doctor; and if Sister Ursula will write a note, as your nurse, it will be better than for me."

" I don't care, only I want to see him," murmured the sick woman restlessly; and Sister Ursula bent anxiously over the pillow, studying the face on which some sort of change was certainly passing.

# CHAPTER XXXV.



## A FEARFUL FIGHT.

"WE had better wake Phenice, and send her for the doctor. He said we were to do so, if a crisis came to-night," whispered the Sister to Margaret, who nodded, and was moving noiselessly toward the door, when Camilla spoke out clearly and strongly, —

"And the battle was set, Satan and Death and all their host, against Michael and his angels. Send for the priest, for I fear Him who can slay both soul and body, and cast them into hell!"

There was an awful something in her voice and in the groping of her aimless hands and the dimly seen, disfigured, and inflamed face that chilled Margaret's blood as though she were indeed on the borders of a supernatural battle-ground, and heard the wild cry for rescue and protection of a soul already trembling in the talons of the Destroyer; the air seemed thick with the rustling wings of the combatants; a sense of suffocation, as in an awful presence, fell upon her, — a strange terror, such as she had never known, shrinking and loathing in all her senses, the fear of seeing and hearing those things, unspeakable for horror, which sometimes loom darkly and vaguely through our dreams, or yet more vaguely before the eyes of the soul striving to picture to itself eternal loss and doom, bending, as it were, for one breathless moment over the abyss, then shrinking back to fall trembling in the dust, crying, Have mercy, have mercy upon me a sinner!

The Sister fell upon her knees, whispered a prayer, crossed herself, and rose, pale, strong, and collected.

"Go, please, and send Phenice for both the doctor and the priest. Tell her to hurry all she can," said she; and

Margaret, rousing from the strange terror that had struck her dumb and motionless, sped out of the room, waked the negress and despatched her, saw that a fire and hot water were ready, went into her own chamber, and knelt for a moment with a wild yearning of prayer in her heart, a sudden, swift knowledge of her inability and ignorance of prayer, and of the uselessness at this hour of all else which she had so complacently acquired, and then, strangely meek and gentle for Margaret, went back to the sick room, where Camilla lay in darkness, for her burning eyes could not endure the least ray of light, muttering, fast and fiercely, inarticulate questions, replies, petitions, angry accusations, wild wails for mercy and help, weary moans of exhaustion or despair. The Sister knelt beside the bed, silently praying, and waiting till she could be of use otherwise ; and Margaret, still half-stunned and bewildered in presence of these adversaries of whom she knew so little, stood, tall, fair, and motionless as a statue, in the little circle of light thrown upon the door from the carefully-screened lamp.

The door below softly opened and shut, and quiet, heavy steps came up the stair.

"Thank God! she need n't fight alone any longer," was the cry of Margaret's heart ; but aloud she said nothing, not even when Baruther, entering after the doctor, cast one steady, friendly look of greeting upon her, but did not stop until he leaned over the bed, and gently laid his hand upon the sick woman's head.

"Don't touch her skin. It 's death!" whispered the doctor in his ear. The priest nodded, and remained with his eyes calmly fixed upon that half-seen, hideous face, which no man would have guessed to be that of beautiful Camilla Trevylyan.

Presently the doctor withdrew, beckoning Sister Ursula to follow him to where Margaret still stood.

"It is the crisis," said he. "She will be a dead woman before morning, or she will get well. There is nothing to do for the present, and another woman is lying between life and death in the next street. I will return in an hour.

Give her all she will take of this mixture, Sister Ursula. Mrs. Ufford, swallow a good glass of sherry immediately, and lie, or at least sit down, in the next room until you are wanted."

He was gone, and Sister Ursula brought the sherry and put it to Margaret's lips before she returned to the patient ; but the rest of the prescription was unheeded, for no human power could have persuaded Margaret to leave that room, wherein to her thought, heaven and hell had met to fight out their battle for this soul, whose life had so closely mingled with her own, whose lighter sins she had shared and encouraged, whose blacker crimes she had so coldly and contemptuously visited with her scorn more than her abhorrence.

The night deepened, and with it the conflict. The doctor, pallid and exhausted, came in, watched for a while, then went to lie down in the next room, trying to snatch a little sleep for the morrow. Sister Ursula, silent, ready, and collected, did all that could be done for the poor sufferer's outward comfort, and, in the intervals, knelt beside her pillow in quiet prayer. At the other side stood the priest, his eyes resolute and watchful as those of the general who carefully marshals his forces, and, not despising the foe, feels his own strength, and looks on through the fierce din of battle to a glorious conquest. From time to time he knelt and said a prayer, brief, fervent, and penetrating, and sometimes, when the paroxysms allowed the patient to listen, he spoke to her, but generally stood, his eyes upon hers, sometimes touching her burning head, sometimes with folded hands, an expression of intense concentration of purpose upon his face, marble-white in the obscurity of the place, except as his luminous eyes seemed to gather and shed forth again the feeble rays of light penetrating it.

Of a sudden, Camilla spoke loudly and clearly : " Is Margaret Ufford here ? "

" Yes. Do you want me, Camilla ? " replied Margaret, coming close to the bed, on the side opposite Paul.

" Yes. Listen, all of you. Who are all of you ? "

"Sister Ursula, Mrs. Ufford, and I, are all," said Baruther gently.

"A priest, a nun, and the woman I have wronged! Is n't that enough? I 'd go stand in a church porch, with a sheet and a lighted candle, if I could, but you know I can't! Won't this do?"

She paused; but all there knew that she addressed none of them, and none replied, yet she had her answer; for she rejoined, always in the same clear, loud voice, so different from her usual thick whisper, —

"Yes, I confess to God before all this company, — angels, devils, priest, nun, and you, Margaret, — that I have bitterly, bitterly wronged you, and that I repent and will make amends so far as I can. I wronged you in your husband's love, Margaret. Poor old man! it was no Roman fever that he died of, it was me. I told him that Montefiasco was your lover and that the Duc de Nemours had been, and that you laughed at his senile delusions about you, and I showed him a silly letter that you wrote for me to copy to send to a man I wanted to mystify, and I pretended it was to Nemours " ——

"And he believed you!" exclaimed Margaret, aghast.

"Yes. How could he help it in face of all the proofs I gave? and that was the reason he took you away from Florence so suddenly; and although the brave and loyal gentleman would never treat you ill, or even accuse you, he never was the same to you again, was he?"

"No, never!" said Margaret bitterly.

"And in three months he died at Rome, and it was I who killed him, and I did it to secure Montefiasco for myself, and, after all, he was shot for love of you. But you were in no wise to blame. And I wronged you with Reginald Forsythe. I made him think that you sent for him last summer, and I played upon his jealousy and his suspicions, — yes, made him believe that you had gone too far with poor Jim, so that in the rebound I could catch his heart, for I always loved him. I only succeeded in entangling his senses, and the love he gave me was an insult to any woman " ——

She stopped abruptly, as if listening, and then went on almost in a scream, as if the words were forced from her, "No insult to me, no, for I was a sinful woman already, and I was glad to become his mistress, — yes, tempted him to it, and succeeded, and then, lest he should despise me, told him that you were as bad, and that your conduct had killed your husband, and gave him proofs of that; for poor, imprudent Ufford wrote me a letter, begging me not to let the matter go further, for he wished to shield and protect you in spite of all. I showed Forsythe that letter" ——

She paused again, and again replied, as to an invisible monitor, "Yes, the priest shall write to him, and tell it all : it shall be undone for the living, and the dead know already. What more? I told Elsie all these stories against you, Margaret, and I told her, too, that you were secretly a Roman Catholic, and went to confession to Father Williams in Paris" ——

"But I did n't," interrupted Margaret, glancing at Baruther, who was fixedly regarding her.

"Belinda said so. She watched you in and out of the confessional at the Madeleine " ——

"Yes ; but I only went to ask advice, to try to discover if confession was the comfort I was yearning to find. It was just after that duel and my poor husband's death, and I was wild with grief and shame and remorse. But I was never a Romanist, I never went to confession, I never even knew who the priest I spoke to was until I met him again last summer."

She spoke eagerly, as if defending herself from some accusation beyond Camilla's, and she never moved her earnest gaze from Baruther's eyes, steadfastly fixed upon her, as if reading her very soul.

Camilla, exhausted and almost lifeless, lay back upon her pillows, breathing slowly and heavily. All at once she started up with a shriek, flinging out her hands wildly, as if to ward off an attack, and crying, —

"Off! Off! You shall not have me ! I have repented, I have confessed, I have made reparation, I have begged for pardon of God and man !   You cannot touch me, you shall not pluck me out of His hand !   Save me, save me, O Saviour of sinners ! "

" He hears you, He forgives you, my child ! " exclaimed the priest solemnly.   " He has left power in His Church to absolve every sinner who truly repents, confessing his sins, and, by the power committed unto me, I absolve thee of all thy sins, and declare to thee, with authority, the pardon and peace of God the Father, Son, and Holy Ghost.   Spirit of evil, I command you in that Holy Name to release this woman, and come out of her, for He who has conquered death and hell claims her for His own ! "

He laid one hand firmly upon her head, extending the other with a gesture of superb command, while from his pallid face and luminous eyes beamed a light not of this world, not of man, but such as fell about the apostles when, in the name of their Master, they cast out devils and healed those whom the devils had tormented.

A deep silence fell upon the room.   The sick woman lay all but lifeless, yet serene and conscious, beneath Paul's possessive hand ; Margaret, on her knees, with clasped hands and upraised eyes, felt a strange flood of joy and life sweeping through the dark, dry chambers of her soul ; the sister, calm and steadfast, prayed, giving glory to God that another soul was saved for Him ; and still the priest stood, looking up, that strange light upon his face, — the same light, perhaps, that they of the Council beheld upon Saint Stephen's as the heavens were opened to his eyes.

" Well ! what now ? " asked the doctor softly, as he approached the bed, and, attentively examining his patient, straightened himself to say, with solemn self-gratulation, —

" The crisis is passed.   The woman will live ! "

# CHAPTER XXXVI.

## MRS. BEAUCHAMP BROWN TAKES COUNSEL.

CAMILLA'S convalescence was a tedious and fluctuating one, and hardly was it pronounced enough to relieve her friends from constant care when Margaret succumbed to a very mild form of the same disease, so mild as to never suggest danger to life, and to leave no trace behind when it had departed, but still quite sufficient to keep her in quarantine and to forbid the visits of the outside world.

Mrs. Beauchamp Brown lived the life of an insane pendulum, her vibrations governed by no law but her own whim, and ranging from a frantic grief, terror, and devotion to Margaret — in which she sometimes came as far as the door of the house in Spring Street, and, standing with a carbolic sachet over her nose and mouth, made inquiries, and sent pathetic messages to her niece, down to a condition of frantic displeasure at what she called Margaret's Quixotic folly and selfishness in causing her friends so much trouble and anxiety.

In these days it was that Mrs. Beauchamp Brown sent a peremptory message desiring the Rev. Mr. Rockfort to call upon her that evening; to which she received a prompt and equally peremptory note to the effect that Mr. Rockfort had not time to visit persons at their own houses unless they were ill, but would see Mrs. Beauchamp Brown at the church, after any one of the daily services. At this rebuff the pendulum vibrated more furiously than ever, now declaring that audacity, rudeness, ingratitude, and many other vices had never truly found their home until now, in the person of the Rev.

Peter Rockfort, and that not only would Mrs. Beauchamp Brown die before she would submit to such arrogance, but that she would withdraw herself and her influence from St. Polycarp's at once, and leave it to sink into its original insignificance and poverty.

"I'll go to the Church of the Holy Frescoes, and have a fifteen-hundred-dollar-pew to myself," exclaimed she to Joan, the only *confidante* of her affront; "and on some accounts it is a deal nicer: one can carry one's Unitarian friends there with no danger of their being shocked or disturbed, and nobody expects you to go down on your knees at prayer, or stand up for anything you don't want to."

"I've noticed they don't seem to stand up for anything in particular at the Holy Frescoes," demurely replied Joan, and the pendulum swung violently back.

"Well, my dear," exclaimed Joan's aunt indignantly, "I hope you don't mean that's a recommendation! I'm sure if you listened to Mr. Baruther's sermon about fighting for the faith once delivered to the saints, and not letting one point of that faith, or one form of the respect by which we prove that it is a real faith to us, fall into disuse, you would know better than to uphold a congregation who never testify to any especial reverence for anything, and believe pretty much what they like. I'm surprised at you, Joan! I thought you had profited more by the sound catholic teaching at St. Polycarp's."

Joan smiled, and counted her stitches for a moment, then carelessly said, —

"If we go to Litany at noon to-day, you might see Mr. Rockfort in the vestry afterward, Aunt Phyllis."

"Yes, I suppose I might," replied her aunt meditatively. "You see, Joan, our clergy should n't be expected to make visits like the Low Church clergy, who have no daily services to attend, and don't do half so much among the poor. It is very proper that we should wait upon them when we are well, and they will not be remiss in visiting us when we are sick or poor or in prison."

"Very true, aunt," replied Joan demurely, "and as

we're not very likely to be sick or poor or in prison to-day, perhaps you had better go to Mr. Rockfort at the church."

"I intend to do so," replied Mrs. Beauchamp Brown, with much majesty. "I only wish you young people understood as well as I do the proper consideration and deference we all owe to the clergy, especially to one so active and faithful as Mr. Rockfort."

So, at ten minutes past twelve that day, Mrs. Beauchamp Brown, having with much unction proclaimed herself and her friends miserable sinners, rose from her knees, and ostentatiously avoiding saluting any of her acquaintances on her way down the aisle, sought the vestry, where Mr. Rockfort greeted her with a certain resignation of manner suggesting that he had been thus favored before. Placing a chair for her at some distance from his own, he seated himself, and listened, with the composure of Bunker Hill Monument, to the exordium of compliment upon last Sunday's sermon, of congratulation on the number of attendants at early service, and upon the general prosperity of the parish, owing, as Mrs. Beauchamp Brown gently insinuated, chiefly to her own exertions. At this point Mr. Rockfort spoke : —

"If you have done any good works, don't spoil them by boasting of them," said he. Mrs. Beauchamp Brown colored indignantly, gasped a little, as if she had been dashed with ice-water, and then, vibrating into the meek corner which she occasionally elected to occupy, replied, —

"Always faithful, always bold and honest! Do you know, Mr. Rockfort, that I like you all the better for seeing that you are no more afraid to speak to me than to the meanest creature in this parish. I do admire courage."

"Why should I be afraid to speak to you?" asked Rockfort, in such honest astonishment that even Mrs. B. B. found herself unable to enlighten him, and abruptly said, —

"But all this is not what I came to say. You know

that I consider you my spiritual adviser and director, Mr. Rockfort."

Rockfort drew his brows together and shot a worried glance from beneath them at his worldly disciple.

"Don't use such words without knowing what they mean," said he. "You have n't got up or down, whichever you call it, to the ground where direction is possible. An ostrich with its head in the sand can't be directed."

"'Ostrich with its head in the sand!'" echoed the lady in angry bewilderment. "What *are* you talking about?"

"Natural history. What did you come to say?"

"Upon my word, Mr. Rockfort, I wonder that I came at all, or that I ever come, when you are invariably so rude to me."

"I do not mean to be rude, but I have really no time for anything but real work. If you have any to propose, or if I can help you in any way, please tell me at once. If you would be simple and honest, you would not find me rude."

"Well, simply and honestly, who is Paul Baruther?"

"Assistant clergyman of this parish."

"Pho! Is he a gentleman?"

"He is a priest, — the highest rank a man can boast."

"Well — but " ——

"I don't want to be rude, but if your business with me is only to gossip about Mr. Baruther, I must ask you to excuse me."

"Evidently, priest and gentleman are not synonymous terms in your dictionary," exclaimed Mrs. B. B., her head vibrating so that the ostrich plumes upon her hat rustled as if still appertaining to the fowl of which Rockfort had spoken.

"Is that all?" asked he, glancing at the clock.

"No, it is n't all, Mr. Rockfort. I had a plan, — a plan that would be of great benefit to the Church, and give it a place in Boston that it never has held yet ; but since you have n't time to listen, and only laugh at me or insult me when I try to explain, I 'll give it up, yes, and give up the plan, and perhaps give up the Church and everything.  I don't care, I 'm sure, if you don't."

She rose with a breeze and flutter that shook the robes hanging upon the wall, but never shook the calm of the Rockman's face.  Slightly pointing to a chair, he said in his quietest and coldest tone, —

"Will you be so good as to sit down, Mrs. Beauchamp Brown, and try to think and speak as befits a woman of your age and position?  What is the good of this outburst of arrogance and ill temper?  Whom does it hurt?  Not me, and not the Church,— only yourself.  If you really have a plan for helping on God's work in His Church, and drop it because you don't fancy me, you make me of more importance than you do Him.  Do you mean that?  O woman, woman, hate me if you will, but don't lose your own soul by ingratitude to Him!  Give to God, work for God, glory in God, and thank Him that He permits you to do it.  Don't turn aside from the Divine Beauty to contemplate the unworthiness and unloveliness of His servant!"

Very seldom, very seldom indeed, did Peter Rockfort speak out like this; very seldom did any human being catch a glimpse of the sacred fire that burned, night and day, upon the altar of his heart, — the strong, sweet vein of tenderness lying deep down beneath the flints and shards of the upper surface.  To very few did this strange man reveal — and never voluntarily — that he possessed a capacity for love befitting the grand proportions of his nature, physical and spiritual ; and that, disdaining any mortal end, this love was, day by day, poured out, a costly libation, upon that hidden altar where burned his life.

Had Mrs. Beauchamp Brown possessed eyes to see, or ears to hear, or a heart to understand, she might, as she glanced at that momentarily illuminated face, and caught that tone, have learned more of Peter Rockfort than most persons learned in a lifetime ; but she had not.

A vague surprise, a sort of sympathetic wish to do great things for God, a shadowy discontent, and shame at her own life, stirred the surface of her mind, but never reached below. At sixty it is a little late to begin to remodel a character, and Mrs. B. B. had not even got so far as to know that hers needed it.

So she laughed a little nervously and held out her hand, saying, " I always have to give in with you, Mr. Rockfort, and I do believe that 's the reason I like you so much ; for I do like you, in spite of everything."

Rockfort turned a face of gray granite upon her, and waited in silence. Unabashed, she went on : —

" I 've been thinking that it would be a good thing for me to build a church, and make Mr. Baruther the rector, and marry him to Margaret. There, it 's all out ! "

Again she succeeded in stirring that stony face, and now it expressed unbounded astonishment and horror.

"Marry Mr. Baruther to Mrs. Ufford ! " echoed he. " Absurd, monstrous, impossible ! "

"Why absurd, monstrous, or impossible ? " coolly inquired Mrs. Beauchamp Brown. " A clergyman ought to be married, you ought yourself : there 's no sense or reason in remaining single, and having all the women of your parish pulling caps for the preference. In fact, I think it 's immoral, and only fostering envy, hatred, malice, and all uncharitableness among your flock. At any rate, I shall have the rector of my church a married man, and Paul Baruther is to be that rector, and Margaret the rectoress, if I can coax her into it, and I think I can : she 's done everything else under the sun and worn it out ; and now she 's got varioloid, and I suppose will lose all her beauty, and has got to go in for something new."

"Baruther won't do it ! " interrupted Rockfort, in a tone of mingled relief and indignation.

" Won't he ? H'm ! " replied Mrs. Beauchamp Brown very significantly. " He goes to that cabin in Spring Street, and spends an hour, every day of his life. What 's that for ? "

"To visit Mrs. Trevylyan at first, and then, you ungrateful and foolish woman, to visit Mrs. Ufford, because she is sick, and needs help. Not for any pleasure to himself, you may be sure. Preposterous!"

"Preposterous it may be, and I may be an ungrateful and foolish woman, Mr. Rockfort," exclaimed Mrs. Beauchamp Brown, her plumes rustling audibly with the nodding of her head. "But you 'll see if I don't carry out my plan, — yes, and leave you and St. Polycarp stranded high and dry, if you make an enemy of me. A hundred thousand dollars, or two hundred thousand, for the matter of that, is a good weapon to fight with, and I will use it too."

"You won't buy Paul Baruther's conscience with two hundred millions of dollars, however," replied Rockfort confidently, and the interview was ended.

# CHAPTER XXXVII.

"OUT OF THE STRONG CAME FORTH SWEETNESS."

EVERY one who has lived to maturity, and lived intelligently, must have noticed with amusement or chagrin, as the case may be, the satirical vein in which Dame Destiny delights. Does a man's soul revel in softness and luxury, in leisure and adulation, in fine houses and galleries of pictures, and does he resolve to sell his early years to Mammon, that in his latter days he may enslave Mammon to his tastes? Destiny pats him on the back and says, "Go on, my dear fellow, toil night and day, give all your heart, all your brain, all your will, to money-getting, and you shall get it — with a vengeance!" At fifty, perhaps sixty years old, the money is his; and he is bent and blear-eyed, sordid and unlovely, and alone in the world, or tied to the companionship of his grub existence, and finds it incapable as himself of becoming a butterfly. He does not care for his fine house, and nestles in one little basement room of it, like a small worm in a big walnut; he estimates his pictures only by their cost, his books by their bindings, and his friends by their incomes. He has sold himself to Mammon, and Mammon has drawn the pith out of him, and thrown aside the dry, empty husk.

Or the girl pines and longs and schemes for a lover, and half ruins her soul in jealousy and intrigues, to get him away from a rival. At last she succeeds, and marries him with the feeling that Paradise is regained for man, and the Golden Age again has dawned on earth.

Five years later, they quarrel about money, about the children, about his evenings out, about her adherence to her mother and sister, about his or her friends, and she says, " I 'd die of a broken heart if I did not know it would please you better than anything else I could do," and he rejoins, —

"Yes, you 'd rather disappoint me than please yourself, any day."

Or an honest, simple man fancies what a great and good thing it must be to become President of the United States, and some luckless day two wearied parties unite on him, as inoffensive to either ; and the next happy day he sees after his Inauguration is the day when he shakes the dust of the White House from his feet, or lies murdered in its precincts.

Not quite so grim as these pleasantries of Clotho and Lachesis, but still after the same order, was the present epoch of Margaret's life.  She whose study through all her years had been the gratification of æsthetic tastes, especially in her personal surroundings, she who had lain in the silk and fed on the rose-leaves of life, who had shut her proud eyes and turned away her dainty feet from every form of disease or poverty or degradation, who had found an admirer or a servant at every turn, and while despising the adulation and hardly noticing the service, had come to regard both as essentials of existence, — here was she in poverty, in sickness, a prisoner and friendless, and yet breathless and radiant with joy, feeling that never until now had she known what it was to live, never had any of the palaces in which she had dwelt from time to time shone as fair in her eyes as this mean little house in a squalid quarter of the city ; never had ivory and ebony, buhl and marquetrie, combined to give her one tithe of the joy that hung like a drapery, and illuminated as with rare arabesques the pine chairs and tables, the chintz-covered couches and lounges, of her present abode.  Her table was most plainly, and during her half-illness, meagrely supplied with such articles as Phenice could cook and Sister Ursula allowed ; yet what triumph of Vatel, what imperial wines or celestial teas ever reproduced the nectar and ambrosia of the gods, as did those basins of broth, those slips of toast, those weak, weak cups of very ordinary Oolong, on which dainty Margaret for a while subsisted? Phenice, her only servant, was unlearned in the finer branches of servitude, and in her zeal became even more clumsy and noisy than nature had intended; she broke Margaret's hand-glass, smashed two of the gold-topped bottles of her dressing-case, and having quietly carried away and washed the ivory-backed brushes, laid them in a hot oven to "dry off nice," and ruined them forever-more: but Margaret lavished smiles and kind words upon her, and in the end made her a present of the house and furniture in Spring Street, where she keeps a lodging-house at this very moment. Visitors of course were absolutely forbidden; but this child of the world and queen of society had never, in all her life, blushed and thrilled at hearing the door-bell ring, and steps ascending the stair, until now, when the visitor could be no one more exciting than the doctor or the priest.

Sister Ursula, most silent, most unexpansive, most prosaic of good and devoted, but uninteresting women, was made the recipient of such floods of fascination and witchery as princes and peers had never evoked from their imperial and imperious idol, though they had grovelled in the dust at her feet.

Was it not an irony of Fate?

Paul and Margaret did not speak of love. Both had suffered so much, both had waited so long and in such agony of suspense, and both were endowed with such exquisite keenness of sensibility, that it was a luxury to dally for a while upon the threshold, to stand and look at the rose in whose heart they would presently bury their intoxicated senses. What need of words for those whose eyes could talk, what need of closer caresses for those whose clasping palms sent thrills of joy through the remotest fibre of the being? Looking upon love from the epicurean side, craving it as an æsthetic enjoyment, lovers delicately constituted enough to appreciate these hours of unspoken yet confessed love, find in them the keenest enjoyment which love in any stage has to offer. "Thought is deeper than all speech, feeling than all thought," and so soon as one tries to reduce, first to thought, and then to speech, the subtilest, most intangible, yet most powerful feeling of our nature, one loses very much of its penetrative charm. The essential delight of a bottle of royal Burgundy is in the bouquet of the first glass before ever it has touched the lips, not in the dregs of the last glass. When Eve beheld the apple, that it was pleasant to the eyes and to be desired that it might make one wise, she desired it so vehemently as to sell her life for it; but with the last morsel came the curse, and one name of that curse is Satiety.

However, it was no such cold-blooded philosophizing that kept these two lovers silent. Margaret was silent because she was absolutely content already, and because, being a woman, she could not well have declared it had she been less content; and she was silent because Paul willed that there should be silence, and the sweet surrender of her own will to his was one of the subtilest joys her proud nature could ever know.

Paul was silent — why? From a dozen reasons, — the most powerful, that he felt it right to be silent until Margaret was restored to her own home and kindred; also, no doubt, his intense and reticent nature loved to feast for a while upon this joy, so long denied, so hardly won, in the solitudes of his own heart, and dreaded the moment when the eyes of the world should invade even the outermost courts of that sanctuary; also, a sense of delicacy and of fitness forbade that the first words of a pure and sacred love should be spoken within ear-shot of the poor, fallen, wrecked, and broken woman, struggling back to life in the next room; perhaps, too, the priest, who had resolved honestly and conscientiously and after much prayer, that the holy estate of matrimony and not that of celibacy was his path to God, felt a little shy of the grave-eyed Sister who had chosen the harder road. At any rate, he never spoke a word that Sister Ursula might not have heard, and spent quite half of his time, when in Spring Street, with Camilla, who clung to his presence with a painful tenacity, and would lie for hours, her great, cavernous eyes fixed upon his face, listening as he read or talked to her so gently, yet so faithfully, of the things she had need to hear and consider.

Only one day she asked, with a little discontent, " What were you reading to Margaret, yesterday? It sounded like poetry. I like poetry, too, but you never read me any."

" It was the Lyra Innocentium," said Paul quietly, but with a significance that she felt ; and, with a sudden crimson upon her poor, scarred face, she exclaimed, —

" And the songs of innocence are not for me ! Why, oh, why, did you drag me back to life when I was all but dead ? "

" Would it have been better for Mary Magdalene if she had died just before she came to weep at the feet of her Saviour, and hear His words of pardon?" asked Paul gently ; and she, turning her face down upon her pillow, moaned out, —

" Go now, go to Margaret, and read the Lyra Innocentium if you like. Leave me alone, — always, always to be alone ! "

" Indeed, I sha'n't," replied Paul cheerily ; " and there is something in the Lyra, which I have here in my pocket, that I should like of all things to read to you."

So it was almost an hour before he came into Margaret's room, to touch her hand and look into her eyes, and say, in a voice that brought the color to her cheek, —

" I must say How do you do and Good-by, Margot. I have used all my time in Mrs. Trevylyan's room, because she needed me, and I did not believe you did. Was I right ? "

" Not right in thinking I did not need you, but quite right in denying me for her sake if she needed you most."

They looked at each other for a moment, — two grand and tender souls holding such converse as the angels may, — then he closed her soft hand in the firm and possessive clasp of his own strong palm, and went away for all that day.

Sister Ursula, softly entering the room some moments later, could not imagine why Margaret lay with her right hand over her lips, or why she should blush so rosily in being caught in that attitude, nor yet what was the source of the smile of serene content, and the look of hidden joy in her eyes, as she replied to the Sister's questioning, that Mr. Baruther had not been able to make her his usual visit this morning, but had spent all the time with Mrs. Trevylyan.

"I met him on the stairs, and he said you would probably go home by day after to-morrow. He is going to see Mrs. Beauchamp Brown this afternoon, is n't he?"

"I don't know. He did n't say anything to me about it; but if he told you, I suppose it is to be so," replied Margaret contentedly.

"What! did n't you arrange about returning home?" asked the Sister, amazed.

"No, Sister, I never spoke of it," said Margaret, with a delighted smile. "I suppose Mr. Baruther arranged it all with the doctor. He will tell us to-morrow."

# CHAPTER XXXVIII.



MR. ROCKFORT meditated upon his interview with Mrs. Beauchamp Brown, at first with feelings of simple annoyance, through which presently loomed a vague terror and suspicion. Baruther could not be bought, — on this point his convictions never wavered ; nor could the Rockman's grand nature entertain jealousy or envy of his brother's success. Already he was accustomed to seeing the world throng to Baruther's sermons, while his own congregations were mostly the poor, the ignorant, the criminal, the children of Ham ; and he gave thanks to God, who had divided to each of his servants such gifts that all men might be reached by them. If Mrs. Beauchamp Brown chose to expend her fortune in building and endowing a church of which Baruther was to be rector, his friend would be all the better pleased that two houses should rise where only one had stood before, and would glory in the spread of the kingdom, though it were at his own cost.

But that Paul Baruther should marry ! That was the grisly shape haunting Rockfort's fancy. That was the terror which finally devoured all annoyance, all other feeling in the matter, and at last resolved him to speak boldly to his friend — breaking the silence which by tacit agreement had endured between them upon this subject ever since the conversation at Plum Island, terminating in the catastrophe with Moses Barnes.

That evening the two men sat together in the library of their little rectory, each with a book open before him, each with his mind revolving a subject far enough from the matter of that book, each meditating how best to broach that subject.  Rockfort was first to begin.

"Mrs. Beauchamp Brown was with me yesterday, Baruther," said he, turning a page and glancing down it.

"Indeed!  And what did she have to say?" asked Paul sharply, wheeling his chair so as to face his friend, and throwing his own book upon the table.

"Various things.  Among the rest, that she intends building and endowing a handsome church for fashionable people, and procuring the rectorship for you."

"I should not accept it.  I told Mrs. Beauchamp Brown so to-day."

"Oh!  She spoke to you?"

"Yes."

"And did she advance any other plans for you?"

"No: no, I don't think she did."

Rockfort glanced up with a look of inexpressible relief ; but there was that upon his friend's face which struck like a sword of ice to his very heart, and blanched his strong face to the color of ashes.  He said nothing, and presently Baruther spoke again.

"No, she did not propose any other plan, but I did."

"Well?" demanded the other, in his harshest tone.

"I proposed to become the husband of Margaret Ufford," said Paul, in a sort of wonder at the sound of his own words.

Rockfort leaned an elbow on the table and hid his face in his hand.  Paul glanced at him uneasily, and then a look of light and strength grew upon his own face, and he quietly said, —

"Our Lord's first miracle was at the marriage at Cana, and St. Peter, whose namesake you are, was a married man."

"And St. Paul, your namesake, was a celibate, and wrote that it was better all men should be as he."

Paul rose, and stood before his friend with outstretched hand.

"Don't let us sit here, hurling Scripture at each other's heads, until both forget the brotherly love that

Scripture everywhere teaches," said he. "I know all that you could say, and I have said it to myself, not once, but hundreds of times in the last six months, for there never has been a day since last July in which I have not meditated and prayed upon this subject; and the end of all is, that I am firmly convinced God has not called me to serve him in the celibate life. You decide that He has called you, and, having chosen it as your own, you naturally think it the best, and wish it for me as well; but you would not have me vow myself to it, feeling that my heart was not in it, would you?"

"Surely not. But I hoped you had the vocation for the higher life."

"Don't say that, Rockfort! Don't claim the title of 'higher' for any life in which the great mass of men, even the great mass of the clergy, find it impossible to serve God. The higher life is the life nearest to Him, and I am steadfastly convinced that for me the life most in accordance with His will is the holy estate of matrimony. I wish I could have your approval of my decision, old friend."

He held out his hand again, with a wistful tenderness in his eyes contrasting strangely with the iron determination of the lower part of his face.

Rockfort looked at him steadfastly for a moment, and a sort of agony passed over his own face, — the death-agony of the hope he had nurtured deep in his silent heart. Then, grasping Paul's hand in a gripe whose power he did not know, he muttered hoarsely, —

"God's will be done. God bless you in all ways!" and abruptly left the room.

Not another word ever passed between these two men upon this subject, nor was the cordiality and confidence of their manner, or perhaps their feeling, in any way diminished; but from that night an indefinable change passed upon Peter Rockfort's life, — an added grayness to the granite of his face; an added severity to the austerity of his manner; an added keenness and depth to his exhortations to repentance, his warnings of loss and doom to those who fail to achieve the best purpose of their lives. The one instance in which he indulged himself in expression, the one concession to that craving for sympathy stirring even in natures as sternly repressed as this, was peculiar. Being summoned to preach to a scant and unlearned congregation, in a little town of New Hampshire, he took for his text : —

"I am distressed for thee, my brother : very pleasant hast thou been unto me : thy love to me was wonderful, passing the love of women." And from these words he preached a discourse upon the love of man for man, so glowing and eloquent, so pathetic and so real, that the few who heard and understood him spoke of him ever afterward as, "That man who loved his brother."

# CHAPTER XXXIX.

### A WHIFF OF EDEN, ALSO OF JOANSVILLE.

AT the end of Mrs. Beauchamp Brown's suite of
drawing-rooms was a little boudoir, screened from
the rest of the apartment by curtains, and here Margaret loved to sit, and here she stood, on the morning
after her return home, listening, with bent head, and a
nervous smile upon her lips, to the sound of footsteps
advancing up the long room. She looked very beautiful in the soft light of the tinted window beside her; a
little pallor, a little delicacy of outline, — tokens of her
late illness, — added a softening charm to the regal beauty,
sometimes a little oppressive by its very regality, and
the expression of hesitation, almost timidity, visible even
in the fluttering fingers toying with the roses upon the
table, added the last charm to this new phase of proud
Margaret's ever-changing, ever-triumphant loveliness.

The steps drew near, paused at the curtain, then
entered; and Margaret, only half-regaining her usual
poise, raised shy, sweet eyes to greet her visitor, and
murmured something, — she knew not what, he cared
not what, for thought is deeper than all speech, feeling
than all thought.

The cold, trembling little hand fluttered out to meet
him, and he took both it and its mate, and, holding them
fast, looked down at her with a proud, possessive smile, —
a smile before which her own eyes drooped, her lips
quivered between joy and tears, the lovely color crept
over cheek and chin and brow. At last he spoke, and
in this great, wonderful crisis of his life, this rush of
strange, incredible new emotion, he found no words

newer than Adam may have said to Eve in Paradise, and millions of Adams, each in his own Paradise, have said since, each to his own Eve.

"Do you love me, Margaret?"

"You know that I love you, Paul."

He put his hand under her chin, and gently raised it until all the glory of her beauty lay beneath his eyes, — the fair, conquered kingdom, joyously waiting for its conqueror to come and take possession of his throne, — then he stooped and kissed her.

Did it ever occur to you to imagine the sensations of Adam and Eve the first time their lips met?  The first kiss, in the world that God had seen was very good but not yet perfect; for men and women as yet were not, and the kiss of love, pure, unsullied, hallowed yet most fervent love, had never yet been given, the perfection of Paradise had not been reached.

"Margot," said Paul presently, holding her at arm's length, and looking at her, "I am glad that you are so exquisitely beautiful, so perfect in shape, so noble and grand of bearing.  If you had been a little and insignificant woman I should have been afraid to marry you, lest my ideal might become dwarfed through love of you.  Now I shall try to educate the souls of all women to the beauty and stature of my wife, for the body should be the exponent of the soul."

"Then little women will still have little souls, after all your education," said Margaret gayly, and they laughed like two children at their own nonsense; then Margaret, clasping her hands, laid them upon his breast in a pretty gesture of shy caress, and looking up at him, said, —

"And I am glad that, though I am tall, you are taller, and if I have good looks, you have better looks, infinitely better than beauty; for you are not handsome, Paul; at least,"——

"Nay, don't qualify.  I'd much rather be left, 'not handsome;' so that you like to look at me, that is."

"Well — yes — I think, I'm not quite sure, but I *think* I like to look at you, Paul."

And again they laughed. Oh, Paradise must have been a very simple place, and there's a good deal more than a jibe when we speak of a fool's paradise, especially if, with the Irish, we call a fool an innocent. "Unless ye become as little children," you know.

An hour later, Mrs. Beauchamp Brown, who had mounted guard in the front drawing-room, like a dragon, and allowed no one to enter on any pretence, approached the curtained doorway, coughing dramatically; but nobody heard the cough, and Margaret was exclaiming eagerly, —

"O Paul, do you remember"——when her aunt's voice, a little dryer than usual, interposed : —

"If you two people have begun on the 'do you remember' chapter there's no more use in waiting for you to finish than for the river to run by ; and Tom Sneyd was asked to lunch, and as we had to wait for you, he has occupied the time by proposing again to Joan. What's to be done with him?"

"I should say, give him his lunch at once and try to restore him to reason," suggested Margaret, coming out into the drawing-room followed by Baruther, who shook hands with Mrs. Beauchamp Brown, and murmured some sentences in her ear, whereupon that lady startled him by presenting a very powdery cheek for the salute which, after some meditation, he bestowed upon it, and remarked, —

"You're dear good children, both of you, to carry out my little plans without any fuss and opposition."

Paul and Margaret exchanged a look, but said nothing ; in fact, words would only have weakened that communication.

Mrs. Beauchamp Brown majestically led the way to the dining-room, where Sneyd and Joan already waited, and announced the double engagement in a characteristic manner.

"One pair of turtle-doves on this side the table, and the other on that, if you please ; and I beg all four to remember that I, here at the head, represent the world, and the world don't like turtle-doves."

" My dear Mrs. Beauchamp Brown, you represent the wisdom of the serpent, which always combines so satisfactorily with the innocence of the dove," suggested Paul ; and the lunch went on with all decorum, but with innumerable side-glances and speeches and innocent equivoques, to which Mrs. Beauchamp Brown, with Arabian hospitality, closed her eyes, and did not open her lips.

" And now," said Sneyd, as the party returned to the drawing-room, " I want to give you an idea of mine."

" Had n't you better keep it for your own use ? " saucily inquired Joan, who, in the joy of having at last decided the question that had fretted her for six months, and kept both her and her lovers in a succession of hot waters outnumbering those of a Turkish bath, glowed like a rose in freshest beauty, and darted in and out of everybody's conversation like a humming-bird.

Sneyd received her suggestion with a delighted grin, but proceeded without answering it, —

" The reason I came to-day especially, to speak to — to Mrs. Beauchamp Brown and Joan, and try to settle matters for us two, is that I have a proposition from my father to go home and take charge of some mines they have just opened on a lot of wild land bordering on the Mississippi, which he bought a good while ago, partly for the lumber, partly because he thought of building a town there ; the town never came to more than a village, but in cutting the lumber off, they have struck coal, and very likely oil too.  At any rate, people are already thronging there, and as it is on the river and a good landing, it will grow immensely, and may become a very important place.  At present it has n't even a name beyond Sneyd's Landing, and I 'm going to call it after Joan in some way " ———

" Joansville is at once novel and euphonious," suggested that young lady demurely.  " Only it will always be spelt J-o-n-e-s-ville."

" I did n't suggest Joansville, my dear," replied Sneyd, with another grin.  " But you and I can quarrel about the name in private , at present I wish to tell Mr.

Baruther my idea.   La Branche and I were talking about it all; and as my father is willing to make over this property to me at once, as my share of his estate, I have offered La Branche a partnership, and he will live at New Orleans through the winter to receive the shipments I shall make from —Joansville, if you like. Then in summer he will come up there, and one or other of us can be away at the seashore or mountains all through the warm weather.   My father will advance the money to build a couple of suitable houses and also, I don't doubt, —and now, Mr. Baruther, I come to the idea, —a church and rectory."

"And if your father builds forty churches and eighty rectories, what under the sun has Mr. Baruther to do with them?" demanded Mrs. Beauchamp Brown, her head nodding vehemently.  "I have plans of my own for Mr. Baruther, especially if my niece is to be Mrs. Baruther.   Don't count them in to your Western Utopia, if you please, Tom Sneyd."

Tom looked bewildered and dubious, Joan flushed angrily, and bit her lip to repress some hasty words, Margaret smiled half-approvingly at her aunt, and Paul, turning his persuasive smile upon his hostess, said, in a tone of gentlest and most veiled yet irresistible authority, peculiar to himself, —

"But Mr. Sneyd may make his proposition before we quite reject it, may he not?"

"Oh yes, he may propose," grumbled Mrs. B. B. "But he can't dispose any more than any other man."

"Or woman," added Paul, with another smile.  "Well, Mr. Sneyd?"

"Why, I don't know that it's worth while to go on," said Tom ruefully, "if Mrs. Beauchamp Brown is going to offer some brilliant city parish, —and of course she has money and influence to set up anything of that kind that she fancies; but my idea was, that you are so powerful among all sorts of people, and don't care a button for rich or poor, fashionable or vulgar, gentle or rough, but find some way to manage and control them all, —that you would be a tremendous power for good in such a place as this is going to be.  Miners are always a rough set, and there will be worse than miners in a place right on the river ; the blackguards that swarm on the Mississippi boats will flock to a place where money is going to flow freely and carelessly ; and then there will be a better class of people, who will need moral support and comfort, — engineers, architects, merchants, with their families, if we make it fit for families.  My idea is," — and honest Tom, warming to his subject, began striding up and down the room, — " my idea is to build up this place to be something very different from the God-forsaken mining and oil-centres that so often disgrace our western country, — towns where there are seventy gambling hells and one Methodist meeting-house, not to mention "——

" Well, don't mention them," sharply interposed Mrs. Beauchamp Brown.  " You mean to collect a company of saints and angels to dig coal and pump oil, and persuade Paul Baruther to go and be head saint.  I suppose Margaret and the miners' wives will go round singing hymns at the bar-room doors of an evening, won't they ? "

" Oh, of course you can pick me and my plans all to pieces, and make me look like no end of a fool, as very likely I am in most things," said Sneyd good-naturedly, although he had turned very red.  " But there's no doubt that a clergyman of the right sort could go to a place like that, and in a year's time considerably influence the census of saints or devils.  No doubt, it will be hard work and plenty of it, and giving up a great deal, all this sort of thing," — and he waved his hand around the room, — " and society, except as we could gather it about ourselves ; and the feeling of being in the civilized world that one can't get, out of a large city, and lots of things beside ; but then it's a grand work for a strong man to undertake, and Mr. Baruther is my idea of a man who is meant to do grand works for God without much counting of the cost to himself, and so "——

"And so you did him a great honor in proposing the post to him, and I think he will accept it with much gratitude, but cannot say yes or no until he has considered and taken counsel upon a matter involving another life than his own."

So spoke Paul, with a glance at Margaret, who met it with startled and questioning eyes, but in a moment rose and came to stand beside him, saying quietly, —

"Whatever you think best, Paul, will be best."

Mrs. Beauchamp Brown saw the action, heard the words, and, covering her face with her hands, burst into perhaps the only hearty, genuine tears she had ever shed, while she sobbed out, —

"O Meg, Meg, I did n't think you 'd do it! I did n't think you 'd desert me in my old age!"

"It won't be half so far as if I had gone to Madrid, auntie darling," whispered Margaret, with her arms around her aunt's neck.

"Ay," moaned the woman of the world, carefully drying her eyes, "but then you would have been an ambassadress, and I could have borne it."

"And she 'll be an ambassadress now, dear Mrs. Beauchamp Brown," said Paul softly, "and every grace and every charm with which she is so lavishly endowed will be another weapon to win men to allegiance to her Royal Master. She will be a greater power at Joansville than ever she could have been at Madrid."

# CHAPTER XL.

TWO WEDDINGS.

"I BELIEVE the very smoke-jack and warming-pan will come down out of the garret, and set themselves up to thwart my plans!" exclaimed Mrs. Beauchamp Brown, as she hastily entered the library, where Paul and Margaret sat at a table covered with plans of churches and dwelling-houses, for Margaret had resolved to make a marriage-offering of a little church and rectory, built of the sandstone abounding in the vicinity of the nameless town which she already spoke of as home.

"Why, what's the matter now, Aunt Phyllis?" asked Margaret, rising, and going toward her, with a bright smile.

"Elsie's the matter," replied her aunt pettishly. "She won't be married! La Branche came to me this morning with positive tears in his eyes, and said that ever since she came home from the Sisters she had been queer and upset, and last night announced that she had resolved to become a Sister, and, of course, never marry. Now do you wonder that I am provoked?"

"Paul, you must talk to her," exclaimed Margaret confidently.

Paul drew vague lines with his pencil on the blotter, and did not reply. The two women looked at him in astonishment, and Mrs. Beauchamp Brown indignantly demanded, —

"Did you know of it, Mr. Baruther?"

"No — I did not; but I am not surprised."

"Why?"

"She has that temperament, and the life in a religious house is very attractive. Most girls of Elsie's character

would be fascinated, and suppose that they had a vocation. She would be undeceived in six months."

"Then you don't approve?"

"Approve what? I heartily approve and admire the
religious life if a person has a genuine vocation for it; but,
of course, I quite as heartily disapprove the adoption of
such a life by one without such a vocation."

"Well, talk with Elsie, and see what she has to say.
She is in my morning-room at this minute," said Mrs.
Brown eagerly; and Paul went with strange reluctance.

Why his reluctance? Why Elsie's pallor and low spirits,
and resolve to devote her young life to celibacy, poverty,
obedience, and good works in a Sisterhood? One must not
profanely penetrate the recesses of a pure and virginal heart,
never as yet unfolded to any eye, save that of God; but
Joan, hearing all this talked of, silently remembered how
constant Elsie's attendance at church had been of late, and
how, when Paul preached, the young girl had sat as one
wrapt beyond all consciousness of time and place, gazing
up into his face, her color coming and going, her eyes
kindling with fervor or drowned in tears, her whole soul
swayed by his word and at his will. She remembered,
too, how often she had been to him for counsel and private instruction; and, although the counsel had been of
the wisest and the instruction of the soundest, Joan
shrewdly suspected that, all unconsciously to the teacher,
the pupil had learned more than church history, more
than simple rules for her daily life, from those eloquent
lips.

Did Paul guess as much? And had he, like Joan,
remarked that, since his engagement was announced, Elsie
had remained almost always in her own room, until now
that she came forth with this new plan of life?

What Paul knew, or what he guessed, in this and many
other matters, however, he kept safe in his own heart;
and his interview with Elsie was never repeated by either,
nor was the child seen again that night.

When Paul came downstairs, he was very pale and
very grave; and to all Mrs. Beauchamp Brown's eager
questioning, only replied, —

"I trust all will be right. I would not talk to her any more about it to-night if I were you."

The weddings came after Easter, and were very different: Margaret's, absolutely quiet and unpretentious, at eleven o'clock in the forenoon, with only a dozen or so of spectators, and a celebration of the Holy Communion.

Mr. Rockfort officiated, and Mrs. Beauchamp Brown afterward insisted upon his assurance that he was perfectly well, for, as she several times declared, "no ashes were ever grayer than your face, and your voice shook like the tremolo stop of the organ."

Joan's wedding was in church, also, but of a very different style, — profuse in lights, in flowers, in music, in trailing masses of silk and satin and lace, in crowded pews, white-favored ushers, Elsie as a bridesmaid and La Branche as best man, and a right-reverend bishop, besides the Rev. Mr. Rockfort, to officiate. Lovely, glowing, rosy, bright-eyed Joan! We see her now, pacing up the aisle of the grim old church, the bridal veil softening, not hiding, the rich glow of her beauty, the shimmering lace and satin of her dress trailing about her slender, shapely form, leaving the pretty feet to steal in and out "like little mice," as they bore her on toward the tall, manly young fellow who awaited her, with such eager eyes, beside the altar-rail. Pretty Joan! Dear Joan! Wish her Godspeed on her life's journey, dear people, do!

"Now, Elsie, are n't you sorry you did n't decide to be married at the same time, and have a share in all this fuss and feathers?" demanded Mrs. Beauchamp Brown, when they were at home again; and pale, pretty Elsie smiled in her moonlight fashion, and said, —

"No, Aunt Phyllis, I think it will be better to spend this summer quietly at home with papa and mamma, and in the autumn be married in our own little church by my own dear father. Cyprian says we can go directly to New Orleans then, and it will be better than to be at Sneyd's Landing for the present."

"Sneyd's Landing!" echoed Mrs. Beauchamp Brown. "I wish they would hurry and name that place, even if they call it Joansville."

It was decided that Sneyd and his wife should proceed at once to Louisville, where Joan would make a visit upon her new relatives, while Tom could travel back and forth between that gay little city and the mines ; and Baruther and Margaret would stay for some time longer in Boston, giving Mr. Rockfort time to make other arrangements for an assistant at St. Polycarp's, and also for a house to be finished wherein they might fitly dwell during the building of the rectory of the Church of the Holy Cross, as the prospective outpost was already named.

Thus it came about that Joan, staying for some days in New York, and diligently sight-seeing in that great Babylon, was taken by an enthusiastic church-friend to see the House of Mercy on 88th Street, and was much impressed by its noble situation, commanding the sweep of the Hudson, by the dignity of the old colonial house, built by a Knickerbocker as his private residence, and the grave beauty of the chapel, fitly named for her whose sins were forgiven because she loved much.

In the sewing-room a class of girls and women were engaged in various branches of needle-work, under the direction of a lady dressed in deep black, with a cap upon her head. As Joan and her companion, escorted by one of the Sisters who have charge of the establishment, entered the room, this lady glanced at them, then, moving hastily to the window, remained with her back to the visitors until they had left the room. In the one glance she caught of her face, Joan noticed that it was dreadfully scarred and distorted, as if by small-pox, and at first supposed this to be the reason of her avoidance of the eyes of strangers ; but as she again glanced pityingly at that shrinking figure, something familiar in its outline, something about the hand resting upon the window, — an air, a suggestion, she knew not what, — set shrewd Joan a-thinking, and by and by she carelessly asked of the Sister, —

"Who was that lady in charge of the girls in the sewing-room ?"

"A lady visiting us, and kindly helping in our work," replied the Sister, in that manner, gently discouraging further questioning, which seems part of the education of a Religious.

Joan took the hint, and a couple of months later asked Mr. Baruther, —

"What ever became of Mrs. Trevylyan? Do you know?"

"She is living retired from the world, and engaged in good works," said Paul, in exactly the same tone the sister had used. Joan meditated for a moment, but could not deny herself the satisfaction of letting him know that she had the secret, so quietly said, —

"A friend of mine took me to the House of Mercy while I was in New York. I was very much impressed with all I saw."

Paul fixed his eyes upon her own for a moment, then said, in a voice conveying more than its words, "I suppose you know that a point of honor among those admitted to visit religious houses is never to repeat outside anything they may see of the life there."

"I understand," replied Joan shortly, then added, "but I saw nothing there that I do not heartily approve, and wish well with all my heart."

"It is a great and good work, and a blessing will follow those who carry it on," replied Paul, and that was all.

Belinda McVie Beauchamp, having taken Camilla's disease, died in the hospital, quite alone except for a hired nurse ; for her husband was afraid of contagion, and she had no friends.

Well, the Church of the Holy Cross was finished, and accepted by the bishop of that diocese. The rectory was finished and furnished, not like Mrs. Beauchamp Brown's house on Beacon Hill, but with a quiet elegance befitting its inmates, and with plenty of books, musical appurtenances, and pictures, whose mere money-value would have bought the little town and even the mines twice over ; for both Paul and Margaret believed that missionary work calls for the very best material and workmen, and that he who would put himself in sympathy with the mass of men must cultivate them up, and not lower himself down. Excelsior is a word of manifold development.

Was Margaret happy? Ah, was she not? See her, standing in the bay-window of her pretty drawing-room, a perfect bower of blossoming plants, her head upon her husband's shoulder, his arm around her waist, her hand in his. They were looking at a sunset, and as the glory began to fade, she raised her head and looked into his eyes. They met hers steadfastly, and the love each told to each has no earthly words to phrase it. It is the unforgotten language of heaven, never translated into the clumsy dialects of this world.

After their eyes their lips met, and then, with a deep sigh of perfect content, Margaret wound her arms about his neck, and nestled closer to his breast.

Was she happy, think you?

That was five or six years ago, and she is happier now, with children growing about her, and a grand, broad work before her, for she is in everything Paul's helpmeet, and he respects and consults her opinion at every turn, quite as much as if she were not a most obedient and dutiful wife, making glad oblation, day by day, of her own will and her own pride, to him who is her head as Christ is his.

Joan made a charming lady of the manor. The mines were a marvellous success, and money flowed in upon the owners in Pactolean streams. Sneyd built himself a lordly mansion, and entertained guests and sight-seers in true royal fashion, his hearty, genial manner and unfailing spirits making him the ideal host, while Joan's beauty, grace, and sprightliness, not to mention a solid substratum of womanly dignity, fitting her admirably for her own position.

La Branche and his wife visited them from time to time, but Elspeth liked best to remain in New Orleans whenever the weather permitted, and Margaret often spent several weeks of the winter with her.

Mrs. Beauchamp Brown set up a cat, — true Persian and very cross; also a companion, whom she entertains for hours with panegyrics upon "my niece, Mrs. Baruther," and the glories of the town which to this day she persists in calling Joansville.

But with all her eccentricities and wilfulness, and all the

worldliness that never will leave her until she leaves the world, Mrs. Beauchamp Brown entertains a true, loyal, and practical friendship for Peter Rockfort, who in turn has learned to tolerate and accept, with only a mental protest, a great deal that used to call forth indignant speech ; and although he still speaks his mind with the utmost honesty, it is not often his mind to say anything harsh to the odd, devoted, and most generous woman between whom and himself is firmly established that best of all friendships, one based upon mutual good deeds and hearty respect.

She still cherishes the complacent belief that it is to her influence that St. Polycarp's parish and rector owe their position and prosperity, and when it is called in her hearing, " the poor man's church," she sometimes says, with a sagacious nod, " It 's very true the poor profit by it, but if some of us who are not so poor did n't pay the coal and gas bills, I 'm afraid the poor man's church would freeze out the poor man pretty effectually.  The poor are an expensive luxury, whether you take them in the food and firing way or in the religious way.  It is a great privilege, of course, but — it costs."

Do you want to see Mrs. Beauchamp Brown, and to both see and hear the Rev. Mr. Rockfort?

Go to St. Polycarp's next Sunday morning, and if you see a tall, stern man in the pulpit, and presently hear your own pet and hidden sin anatomized, discussed, pitilessly scorned, and then cauterized, wisely and healingly, that is he.

And if you see a stately lady, with white hair, a complacent expression, and a great deal of velvet, lace, fur, and diamond about her, who listens to the sermon as if it were a prize essay, and she president of the society before which it is delivered, that is she.  If you are not quite sure, wait for the offertory, and see the double-eagle gold-piece she always drops in with a satisfied little nod.

Note, too, the exactness with which she stands, kneels, or sits at the appropriate moment, the depth of her genuflections, and the severity with which she represses any attempt at conversation on the part of a stray visitor from the Holy Frescoes or St. Iamblichus, parishes whose practices and manners she has forgotten as completely as the country lass, become a city milliner, forgets the identity of that horrid creature with horns that cries " Moo ! "

And if, having gone once for curiosity, you go again and yet again for something better, then shall the little book have done its work, and bring a blessing both to reader and author.